EMERGENCE

EMERGENCE

Justice Hawk

iUniverse, Inc.

New York Lincoln Shanghai

Emergence

Copyright © 2005 by Justice Hawk

iUniverse books may be ordered through booksellers or by contacting:

iUniverse
2021 Pine Lake Road, Suite 100
Lincoln, NE 68512
www.iuniverse.com
1-800-Authors (1-800-288-4677)

ISBN: 0-595-34441-0

Printed in the United States of America

To all those who have asked the question...

ACKNOWLEDGMENTS

First and foremost, Renee Szeligas and her staff deserve the credit for encouraging this novel into fruition. It is difficult to engage a subject so profound without unrelenting support. Second, Mark Weinstein submitted graphic design ideas for the cover.

PREFACE

Throughout the ages, one question has occupied the mind of humankind. Various anomalies throughout these ages have spawned a number of responses. Religion, in one disguise or another, has been at the forefront. Persuasively, these responses, by design, have provided a cloak of security, calming the angst emerging from this question. This story revisits that question.

Whether your preference is religion, science or occult, this story attempts to unravel the narrative of their interdependence. Although one might query the very existence of interdependence amongst religion, science and occult, this story meanders into the realm where interdependence flourishes.

Was the religion of the recent millennia that different from the occult of the shaman? Was the science, after the renaissance, any more foretelling than the contemporary religion? How closely related are faith and reason? Why was the shaman so convincing? Recall, the shaman was able to capture the imagination of his or her tribe. Recall, religion captured the imagination of a people or a nation. Recall, science has captured the imagination of the civilized world. What is it about religion, science and occult that enables imagination to be captured?

Aristotle, despite obvious experimentation to the contrary, held the imagination of the civilized world for nearly two millennia. Paul of Tarsus' narratives, despite historical evidence to the contrary, have captivated the Western world for nearly two millennia. Why?

Humankind has been unable, or unwilling, to shake the shackles of these gripping responses. Experience has shown that when one shackle is loosened, humankind rushes to bind itself into another more alluring entrapment. Why? What is it about these responses that ensnare us? Why do we accept them so willingly? Do we need them in order to survive?

Like Dostoevsky's *Grand Inquisitor*, this novel revisits those questions. Dostoevsky revisited the great questions of the Western religion; whereas, this novel unearths the greatest question of all. Since the beginning of time for humans, this question has lingered. Religion, science and occult have attempted to distance the response to this question with narrative upon narrative, until the question submerged beyond the angst of its lingering. Some, like Tolstoy, have equated religion and occult to opiates. Science out of current preference was sparred that labeling. Nonetheless, as this novel will unfold, the opiate labeling for science is inclusive. Religion, science and occult have served as opiates with respect to the question. One mental endeavor merely reorients awareness away from the directions or preferences of the other two. In the end, submerged beneath layers and layers of narratives, the question remains unanswered, frothing with angst.

In the hopes of providing some clarity to the question of the ages, this novel unfolds in various levels of awareness.

I hope you like the story!

Note of caution: Those with deeply rooted religious beliefs should refrain from reading this novel.

CHAPTER 1

▼

One thing I enjoy about Manila is to be able to relax on my balcony overlooking Rizal Square. Nothing beats the taste of an ice cold San Miguel, as the sounds of the street traffic serenade me. Just prop my feet up on a cushion and allow the city noise to take my consciousness wherever it desires. Most of the sounds are unintelligible to me, a mixture of the various Malay-related languages of South East Asia interspersed with the constant cacophony of the jeepnies.

Jeepnies are jeeps and other small, engine vehicles that have been converted into makeshift buses. With their multiple-array of colors, they appear like tropical macaws squawking their advantages. Thousands of jeepnies parade the Square in the evening. It reminds me of Brazil during carnival.

The balcony of my second floor suite provides an excellent vantage point with which to enjoy the bustling of the Square. Manila throbs in the evening. A cool breeze from the harbor allows me to endure the tropical humidity all through the night.

A large mosquito net encases the balcony to deter the local insect life. Some nights, the net is tested by the weight and determination of the buzzing creatures. Fortunately, they make good netting in the tropics.

My suite is a typical bachelor's paradise: one bedroom, one bath, one living room and a large kitchen/dining area. Second floor means a walk up corridor in this old, two-story building. The first floor contains an international cuisine restaurant. Certainly, it does not qualify for five stars, but it would for three stars. In the tropics, five star restaurants are reserved for the more up-class or affluent neighborhoods.

Rizal Square dates back to the turn of the 20th Century. Most of the buildings are post-World War II era to mid-1960s. Only a few of the buildings have been renovated to late-20th Century standards. Most notable is the Manila Hotel, located a good stone's throw from my balcony. General MacArthur maintained his headquarters in that hotel.

History emerges everywhere around Rizal Square. Since the designs of the building have undergone few changes, one can feel the past unfold by just contemplating on the facades. The Spanish galleons moored in the harbor just past the upper boundary of Rizal Square. Gold, bound for a transpacific crossing, was horse-carted along the dirt roads of the pre-Square era. Spanish military assembled on the open grounds of what is now called Rizal Park. Where band members form to please the weekend visitors, soldiers with sabers and bayonets marched.

Across Rizal Square lies the formidable walls of an old Spanish fort. Manila must have been a grand place when that fort was in operation. To me, the fort is a marvel of Romanesque architecture: solid concrete, I mean solid walls. Those walls are impenetrable. It would have taken a million cannon balls to penetrate those walls. It is no wonder the Spanish maintained their grasp on this island nation for centuries.

To the local Filipinos, the fort is the last reminder of slavery. Strange how one landmark can present such different imagery for two different cultures? I see beauty while others see the despicable aspects of humanity. Yet, the fort still stands.

Rizal Square is named after the patriot, Jose Rizal, who stood against the Spanish at the turn of the 20th Century. The Square contains his statue, depicting his last act of defiance to the Spanish, as they were about to execute him. From the stories about him, Jose Rizal was a true hero. He stood for something in no less a manner than Socrates. Thank God, there are people like that in this world.

This evening, my consciousness' wandering is restricted to the contents of a fax that I just received from the Asian Development Bank (ADB). I do some work for the Bank whenever they need something looked into that lies outside their normal channels. It is a good deal for me. I get to lounge around Manila at their expense. Actually, it has been over two years since they asked me to do something. That is a fantastic deal: a free flat in the heart of Manila with all expenses and a generous stipend.

If someone has never spent time in Manila, then there is no way that I could describe the benefits. Truly, I thrive as well as any US Mainland playboy. Of course, I have to limit the number of times I frequent certain establishments. The locals are staunchly Catholic. My carousing about with an ample supply of young ladies does irate the young men. A tourist can get away with my kind of antics, but to live here permanently requires some discretion and a keen eye for caution. Fortunately, I have both.

According to the fax, the ADB has directed me to be ready to check out some problems with a forestry project in New Guinea that they underwrote. If what I am reading is correct, the project is behind schedule for what they describe as "unforeseen difficulties" and some missing workers. I have to chuckle at the thought that anyone working in the deep rain forest areas of New Guinea might just decide to walk away. It is certainly understandable to me that the Bank's client would have foreign workers missing. Well, I will check with the Bank tomorrow and get some clarification.

If the Bank needs me to go to New Guinea, then I might as well resign myself into going. One of my college buddies got me this job, and I cannot let him down. It is just too sweet a deal. I certainly owe this guy for this job. Working 9-5 was not for me. Working at half this stipend was not for me either. Well, a few days or a week in the rain forest cannot be that bad. I can handle it. I wonder if I have to know anything about trees. God, I hope not. Botany was not exactly my favorite subject in college. Even if it was my favorite subject, these are tropical trees. This tropical tree stuff is a species of botany all in its own. The brief from the Bank should give me enough background.

Another cold San Miguel returns me to the peacefulness of the evening. I quickly forget the fax and eye the young lovelies making their way down the street below. Truly, this town is paradise for a middle-aged man with a few dollars in his pocket.

Long nights are common in Manila. Either I sip San Miguel on my balcony until the alcohol succumbs me, or I bar hop until morning in the company of the most accommodating of female companions. Despite its allure, after a year or so, it does get boring. A void seems to form deep inside me, craving excitement. I long to get away and indulge in the thrills of life. Soldiers of fortune often express a similar sensation that drives them into dangerous adventures.

Life has been good to me in Manila. As a kid, I never dreamed that life could be so giving. I suppose long into my old age, if I live that long, I will cherish these years. It is hard to imagine life getting any better than this. I suppose I am like someone's cherished pet that gets overly pampered. Lounging around all day, prowling for love and excitement at night and coming home to replenish and rest, how could anyone beat that? This is a dream job!

No matter what time I decide to turn in, like sunrise to birds, the jeepnies honk life back into me in the morning. It seems like clockwork. These colorful, ragtag, rust buckets on wheels are running by 6:00 AM, each and every morning. They never take a day off. Like gazelles cautious of lions, they are hustling about making the most of their day.

These people do not have job security or pension plans. They make do as they can. Most jeepny drivers do not own their vehicle. They rent it. They get to keep what they make over the daily rent. Some have to share a percentage of what they make over the rent as well. The rental system dates back to the rickshaw driver arrangements. They have no unions. In Asia, the King of the Bums makes the rules.

King of the Bums refers to the top underworld person. Each city in Asia has a King of the Bums. It is this king that makes the cities run smooth. Of course, in order to run smoothly, the king has to be paid. Each and every establishment pays tribute to the king. Failure to do so is not an option. Unlike the huge and costly police forces of the West, Asia has this millennia old system. It works fine. Young rascals think twice before offending the king. Like the Chinese penal system, most offenses are punishable by death. Death means summary execution.

Locales where the rascals become a nuisance are those where the local population has tried to adopt the ways of the West with their accompanying judicial system. Asians know that those bent on a life of crime are little persuaded, if not truly encouraged, by short periods of incarceration. Immediate death, on the other hand, is a persuasive alternative.

Breakfast, before any travel into the administrative center of Manila, has to be light. A slice of papaya and small cup of instant coffee is the intake limit. The administration sector is not as well cooled. During the day, this area is drenched in humidity. The height of the buildings and their unorganized arrangement hinders the effect of the cooling harbor breezes. Any further consumption would bring on a torrent of perspiration. Also, it is best to catch the early jeepnies before the tropical sun can begin to warm the city.

Jeepnies are the choice of transportation, because they are cheap and travel almost anywhere. At the cost of a peso for a ride into Manila, how can you beat that? A peso is about 4 cents American. The jeepny will drop me off right in front of the ADB.

The passenger section of the jeepny is open air, resembling the flatbed area of a small pickup truck with bleacher like seating on either side. Eight to ten people can be seated reasonably comfortably. In Manila, most jeepny drivers speak enough English. They know the major drop off locations. You just need to mention one of those locations, and you are sure to get there.

This morning is no different. A quick shower, don loose-fitting, tropical attire and nibble on some papaya as I sample a cup of instant coffee prepare me. I seldom percolate or drip my coffee. A hotplate arrangement is quick and easy. In no time I am out of my flat and waving down a jeepny.

Jeepny drivers adore seeing me on the street. They know I will tip them an extra peso whenever I ride. As they pull up to the curb, they always greet me with some Filipino slang. Whatever it means, I suspect it is courteous. They often call me "Big Man Joe." Actually, I am not that big, but I am considerably larger than these people. Most are less than 5'4" (163 centimeters) in height with a slender build. My American-football-tackle shape and height tower over them.

My size concerns them, because I have often experienced a strange behavior on their part. A few times when I have passed through a security sentry, the inspector has felt the muscles in my upper arm in a strange way. His fingers dig deeply into my muscles, kneading them. At first, I thought he was performing a thorough inspection of my body, but as the finger-kneading experience repeated itself in other circumstances, I began to realize that he was feeling my arm in a manner that a butcher admires a piece of meat. It is an eerie sensation to imagine someone admiring you for consumption. The experience has left me with a feeling of distrust for these people.

This morning, as I emerge from the building that houses my flat, a familiar jeepny driver greets me. He seems to have been waiting for me. I barely step on the sidewalk, as he pulls up. He shouts "Big Man Joe, you need a ride?" The entire passenger section erupts in laughter. Obviously, there was more said before he offered his services. To me, his enjoyment at my expense is of no consequence. He fills his jeepny for 40 cents American and fights the crowded Manila inner-city traffic. At that rate, he needs a laugh anyway he can get it.

I just board the jeepny, settle into a seat near the front of the passenger section and exchange facial greetings with the other passengers. Most are women going to work. From their dress, I suspect that they are schoolteachers or office workers. The ride is quiet, despite the constant blare of honks from jeepnies trying to out vie each other for position in order to get to their destinations quickly. Current Filipino songs from the radio soothe the ride. I am particularly fond of one called *"Maganda Oumaga."* It happens to play, carrying me away to a special place immersed in fond romance. Within about fifteen minutes, the jeepny driver pulls up in front of the ADB. He calls out the destination. As I am disembarking, he pleads for an additional tip and asks when I will be returning. I succumb and present him with another peso. Twelve cents is not much for a ride. I know he is taking advantage of me, but what the heck he earned it. He got me here quickly and safely. The passengers see me as an easy mark. To me, I pity them. They toil all day, in unbearable humidity, for the change in my pockets.

The ADB resembles every other government building in Manila: solid concrete, Doric columns with an artistic entablature. The Bank actually is not a bank, as one would commonly know one. You cannot get a passbook and save money here. There are no tellers, *per se*, to draw out money. The money that the Bank does handle is more in the form of electronic transfers from the major lending institutions of the world: International Bank for Reconstruction and Development (IBRD), World Bank (WB) and the International Finance Cooperation (IFC). The Bank also has some nebulous relationship with the International Monetary Fund (IMF). The ADB acts merely as a conduit for these funds, as they are applied to developmental projects in the less developed countries (LDC) of Asia. Nevertheless, the Banks handles a good deal of money and has an ample supply of employees and consultants. My category, very loosely speaking, is consultant.

Once inside the columned arcade and the glass barrier, refreshing air conditioning greets me. First, a security check is required. Manila is surrounded by roving bands of Muslim terror groups. Since the ADB is the only presence of Western capitalism in Manila, it has become a prime target. Sooner or later, hopefully after today, these security checks will pay off in repelling an attack on the institution.

Security Officer "Joe Del Rosi, is it?"

I recognize the security officer; "Yes, it is, good to see you, again."

Security Officer "What's your business here, Joe?"

Joe "I'm here to see Director Watson."

Security Officer "You need an appointment, Joe."

I manage to retrieve the fax from my valise; "Here you go. I got this fax yesterday, directing me to report here for a briefing."

The Security Officer looks over the fax; "This sounds like you will be traveling, Joe."

Joe "It sure does, doesn't it?"

The Security Officer clears me to enter, hands me back the fax and directs me to Director Watson's office.

As I leave the security post, I marvel at the strange design of the marble flooring of the ADB. Why someone would waste so much money on designing a floor made out of marble just simply amazes me. I suppose, when you are a bank, you have to keep up with the times.

Director Watson's office is on the first floor at the far end of the second corridor. His secretary, a shapely, young Filipina, acknowledges my entrance and tells me to go right into his office. For someone with Watson's stature in the Bank, you would think he would deserve more than four, unadorned cement walls. There is not even a certificate of his college accreditation on the wall. His desk looks more like a pillbox than an administrative tool. The furniture in the room is old, mostly made from local rattan. The fan on his desk is in dire need of dusting.

I enter his office to a cheerful sound, "Joe! My God, how long has it been?"

Joe, as I extend my hand, "Too long, I suspect."

Watson "I see you got the fax. Actually, I didn't expect to see you for another week. You must be bored to death to come in this quickly."

Joe "Well, I suppose that's part of the reason."

Watson offers me a seat in one of the rattan chairs with a cushion back. These chairs are extremely relaxing. As we sit and reminisce old times, his secretary brings in some ice cold tea.

Bob Watson and I were college roommates. He majored in business, international finance actually; whereas, I majored in the 60s. My curriculum was as diverse as my interests. I made him laugh when he needed to smile, and he never forgot me. Thank God for that!

Watson, after an ample time of refreshing our friendship, "Joe, I called you in, because we need someone to go down to New Guinea and help out with one of our development projects. As you read from the fax, our client is clearing an area intended for use as a natural gas train substation. Apparently, the local population has some animistic notions that the trees are revolting against the deforestation and some of our and their people are being devoured by spirits."

I slowly lower my glass of ice tea onto his desk and gulp, "We have people missing down there?"

Watson, he pauses before he continues the conversation, "Actually, Joe, we have quite a few people missing."

Joe "Quite a few, what does that mean?"

Watson "Joe, it could be in the hundreds. We are not sure. The project has been going on for a few years now. At first, we felt that these people were just walking off the job. As for the locals, they have the Australian equivalent of a walkabout down there, so no one ever knows when they come and go. But, we have a lot of people unaccounted down there. They are there one day, then they are gone, seemingly forever, the next. There are no bodies and no traces of foul play."

Joe, somewhat concerned, "You want me to go down there and check this out for you, do you?"

Watson "Joe, you understand these animistic people. You practically live with them. Maybe your presence will assure them that whatever is going on down there, it is not the trees eating them."

Joe smiles, "Like a cultural attaché for Neanderthals, you mean."

Watson chuckles, "Something likes that, yes."

Joe "Bob, my experience with these Malays is limited to drinking, carousing and fucking them. I really do not know their culture that well."

Watson "Joe, you make them smile. They feel comfortable with you. You are not a suit, like me. They will trust you. That is why you are perfect for this assignment."

Joe "Bob, people are going missing down there."

Watson "That seems to be the case, but we have not been able to ascertain any foul play. We suspect another reason. Papuan rebels frequent the area. They are well known to be in opposition to any development. They could be kidnapping them. We need to find out what is wrong."

Joe "That's probably the case."

Watson "Joe, go down there for a few days, and check it out. Give me an assessment, and you are back here by the end of the week. It is a midnight run, Joe."

Joe sensing closure to the discussion, "Sure, Bob, I can do that. Anything else I need to know?"

Watson looking over his file, "Oh yes, check out this uncuttable tree report."

Joe nodding his head, "Of course, I will take special interest in the uncuttable tree."

Watson stands up and shakes my hand: "My secretary will have your travel documents and financial affairs delivered to your flat by tomorrow. You have a good trip."

As I leave Watson's office, my mind races back over our conversation. This has to be the weirdest assignment that I have ever heard. Bob should change tea brands or something. My God, I am traveling to assess people-eating, uncuttable trees! I can handle this with or without an ice chest of San Miguel.

Since it is still morning, I have time to replenish my travel-consumables: shaving cream, toothpaste, deodorants, etc. There is a department store not far from here. The walk would do me good. I might even be able to pick up a few tropical shirts. The fancy ones printed with lots of jungle life impress the natives. They are darn good for barter as well. You never can tell what kind of trouble greets you in the jungle.

The morning passes as my shopping bag fills up. Actually, by noon, I have two shopping bags. It is amazing how much your mind works to imagine every conceivable thing you might need on a trip. I even got some fresh shoe polish. After purchasing the polish, I decided that I needed the accompanying brush and kit. Think of it, after three days in the rainforest, will I ever need to polish my shoes? I will be wearing jungle footwear that, undoubtedly, will be ankle deep in mud.

Exiting the department store, the same jeepny driver that took me to the Bank greets me. I swear he has been waiting all morning to take me back. He offers me a "special" fare to take me back directly. "Special" fares costs more, much more actually, but you have the jeepny to yourself. It resembles a taxi ride in a Mainland USA city. Today, I graciously accept his offer. With my two shopping bags, I am in need of special travel arrangements.

On the way back to my suite, the jeepny driver plays popular American tunes on his speaker system. There is an American military station in Japan that he dials. The reception is good, despite the sudden signal breaks from being shielded by the large, cement buildings of Manila's administrative district. Each song brings back memories of where I was and what I was doing at the time the song was popular. Sometimes, the song reminds me of whom I was with at the time. Those are special songs.

At my building, the jeepny driver offers to assist me to carry my bags upstairs. Why not? It costs just a few pesos more, and he needs the money. As we climb the stairs, he inquires if I will be gone long. When I mention the trip is for just a few days, he seems relieved. I guess he counts on my generosity to make ends meat. I have never experienced a life filled with such depravity. As he is about to leave, I tip him 20 pesos. His face glows at the sight of the 20-note in his hand. To me, it is less than a dollar. We bid farewell.

Closing the door, after the jeepny driver departs, I immediately turn on the air conditioner. My AC unit is huge, so the room cools in a few minutes. For the next few hours I will be loading my travel bag. As usual, I have purchased too many items for the trip. As common sense and the capacity of my travel bag dictate, I begin triaging my belongings that I intend to take. I prefer travel bags, because they can be stowed in the overhead bins of the passenger compartment. Traveling through LDCs with suitcase-like luggage presents too many problems for mishandling. Travel guides are replete with horror stories of passengers being stranded without their belongings in areas where replacements are limited. Often, the next flight to these areas that could reunite the passengers with their luggage is a week away. Isolated locations are just that, isolated.

By late afternoon, my travel bag is loaded. I am ready to go. I settle into my recliner with a cold San Miguel in the comfort of air conditioning. Before I can empty the bottle, I am sound asleep. Soon the discomfort of the recliner wakes me and encourages me into my bed. Getting up so early and braving the humidity and bustle of Manila must have drained my energy. I am not use to it. Seldom do I wake before 10:00 AM in the tropics.

Darkness greets me when I finally awake. It is mid-evening. Tonight could be my last free evening in Manila. Before I leave, I need to embrace a CLEO to charge my batteries, so to speak, for the upcoming period of abstinence.

A CLEO refers to a young lady of the evening, officially classified as a Client Liaison Entertainment Officer. These arrangements are popular all over East and South East Asia. They have different identifications, of course. I will call them whatever they prefer to be called. The performance is the same. And, satisfaction is guaranteed whatever they are called.

A quick change of clothes into more relaxing evening attire and I am out the door, down the staircase and into the street waving down a jeepny. Tonight's jeepny is different than the earlier one. These passengers are night prowlers, anticipating an evening of bar hopping. As for me, I am headed for the CLEO center in Metro Manila.

The passengers erupt in laughter when I tell the jeepny driver the location I am headed. Some even pat me on the shoulder and add a comment: "good choice, my friend." The rest of the ride, the other passengers and I share experiences at different bars in Manila. Interestingly, there are some establishments that I have never heard about that seem to come up continually in the conversation. They seem to be favorites for the locals. My location is a bit high priced for them, so I understand their attractiveness to the less expensive bars. Nonetheless, I promise the other passengers that I will check out their recommendations.

Sooner than expected, the jeepny driver pulls up in from of my chosen destination. He offers to take me back when I am done. I tell him I will spend a few hours here. He does not seem to matter. I give him an approximate time, and he says he will be available. It is that way in Manila. He knows I am a good fare and that I will tip him handsomely.

The CLEO club is guarded with armed security personnel. Many foreigners frequent this establishment. The security personnel check my identification and frisk me for weapons. I am Italian, so I look something like a West Asian to them. West Asians resemble the Persians-looking terrorists that travel with Abu Sayyad.

Abu Sayyad is the terrorist organization from Mindanao with ties to Al Qaeda. Mindanao is the island just south of Luzon. Manila is on Luzon. The people on Mindanao are more Persian in ancestry than Malay. How that came about, I do not know. I guess in the days of Alexander the Great, Persians fleeing his eastern advance must have traveled to Mindanao for sanctuary. Anyway, people of Persian ancestry are living in the Philippines.

Once inside the establishment, I am greeted by a horde of overly zealous CLEOs. Some of them, I have had the pleasure of experiencing their services. They remembered me. One in particular, Angelina, remains a special favorite of mine. Angelina is a 5'2" gorgeous, Malay-looking Filipina with long hair down to her waist. She cannot be more than 25 years old. She is quite articulate in English. In the club, she performs often as an exotic dancer on weekends when the club fills with clientele. This being a week night, she will simply be at my service.

The mamasan comes over and asks my preference. I select Angelina and make the usual arrangements for her services. Mamasan is the name given to the head mistress in these kinds of establishments. Though mamasan is a Japanese term, it is used all over East and South East Asia. Apparently, the desire for "comfort women" created the mamasan role during World War II, and it remained.

A CLEO can be classified as midway between a "comfort woman" and a *geisha*. Where a *geisha* truly entertains her client, a "comfort woman" attends directly to his sexual desires. They all get paid for their services. It is the extent of the services that determine the classification. After being immersed in Asian culture for a year or so, one seems to be able to distinguish between the three quite easily.

Angelina, after being released by the mamasan, escorts me to a cushioned area where she brings us drinks. She remembers my fondness for ice cold San Miguel. The club keeps the establishment well air conditioned. One soon forgets the humidity of the area and the drone of mosquitoes for the comfort of a beautiful woman. Angelina sips from a freshly opened bottle of wine. It is a house specialty wine, watered down to keep the girls alert. It is understandable. You do not want the girls falling down, slobbering and barfing on their clients.

Immersed in the melodies of soft music, Angelina and I remake old acquaintances. I recall the comfort of her embrace, and she remembers how I quickly come alive. Soon, we are off to the interior of the establishment where soft pillows and perfume complement the talents of the CLEOs.

There is something about a long-haired woman that excites me. It is the connotations that come with the vision more than the feel. Long hair feels odd and less desirable; more so, as it barriers the feeling in my hands against her flesh. My trick to maintain my desire is to reach under the hair and allow my hands to follow the contours of her body. The sensation of soft skin on my hands arouses me. The accompanying feeling of moist lips gently mouthing my skin drives me to the extreme of desire. Angelina knows this about me and takes her time slowing my breath. Moments like these seem to last forever. Long after I have left a woman like this, I can recall how she held me between her lips. How she marinated me. How I disappeared within her. How she wrapped herself around me and held me firmly until I was expended.

One needs these moments to remember how wonderful life is. Before a long journey, these moments reminds us of what we are leaving behind, insuring we will return. Yes, I will return to Angelina. How could I not? Maybe, when I return from this assignment, I will ask the mamasan for a more permanent arrangement with Angelina. She is becoming that age where the mamasan might consider retiring her. I always have thoughts like these after a CLEO session. But, I truly like Angelina. I would enjoy sharing coffee and papaya with her in the morning.

CHAPTER 2

▼

NEW GUINEA, REPUBLIC OF INDONESIA

From the air, Sentani looks like a barren area with large strips of land cleared for no apparent reason. There must be twenty or so large strips, the size of many football fields in tandem. During World War II, these strips acted as runways for Allied bomber aircraft.

Sentani is located on the northern tip of the island of New Guinea, adjacent to the main settlement area of Jayapura. Currently, this portion of New Guinea is under the jurisdiction of the Republic of Indonesia. Little is known about this part of the world. First, few people care about it. Second, the Indonesian over-lords keep the ongoings here under tight control. Third, the American mining company, located in the southern sector of the island, releases little information about their activities. Fourth, the interior of the island is randomly meted out between the insurgent forces and the foreign forestry companies. Fifth, the inter-national arrangements to exploit the island's natural gas reserves necessitate a cloak of secrecy.

Today, one runway remains active for the ingress and egress of foreign con-cerns and the movement of Indonesian officials. Security at the airport is in a heightened status over the calls for independence from the local population. Insurgent raids into the areas surrounding Sentani Airport are common. The air-plane that I am on will land at Sentani.

Being not far from the equator, I am attired with loose-fitting clothing to accommodate the tropical humidity. Since Sentani is not altogether that different a climate from Manila, I should be able to withstand the slight differences.

After landing, the plane taxis to a special area of the runway set aside for security inspections. Smuggling firearms is common. An assault rifle will bring a handsome exchange value with the rebel forces.

As I disembark the plane, Indonesian officials greet me and provide for special treatment through the custom and security checks. It is a good thing that they do so, because these Indonesian inspectors, all military commandos, seem fanatical about their jobs. One look into their eyes conveys quickly that they would kill you for the slightest infraction. These are serious people.

Upon clearing the airport inspections, I am brought to the government offices for a briefing. The offices resemble refurbished remnants from General MacArthur's World War II arrangements. Scraps of old maps from the era still cling to some of the walls. The furniture seems right out of a scene from a B-29 bombing run briefing. The entire office complex reeks of the ambiance of past decades. At any moment, I expect to see an officer from the 1940s enter the room donned in a full flight suit.

A liaison officer for the World Bank, a colonel in the Indonesian army, provides the brief. The colonel is an elderly gentleman. I suspect he received this post as a result of family and political connections. He seems too old to be a line officer with the army. The colonel that I saw overseeing the inspections at the airport was at least ten years his junior.

Colonel Ulang "Mr. Del Rosi, allow me to welcome you to Papua."

Papua is the name of the Indonesian province that shares half the island of New Guinea with the Independent State of Papua New Guinea.

Joe "Thank you, Colonel."

Colonel Ulang "Is this your first time to New Guinea, Mr. Del Rosi?"

Joe "Yes, it is, Colonel."

Colonel Ulang "I see. As I understand, you will be traveling into the interior to ascertain some unusual reports from one of the World Bank projects, is that correct?"

Joe "Yes that is my assignment. I will just be confirming some reports."

Colonel Ulang "One word of caution is in order. Rebel forces operate in the area where you have been assigned. You should make every effort to stay clear of them. They are quite unpredictable. One day they may treat you like royalty, yet the next you may find yourself as a hostage. Killing of hostages is common. Once you have been taken hostage, the Indonesian army does not have the manpower, or the directives, to go in an attempt to extricate you from the rebels."

Joe "I understand perfectly, Colonel."

Colonel nodding his head, "Good! I will send an ununiformed, armed cadre of my soldiers with you into this area. Please remain within their sphere of protection and follow their instructions."

Joe breathing a sigh of relief, "I certainly will, Colonel."

Colonel Ulang introduces one of his officers, Captain Djarmat.

Colonel Ulang "Captain Djarmat will lead the cadre that accompanies you. He speaks perfect English and can be relied upon as your confidant."

I shake hands with Captain Djarmat. He is my height, much more physically fit with a serious look in his eyes. I can tell that he has seen death, close at hand, many times. He reminds me of a butcher admiring the latest arrival of cattle. This man looks dangerous. I pray he remains on my side.

The brief continues for another hour or so, mostly a review of the local maps of the area. Colonel Ulang knows this area well. He must have been a field commander in this region earlier in his career. The sector of our concern consists of rainforest for the most part. A few streams traverse the area, mostly tributaries from the Sepik River. The colonel reminds me that a majority of the rainforest has been cut. I should expect to see large tracts of freshly cut timber.

After the brief, Colonel Ulang leaves me in the custody of Captain Djarmat. Quickly, Captain Djarmat readies a jeep and a military transport truck. The soldiers, accompanying us, load my travel bag into the back of the truck and board the vehicles.

Captain Djarmat "Come, Mr. Del Rosi, we need to be going. It will take us most of the remaining daylight to reach our destination."

Joe "Sorry, I hadn't realized that it was that far away."

Captain Djarmat chuckles, "On a super highway or improved road, it would not be that far. However, as you recall from the maps, the latter part of the trip runs through freshly cut timber areas. Those roads are not solid. They have been bulldozed simply for moving logs. After one rain, the roads erode a good deal, leaving them with abundant potholes. Come let's get going."

Captain Djarmat and I board the jeep while the remaining soldiers board the truck. Soon, Captain Djarmat signals the group, and we are off.

The roads in and close to Jayapura are well maintained. After about three miles or so outside Jayapura, the dirt roads commence. They are well-worn roads from constant usage by heavy vehicles. It is a good thing the captain knows where he is going, because the jungle vegetation masks the countryside from the road. It gets worse as we veer onto a single lane road.

Captain Djarmat breaks the silence, "I understand you are from Manila, Mr. Del Rosi, is that right?"

Joe "Yes, I am assigned there. Originally, I am from the States."

Captain Djarmat "I know you are from the States. Which one?"

Joe "Illinois."

Captain Djarmat "Is that where Chicago is located?"

Joe "Yes."

Captain Djarmat "Have you been to Chicago?"

Joe "Yes, I spent some time there after college."

Captain Djarmat maneuvering the jeep to avoid some road erosion, "How did you end up in Manila?"

Joe "A friend of mine from college got me the assignment. We were good friends in college and often shared some of the same study groups. He got assigned to Manila and asked me to come along."

Captain Djarmat smiles, "I need a friend like that to get me out of this place."

Joe "Have you been assigned here along time?"

Captain Djarmat "I'm going on five years now. Three years were line duty in the southern sector. The last two years have been here in Jayapura. Jayapura is much better than the south."

Our conversation is interrupted as we come upon a military checkpoint. The soldiers at the checkpoint salute and speak with Captain Djarmat. I do not understand their language; although, it does resemble the language in Manila. In an area off to the rear of the checkpoint area, I notice two soldiers interrogating a native. The native has his hands tied behind his back and is kneeling down. Suddenly, one of the soldiers pulls out a revolver and shoots the native in the head. The gunshot startles Captain Djarmat.

Captain Djarmat, as he dismounts the jeep, "Stay here, Mr. Del Rosi, stay in the jeep."

I watch Captain Djarmat walk over to the soldier who just shot the native. The captain appears angry and seems to be admonishing the soldier. As he is turning to come back to the jeep, Captain Djarmat suddenly reverses direction and slugs the soldier in the head. The soldier's helmet falls to the ground. The soldier is definitely shaken from the unexpected blow. Captain Djarmat returns to the jeep.

Captain Djarmat after he settles into the jeep, "Mr. Del Rosi may I impose upon you to disregard what you just witnessed."

I am stunned by the remark. I just witnessed a summary execution.

Joe stuttering "Yes, of course, Captain."

Captain Djarmat signals for the vehicles to proceed.

After a mile or so of driving, Captain Djarmat says, "The soldiers were interrogating a known member of the rebel forces. They have been instructed to bring any captives to their battalion intelligence officer. I needed to reinforce their orders. I hope you understand."

Joe extremely nervous, "I understand, Captain."

At that moment, I realized that the captain was apologizing for hitting the soldier and not for the summary execution. I will need to get use to this place very quickly.

Another checkpoint is passed without incident. As we continue inland, we encounter natives walking outward. Many seem to have an exorbitant amount of belongings with them. Even the children are laden down with items. Captain Djarmat does not say a word. I am surprised, because he has had a comment for every nuance we have encountered along the way.

A few more miles inland, we come upon the eroded logging roads mentioned at the start of trip. The potholes are evident everywhere. Captain Djarmat slows down the jeep, as he begins to maneuver through the damaged road. Each time one of our wheels lands in a pothole, I feel my spine react to the drop and bounce of the jeep. After a mile or so of this treatment, I appreciate how a cowboy feels riding upon a bucking bronco. I fear my spine will never recover from this experience. My kidneys are becoming sensitive to the sudden and extreme bouncing of the jeep. One pothole we stumbled into almost ejected the captain and me from the jeep.

Joe "Captain, can we rest awhile to allow my spine to recover?"

Captain Djarmat "I'd love to, but we must make the encampment before nightfall. We have to keep going. Relax; it is just a few more miles."

The road does not improve for the next few miles. Actually, it gets worse. We begin to slide as well as buck. The sliding sensation really aggravates my kidneys. I doubt that I will be able to walk tomorrow. The truck behind us seems to move in every which way as well. From the sudden bulges in the canvas covering, the soldiers riding in the rear are being tossed out of their seats. This is a terrible road.

Once the road solidifies, I get an opportunity to see the cleared vegetation to either side. As far as the eye can see, all the vegetation, including trees, has been cleared. This cleared area is ripe for erosion. No precautions have been taken to protect the topsoil. A heavy rain will wash it away.

We make better time on the solid road. Captain Djarmat informs me that this is recently cleared lands. It will take a few rains before it resembles the trek we just passed over. I acknowledge our good fortune.

Joe "Captain, how much area do they need to clear for a depot?"

Captain Djarmat surveys the surrounding area before answering, "The logging company has a deal with the government to clear the area in return for timber access. The government allows them to extend the clearing two kilometers in each direction from the intended path of the train and depot. That is why you see so much of the rainforest removed."

Joe "Why does the government allow the logging company such leeway?"

Captain Djarmat, as we sight the encampment, "The government gets the logging company to clear the train route and depot area for free. See, the logging company gets paid in timber and not in cash. It is a common practice in this part of the world."

As we pull into the encampment area, I realize that the ADB allocated funds for the clearing of the road and depot area. I wonder where those funds went.

The encampment is a tent city. There is not one permanent structure in the area. From what I can tell some one hundred or so loggers and support staff are milling about. It is just before sunset. Captain Djarmat just made it. There are few lights rigged around the encampment. Most are floodlights, powered by a small diesel generator. Food is prepared on campfires in large metal pots. Tea is the beverage of choice. Water is issued from one of the trucks, loaded with huge water bottles. All the workers carry canteens.

Captain Djarmat "Mr. Del Rosi, we will camp tonight and inspect the area tomorrow. You and I will sleep in the truck. I hope you don't mind. It beats sleeping on the ground here. My men will have a tent and watch over us through the night."

Captain Djarmat wastes no time issuing the night orders to his men. Three of the soldiers begin pitching a tent while the fourth takes up an M-16 and begins patrolling the area where we will sleep. Darkness falls upon us quickly. I never realized how dark it got. Thank God for the few floodlights, or we would not be able to see each other. I feel sorry for the night guards, the mosquitoes descend upon us as if they had been starved for months. Even after I entered the rear of the truck, protected by a mosquito net, I could hear the night guard constantly slapping his neck. This is a miserable place. Despite the canvas cover, my body responds negatively to the dampness from the moisture collecting upon the canopy.

The comfort of the warm blankets laid upon the truck's benches does little to reduce the soreness in my back. I sleep little during the night. The strange sounds, emanating from the surrounding jungle and the drone of the mosquitoes, keep me awake. Captain Djarmat, on the other hand, sleeps like a babe. Will I survive this for two days?

It is daylight when Captain Djarmat awakes me. I must have slept some, as morning approached. My back still aches though. Captain Djarmat offers me a mess kit pan with some water for refreshing and shaving. Fortunately, I brought my cordless, electric razor. He tells me when I am ready one of the soldiers will bring me a cup of hot tea.

Before he is about to exit the truck, Captain Djarmat asks, "Did you hear anything unusual last night?"

Joe "No, I just heard the jungle sounds, until I finally slept. They were quite loud."

Captain Djarmat "Besides the macaws, the monkeys on New Guinea are the loudest in the world."

Joe "Is there anything wrong?"

Captain Djarmat just stares at me, says nothing and exits the truck. Through the canvas drape covering the rear of the truck, I can see the captain discussing something seriously with three of his men. The captain seems disturbed. Something must have happened last night.

There is nothing like having an electric razor in the jungle. It sure beats using a straight edge and cold water. I refresh and exit the truck. It is a humid morning, but it is sunny. The sky is a perfect blue without a cloud in sight. A few mosquitoes greet me, but I quickly brush them away. As I exit, one of the soldiers attends to my tea.

Before walking three steps, the soldier has a cup of hot tea for me. He says something to me that I can only decipher as "good morning."

Joe "Good morning. Thank you for the tea."

The soldier just smiles and repeats a similar phrase to the first one he uttered.

Sipping my tea, I scan the depot area. It is truly an island of men and equipment in an ocean of devastated vegetation. As far as the eye can see back toward Jayapura, vegetation has been bulldozed down. Tree stumps dot the landscape. Somehow, they remind me of bomb craters. The track the loggers took is easy to distinguish. Your eye just needs to follow the four-kilometer span carved out of the jungle back toward Jayapura. I wonder where the animals go that used to live here.

Captain Djarmat approaches me with a Caucasian fellow. He is a rough looking character that obviously has spent too much time in the jungle. His attire looks like he has not changed clothing in a week or more.

Captain Djarmat "Mr. Del Rosi, this is Bradley Connors. He is the civil engineer overseeing the onsite work here at the depot."

We shake hands. His hands are rough, like he cut all this vegetation himself by hand. His handshake is firm as well, giving me the immediate impression that this man says what he means.

Connors "Brad will do fine, Mr. Del Rosi."

Joe "It's Joe Del Rosi. Joe will be fine as well. Good to meet you."

Connors "OK, Mate, I take it you are here to assess our problems, is that right?"

Joe "Yes, the Bank has asked me to check all this out."

Connors "OK then, let's get a move on. I'll show you around."

Just as we are about to walk toward the area of concern, a military transport truck honks its horn to clear the way.

Connors pulling me aside, "It's best to let this bloke go by first."

The military truck pulls into a spot not far from our location. Soon, the truck is surrounded by a horde of Malay-looking workers. A few climb inside while others form a line, leading to a huge tent. In seconds, semi-frozen and fresh meat parcels begin making their way down the line into the tent.

Connors "That's our fresh supplies. A water truck should come tomorrow morning."

Captain Djarmat accompanies us. The soldiers remain by our truck. As we walk, another military officer distracts Captain Djarmat. As they discuss something in their language, Connors takes me aside.

Connors in a lower voice, "Listen, Mate, whatever you think of the captain, he's a good man. He will keep you alive out here. You do whatever he tells you. This place is dangerous."

Our conversation is interrupted by the return of the captain. We continue on our walk to the site of interest.

Connors breaks the silence, "I'm sorry to hear about your man last night, Captain."

Captain Djarmat, slow to respond, "We are still looking into that."

Joe "What happened?"

Captain Djarmat and Connors remain silent. We just keep walking. I realize that all morning, since I woke, I only observed three of the soldiers. Something must have happened to one of them. The soldiers are always close together.

The walk to the site is difficult. The topsoil is damp, allowing our feet to slide every now and then. There is little vegetation left to retain the soil. Connors almost falls on one occasion. Captain Djarmat, the sure-footed one, reacts in time to catch his fall. Although we only walked a few hundred yards, it seemed to take forever. My thighs are sore from the trek. I may have even pulled a muscle in one of my thighs.

Sure enough, near the middle of this square-kilometer, cleared area rests one lone tree. From a distance, it looks no different than those trees already cut and piled up alongside one boundary of the area. As I look into the distance for comparison, at least a thousand trees resemble this one. So what is the problem?

Approaching the tree, Connors makes obvious comparison comments with other trees. He then goes into a long story about how they tried to cut it down.

Captain Djarmat circles the tree and asks, "Have you tried dynamiting the roots?"

Connors "Oh yes, Captain, we tried that too."

Joe "What kind of chainsaws were you using?"

Connors "We used the top of the line variety that we have used everywhere in South East Asia. Then, we brought in some heavy duty types from Canada. They all failed. Remember, these are tropical timbers and not the hardwood variety found in the northern climates."

I reassess the tree and confirm that it appears to be a tropical timber. Captain Djarmat likewise concurs.

Joe "Brad, have you ever run into a problem like this before?"

Connors "No, I've run into some trees with stubborn roots before, but never anything like this. Let me show you something unusual."

Connors makes his way to the rear of the tree where he points out a small portion of the tree where some of the bark has been removed.

Connors "Look at this part of the inner tree. Now, the bark looks like tropical timber, but this part looks very different. Notice how clean it is. We stripped the bark off yesterday. Look at how strangely it is mending."

I place my hand on the inner tree. It feels warm. On another note, it does not feel like a tree. I ask Captain Djarmat for his impressions.

Captain Djarmat after feeling the inner tree with his hand, "I agree. It feels different. The texture somehow feels different."

Captain Djarmat removes a bayonet from a sheath he carries on his side and attempts to cut the inner tree. Surprisingly, he cannot even make a mark on the tree. He tries a piece of discarded bark from the tree and cuts it easily.

Joe amazed, "Brad, what happens to the chainsaws when you try to cut the tree?"

Connors "Some chainsaws have their blades bent while others have their teeth cleaved off entirely. In either case, the chainsaws become inoperative in a matter of seconds."

Connors shows us one of the discarded chainsaws with bent blades, left near the tree by an earlier work crew. This particular chainsaw is one employed almost exclusively in the deep forests of Canada. It should have cut through this tree with ease.

Captain Djarmat "Mr. Connors, how long did it take the loggers to cut through the other trees that look like this one?"

Connors "Those trees were cut clean through and toppled in less than thirty seconds."

Joe "Well, before I report this to anyone, I will need to see a demonstration."

Connors "Fair enough."

Connors turns around and hollers something in some Malay dialect to the loggers. One logger approaches with a chainsaw like the damaged one on the ground. Connors gives the logger some instructions, and the logger pulls on the starting cord to get the chainsaw working. A loud cylinder cycling sound disturbs our ears. The logger allows a few minutes for the machine to warm up.

Connors cautions us to move out of the way of the ejection route of the chainsaw and then signals the logger to commence cutting. The logger has no sooner touched the inner tree with the revolving chainsaw blade that the machine stops operating. The machine ceases to operate. When the logger retracts the chainsaw, the blades are bent. The machine stopped operating, because the bent blades jammed the revolving chain in its housing.

Connors looks over at me and says, "Good enough Mate."

Joe "Yes, that will do quite nicely. Thank you."

Connors dismisses the logger. The three of us just stare at the tree. Truly, we are at a loss as to what to do and say about this. I begin sizing up the entire tree. In height, it is probably fifteen to twenty feet. It has few branches extending out its trunk, and those branches are near the top of the tree. There are leaves on the branches. At most, the tree is two feet in diameter near the base. There are no roots protruding up from the ground. That seems strange, since the locations where similar trees where cut down have protruding roots.

Joe to Connors, "What can you tell me about the roots, Brad?"

Connors "We didn't find any roots running out away from the tree. There seems to be one main root, as best we can tell, and it goes straight down into the earth."

Joe "Have you tried to pull it up by its root?"

Connors "Try? First, the root goes straight down. For how far, we have no idea. We even tried dynamite and acid. Nothing worked?"

Joe "Acid?"

Connors "Sometimes, if you spill battery acid on a root, it will soften up. Or, the acid will eat through enough to allow you to remove the root. The battery acid didn't even scratch the root."

Joe "This was sulfuric acid, right?"

Connors "That's right, sulfuric acid from a fully charged batter. It would be hard to find anything more corrosive than that out here."

Joe "Listen, I will have to get my thoughts together here. This is too much to absorb at one time. Do you have any suggestions, Brad?"

Connors "None, Mate. I've tried everything I know. I'm stumped."

Joe to Captain Djarmat, "Is there anything that you would like to add, Captain?"

Captain Djarmat "The sooner we tell the authorities about this the better. This tree is way beyond anything that I have ever experienced. Besides, there are too many unexplained occurrences out here. We need some specialists in here to unravel all this."

Connors interjects, "I agree. We need a tree scientist to tell us what this is, and how to get out of our way."

Joe "OK, OK, what type of communication do we have here?"

Captain Djarmat responds, "We have shortwave communication with the military outpost in the area. The outpost can relay any information from us to Jayapura."

Joe to Captain Djarmat, "Can I send a confidential message to the Bank from Jayapura?"

Captain Djarmat "I can insure that the message goes out in a confidential fashion. Colonel Ulang will send it priority traffic to the ADB in Manila. Just draft the message you want to send, and I will attend to it."

The walk back to the truck is easier on our footing. The tropical sunlight has evaporated much of the moisture in the topsoil that troubled us so much in the morning. As we approach the truck, the soldiers seem eager to greet Captain Djarmat. Connors, noticing the soldiers' need to discuss something important with the captain, invites me into his tent for some tea.

Entering Connors' tent is an experience. The man has no sense of organization. Truly, he has been living out of this tent for quite some time. Unfolded clothing is draped everywhere. It is hard to move about inside the tent without brushing up against some article of his clothing.

Connors clears a space on the only table in the room. The table is one of those card tables with patches of green felt. I bet he lifted the thing from some makeshift casino in the jungle somewhere. He opens one of his private water bottles. The bottle must hold twenty gallons or more from its size. Filling two metal canteen holders, he proceeds to heat the water up on a sterno type camping heater.

Connors "Would you care for some tuna fish? It is fresh from the canneries in Samoa."

Joe smiling, "Do you bring your own rations out here?"

Connors "Trust me, Mate, you are better off with a diet of my tuna than eating the meat from the chow tent. The meat they serve in the chow tent is bush meat."

Joe "What is bush meat?"

Connors "If you notice, you are a long way from civilization out here. You probably also noticed how difficult it is to get out here. Just think of what the cooks have to do to get fresh provisions out here. The only two locations from here that could supply fresh meat are the military outpost and Jayapura. Now, the military outpost only feeds the troops. That leaves only Jayapura for our fresh supplies. The cooks have to make do. You may have noticed the lack of an abundance of jungle life, mostly a lack of mammals."

Joe "Do you mean they serve the monkeys to the loggers?"

Connors clears his throat: "You would be lucky, if you only ate monkeys. Did you see any natives on your way up here yesterday?"

Joe recalls with clarity the native that was executed and the natives with their belongings leaving the area. A sudden sense of disgust overcomes him. The thought that humans were being tossed into the meat pool was too much for him to comprehend.

Joe "Are you serious? They would serve human meat."

Connors "The bush meat trade is common in every deep jungle forestry project. Essentially, it is the only source of fresh meat. It is just too difficult and way too costly to ship fresh meat into these distant areas. That's why I bring tuna fish. Natives in this part of the world carry mad cow disease. Remember, they were once cannibals. If you eat them, your brain accumulates the disease."

Joe grimacing, "Sure, I will try some of your tuna fish."

Connors "While you are here in the encampment, feel free to dine with me whenever you like."

The water is steaming. Connors turns off the sterno oven and adds a tea bag to each canteen holder. He hands one of the canteen holders to me.

Connors "Here ya go Mate. You'll like this tea."

As I listen to Connors relate the situation here in the encampment, I sip his tea. It is quite good. It is hard for me to get the bush meat trade and its implications out of my mind. The Bank allocates funding for fresh supplies to these logging projects. Where does that money go?

Connors reminds me to draft a memo about the tree. As I attempt to write, Connors provides a constant supply of ideas. Before long, I have a basic draft. In essence, I request a tree scientist to assist us in identifying this tree. The draft contains all our failed attempts to remove the tree. I request additional assistance, as the Bank deems necessary. After some deliberation, I recommend Class 3 containment.

Class 3 containment will require military isolation of the encampment and the removal of all unnecessary workers. I realize that this is a drastic step, but I feel we need to ascertain positively what we are confronted with before proceeding.

Once completed, I exit Connors' tent to locate Captain Djarmat. He is with his troops near the truck. As I approach them, they silence their conversation.

Captain Djarmat looks over the draft closely. He seems to freeze on the Class 3 containment part.

Captain Djarmat "Mr. Del Rosi, I feel that a higher containment level might be required."

This response shocks me. I was pushing the envelope with Class 3.

Joe "Why should we be so cautious, Captain?"

Captain Djarmat "My men found the helmet and M-16 of my soldier near the periphery of the encampment. I have a soldier missing. There was no sign of a struggle. Something very strange is going on here."

Joe "Could your soldier have been kidnapped?"

Captain Djarmat "Perhaps, but if that were the case, the kidnappers would never have left the M-16. The M-16 is worth more than my soldier to them."

Joe "Could he have just walked off?"

Captain Djarmat "No, I have known this soldier for years. He is professional and intended the military to be his life's calling. He would never leave his post."

Joe "I see, and there was no sign of a struggle."

Captain Djarmat "There were no signs at all. He just disappeared without a trace."

Joe "OK, change the containment level to Class 4. Wow, this will shake up a few people."

Captain Djarmat handing me an M-16, "Take this weapon for your protection. I will leave immediately in the jeep for the military outpost and get this message off to the authorities and the ADB. One of my solders will accompany me. The other two will remain with you through the night. They have been directed to guard the truck while you sleep."

Joe "I have never used an M-16."

Captain Djarmat takes the weapon from me and begins to describe its operating mechanism. The gun jams. He tries to arm the operating mechanism a second time. It jams again. He calls to one of his soldiers to assist him. The gun still jams. He orders the soldier to disassemble the weapon and check out what is wrong.

Captain Djarmat "Just a moment, my soldier will have the weapon operating shortly."

Joe "Do these guns jam often?"

Captain Djarmat "No, we clean them daily and insure that they are operating correctly."

After about fifteen minutes, the soldier returns and reports something to Captain Djarmat. Captain Djarmat seems disturbed by the report.

Captain Djarmat turns to me and says, "The soldier found the chamber out of alignment. The operating mechanism will not operate properly."

Joe "How could that happen?"

Captain Djarmat excuses himself and walks over to his troops. He discusses something with them quite intently.

Captain Djarmat returns and says, "The soldiers insist that they were together when they cleaned and inspected their weapons last evening. The M-16 was operating properly before the soldier took his watch. Somehow, whatever happened to my soldier caused the chamber to be out of alignment."

Joe "Is that something difficult to do?"

Captain Djarmat "The chamber, made of strong steel, is bent. And, there is no sign of a struggle. That is near impossible."

After some deliberation with his troops, one of the soldiers hands me a sidearm weapon, a .38 caliber revolver.

Captain Djarmat and one of the soldiers board the jeep. As they are driving off, the captain tells me to keep the sidearm with me all through the night. The captain assures me that he will return tomorrow with help. I watch his jeep drive away.

CHAPTER 3

▼

ASIAN DEVELOPMENT BANK, MANILA, PHILIPPINE ISLANDS

At 3:00 PM in Manila, a secretary informs Bob Watson that the president of the ADB desires his presence in the main boardroom. The secretary conveys to Mr. Watson that he needs to bring all the files on the forestry project in New Guinea with him.

The president's office is on the top floor of the Bank. In an air conditioned building, it is a nice leisurely walk. Rather than try the elevator, truly the slowest in Manila, Bob decides on the stairs. The file on the forestry project is quite small. It can be cuddled easily under a shoulder and carried anywhere. It is surprising though that the president would take such an interest. Actually, it is the first time in all Mr. Watson's years at the Bank that the president has asked to see him.

Bob is in pretty good shape from all the sports activities in which he participates. As he makes his way to the president's office, he marvels at how someone could have recreated the intricate marble design in the third floor to be in consonance with that of the first floor. This artist truly was another Michelangelo.

The president's secretary tells Mr. Watson just to enter the office area. As he enters the room, Bob realized that the most senior members of the Bank are present. From their expressions, it is too obvious that they are expecting him.

Watson "Mr. Yoshihara, you asked to see me. I brought the New Guinea forestry project file."

The members are seated around a mini-board table, made from cherry wood. Its deep, rich color and fine texture immediately evoke a sense of affluence.

President Yoshihara "Please, Bob, take a seat. I trust you know all the other members present."

Watson looking around the board table, as he takes a seat, "Yes, I do."

The chairs consist of thick cushioned leather. One easily could succumb in their relaxing grip.

The president's secretary closes the door to the office.

President Yoshihara "Now that Bob is here, we can start. First and foremost, whatever we discuss in this room, henceforth, will be considered confidential. No one, and I mean no one, outside the people in this room should hear a word of what we are about to discuss."

Watson is stunned. He has never been summoned to such a meeting. Actually, he has never been in the same room with these upper ranking officials of the Bank during his entire tenure.

President Yoshihara "This meeting concerns our forestry project in New Guinea. As many of you are aware, we have encountered some curious delays. I am here to tell you that we now have another delay. That is the bad news. The good news is that the World Bank has allocated us additional funding."

The room members seem confused about the president's announcement. Yet, no one asks for clarification. After a pause, the president continues.

President Yoshihara "The Indonesian government has directed that the forestry project is now under Class 3 containment. I realize that Class 3 containment is a drastic step; however, they are evaluating the situation for even a more severe containment classification."

Watson interjects, "Mr. President, I just sent one of our consultants down there to evaluate the reports that we had been receiving. I have not received his report. He should be back in a few days."

President Yoshihara "Mr. Watson, it was Joe Del Rosi that initially recommended Class 3 containment."

Watson is stunned; "When did you find this out?"

President Yoshihara "Del Rosi's recommendation was an enclosure to the confidential fax that the Bank received today."

Watson realizes now that he is on the spot to support or denounce Joe Del Rosi. This could mean his job, if Joe just went nuts.

President Yoshihara "I would like an assessment of Joe Del Rosi. I understand you have been keeping him around a few years. Can his assessment be relied upon?"

Watson clearing his throat, "I have known Joe Del Rosi for a long time. He would never make a call like this, if he were not absolutely certain of the situation. There must be something serious happening down there."

President Yoshihara smiles, "Well, the Indonesian government believes that Mr. Del Rosi is correct. Tell me, Bob, what is Del Rosi's background?"

Watson "Do you mean formal education?"

President Yoshihara "Yes, tell me about his education and all else you can about him."

Watson leans back in his chair and loosens his tie, "Well, Joe Del Rosi and I attended the same university together. We were part of the same study group. I can attest to his objective approach to sensitive matters. He would have made an excellent research scientist. He did not pursue that goal, because he was interested more in philosophy than science. He has a general liberal arts degree with minors in biological sciences and philosophy. Rather than continue his studies, I persuaded him to come out here and assist me. I believe, he enjoys living in Manila"

President Yoshihara smiling, "Yes, I have been told that Manila seems to keep him occupied. That is why I am puzzled as to why a man of leisure voluntarily would quarantine himself in New Guinea, rather than just go through the motions down there in order to get back to what he enjoyed most. That truly confuses me, Bob."

Watson lost in thought over the president's implication, "It confuses me, too. He must really have been taken in by what he has uncovered."

President Yoshihara "What I have from the Indonesian Ministry of Information is that there exists a tree of unknown origins that seems to defy all attempts to remove it. Second, a professional soldier...an elite commando...disappeared while patrolling the area in the vicinity of the tree. There are other reports of loggers and natives going missing as well. The Indonesian Army voiced serious concerns about the situation. All personnel who have visited the site, containing the tree, have been quarantined. Those soldiers guarding the quarantined individuals have been given the order to shoot anyone trying to escape the quarantine."

Watson shocked, "My God, what is going on down there?"

President Yoshihara looking through the fax, "The tree, in outward appearance, resembles the other tropical trees in the vicinity. Once the bark is removed, the inner tree is uncuttable. Del Rosi witnessed a chainsaw destroy itself trying to cut the tree. In order to soften the tree's roots, battery acid was poured onto the roots. The roots were unaffected by the acid. Dynamite was unable to damage the roots in anyway. This tree seems to be indestructible."

President Yoshihara looks around the room and says, "Gentlemen, we have never encountered a tree with this tenacity. The Indonesian government will ascertain everything about this tree before the quarantine is lifted. The good news for us is that the World Bank has agreed to give us an open check to finance this investigation."

The room members smile at the thought at having such financial power. To them, this tree is a dream come true. An embarrassing project is now center stage, financially.

President Yoshihara "OK, first on the agenda is the Indonesian investigative team. The team leader will be Dr. R. M. Leong of the University of Penang."

One room member exclaims, "Do you mean Rachel Leong, Mr. President?"

President Yoshihara looking through the enclosures, "The fax just mentions R. D. Leong."

The room member "Mr. President, that would be Rachael Monroe, formerly a Kiwi that married into the wealthy Leong family of Djakarta."

President Yoshihara "I still do not follow your concern."

The room member "Mr. President, Rachel Monroe headed up SETI in New Zealand."

SETI refers to Search for Extraterrestrial Intelligence…the search for outer space aliens.

President Yoshihara stunned "Oh my, this could really backfire on us."

Turning to Watson, President Yoshihara says, "Bob, I want you to reply to Del Rosi's fax. Tell him to provide us daily feedback on the events down there. And, please alert him to Dr. Leong's background as discretely as you can. All we need to have is for an alien sighting hit the international press."

Watson "I will, Mr. President."

President Yoshihara "Bob, you will continue to be the lead contact on this project. Keep me updated."

After an hour of deliberation over specific assignments and responsibilities for this project, President Yoshihara thanks the other members for their participation and closes the meeting. As the members are filing out of the room, the president asks to see the file on the New Guinea project. This request is a delay tactic designed to keep Watson in the room. After a few minutes have elapsed since the last member left the room, the president signals for his secretary to close the door.

Thumbing through the file, President Yoshihara says, "You are an American, Bob, and I am Japanese. Both our countries have an interest in this anomaly that goes far beyond our assignments here at the Bank. Don't you agree?"

Watson "Yes, I can see that unfolding."

President Yoshihara nodding his head in the affirmative, "Good! Given our mutual recognition of this fact, I am going to ask you to keep me personally informed. My country, as well as yours, will want to be a part of any decision that evolves from the findings of this investigation."

Watson leans forward, "You can count on my loyalty, Mr. President."

President Yoshihara "Let me share an unfortunate issue with you, Bob. Although our man, Del Rosi, is the lead man on the ground in New Guinea, he is hamstrung by communication. You see, all his communications to us travel via the Indonesian Army. The Indonesian Army insures that the Indonesian Ministry for Information gets to see Del Rosi's message traffic before it is transmitted to us. For instance, the message that was communicated to the Bank was addressed to you, Bob. The Ministry of Information merely reassigned the destination to me."

Watson surprised, "I am not sure we can improve upon that situation. As I understand that portion of New Guinea does not fall under the footprint of any of the currently available communication satellites. That is why I did not equip, Del Rosi, with a direct satellite cellular phone."

President Yoshihara looks up at the ceiling intently, deep in thought. Suddenly, he lowers his eyes and stares at Watson, "I have an idea. This new woman scientist, Leong, would have privileged communication with other world scientists. We need to convey to Del Rosi to befriend this woman and have her communications copied to us."

Watson shaking his head, "It would be difficult to get her to compromise those communications."

Both men appreciate the problem. They think on the matter a few minutes.

Watson suggests, "What if we asked Leong to copy an imminent scientist in Japan?"

President Yoshihara smiles, "Yes that would do it nicely. Yes, Bob, that is the solution. Actually, that solution improves on my concerns. This way, the communication to my country would not be hampered by the Bank."

Watson says nothing, but he suspects that the president had this intention in mind all along. He just needed it to be my idea in order to distance him from the process. The Japanese mind is not all that difficult to decipher.

Watson nods, "We just need a name of an imminent Japanese scientist to provide Del Rosi in our response."

President Yoshihara, acting as if rushed, "Give me a few hours to work this out with my government. I'll have a name for you before the close of business today. We need to respond to Del Rosi quickly. In the meantime, please begin to draft our response."

President Yoshihara hands back the New Guinea file. The gesture signals the end of the discussion. He has accomplished his objectives. Watson takes the file and proceeds out of the room.

After Watson has left the room, President Yoshiraha has his secretary make the connection with the Ministry of Information & Technology in Japan. The call is being placed to a Mr. Kajioka.

President Yoshihara "Mr. Kajioka, I just called to inform you that a Japanese scientist will be requested for this affair in New Guinea."

Kajioka "That is excellent. We will proceed as planned. I have cleared it with the Foreign Ministry. Our man will be Yanagi."

President Yoshihara "There is one more item that we need to address: communication. My project manager informs me that satellite communication is limited in this area."

Kajioka "Let me assure you that it is not. We already have addressed that problem. There are windows of opportunity for us to transmit from the area."

President Yoshihara "That is good news, because the project manager seemed certain that there was no satellite coverage."

Kajioka "I am sure that with his restricted knowledge of the outer atmosphere communication systems that he would think that to be the case. Let me assure that it is not the case."

President Yoshihara "I trust in your confidence, Mr. Kajioka. While I have you on the phone, this Yanagi fellow, is he with your department?"

Kajioka "No, Yanagi works with the Science & Technology sector within the Foreign Ministry. The Foreign Ministry felt that a trained operative would be best for this assignment."

President Yoshihara "The other scientists will be cautious of an unaccredited colleague, don't you think?"

Kajioka "Dr. Yukio Yanagi is an accredited colleague. Actually, he was assigned with Dr. Leong on a prior project. Dr. Leong will identify him, immediately. This was another reason why he was chosen."

President Yoshihara "I trust that Dr. Leong is unaware of his collateral duties with the Foreign Ministry."

Kajioka "She may suspect his dual functions. That is a chance we are willing to undertake, because she would be hesitant to reveal this fact."

President Yoshihara "Why would she hesitate?"

Kajioka "Dr. Leong hesitation is a matter I am afraid that I cannot discuss with you."

President Yoshiha sensing the tone of Kajioka's voice, "I see. Well, in that case, that is all the news that I have for you, right now."

Kajioka "We will proceed as planned. Once our man is in place, we should limit the communication between us, so as not to awaken suspicions and invite eavesdroppers."

After the telephone communication terminates, President Yoshihara contemplates the issue of Dr. Leong. She must be a foreign operative. But for whom would it be? She has all the support of the Indonesian government. Therefore, she must work for New Zealand! That must be why Kajioka abruptly silenced the topic. This New Guinea affair will evolve into an international cloak & dagger operation. Fortunately, my involvement ends after I supply the name of the Japanese scientist. Thank the Beloved Buddha for that! I pray for that poor fellow we sent down their on a cursory inspection mission. He will be incarcerated there forever, it seems. What a hellhole that will turn out to be for a Manila man of leisure!

Watson labors over the correct wording of the response to Del Rosi. He must insure that the wording is distant, yet sufficiently comprehensible to Del Rosi that he acquires the Bank's intentions. Not having been trained in the evasive writing, Watson experiences the difficulty with such a task. Despite the challenge, he managers to create a working draft just before the close of business.

Sensing the time, Watson quickly rushes the draft, personally, to the president's office. As he approaches the president's secretary, once again, she gestures for him just to enter the president's office. Once again, he is surprised by the lack of protocol. The president is expecting him. Watson has never received such treatment in his entire tenure with the Bank.

Watson entering the room, "Excuse me, Mr. President, I have the draft for you."

President Yoshihara gesturing for Watson to close the door behind him, "Please, come in."

Watson takes a seat near the president, as he hands over the draft. President Yoshihara peruses the document a few times.

President Yoshihara "This looks good, Bob. Will our man be able to decipher our intentions? The way this letter is worded, a Bank employee would have some difficulty comprehending our intentions."

Watson running his index finger across his lips, "Del Rosi and I were in the same study group. We would communicate in such a manner when we needed a break. Please note that I have inserted a keyword in the salutation of the transmittal that will alert Del Rosi as to the hidden agenda contained herein."

President Yoshihara "Which keyword is that?"

Watson, leaning over the draft, points with his index finger to the BSc in the salutation, intended to identify Del Rosi's accreditations.

Watson "BSc, as you know, refers to a Bachelor of Science degree in the accreditation of the British Empire. Del Rosi does not have a Bachelor of Science degree. He has a Bachelor of Arts degree or BA. Del Rosi knows that I am aware of his credentials. The BSc will alert him to be cautious, and that I am conveying to him sensitive information."

President Yoshihara "I see. I would never have suspected such a subtle cue."

Watson smiling, "Few people would suspect. First, few would have the knowledge of Del Rosi's credentials, because an economics degree, a fundamental requirement for employment with the Bank, is a Bachelor of Science degree or BS in the United States."

President Yoshihara admires the draft and concludes that it will do nicely. The two men discuss the transmittal process. It is agreed that the Bank will forward a copy of the transmittal to the Japanese Foreign Ministry requesting a tree scientist to represent the Bank's concerns. Another copy will be forwarded to the Indonesian Foreign Ministry requesting their cooperation to allow a Bank-appointed scientist to assess the tree in question. The main copy will be sent to the Indonesian Ministry of Information as a response to the fax that they sent to the Bank.

Watson "Won't we need to supply the name of the Bank's scientist?"

President Yoshihara "The Japanese Foreign Ministry will handle that concern. Trust me, getting involved in a Japanese selection processes would create more trouble for the Bank than we need right now. It would behoove us to stay clear of the Foreign Ministry's affairs."

Watson thinks on the matter a while then concedes to the preferences of the president.

The president requests the secretary's presence in the room. A few changes are made to the draft in order to accommodate Japanese accepted phrases for ease of translation. The president instructs the secretary to type the message in English,

Indonesian and Japanese. A cover letter, officially requesting a Japanese scientist, will be attached to the message sent to the Foreign Ministry. The intention is to transmit the message to all parties, this evening.

Watson is amazed at the pace with which this matter is being attended. Usually, the Bank is noted for doting forever over minor details.

CHAPTER 4

▼

TREE SITE, NEW GUINEA

Although it felt uncomfortable sleeping next to an inoperative M-16, the night passed without incident. Apparently, Joe's ears acclimatized to the jungle noise. Sporadic rain showers tapped on the truck's canvas. Some laughter, now and then, burped out from one of the loggers' tents. Morning found everyone present.

A cup of hot tea greeted Joe, as he pushed aside the canvas cover to exit the truck's rear. The two soldiers attempted to converse with Joe, but their lack of an understanding of English was their undoing. Joe, on the other hand, could make out a few of the words of Bahasa Indonesia. Those words had similar sounds to some he had heard in Manila. Trying to communicate over tea, at breakfast time, without a common language is difficult. The trying does keep the mind active and provides the added benefit of relieving your thoughts from the dangers at hand.

By mid-morning, as promised, Captain Djarmat returns with a convoy of Indonesian soldiers. From the number of trucks, following his jeep, an entire Battalion must have been summoned. The peacefulness of the loggers' living was about to change. As the first few trucks pulled into the encampment, the soldiers disembarked and formed up. The remaining trucks were empty.

Connors, making his way to Joe's truck, in a hoarse Australian query shouted to Joe, "What do you make of this?"

Before Joe could answer, Captain Djarmat bellows out an order for the troops to round up all the loggers. The troops consist of about half of a company in strength, some fifty or so.

Connors joins Joe and the two soldiers. As they watch the herding up of the loggers, Captain Djarmat comes over and explains the situation. The loggers will be quarantined at the military outpost. Connors and Joe are to remain at the site with a detachment of soldiers. Then, Captain Djarmat relays the bad news.

Captain Djarmat "I am sorry to have to tell you this, Mr. Del Rosi, you are to be quarantined, as well, here at the encampment. You will not be departing as you had planned. Unfortunately, I have no estimate of when you may be allowed to return to Manila. As it stands, right now, we are all here for the duration."

Joe somewhat disturbed by the news, "Does the ADB concur with this?"

Captain Djarmat "It is not the Asian Development Bank's decision. It is the decision of the Indonesian government. I am sorry, Mr. Del Rosi."

Captain Djarmat begins to turn to speak to Connors, but Connors acknowledges, "No need, Captain, I understand. I'm here for the duration, as well."

Joe "Can you tell us anything more, Captain?"

Captain Djarmat "Once the loggers have been evacuated, helicopters will bring in equipment and supplies. I understand that a team of scientists will follow soon thereafter. That is about all I know for now."

Joe "Captain, I only packed for a few days. Is there any chance I could acquire some additional clothing and personal supplies? I brought a cordless electric razor."

Captain Djarmat smiles, "Of course, Mr. Del Rosi, I will have one of the soldiers fit you for some uniforms. As for the electric razor, without a re-charger, you will have to use a straight edge."

Connors breaks in, "Joe, I got an electric razor. You can use mine, if you don't mind."

Both Captain Djarmat and Joe notice Connors' beard and realize the razor might be an extinct relic. It is difficult for the two of them to prevent from smiling at Connors' offer.

Joe manages a response, "Thank you, Brad. I appreciate the offer and will take you up on it."

By noontime, the soldiers have assembled all the loggers in the trucks. Captain Djarmat orders a first lieutenant to return the convoy to the military outpost. As we watch the trucks depart, Captain Djarmat and Connors join the two soldiers and Joe for a cup of hot tea. The remaining soldiers begin cleaning out the vacated, logger tents for their new guests.

Despite the outward appearance of control at the encampment, Captain Djar-mat, Connors and Joe realize that very little has been uncovered about this unusual tree and the reasons why so many people are missing. A sense of one's last days seems to overcome the thoughts of each of these individuals. To Captain Djarmat and Connors, both of whom have extensive experience in these wild, unpredictable areas, the anxiety is not uncommon. To Joe, however, this situation is downright frightening.

Joe nervously asks, "Captain Djarmat, did you hear any news about the tree while you were at the military outpost?"

Captain Djarmat shaking his head, "No, I did not. When I left the outpost to return here, we had received a reply from the Asian Development Bank. All I have read in the transmittals is that a tree scientist is being flown in."

Connors smiling, "I can't wait to see the look on the bloke's face when he checks this tree out."

Captain Djarmat chuckles, "Sorry to break the news to you, Mr. Connors, but the tree scientist that is coming is a female. Do not harbor any preconceptions about this woman. She married into a wealthy family from Djakarta."

Joe surprised, "They are sending us a woman."

Captain Djarmat "That is what I am told, Mr. Del Rosi. Apparently, she is a resident expert on tropical trees."

Connors even more surprised, "She's from Indonesia, is she?"

Captain Djarmat looks at Connors sternly, "Yes, she is from Indonesia, and she is the government's selection. Like I spoke earlier, she is to be accorded the respect due a scientist and representative of the Republic of Indonesia."

The serious tone of Captain Djarmat's voice reaches home for both Connors and Joe. The Indonesian Army soldiers will surround this woman at all time. In essence, she will have technical command over the entire encampment.

Having a woman in charge is no big deal to Joe; however, for Connors, this will take some time getting accustomed. Connors hails from a strong patriarchal society, Australia. Although there are woman leaders in Australia, they are uncommon and usually relegated to politics. Some American companies have stationed female, senior executives in Sydney; however, the interface personnel with the engineering corps always have been men.

A second lieutenant reports to Captain Djarmat that the encampment has been cleared out for the new arrivals. Captain Djarmat selects a special tent that will lodge the incoming tree scientist. A soldier will be posted, around the clock, near the entrance to the tent. Joe can tell from Captain Djarmat attentiveness to every detail concerning the tree scientist that she is an important person.

By 3:00 PM, the first helicopters begin to arrive from Jayapura. Captain Djarmat rejoins his men to coordinate the landings.

These helicopters are loaded with equipment. One of the helicopter crews unloads a new generator. The sight of this machine brings a smile to both the faces of Connors and Joe. Connors attempts to read the generator's shipping label, but a soldier deters him at bayonet point.

Connors, retreating from the bayonet slowly, says something in Indonesian that causes the soldier to smile. Seeing the smile on the soldier's face, he returns to where Joe is standing.

Connors wiping his brow, "I hadn't realized that they would be so touchy. That was close."

Joe exhaling, "Yes, it was close. If they don't want us to see anything, why are we still here?"

Connors explains, "I am the current resident expert, and you are the Bank's representative. Captain Djarmat oversees the soldiers. The Bank assigned him as your protector. In a sense, you brought Captain Djarmat an express route to promotion by coming here. Trust me, Mate, the Captain is in your debt for this."

Joe "Isn't the Captain a little junior for an assignment like this one?"

Connors clearing his throat, "You bet he is, but he is assigned to you. You represent the financing for this project. He will never let you leave here until all this is wrapped up. This could mean a spot promotion to major or even a leap in promotion to lieutenant colonel for the Captain. An assignment, such as this, warrants a colonel in charge at the encampment. Captain Djarmat knows this too well. Mate, I suspect the Captain already purchased his major's bars in Jayapura before you departed for this site."

Joe smiling, "I'm happy I could enhance his promotional opportunities."

Connors chuckles, "I think someone else is looking out for the Captain's career. This is a sensitive assignment. If it goes south, the upper command can point the blame on the Captain's inexperience. If it succeeds, then the Captain gets promoted. Think of it, Mate, you ever see a tree like that? Or, for that matter, you ever see anything withstand what we witnessed?"

Joe shaking his head, "No, I can't say that I have, but I'm not experienced with materials."

The conversation is interrupted, as more helicopters approach the encampment.

A captain emerges from the first of the new set of helicopters to touchdown. Huddled down, with one hand on his hat and the other filled with dispatches, he scurries immediately toward Captain Djarmat. Fortunately, after the trucks carrying the loggers departed, the captain ordered his soldiers to dampen the ground in order to limit the amount of dirt entrained airborne by helicopter blades. The conversation between the two captains is brief. Captain Djarmat opens the dispatch bag and rifles through the contents. One letter captivates his attention. The other captain returns to the helicopter and commences organizing the offload of all the copters.

Captain Djarmat walks over to where Connors and Joe are standing, "Mr. Del Rosi, this letter is for you."

Joe taking the letter from the captain, "Thank you, Captain."

The letter is a fax transmittal from the Bank. He reads the letter, as Connors eavesdrops over his shoulder.

When Connors sights the name R. M. Leong as the tree scientist, he exclaims, "Bloody bitch!"

The sudden burst of expression from Connors startles both Captain Djarmat and Joe. The intense stare from Captain Djarmat returns Connors to his senses. Connors recalls Captain Djarmat caution to be respectful toward an emissary of the Republic of Indonesia.

Joe "Do you know this woman, Brad?"

Connors, now composed, "I sure do, Mate. She's a Kiwi. Her maiden name was Rachael Monroe. That is what the "R. M." stands for in her new name."

Captain Djarmat remains silent. It is a silence that restricts Connors' comments like the sudden appearance of a stiletto in a chic nightclub.

Joe confused, "What's her story, Brad?"

Connors exhaling, "Well, Mate, she's competent, if that is what worries you. I'll reserve any further comments until after you have met her."

Captain Djarmat's smile indicates his pleasure with Connors' response.

While Captain Djarmat, Connors and Joe continue to converse, the helicopters are unloaded. Some office equipment is carried into the tent reserved for the tree scientist. One of the helicopters carried only technicians, assigned to electrically and electronically set up the encampment for service. The majority of the technicians run cables into and out of a series of tents. Captain Djarmat informs us that those tents will contain the assessment equipment. The technicians perform their tasks, swiftly. They must be some form of elite force designed for such occasions. Their motions seem habitual, like they have done this many times. Connors remarks, in amazement, at their efficiency.

Within an hour, the assessment tents and the equipment are operational. Even the new power generator is up and running. To Joe, the encampment takes on the appearance of high-tech display center at a state fair. The senior technician, a first lieutenant, requests a sign off from Captain Djarmat that the encampment is electrically powered and operational. Captain Djarmat tours the facility with the first lieutenant and approves of the set up. By 5:00 PM, the helicopters are revving up their blades for departure.

While Captain Djarmat is inspecting the set up, Joe re-reads the transmittal from the Bank. He notices with concern the error in the salutation. Similar errors, in Bank memos from Watson, signaled instances of caution. Undoubtedly, one of those instances is unfolding.

Following a number of re-reads, Joe only can comprehend the statement toward the end of the transmittal that he may be marooned in New Guinea for an indefinite period of time. Whatever else Watson is trying to communicate is not yet clear to him. The fact the Bank is sending a scientist of their choosing is understandable.

Joe's reading is interrupted by Captain Djarmat appearance near him, "Mr. Del Rosi, Dr. Leong will arrive tomorrow morning with the next convoy of helicopters."

Joe "Captain, just so you know, the Bank is sending a scientist as well."

Captain Djarmat smiles, "I am aware of that. The first lieutenant briefed me. This other scientist is Japanese. Not to worry, Mr. Del Rosi, he is conversant in English. Also, he has worked on assignment with Dr. Leong."

Connors interjects, "What's this Japanese scientist's name?"

Joe "The fax doesn't mention a name."

Captain Djarmat smiles, "His name is Yanagi. He will arrive in a few days."

Connors looks over at Joe and shrugs his shoulders. Joe just received the transmittal from the Bank, and yet, the captain knows more than Joe. Indonesian Army intelligence deserves respect.

Before Captain Djarmat returns to his troops, he comments, "Mr. Del Rosi, there are fresh uniforms for you to change into in the tent next to the tree scientist's tent. You can relocate all your belongings to that tent. It will be your new accommodations. Oh yes, a new electric razor with a charger has been provided to you, compliments of the Indonesian government."

After the Captain leaves the group to attend to his men, Connors whispers, "Mate, I would be careful from here on out. When the Indonesian Army knows more than the international institutions, there is cause for concern. The Indonesian government has their elite, foreign-intelligence staff working overtime on this situation. Be careful of all your communications with the Bank. Trust me, Mate, those communications are being monitored."

Next morning, Joe awakes to the guttural sounds of Connors fumbling about outside the tent trying to prepare some breakfast concoction. The tent was an improvement upon the back of a military truck. An air-mattress under your sleeping bag does wonderful things for the back. This jungle-quarantine might not be so bad after all.

Connors greets Joe with an offer for some breakfast with tea. One look at Connors' entrée discourages Joe. He settles for tea with the accompanying comment that he seldom eats breakfast. The comment pleases Connors. While Joe settles in for tea, Connors selects and devours portions of the mysterious items right from the pan. Seeing Connors enjoying the meal deters Joe from commenting on the cuisine and the etiquette. Joe's conclusion is that Connors has been in the jungle too long.

Captain Djarmat joins Connors and Joe for a cup of tea. Connors offers the captain a sample of his entrée. The captain, like Joe, comments that he seldom eats breakfast. As Connors cleans out the contents of the pan, the captain and Joe just smile at one another.

Captain Djarmat sipping his tea, "I stopped by this morning, gentlemen, to remind you that the scientific team will arrive this morning, and to inform you that Jayapura has alerted us that there have been many more disappearances in this sector than any other in New Guinea. As cautioned before, you should remain within the confines of the encampment."

Connors and Joe just nod in acknowledgment.

Captain Djarmat turns and looks at Connors, "I expect this to be the last time you venture outside the encampment to catch cuscus, Mr. Connors."

Connors gulps, "OK, Captain."

The captain finishes his tea and bids us good morning.

After the captain departs, Joe queries Connors, "Was that a jungle rat, you ate for breakfast?"

Connors surprised, "Hey, Mate, they are delicious. You should have tried some."

Joe grimacing, "Brad, I never acquired a taste for rat. I have heard that cuscus is a delicacy, but it is one that I avoid."

Connors smiling, "After you have been out here a while, you'll change your mind. The restaurants in the jungle have no star ratings; let me assure you. Besides, at least with cuscus, you know what you are eating."

Connors and Joe continue to chitchat over tea, until helicopters are seen coming over the tree tops on the horizon. These helicopters appear different than the others. First, they do not have M-16-toting soldiers bulging out the sides of the cargo section. Second, they are not heavily laden. Third, there are no cargo meshes attached to the portals.

Connors and Joe observe the soldiers in the encampment scurry about clearing a landing site. It is amazing how soldiers seem to spring into action for short durations then resume their normal meandering form of existence. Combat habits must condition them to perform in that manner.

There are three helicopters. A Caucasian woman exits the first helicopter to touchdown. She is attired in a similar military uniform, as the one provided to Joe by Captain Djarmat. To Joe, she is quite attractive. She stands about 5'8", slender, but athletic in appearance, with jet black hair. Captain Djarmat greets her and escorts her to meet Connors and Joe. The introductions are quick. She shakes hands with both Connors and Joe. Her mannerisms are professional, but one can sense her disdain for their presence. It is obvious that she prefers the company of fellow scientists.

After the meeting with Connors and Joe, Captain Djarmat escorts Dr. Leong to her tent. Joe notices that Dr. Leong treats the captain, as if he were her servant. Her demeanor will not go well out here. Connors comes to the same conclusion.

Connors exhaling, "Well, Mate, you've just met the bitch. What do you think?"

Joe likewise exhaling, "I think it is going to be a long quarantine."

Captain Djarmat comes over to Connors and Joe, "She will see us, now, to get acquainted with this tree problem. Come, she wants us in her tent."

Entering Dr. Leong's tent, she quickly seats us into the folding chairs provided around her simple card table. Captain Djarmat introduces Connors as the more knowledgeable and experienced with the tree. Connors commences to provide Dr. Leong the background information and his assessment of the tree. As Connors relates the information, Dr. Leong poses queries, now and then. She seems quite knowledgeable and certainly inquisitive. After Connors delivered his assessment, Dr. Leong requests to examine the tree with the three of us.

Captain Djarmat escorts the group to the tree. Soldiers patrol an imaginary circumference some twenty meters around the tree. As we approach, the captain signals for the soldiers to allow us entry. Once inside the imaginary perimeter, Dr. Leong walks around the tree, taking mental notes of certain peculiarities that she notices.

Turning suddenly, Dr. Leong says, "Captain, I thought the report mentioned that a portion of the bark was removed during the attempts to cut this tree?"

Captain Djarmat "Yes, Dr. Leong, a portion of the bark was removed. It should be somewhere near the base of the tree."

Dr. Leong looks carefully, twice, at the entire base of the tree. She sees no removed bark. Actually, to her, the bark has not even been bruised.

Dr. Leong "Perhaps, you are mistaken, Captain. The bark on this tree is untouched. Did you bring me to the right tree?"

Connors interjects, "Doctor, I witnessed the bark removed."

Joe "I witnessed it removed, also, Doctor."

Dr. Leong looking at the three men intently, "Well, gentlemen, come look for yourselves. This tree bark is untouched. I hope that this is not some kind of a joke, because I assure you that serious ramifications will befall the entire crew at this encampment."

The three men look over the tree. The tree bark is, as Dr. Leong reported, untouched."

Joe nervously states, "Dr. Leong, I am the Asian Development Bank representative here, and I personally witnessed the loggers remove some of the bark along the base of this tree. The bark was removed at my direction as a credibility check prior to announcing this anomaly."

Dr. Leong sensing Joe's truthfulness, "I am sorry, Mr. Del Rosi, if anything I said was taken improperly. I only meant to point out that the bark has somehow regenerated itself."

There is a sense of sweetness to Dr. Leong's apology. She is human after all. Joe senses a breakthrough with this woman. Perhaps, the jungle quarantine will not be miserable.

Joe "There is no apology needed, Doctor."

Dr. Leong tips her head in acknowledgment.

Joe turns to Connors, "Brad, would you do us the honors and cut off a piece of bark from this tree?"

Connors nods, "Sure thing, Mate."

Connors removes a survival knife from its sheath attached to his belt and commences to slice off a piece of the bark.

Upon removing the bark, he hands the piece to Dr. Leong, "There you go, Doctor."

Dr. Leong prior to accepting the bark dons a pair of rubber gloves, "Thank you, Mr. Connors."

The doctor takes a good deal of time admiring the bark. To Joe, her intense stare at the bark reminds him of a sexual encounter with Angelina in which she admired a portion of his body. I suppose women act the same when they encounter something that they admire. Suddenly, Dr. Leong begins to evolve into a different entity in Joe's mind. This new entity is desirable. Fantasies begin to pour into Joe's stream of consciousness. Joe's body likes this woman.

After what had to be twenty minutes of perusing the surface texture of the bark, Dr. Leong exclaims, "This is not natural tree bark. This bark has been fabricated to appear like tree bark."

Captain Djarmat stunned, "Gentlemen, what Dr. Leong just said is not to be repeated. Do you understand?"

The tone of the captain's voice is self-explanatory. Connors and Joe acknowledge the obvious order.

Dr. Leong to Captain Djarmat, "I'm sorry Captain. I just spoke out loud. It will not happen again."

Captain Leong sternly, "See that it does not Doctor. I am under strict orders here."

Dr. Leong pleads, "Captain, I will need someone in which to confide my impressions. You must allow me to converse with these two gentlemen."

Captain Djarmat thinks this request over for a moment then says, "I will allow you to converse with these two gentlemen. However, I must insist that your conversation be limited as much as possible. You must understand the severity of the situation here."

Dr. Leong smiles, "Thank you, Captain."

At which point, Dr. Leong says to Connors and Joe, "We got off on the wrong foot earlier today. My name is Rachel. Please just call me Rachael."

Connors shakes her hand: "Brad is fine for me."

Joe "Joe will do for me, Rachel."

Captain Djarmat just shakes his head.

Dr. Leong pauses a moment to think about the situation, then she says to the Captain, "Captain, I am going to observe the tree a while today. Could you have some of your men provide me with a shade covering…like an umbrella…a folding chair with side table and some tea?"

Captain Djarmat smiles, "I certainly will Doctor. Will you require the company of these gentlemen?"

Dr. Leong "No, I want to observe this tree by myself in silence. I want to allow my senses to provide me an impression of what we are dealing with here. After I am done observing the tree, I will meet with these gentlemen and discuss my impressions with them in your presence, Captain."

Captain Djarmat nods in acknowledgment and escorts Connors and Joe out of the guarded periphery area back to their tents.

While the soldiers are assembling her observation post, Dr. Leong places the piece of bark into a plastic bag, labels the contents and scribbles down some instruction for testing the material.

Dr. Leong, as Captain Djarmat comes to inform her that her umbrella site has been erected, tells him, "Captain, on the next helicopter, have this sample sent to my laboratory at the University of Penang. I have instructions on the label. My laboratory is expecting samples from the site to be tested."

The University of Penang is located in the city of Penang on the island of Sulawesi, one of the major islands in the Indonesian archipelago.

Captain Djarmat taking the sample, "Yes, Doctor, I will see that it is on the next flight."

Captain Djarmat escorts Dr. Leong to the umbrella. It is a huge beach umbrella that Dr. Leong brought along with her. The table and chair consist of more comfortable materials than those in Dr. Leong's tent.

Settling into the chair and adjusting the umbrella, Dr. Leong commences to contemplate on the tree. No sooner has she sat down that soldier arrives with a cup of tea. Captain Djarmat admires Dr. Leong's organization. Had his parents not forced him into the military, he could see himself as a research scientist. As it is, he acquired an engineering degree from the same university that Dr. Leong lectures.

Dr. Leong takes a long time scoping out the bark of the tree. She makes note of the fact that, unlike similar trees in the surrounding jungle, the branches on this tree congregate at the top. Most of the tree trunk is devoid of any type of protrusions. She is particularly concerned about the lack of surface imperfections in the bark along this branchless section of the tree. Every tree in the area contains scars of one form or another. This tree has no blemishes at all.

The branches at the top of the tree form a sort of canopy. They seem more designed for shielding the tree than any photosynthesis advantage. Speaking of photosynthesis, the leaves on the branches are at an odd angle for this time of day. The other vegetation around the site, even the blades of grass, is aligned to absorb the maximum amount of sunlight. Yet, the leaves on this tree orient to another direction. It is as if this tree is unconcerned about photosynthesis. Since photosynthesis is the means by which plants acquire energy necessary to sustain life, this tree must operate on another principle. Dr. Leong concludes that this tree is not a photosynthesis-related life form. But, all trees are photosynthesis life forms.

Sipping the last of her tea, she requests a refill. A soldier is quick to accommodate her request. Orderlies in five-star hotels are not this fast. She is impressed with Captain Djarmat's control over the soldiers.

Dr. Leong asks herself over an over why this tree would sprout branches and leaves, if it had no intention of utilizing them. She recalls Connors removing a knife from its sheath and concludes that the bark of the tree, with its extension into the branches, is some form of sheath designed to camouflage the exact nature of whatever this thing is. She realizes the implication of this line of thinking. Definitely, more tests will be required before she utters anything about her assumptions to anyone other than Captain Djarmat.

Enjoying her tea, she allows her stream of consciousness to concoct an array of bizarre ideas about the tree. If the bark is in fact merely a sheath, then the roots will reveal the true nature of whatever this thing is. From her observations, she seems certain that the camouflage notion has merit. The tree just does not exhibit the correct properties as other plant life in the surrounding area. Actually, to Dr. Leong, the tree does not exhibit any properties of plant life on this planet. At a minimum, she should confide in Captain Djarmat that Class 4 containment should be activated. If this tree is an alien species of plant life, then the encampment and everyone that has come in contact with it has to be placed under strict quarantine.

Finishing up her second cup of tea, she calls for Captain Djarmat. A soldier approaches and asks if she desires another refill. She accepts.

Dr. Leong standing up and stretching, "Captain, I will need to examine the roots. Could you have Mr. Connors assist me?"

Captain Djarmat orders one of the soldiers to fetch Connors.

After the soldier departs, Dr. Leong whispers to Captain Djarmat, "Captain, I believe that Class 4 containment is in order."

Captain Djarmat matter-of-factly, "Doctor, I came to that same conclusion a few days ago."

Dr. Leong surprised, "You were right, Captain. We are confronting something here that defies our previous understanding of plant life."

Captain Djarmat "Do you think the disappearances are somehow connected to this tree?"

Dr. Leong "It is quite possible, Captain. This tree requires some form of energy input to sustain itself. I have discounted photosynthesis, so the tree must be acquiring its energy in another manner. Animals need to devour other animals or plants in order to acquire the energy that they need to sustain themselves. It quite possibly could be the case that somehow this entity is devouring people in some manner for sustenance. It definitely requires an energy source in order to survive."

Connors and Joe are sampling from a family-size tuna can when a soldier appears and requests their presence at the tree.

Connors removing some tuna juice from his lips with his index finger, "That didn't take long, Mate. I guess the good doctor needs us. What did you think of the tuna?"

Joe "It was fine, Brad. I especially enjoyed having my own spoon to scoop out the mayonnaise to add to the tuna chunks."

Connors smiling, "Mate, in the jungle, you learn to make do. I always carry two spoons. Shall we join the good doctor?"

Joe standing up, "I suppose that we should."

As they are both about to leave, the soldier says to Connors in Indonesian that only he was requested and not the Bank representative."

Connors to Joe, "Sorry, Mate, the good doctor only desires my presence. You can finish off the tuna, if you like."

Connors exits the tent with the soldier, as Joe sits back down and continues to sample the tuna.

The soldier escorts Connors to Dr. Leong's table. Graciously, Dr. Leong invites him to join her under the umbrella.

Dr. Leong "Mr. Connors, I would like to inspect the roots. What can you tell me about them?"

Connors, as he adjusts his chair under the umbrella, "Doctor, there are no roots *per se*. There is only one root. It travels straight downward into the earth."

Dr. Leong "Are you certain that there are no branches sprouting out from this main root?"

Connors "As far as we could tell from the depth that we dug around the root, there was no sprouts at all. There was one single root directly below the trunk of the tree."

Dr. Leong "Can you dig a little around the root, so that I can inspect it? I will need to visualize this root."

Connors requests a shovel from one of the soldiers.

Connors "Of course, doctor, I understand."

Dr. Leong continues to sip her tea. When the shovel arrives, Connors excuses himself and commences digging up around the tree. Dr. Leong remains seated, admiring Connors work. Connors requests no assistance from the soldiers.

Within twenty minutes he has a hole about a meter deep dug around the circumference of the base of the tree.

Connors wiping some sweat off his brow, "This should be deep enough, Doctor. Come take a look for yourself."

Dr. Leong, setting down her teacup, walks slowly up to the hole that Connors just dug. Slowly, she views the shape of the single root, as she travels about the circumference of the tree.

Dr. Leong stops in front of Connors, "Yes, Mr. Connors, I see what you mean. Can you dig a little deeper, say another meter?"

Without comments, Connors commences to dig deeper. At about half a meter deeper, Dr. Leong notices how the bark-color of the tree begins to fade and a lighter, more lustrous, material begins to appear on the surface of the root.

Dr. Leong to Connors, "Mr. Connors, did you notice this strange coloring on the root when you dug around it earlier?"

Connors, stopping his digging for a moment, "Yes, Doctor, we did. It gets quite light in bark-color a few meters down. After that it assumes a kind of a light, reddish-black color."

Dr. Leong surprised, "Could I impose upon you to dig to that reddish-black color?"

Connors chuckles, "You could impose upon me, Doctor, but I am afraid that I would be too pooped by then."

Dr. Leong Smiles, "Of course, I understand."

Dr. Leong turns and calls to Captain Djarmat, "Captain, can I beseech your assistance?"

Captain Djarmat hurries to Dr. Leong's location, "What can I do for you, Doctor?"

Dr. Leong "Captain, can you have some of your men assist Mr. Connors to unearth the gravel around the root to the point where the root color changes? Mr. Connors informs me that it some two or more meters down."

Captain Djarmat orders two of his men to get shovels and commence digging. Like automatons, the two men scurry off to get shovels. In no time, the hole is dug, and the tree root is open to inspection.

Dr. Leong climbs down into the recently dug hole to inspect the root. It has the reddish-black color ascribed by Connors. She places her hand on the root where it is reddish-black in color. The root is warm to the touch. This is abnormal. The root should be cold.

Dr. Leong, as she climbs out of the hole, "I am satisfied, Captain. Your men can fill in the hole now."

Dr. Leong returns to her seat under the umbrella and requests that Connors sit with her a while. For some fifteen minutes, Dr. Leong remains quiet. Connors sips tea and allows her to contemplate her observations in silence.

Dr. Leong, as if just speaking out loud, "The tree root is warm to the touch."

Connors nods in agreement, "Yes, Doctor, we discovered that as well. The part of the tree under the bark is warm, too."

Dr. Leong still deep in thought, "It should be cool. Actually, it should be quite cool, since it does not employ photosynthesis. Where is this warmth coming from? Also, the inner tree is rigid and solid. We already have proven that whatever type of wood this tree is made of it is near indestructible."

Connors "That would be my assessment as well, Doctor."

Dr. Leong, nodding in acknowledgment of Connors' conclusion, "That will be all I need from you at this time, Mr. Connors. Thank you for assisting me and your comments."

Connors smiles and walks back to his tent.

Dr. Leong summons Captain Djarmat, "Please join me, Captain. We have some issues to discuss."

Captain Djarmat requests refreshed tea for Dr. Leong and a cup for himself.

Dr. Leong "Captain, this is not a tree at all. This is something else disguised to look like a tree. Why? I do not know. But, what we are looking at is no tree. This thing is not any form of plant life."

Captain Djarmat "I would tend to agree with you, Dr. Leong, but why would anything disguise itself as a tree?"

Dr. Leong inhales deeply, "Captain, I fear that there will be far more questions, like yours, than answers for a very long time from here on out. I have no idea how to respond."

Captain Djarmat "The Bank appointed scientist will arrive tomorrow, maybe he can shed some light on this."

Dr. Leong exhales, "I sure hope so, Captain; otherwise, we are in for a world of serious investigative effort. You should prepare your higher command for the worst, Captain. I have never encountered anything like this in my entire professional career."

Captain Djarmat, setting his teacup down, exhales forcefully, "I will inform them right away, Dr. Leong. I was afraid of this."

CHAPTER 5

▼

With morning, nowadays, comes the fresh scent of mosquito repellant. The Indonesian soldiers have developed an excellent chemical for discouraging mosquitoes. The chemical has a kind of unmistakably sweet odor. About an hour and a half before dawn, they begin applying the compound around the encampment. In the evening, they do the same about an hour and a half before sunset. Since mosquitoes, especially those carrying malaria, are most active in the period an hour before and after sunrise and sunset, the chemical provides its greatest deterrence in those few hours following application.

Connors has prepared some warm biscuits with our morning tea. A little fruit preserve, spread on the biscuits, does the trick. Dining with Connors, coupled with a great deal of imagination, resembles a continental breakfast at any South East Asian sea resort.

Shortly after dawn, our tea and biscuits is interrupted by the whooping sound of helicopter blades coming over the tree line. Connors and Joe observe Captain Djarmat organizing his troops into landing-assist groups for the copters. The copters provide some much needed breeze, as they settle onto the surface of the encampment. No sooner have the copters set down that the unloading process begins anew. One of the soldiers carries a mailbag to the lead copter. Captain Djarmat spends some time discussing something with the lead copter's pilot.

After the copters have been unloaded, a medium height, slender, Japanese-looking gentleman emerges from the last copter to set down. He seems over-burdened with canvas bags. Captain Djarmat issues orders to some of his soldiers to assist the gentlemen. The soldiers end up carrying all his canvas bags while Captain Djarmat escorts the gentleman to meet with Dr. Leong.

Connors to Joe, as they devour warm biscuits, "I suspect that gentleman is the Bank's scientist, Mate."

Joe "The message that I received from the Bank told me someone was coming."

After the gentleman and Dr. Leong have chatted a while, Captain Djarmat walks the gentleman over to Joe's tent.

Captain Djarmat, as he approaches the tent, "Mr. Del Rosi, this is Dr. Yanagi from Japan. He has been appointed as the Asian Development Bank's scientific representative on site."

Joe extends his hand, "A pleasure to meet you, Dr. Yanagi. Until you arrived, I was the Bank's representative on site."

Dr. Yanagi "You will remain the overall representative on site, Mr. Del Rosi. My assignment here is to act as the scientific liaison, only."

Joe looks over at Connors, "I'm sorry, Doctor. I was under the impression that you were here to relieve me."

Dr. Yanagi smiles, "On the contrary. Mr. Del Rosi, I am here to assist you. You will remain in command."

Connors chuckles: "Care for some more tea, Mate? Can I offer you a cup of tea, Doctor?"

Dr. Yanagi "No thank you. I need to get settled in."

Connors to Captain Djarmat, "Care for tea, Captain?"

Captain Djarmat "I will take up your offer, after I get the Doctor settled in."

For the first time, Joe realizes that he is to be marooned here for the duration. With him in overall command, Dr. Yanagi can come and go as he pleases.

Dr. Yanagi turns to Connors, "I am sorry, sir, but I did not get your name."

Connors "Brad Connors, Civil Engineer for the encampment, Doctor."

Dr. Yanagi nods, "Of course, every site needs a civil engineer."

Captain Djarmat adds, "Mr. Connors was the first on site to inspect the tree, Doctor. We felt his experience would be valuable to the investigation."

Dr. Yanagi "I understand, Captain. Shall we attend to my luggage and get set up?"

Captain Djarmat escorts the doctor to his tent. Connors and Joe continue enjoying their biscuits and tea.

Once inside Dr. Yanagi's tent, Captain Djarmat explains the regulations imposed upon the encampment. With emphasis, the captain stresses the importance of not wandering out into the jungle. The missing persons' issue seems to interest the doctor. He asks if a descriptive list of the known missing persons has been compiled. Captain Djarmat informs the doctor that he has requested the latest data from the authorities in Jayapura.

After Captain Djarmat departs the tent, Dr. Yanagi locates his special transmitter. The device resembles a hand-held cellular phone. The doctor checks the device for proper operation. It is too early to transmit. He will need to wait another few hours in order for the footprint of the satellite to pass within the range of the transmitter. In the meantime, Dr. Yanagi decides to visit Dr. Leong.

Dr. Yanagi is surprised by the attention that he is receiving at the encampment. The constant presence of an armed soldier wherever he goes outside his tent will become a problem during transmitting periods. He decides that, if he must, he will transmit within the confines of his tent. Since the device permits typed messages, if need be, he can make his reports in that venue.

At Dr. Leong's tent, a soldier on guard announces his arrival to Dr. Leong. Dr. Leong is quick to come to the foreground of the tent and invite Dr. Yanagi inside. The soldier permits his entry.

Dr. Yanagi "Sorry to bother you, Doctor, I thought I would get caught up on the situation here."

Dr. Leong motioning to a chair at her table, "Please, sit down, Doctor."

Dr. Yanagi settles in and asks, "Have you been at the site long, Doctor?"

Dr. Leong "I have been here just a few days. Connors has been here since the beginning."

Dr. Yanagi "Mr. Connors, is he an Australian?"

Dr. Leong thinks for a moment, "I believe that he is. He is one of those people that you always seem to find on sites like this one. He is a regular bush person."

Dr. Yanagi "What about the other fellow, Mr. Del Rosi?"

Dr. Leong "I cannot say that I have ever seen or heard of him before. He is a finance person for the ADB."

Dr. Yanagi "What do you know of this Captain Djarmat?"

Dr. Leong smiles, "He is very capable. Despite his junior rank, he is experienced and can be trusted. If you need anything, he will produce it. He is a good person to get to know."

For the next thirty minutes or so, the doctors discuss the tree. Dr. Leong provides Dr. Yanagi a thorough overview of the situation. Soldiers enter the tent during the conversation to refresh their tea. Dr. Yanagi comments on the service being better than the hotel-resorts in Indonesia.

As they continue their conversation, rain droplets massage the canvas covering of the tent. It is a soft rain that is common in the tropics. Some travelers refer to it as liquid sunshine. The rain clings to your clothes just long enough to cool you, before the sunlight evaporates it.

After the rain stops, Dr. Yanagi asks to see the tree. Dr. Leong walks him over to it. Soldiers accompany both the doctors. The soldiers do come in handy. When they arrive at the periphery of the tree, the soldiers acquire permission from the boundary guards to allow the doctors around the tree.

Dr. Leong is surprised to see the bark that had been cut away yesterday by Connors already on its way into regeneration. She points this out to Dr. Yanagi.

Dr. Yanagi "You say you stripped this bark yesterday, is that correct?"

Dr. Leong nodding her head up and down, "That is right, Doctor. I saw Connors cut this bark yesterday."

Dr. Yanagi climbs into the hole dug around the tree. He feels the root and the bark.

Dr. Yanagi "You are correct, Doctor. The root material is different than the material comprising the bark. This is strange indeed. Did you notice the warmth emanating from the root?"

Dr. Leong "It is the same warmth we felt coming from the inner portion of the tree under the bark. The tree is warm, Doctor."

Dr. Yanagi "Do you have any idea how far this root extends into the earth?"

Dr. Leong "We have not gotten that far into our investigation. We just uncovered what you see now, yesterday."

Dr. Yanagi climbs back out of the hole.

Dusting himself off, he says, "This is not a tree. Question is: what is it?"

Dr. Leong "I have no idea, Doctor. I consider myself an expert in tropical forests, and I have no idea."

Dr. Yanagi exhales, "We need to come up with some answers, before the whole world finds out about this tree."

Dr. Leong, pointing to the upper branches, "There is one more thing, Doctor. Notice how the leaves on those branches do not follow the sun."

Dr. Yanagi looks from different angles at the leaves, "This thing does not employ photosynthesis. Why is it warm?"

Dr. Leong "That is what is even more puzzling, Doctor. Creatures that do not use photosynthesis have to eat things in order to maintain their body temperature."

Dr. Yanagi, trying to hide his shock at the suggestion, "I understand your concern, Doctor. This thing could be very dangerous, indeed."

As they are pondering Dr. Leong's comment, Captain Djarmat joins them. He informs them that his soldiers have just set up the field radio. Communication between the encampment and Jayapura is now possible. The news pleases Dr. Leong. With Jayapura on-line, she can communicate with her laboratory at the University of Penang. The news is not as welcomed with Dr. Yanagi.

Following the tree inspection, Dr. Yanagi proceeds to his tent. He asks the guard posted outside to insure that he is not to be disturbed while he attends to his affairs within the tent. When he is sure that all is quiet outside his tent, he opens his mini-transmitter and begins to type. The type is in an abbreviated form of *kanji* for diplomatic code purposes.

Kanji became the script of Japanese writing, after Japan divorced from the Chinese script.

Dr. Yanagi's transmittal is short. In translation, "Arrived. Tree alien. Satellite depth probe required. Dangerous." The device flashes a green light after transmission, indicating that the communication was received satisfactorily. After the transmission, Dr. Yanagi carefully hides the device in one of his canvas bags. Unfortunately, the device can only transmit. The only feedback is in the form of the green flashing light indicating his communication was received. Actual feedback will come in the form of dispatches in the daily helicopter lifts into the encampment, or in the form of coded messages, embedded in routing communications with the site.

The rest of day, Dr. Yanagi busies himself with stowing his tent and arranging his things. He has some scientific equipment with him, but he now realizes how useless it will be. It will be difficult to assess the true nature of this tree without specific equipment. Getting that equipment into the site, without alerting anyone as to its purpose, will be next to impossible. He begins to appreciate the insurmountable task at hand. How can he possibly perform his assignment without divulging his results to the entire world? What he needs is an ally. He thinks of the American. This Del Rosi character would appear to be the most receptive to enlistment. Connors, the Australian, has been in the bush too long. What is more is that he is not too sophisticated. He is a person of the land, so to speak. Dr. Yanagi also sensed a bit of racial resentment from Connors. I guess the past Great War upset a lot of Australians. Connors may have had relatives who were incarcerated in South East Asia during the war. That experience is usually what riles Australians the most about Japanese. Dr. Yanagi discounts Dr. Leong, completely. She could be an agent for the New Zealand government. The Japanese Foreign Ministry thought so on his last assignment with her.

A soldier, relaying a message that his presence has been requested for a reception in Captain Djarmat's tent, interrupts Dr. Yanagi's thoughts. He graciously accepts.

Upon entering Captain Djarmat's tent, he is greeted with a glass of wine. Dr. Leong, Connors and Mr. Del Rosi are already present and seated around a center table. The center table contains fresh samplings of fish, biscuits and some cheese.

Captain Djarmat seats Dr. Yanagi next to Dr. Leong. The reception commences with a toast to the Republic of Indonesia, followed by courtesy toasts to Australia, Japan and the United States. Mr. Del Rosi manages to toast the Asian Development Bank for the accommodations. From the manner in which Mr. Del Rosi proposes the toast, one is not certain if it is sincere or in jest. Nonetheless, the reception proceeds amicably. Wine in the tropics has a way of ameliorating discomforts.

Dr. Leong is attired quite comfortably for the reception. Rather than her usual jungle fatigues, she has chosen a light Indonesian dress that seems to flow softly with the slightest breeze. Joe Del Rosi is quick to notice how the dress reveals Dr. Leong's physique. The wine and the breeze evoke a sense of wanting within Joe. Interestingly, Dr. Leong does not mind Joe's sudden infatuation. One might even conclude that she attired for him this evening. Dr. Yanagi also notices the chemistry working between Del Rosi and Leong. Certainly, this attraction could be beneficial to his intentions. Mr. Del Rosi might welcome his assistance in facilitating a clandestine rendezvous with Dr. Leong.

Connors is too interested in the wine to notice anything else. It is so true of overly-extended, forward deployed individuals that simple enjoyments sate their expectations. Dr. Yanagi will use this strange coupling to his advantage. Wine will cover a lot of distance between the site inhabitants and himself. Of course, the ever-watchful Captain Djarmat will take other incentives. He and his soldiers do not partake, other than for ceremonial purposes, in the festivities so alluring to Connors, Del Rosi and Leong.

For the evening, the topic of conversation is distant from the tree and their predicament. It consists of a light-hearted talk of places that they have experienced, mostly in the Indonesian Archipelago. One hotel on the island of Bali seems to be the center of attention. Apparently, all those in the tent spent time in that hotel and had the pleasure of enjoying Bali.

By midnight, the reception winds down. Soldiers escort the guests back to their tents. Connors takes some persuasion. Eventually, a soldier leads Connors with a wine bottle to his tent. Like a donkey following a carrot, Connors never takes his eyes off the bottle. The soldier allows Connors to sleep with the bottle and bids him good night.

Ministry of Information & Technology, Japan

Mr. Kajioka reads over the transmission from Dr. Yanagi. Despite the content of the message, he decides to further investigate prior to alerting anyone outside the small circle of associates in the need to know on this matter. He will make a call to Ministry of Foreign Affairs for assistance on the tree probe. His classmate from the university will be willing to assist him. He calls on Mr. Takeda, a jovial fellow with a penchant for intrigue. Mr. Takeda is a senior bureaucrat in the Science & Technology Division of the Ministry of Foreign Affairs.

When Mr. Kajioka's secretary has Mr. Takeda on the phone, "It has been a long time my old friend."

Takeda "Is this Kajoaka? Yes, it has been ages. What can I do for you, my old friend?"

Kajioka "Do you still have oversight in the satellite surveillance sector?"

Takeda "Of course, I do. Why do you ask?"

Kajioka "How secure is this phone line?"

Takeda "I am not sure. Do you need to speak more privately?"

Kajioka "Yes, I have a sensitive project in need of attention. Discretion is warranted."

Takeda chuckles and leans forward in his chair, "This sounds like my kind of project, old friend. Perhaps, we could meet in person and discuss it."

Kajioka "It is urgent, old friend. Can we meet in a few hours?"

Takeda sensing the excitement, "Yes, I know a place in the Raponggi District, the Doll House. I can be there in an hour, depending on traffic."

Kajioka realizing that Takeda has taken the hook, "I will be there in one hour."

Takeda "When you enter ask for Candice. She will know that you are there to see me."

Kajioka, sensing that Takeda enjoys the perks of Foreign Affairs, "Candice! I see. Is she an American?"

Takeda "Yes, she is as a matter of fact. She is from Minnesota. You will like her, old friend. She is a wonderful creature. See you there."

Raponggi is the nightlife area of Tokyo. The clientele comes mostly of the affluent business executive circle. Senior government bureaucrats with perks have liberties in the area as well. Rumor has it that the Doll House specializes in Caucasian hostesses, a particular favorite with Japanese businessmen. Although the establishments in Raponggi throb mostly at night, they are open by 2:00 PM and service clientele who manage to skip away from their posts a little early.

Within an hour Kajioka arrives at the Doll House. Upon entering the vestibule of the establishment, he is confronted by a huge doorman who demands to see his membership card. Apparently, the Doll House is a members' only establishment in the afternoon. Kajioka is lost for words. He just manages to mention his appointment with Takeda. The doorman is unimpressed with Kajioka and asks him to leave. Kajioka shakes his head in disbelief that Takeda could be so thoughtless. As the doorman opens the door to allow him to leave, Kajioka asks if Candice is working. Without a word, the doorman smiles, closes the door and allows Kajioka to enter.

A hostess leads Kajioka through another very, thick door into the inner chamber of the establishment. The sound of plastic chips clinking together reverberates through the entire room. Everywhere Kajioka looks there are businessmen gambling. The room contains roulette wheels, blackjack tables, dice tables of every kind, and some games that he has never seen before. The Doll House doubles as a gambling establishment in the daytime. Kajioka is impressed.

The hostess brings Kajioka to a *karaoke* room in the rear of the establishment. The room features cushioned seats, a TV monitor, sound equipment with microphones and a huge, teak, oval table. The hostess asks Kajioka to take a seat. Upon seating, she is quick to ask his liquor preference. For Kajioka, it is Johnny Walker Black Label scotch. As the waitress is about to leave to fetch his drink, he tells her that his friend told him to meet with a hostess named Candice. The hostess just smiles and tells him that Mr. Takeda will join him shortly.

Kajioka finds it strange that as he waits he realizes that he has not seen one Caucasian female in the establishment. He begins to wonder if he mistakenly walked into the wrong establishment. Fortunately, Takeda appears, as the hostess returns with his scotch.

Takeda sitting down, "Good to see you old friend. I see you got passed the doorman."

Kajioka sipping his scotch, "Yes, he was a huge fellow."

Takeda "He was a former *sumo* wrestler."

Changing the subject, Takeda inquires, "What is so urgent, old friend?"

Kajioka "We have a problem in New Guinea. I need a satellite to probe an item of concern."

Takeda learns back in the cushioned seat, "We do not have a satellite that covers that area on its normal orbit. How urgent is this?"

Kajioka "Old friend, the Minister, your boss, is asking?"

Takeda learns forward "Are you serious, old friend?"

Takeda realizes the significance of the Kajioka's request. The Minister of Information & Technology cannot ask Takeda to do this directly without arousing suspicions. This request has to be of the highest significance. Though Takeda oversees the Science & Technology section of the Ministry for Foreign Affairs, his immediate boss is the Minister for Information & Technology when matters of technology are concerned.

Takeda under stress, "Does the Minister know that I am involved?"

Kajioka "I am not sure. He is the one who sent me the order to have it done. What I ask is delicate, old friend. The Minister would be criticized for embarking on this without Cabinet approval. Hence, we have to do it clandestinely."

Takeda "Old friend, it will be difficult to do this. The orbit of the satellite might have to be altered. How sensitive is this project?"

Kajioka "The project has the highest sensitivity imaginable. As you know, I cannot divulge anything to you."

Takeda, looking up at the ceiling obviously distressed, "There is a tracking station in Australia. They might detect that we have altered the orbit."

Kajioka "I never said that the request was easy."

Takeda "What assistance can I get from your office in order to distract the Australians?"

Kajioka "We could arrange for a small delegation of astrophysicists to visit the tracking station. Manning the delegation with "good time" fellows should distract the Australians. As I understand it, the Australians never turn down a party."

Takeda "That is an interesting idea."

Kajioka "The Australian tracking station is in the desolate northern sector of the continent. We have the 'good fortune' of a number of female scientists attached to the department who always complain of being denied overseas, familiarization sojourns. Most of these females were educated abroad, hence, their familiarity with Western ways."

Takeda "If you can distract the Australians, then we could redirect the flight path and conduct the probe. What kind of probe do you require?"

Kajioka "I need a deep-earth probe at specific coordinates."

Takeda "Certainly, our satellite can perform a deep-earth probe. If it is one specific coordinate, it will take us longer to redirect the flight path of the satellite than to perform the probe."

Kajioka "Once you have performed the probe, how soon could I expect the results?"

Takeda "I believe instantaneously. The results would be transmitted to your laboratory directly. So as not to cause an alarm, the Geophysics laboratory in your ministry could be the recipient."

Kajioka nodding, "Yes, Takeda, that will do it. When can you be ready to redirect the satellite?"

Takeda "Old friend, our satellite rotates synchronously with the earth. It is positioned over Southern Malaysia to ease our communications with South East Asia and to monitor the waterborne traffic the Strait of Malacca."

Kajioka, accepting another scotch from the hostess, "Does anyone outside our sphere of communication know of our dual-purpose satellite?"

Takeda "There is no one of which I am aware. That is even more reason why your distraction of the Australians will be important."

Kajioka "What about Singapore, won't they detect anything?"

Takeda "The Singapore station activates for space shuttle tracking. If they do notice, we can explain the diversion as piracy surveillance. The only area that may raise a concern is the outer fringes of the footprint. If we plan our diversion at a time at night in which communication traffic is at a minimum in the periphery of the footprint, we should be fine. For this probe to be meaningful, we will need to be close to the exact coordinates. Otherwise, we would be talking about a miniscule adjustment to the orbit."

Kajioka "How much time do you need to alter the path and return the satellite?"

Takeda "As I see it, two hours should be more than enough time for the entire evolution. Most of that time will be involved in maneuvering the satellite."

Kajioka "I will set this in motion. Give me a few days."

The two men touch glasses and toast to their good fortune. A hostess brings a huge plate of *sashimi* while another hostess serves sample spices for dips. The two hostesses, upon a cue from Takeda, settle in like lap kittens next to the two men and commence liven up their spirits.

Encampment, New Guinea

The morning helicopter lift brings dispatches from Jayapura. One dispatch is from Dr. Leong's laboratory on Sulawesi. Captain Djarmat makes the rounds delivering the dispatches.

Captain Djarmat informs the guard posted outside Dr. Leong's tent to summon her. As Dr. Leong emerges from her tent, Captain Djarmat hands her the dispatch. She seems excited over the quick response from her laboratory.

Dr. Leong opening the dispatch quickly, "This is from my laboratory, Captain. Let us see what they uncovered about the bark sample."

Captain Djarmat surprised, "That was quick. I just put the sample on a copter a few days ago. They must have flown it directly to Sulawesi. I guess we do have priority."

Dr. Leong reads over the contents of the lab report. Basically, her lab has identified the bark as a strange combination of odd silicate compounds and various hydrocarbons. The limitations of the equipment in the laboratory prevent an in-depth analysis of the material. The hydrocarbons listed, for the most part, do not resemble those normally identified with those found in tropical timbers. Most strikingly, there are no hydrocarbons listed that would suggest any form of photosynthesis was being employed by the tree. The silicates, on the other hand, present a complete mystery.

Dr. Leong to Captain Djarmat, as he waits for her to finish reading the cover letter, "My laboratory confirms our suspicions that this tree does not function as other tropical timbers. We have something very odd here."

Captain Djarmat "Can they tell us what this thing is?"

Dr. Leong shaking her head side to side, "I am afraid not, Captain."

The report consists of a few enclosures, so Dr. Leong takes the time to review all the enclosures. The analysis page on the silicate is striking. The silicate contains some rare elements that usually are found in special-purpose structural materials. However, all those structural materials are man-made for the purpose of increasing the strength or toughness. Nature has not evolved that far, as of yet, to incorporate such elements. In closing the silicate analysis section of the report, Dr. Leong is puzzled over why silicates would be found at all within a tree-like structure.

Silicates are silicon-based compounds that resemble beach sand or quartz.

Dr. Leong takes the report into her tent and continues to peruse the contents. Her laboratory performed a quick analysis, so the results are more general than she would expect. Nonetheless, the results give a reasonably good picture of the bark from this tree. It is not nature made. The report indicates that a more thorough analysis is underway and should be available by the end of the week. Unfortunately, she realizes that her laboratory is not equipped to analyze silicon-based materials. Botany is a carbon-based science. All her instruments are calibrated and sensitized for carbon compounds. A geology laboratory can better analyze silicon-based compounds. She considers requesting assistance from the National University's geology laboratory in Djakarta. After some consideration, she realizes that Captain Djarmat could get the sample analyzed much faster than her by using the military to request the National University's participation. She asks the guard to summon Captain Djarmat.

A few minutes pass before Captain Djarmat enters her tent, "You asked to see me, Doctor."

Dr. Leong offering the Captain a seat, "Captain, could I impose upon the military to encourage the National University to analyze a sample of the bark in their geology laboratory?"

Captain Djarmat "Yes, Doctor, I can forward that request to Central Command in Djakarta. I am sure that they will assist us."

Dr. Leong smiles, "I am glad to hear that. Cut sections of the bark off the tree, as before near the base, and rush one sample to Djakarta and the other sample to my laboratory in Penang. Take an additional sample for Dr. Yanagi's laboratory in Tokyo."

Captain Djarmat "After I cut the pieces of bark off the tree, I will radio Jayapura to make the request so that the geology laboratory will be expecting the sample."

Dr. Leong "I knew I could count on the military."

Captain Djarmat "Is there anything else you would like me to add to the request?"

Dr. Leong "No, let us not direct their analysis to any particular focus. I want to get their unbiased opinion. It is important that they report what they find."

Captain Djarmat acknowledges the doctor's wishes and proceeds to carry out her requests.

After acquiring samples from the tree bark, Captain Djarmat seeks the refuge of his tent. He is accompanied by a second lieutenant, assigned to assist him in managing the soldiers. The second lieutenant is a young graduate of the military academy on his first assignment. From Captain Djarmat first impression, the young officer is dedicated. The captain recalls when he possessed such high aspirations. Two full tours in New Guinea dampened the captain's ambitions.

The two officers take a seat while Captain Djarmat opens his dispatch from Jayapura. Interestingly, the dispatch contains an overview, with some analysis, on the missing persons' data that he requested. He hands a portion of the data to the young lieutenant and instructs him to review it. Meanwhile, the captain concentrates on the cover letter and the profile analysis section.

In a rough estimate, some one hundred persons have been reported missing in this sector. Most of those missing can be attributed to the native penchant for walkabouts. A walkabout refers to a person suddenly deciding to journey into the jungle somewhere. Australians, residing in the western sector of their continent, have acquired this habit as well. It is not an uncommon practice. The missing foreign extraction workers present another matter. They certainly would not just get up one day and wander into the jungle. The same holds true for missing Javanese transmigrants and Indonesian soldiers.

Captain Djarmat categorizes those missing by likelihood of being abducted. Over sixty persons fall into this category. Perusing the analysis sheets, the captain determines that, on average or mean, the representative composite of a missing person would place the person at less than 163 cm (5'4") in height with a slender build. Interestingly, those are the only factors that seem to tie the most likely group together.

What puzzles the captain is the reason for these people being missing. They are of no special importance. The native kidnappers would not be attracted to them for ransom. They just simply disappeared.

In conference with the young lieutenant, the captain realizes that the data suggests that no one has ever seen these people again. The rebels that wander about the region have not made any demands or revelations, one way or the other. These people just vanished.

In comparisons with other areas of New Guinea, this area is the most prone for disappearances. Even the young lieutenant finds the results of the analysis strange. More people are hijacked in this sector than in Jayapura. The captain discounts a slave trade, because there are far more likely candidates than these people. Even the macabre hints of the bush meat trade would search for better candidates. To Captain Djarmat, what is so special about slender people under 163 cm (5'4") tall?

CHAPTER 6

▼

ENCAMPMENT, NEW GUINEA

Connors and Joe are enjoying a cup of tea in their tent. Today, the liquid sunshine episodes kiss the canvas often. The two men have decided to remain inside rather than try to evade the raindrops.

Connors "What do you think would cause an M-16 chamber to bend?"

Joe "You are referring to the missing soldier's M-16, am I right?"

Connors "I am referring to any M-16 chamber, actually?"

Joe, shrugging his shoulders, "I have no idea. I have never spent any time in the military, so I have never been around those kinds of weapons."

Connors "Well, Matie, I spent some time with the Corps of Engineers. Part of that time was devoted to small arms training which included the American-made M-16. All I can tell you is that piece of weaponry is very durable. During the Vietnam Era, my unit was assigned to clear areas where jungle battles took place in which the opposing forces came under artillery fire. There were M-16s lying around everywhere. As I recall, none had been damaged by the bombardments."

Joe "Is that right?"

Connors "That is a fact, Mate. They had some surface discoloration and some shrapnel dings, but the weapons operated properly. The sights may have needed to be adjusted, but the M-16s could be fired. Now, the Russian-made AK-47 was not as fortunate. Of course, they may have taken some direct hits."

Joe "The M-16 that I watched being operated jammed, each time they tried to cycle the chamber."

Connors interjects, "And, for certain, the weapon did not come under extreme battlefield conditions."

Joe "The soldiers asserted that they had observed the weapon undergo a field check on the very day that the soldier disappeared."

Connors "So, that takes us back to the original question: What kind of force could make the M-16's chamber jam?"

Joe "As I recall, Brad, the captain said the chamber was bent."

Connors "Was the M-16 irregularly bent...you know, like different angle bends?"

Joe "No, the M-16 was bent in a single small, barely noticeable arc."

Connors, cupping his chin, "That would indicate a single, uniform external force. And, whatever it was, it was quiet."

Joe "So, what produces a quiet, single, uniform external force of sufficient strength to bend an M-16...and make an elite-trained soldier disappear?"

Connors "That is a good question, isn't, Mate?"

Joe "Do you think it has something to do with this odd tree?"

Connors "I hate to think like that, but I am thinking like that. The disappearance of the soldier and this odd tree must somehow be linked together."

Joe "It does seem to follow. I mean the soldier was on guard duty. He would have had the M-16 across his chest when the incident occurred. It would be highly unlikely that the M-16 could be bent without leaving a trace of the soldier."

Connors interjects, "And, without making a sound!"

Joe, "You know, Brad, if something very strong wrapped around the soldier, as he held the M-16, the M-16 might bend. If that something prevented the soldier from screaming, it could at least partially account for what happened."

Connors pauses a moment to consider the wrap around idea, "A torquing, tightening force would do it. But, it would have to have enormous strength. What about the noise? There still would need to be some kind of explanation for the lack of noise."

Joe "Brad, how do those big jungle snakes kill their prey? I don't mean the poisonous ones."

Connors "Poor boy, growing up in the States deprived you of so much of nature's wonder. They are called constrictors. They strangle you to death by stopping the blood flow in the body."

Joe "Wouldn't a constrictor provide a single, uniform external force?"

Connors pauses, "I admit the suggestion does match our question, but constrictors don't come that big. Don't get me wrong, Mate, those snakes are big, but they seldom attack humans. You see the constrictor has to be able to swallow their prey whole. Humans have wide shoulders that would require the snake to have a wide enough mouth to engulf us."

Joe "You mean they don't crush our bones like the movies tell us?"

Connors "Mate, you need to watch less American television. Of course not, the constrictor has a special mechanism inside its skin to detect heartbeat. It tightens its grip around its prey until the heartbeat stops. Once the heartbeat stops, the constrictor swallows its prey. One golden rule of constrictors, don't strangle more than you can swallow."

Joe "Brad, if that is true, then there would be no traces of blood around the constrictor's attack site. Without a heartbeat, we don't bleed."

Connors truly is amazed at Joe's conclusion.

Connors "Mate, by God, I think you are right. A huge constrictor could be doing this. We are cutting away the rainforest that could have been its feeding grounds. The snake has run out of its normal diet and now is hunting whatever is available. But, Mate, it would have to be a big snake."

Joe "How big would it have to be?"

Connors "You know, Mate, it could be a million dollar one."

Joe puzzled, "Why is that?"

Connors "Since the 1930s, one of the Roosevelt foundations has had an offer on the table of one million US dollars for anyone producing a snake that is thirty feet or more in length."

Joe, "Do you think there is a thirty foot snake squirming around out here?"

Connors "It would have to be to bend an M-16, swallow a soldier and not make a sound. Besides, even though it sounds crazy, an Australian biologist has discovered a number of prehistoric animals in this area within the last decade. These were animals believed to have been extinct since before the last Ice Age...over 10,000 years ago. Yet, here they were thriving in the old caverns of this area."

Joe "I think I heard of those animals. They were birds and bats, right?"

Connors "That is right, Mate. They found some birds and some bats. If I recall correctly, they discovered some small mammals, as well. You see, Mate, a huge snake is not out of the imagination. Think of it, who comes into this area? The Indonesian Army has the place isolated. The only humans traveling though this area are the natives who themselves are but one step from the Stone Age. No one understands their languages. They might see snakes like this all the time, but who would they tell."

Joe, refreshing both their tea cups, "This is beginning to make sense, Brad. You think we should share this insight with the Captain?"

Connors "Are you kidding, Mate, we have a million dollar snake here. If we tell the Captain…and don't get me wrong, I like the man…he would take the prize for himself."

Joe "Brad, how do we go about getting this snake out here. It does not seem like a task for a cowboy to just go out and lasso it."

Brad chuckles, "Let me give it some thought, Mate. You are right, Mate, the critter might not take too kindly to captivity."

As the two men laugh over Connors' comment, Captain Djarmat enters their tent and inquires as to the whereabouts of Dr. Leong. The two men, trying to hold back their laughter, convince the captain that they had not seen her. The captain departs the tent with a comment about drinking too early in the morning will destroy Western Civilization.

Checking next on Dr. Yanagi, the captain finds Dr. Leong discussing the tree.

Captain Djarmat "Pardon the interruption, Dr. Leong, but I have your laboratory on the radio."

Dr. Leong jumps up, "That is wonderful, Captain."

Dr. Leong follows the captain out of the tent to the radio communications tent. As she enters the tent, the radio operator announces her presence to her laboratory.

Radio Operator "Doctor, just speak into the microphone. When you are finished talking say 'Over,' so the people you are talking to will know you are finished talking. Only one party can speak at a time with this form of communication."

Dr. Leong "Thank you, I understand the operation."

Dr. Leong "This is Dr. Leong from New Guinea. Over."

Penang Lab "Good morning, Doctor. We have received the new samples that you sent. Lucky thing you sent them, the first sample has decomposed. Over."

Dr. Leong "The first sample decomposed already. Over."

Penang Lab "Yes, Doctor, it is now in liquid form. Over."

Dr. Leong "Have you been able to decipher anything about the decomposed sample. Over."

Penang Lab "Yes, we have. In its decomposed state, the sample resembles a concentrated form of seawater. Over"

Dr. Leong "Did you say seawater? Over"

Penang Lab "Yes, Doctor, the decomposed form resembles a concentrated form of seawater. Over"

Dr. Leong "Does this concentrated seawater contain the same constituents as normal seawater? Over."

Penang Lab "Yes, it does, as well as, a number of other elements and compounds. Over."

Dr. Leong "Are silicates present? Over."

Penang Lab "Yes, Doctor, we have a multitude of silicate compounds in the decomposed sample. It is a very concentrated form of seawater. Over."

Dr. Leong "Can you tell me anything else about the sample? Over."

Penang Lab "One of the researchers has suggested that the high concentration of iron in the sample could indicate a magma source. Over."

Dr. Leong puzzled, "Magma and seawater is that what you are saying? Over."

Penang Lab "We are not certain about the magma, Doctor. The magma idea was a hunch. Over."

Dr. Leong more inquisitive, "What made the researchers make the comment then? Over."

Penang Lab pauses a while before answering, "Doctor, it is not a hunch, it is a form of magma immersed within the silicate compounds. Over."

Dr. Leong "Are you certain that it is magma or not? Over."

Penang Lab "We are certain, Doctor. A check with National University's geology lab on the constituency of the magma suggests an active source below your position. Over."

Dr. Leong exhales, "I understand. Check the new samples and confer with National University's geology lab as soon as you can and get back to me. Over."

Penang Lab "Yes, Doctor, we will. Over."

The radio operator concludes the communication.

Captain Djarmat has overheard the entire communication. He says nothing to Dr. Leong, as he escorts her back to Dr. Yanagi's tent.

As Dr. Leong enters Dr. Yanagi's tent, Dr. Yanagi says, "All good news I hope."

Dr. Leong "My lab thinks we are sitting on top of a volcano."

Dr. Yanagi "Good graces, why do they think that?"

Dr. Leong "They found a heavy iron content in the bark sample I sent them, so they related the finding to magma as the source."

Dr. Yanagi "Well, let us see here, this location does reside on the Ring of Fire. The idea of magma being close to the surface here is not without merit. Besides, right next door, we experienced a plate shift that caused the Aitape Disaster. Volcanoes do erupt frequently just across the border in Papua New Guinea. I would say that your laboratory's suggestion has merit."

Dr. Leong following Dr. Yanagi's explanation closely, "I suppose that you are right. Anyway, bark samples have been flown to your laboratory in Tokyo. If your lab confirms those results, I would feel safer going public with this."

Dr. Yanagi "Of course, I understand. In this day and age, one must be careful with any press release. The public seems quick to ridicule any anomaly. The universities, also, are quite susceptible to public opinion when authenticity is questionable. Rest assured, Doctor, my laboratory should have results in a few days to support you."

Dr. Yanagi uses the excuse that he is making another pot of tea to think over the idea of magma being found in the tree bark. The magma idea is not that far out at all; however, the possibility that it was found in a material disguised as tree bark is most alarming. Why would it be there? He will need to sequester the results from his laboratory. This situation is entering a bizarre stage.

As he mixes the ingredients for Japanese green tea, he comments on the weather to Dr. Leong. She responds slowly as if lost in thought. To Dr. Yanagi, Dr. Leong must be working her biologist's mind overtime in order to make some plausible connection between hydrocarbons and magma. He will let her muse over the topic in silence.

Suddenly, Dr. Leong bursts out, "I forgot to tell you that my lab reported that the first bark sample decomposed into a concentrated form of seawater."

Dr. Yanagi stops what he is doing, "Did you say, seawater?"

Dr. Leong "Yes, they said seawater."

There is a long pause before anyone speaks. The idea of seawater floods Dr. Yanagi's mind with possibilities. This evening, he will transmit this information to Japan. Seawater will be another item to check on the satellite probe.

Finishing the tea preparation, Dr. Yanagi presents a warm cup to Dr. Leong, "Here you go, Doctor, I hope you like the taste. It is a special brand that is hard to obtain."

Dr. Leong settles into her chair and sips the tea. The aroma of the tea conveys the sense impression that the fluid contains a rich soup. Truly, it is delicious, and Dr. Leong comments so to Dr. Yanagi. Dr. Yanagi accepts Dr. Leong's approval in a manner resembling those of his ancestors in the heyday of *Bushido*. The conversation continues with the suggestion of sampling the encampment for traces of seawater. Since the Penang lab is essentially a day away, the idea adheres. The two doctors could go about the encampment and dig up some earth, here and there, to be sampled. Dr. Yanagi's main concern is eliminating contaminants that might filter the identity of the tree. To him, this seawater report is in contradistinction to the magma report. Dr. Leong is hesitant to discredit her laboratory but concedes to the follow up earth samples. She realizes that confirmation from the Tokyo laboratory will enhance her credibility in the scientific community. Dr. Yanagi senses her desire for confirmation, as well. This will become quite useful to him in his ability to maneuver the investigation at the encampment.

Meanwhile, in Captain Djarmat's tent, the captain reviews his latest dispatches. He has asked for the presence of the second lieutenant in order to get his impression on the latest data. For the most part, the data seem to confirm the prior information on the missing persons. The majority of the missing persons have been reported in an area of some ten kilometers (six miles) wide. From the Venn-like diagram displaying the area, Captain Djarmat realizes that the encampment lies on the fringes. The concentration of reports commences to occur some five kilometers (three miles) from the encampment.

The second lieutenant enters the tent. The captain has him take a seat and look over the recent dispatch. As he is about to take a seat, he mentions a report that he received from one of his soldiers.

Captain Djarmat stops what he is reading, "What did you hear?"

Second Lieutenant "One of the soldiers posted outside Mr. Connors' tent heard Connors and Del Rosi talking about a huge snake."

Captain Djarmat "What did they have to say about this huge snake?"

Second Lieutenant "According to the guard, Connors said it was worth a million dollars in the United States."

Captain Djarmat smiles, "You don't say, a million dollars, was it?"

Second Lieutenant "That is what the guard reported. He said it was a huge snake."

Captain Djarmat "I have never heard of such a snake being found in New Guinea, or for that matter anywhere in South East Asia. What else did they say?"

Second Lieutenant "Mr. Connors was going to think more about how to capture it."

Captain Djarmat laughs, "Connors intends on capturing a huge snake and then bring it to the United States, does he?"

Second Lieutenant "Yes, Captain, that is what the guard reported."

Captain Djarmat still laughing, "Did the guard hear how big Connors thought this snake was?"

Second Lieutenant "The guard reported that Connors said the snake would be longer than thirty feet."

Captain Djarmat stops laughing, "That is ten meters! That snake would be a monster."

There is silence in the tent, as the captain ponders what the second lieutenant just reported.

Captain Djarmat smiles, then chuckles, "Let the old Australian bush monkey go after this snake. All my life, I have held the impression that Caucasians were brilliant people. Yet, time after time, I marvel at their intuition and get disgusted with their ability to reason. Does Connors know how strong a ten-meter snake would be?"

Second Lieutenant "According to the guard, Connors was concerned about its length."

Captain Djarmat continues without waiting for the second lieutenant to finish speaking, "Have you heard of those strong men from Sumatra that can perform seemingly more than human feats?"

Second Lieutenant "Yes, everyone has heard of them. I have even seen them perform in Djakarta."

Captain Djarmat "The way that they acquire those strengths and skills is by imitating snakes in training. One exercise that they do is to lie flat on the floor and attempt to squirm, without using their arms or feet. They try to move their body like a snake against the floor. We seldom sense the strength in a snake, because it has no huge arms or legs. However, after one session of trying to squirm on the floor, one appreciates how much a snake's muscular system has to be developed in order to squirm about the way that it does. Snakes are extremely strong. What we see is their effortless ability in maneuvering. We somehow equate that effortless ability into weakness, like the daintiness that we ascribe to culture dancers. Yet, because of their agility, culture dancers are stronger than the average person. The snake appears weak when stretched out; however it is formidable when coiled."

Second Lieutenant awed by the captain's rendition, "What shall we do about Connors and Del Rosi?"

Captain Djarmat smiles: "Let them have some fun. We need some humor around here. However, give strict orders that if a ten-meter snake does appear around the encampment, our men are to shoot it on sight. Take no chances with a monster this size."

Second Lieutenant "Do you think this huge snake could be the cause of all these missing persons?"

Captain Djarmat shakes his head, "No, the snake would have to be much larger. The mouth size, even on a snake that size, would be too small to engulf a

163 cm (5'4") human. I have never heard of a ten-meter snake, so I doubt there exists one that could be larger. Let us get back to more serious matters and commence reviewing these dispatches."

The second lieutenant catches his cue to abandon the snake idea. The review of the dispatches follows in silence. The only sound interrupting the tranquility of the tent is the folding of pages, as each man reads the synopsis of the missing persons' data.

After an hour of reviewing, the captain says, "From this data each and every one of these people just walked off the face of the world."

Second Lieutenant "I read a few were the disappearances did not fall into that category. There was one where a Swiss journalist, on a tourist visa, was seen entering a known area of rebel activity. He had been warned not to enter that area by the military police. That occurrence seems to indicate the journalist was abducted. What is more is that his disappearance falls out of the area designated for most probable disappearances."

Captain Djarmat "Yes, you are right. There are isolated instances like the one you mentioned, but the victim was more than 163 cm (5'4") in height."

Second Lieutenant surprised, "What does 163 cm (5'4") in height have to do with these disappearances?"

Captain Djarmat reluctant to reveal his suspicions so early to the second lieutenant, "The height may have nothing to do with the disappearance. However, an earlier dispatch indicated that the majority of the disappearances were individuals under that height."

Second Lieutenant holding his tongue so as not to reveal his displeasure with being kept in the dark, "I see, so you are creating *modus operandi* for the potential culprit."

Captain Djarmat "Yes, that is what I am doing. I am trying to make some sense of all this by grouping the victims into probabilities. I have accompanied other more senior investigators and marveled at their success with this method."

Second Lieutenant trying not to be presumptuous, "Captain, a height limitation would eliminate many of the probable causes."

Both men pause to look each other in the eye. Without having to say a word, it is obvious that this snake idea has merit. It is just too improbable that such a huge snake could exist without being detected by the military patrols.

Finally, the Captain breaks the silence, "You are so right, Second Lieutenant. The height limitation does, in fact, narrow down the possible causes of the disappearances."

Second Lieutenant "Captain, no blood was ever found at any of the disappearance sites. Does that not seem odd for a case with so many occurrences?"

Captain Djarmat conceding, "Yes, Second Lieutenant, that is odd. Then again, we have a tree that has never been observed before in the center of this encampment. I believe we have to withhold our conclusions, until we know more about this tree. For all we know, this tree could be causing these people to disappear."

Second Lieutenant bracing for a reprimand, "Captain, with all due respect, I believe the snake has more plausibility here than some issue of science fiction."

Captain Djarmat smiles, "You are impertinent, are you not, Second Lieutenant? You might get yourself into a lot of trouble in the military with comments like that one. Fortunately, in my years of service, I have learned to respect such impertinence. It is the mark of dedicated soldier...and a fine officer. One word of caution is in order: do not get carried away expressing your thoughts so freely. Your senior officers will not take too kindly to it. Let me assure you of that."

The two men stare at each other a while, before the captain speaks.

Captain Djarmat smiling, "Second Lieutenant, radio Jayapura for assistance on the size of a snake that it would take to devour a slender-built, 163 cm (5'4") tall human. Please be discreet with this request. Speak only to the officer in charge and insist upon his discretion. We do not need to advertise our suspicions. All we would need is a frontpage article announcing a monster snake in New Guinea. That Australian bush monkey may have a point on silence. We dare not alert the world's soldiers of fortune to a treasure squirming about out here. An invasion by the world's dregs would soon be upon us, distracting us from our assignments."

Second Lieutenant smiling, "I will take care of it, Captain."

Captain Djarmat "See that you do. And, one more thing, wipe that smile off your face, Second Lieutenant."

The second lieutenant exits the captain's tent still smiling.

Captain Djarmat nods his head in agreement as the second lieutenant leaves. Truly, he does so hope that a huge snake is the cause of these disappearances. Right now, the captain desires a natural explanation more than the uncertainty of this strange tree in the center of the encampment.

CHAPTER 7

▼

OFFICE OF THE DEPUTY MINISTER FOR INFORMATION, TOKYO, JAPAN

One thing about the offices of the Japanese deputy ministers who are not considered public personalities is that they are quite bland. In some cases, one might get the impression of having entered a hastily converted luncheon area. The Office of the Deputy Minister for Information is no exception. It is only to the culturally alert that the fine art of Japanese expression of power is noticeable. To a foreigner, unaccustomed to such sensitivities, the first impression is that he has been assigned to a clerk and not a person of importance.

Takeda enters the Deputy Minister's office, "Good afternoon, Deputy Minister. I am so glad that you could see me on such short notice."

Deputy Minister Kawamoto smiles, "As I understand from your memo that this is a matter of utmost importance. How could I refuse?"

Takeda opening and rifling though his briefcase, "I assure you that this is something Your Excellency needs to review."

Deputy Minister Kawamoto "Relax, Takeda, take your time. You are with friends here."

Takeda smiles and slows down, "Thank you, Deputy Minister."

Takeda removes some correspondences that had been forwarded to him via Dr. Yanagi's chain of command. He hands them to the deputy minister.

Takeda "As you can read from the correspondences, a serious anomaly exists in New Guinea."

Deputy Minister Kawamoto "An indestructible tree is it?"

Takeda "Please read the rest of the correspondences, Deputy Minister."

Deputy Minister Kawamoto peruses the rest of Yanagi's correspondences. He ponders their content in silence a while, before he responds to Takeda.

Deputy Minister Kawamoto "I see here that your recommendation is to perform a deep-earth surveillance of the area, is that right?"

Takeda acknowledges the deputy minister with an up and down movement of his head.

Deputy Minister Kawamoto "You know we have to be cautious with the results of this surveillance. You recall our experience with that poor, unfortunate fellow in Iraq over our last deep-earth surveillance. We discover a 245 trillion cubic foot natural gas reservoir. When we try to negotiate the rights to develop it with this fellow, the Americans invade the country in order to acquire the site."

Takeda "Did not this fellow, Hussein, invite military action from the Americans by refusing to allow them to participate in the project?"

Deputy Minister Kawamoto "The Iraqi fellow lived a dream world and supported fanatical Islamic nonsense. There was no way the Americans would allow such a creature to get his hands on an unlimited energy source in order to be able to materialize his visions of domination of South and West Asia. The specter of the last fanatically dictator was too alive in the minds of the Americans. They were right to invade Iraq and remove that reservoir from falling into the hands of those with evil intentions to their country and people. We must be careful in this venture as well, Takeda. The Americans have proven, time after time, their willingness to do anything, even resort to outright aggression, in order to protect themselves from potential threats. I caution you, Takeda, if this surveillance proves disturbing, we will need to inform the Americans, before they seek retribution against us for trying to hide our findings. The Americans still hold resentments against us for attempting to out-maneuver them commercially in Iraq over the natural gas find."

Takeda sensing someone handing him a ceremonial sword with which to commit ritual suicide, "I understand perfectly, Deputy Minister."

Deputy Minister Kawamoto "Good, now, explain to me how you plan to accomplish this surveillance."

Takeda organizing his notes, "Our first priority will be not to alert others as to our intentions or our capabilities. As described in the brief, we will reposition our geo-synchronous, communications satellite over the Malay Peninsula. This will be an in-place positioning that merely rotates the communication satellite. This action should be picked up by anyone watching. They will ascribe the action to some form of maintenance, and it will function to divert attention away from our free-roving satellite. The timing of the rotation of the communication satellite will coincide with our pulse, deep-earth probe of the New Guinea area with the free-roving satellite. As an added distraction, we have arranged for a site-inspection…of an educational nature, of course…of the tracking station in Northern Australia."

Deputy Mister Kawamoto raises his hand to stop the brief, "Have the Australians agreed to this site-inspection?"

Takeda "Yes, Deputy Minister, they have. Actually, they were most receptive to the idea."

Deputy Minister Kawamoto "Is that right? What would make them so agreeable, Takeda?"

Takeda "I prefer to categorize it as a cultural exchange tour, Deputy Minister."

Deputy Minister Kawamoto looks over the section of the brief containing the site-inspection and smiles, "I see we have found some use for all these newly-accredited astrophysicists. Please continue, I understand."

Takeda "The entire probe should last only a few minutes. I believe, with the distractions, it should execute without any ramifications."

Deputy Minister Kawamoto contemplates the brief a moment before he responds, "If there exists any possibility that our deep-earth probe capabilities will be revealed, the probe of New Guinea will be ceased. With that understanding, you may proceed."

Takeda senses the ultimatum in the deputy minister's words. He responds with silence.

Deputy Minister Kawamoto senses that Takeda acquiesces and continues with, "One more item, how much does your operative in New Guinea know about this probe?"

Takeda "He is the one who requested a deep-earth probe; however, he is unaware of how we conduct one."

Deputy Minister Kawamoto sits ups, "Good, you keep it that way. An operative is expendable."

Takeda, sensing the meeting has come to a close, gathers his brief materials and leaves the room. With the support of the deputy minister, he can proceed without interruption.

Entering his office area, Takeda has his secretary notify the section heads of the involved units to assemble in his office for a mandatory meeting.

Punctuality is supreme in Japanese ministries. The section heads scurry into Takeda's office within a few minutes. Some small talk accompanies them about an upcoming baseball game between the Seibu Lions and the Yamato Giants.

Takeda commences, "If we could dispense with our admiration for the Giants momentarily, I have some important news to promulgate."

The section heads quiet down and listen.

Takeda "A deep-earth probe has been approved for Northern New Guinea. I want this to happen in the next few days. We have an anomaly that needs to be identified. The composition of the anomaly is uncertain, so we will need to employ a wide range of frequencies. Also, the probe is classified Top Secret. No one outside the senior operators that you select will have any knowledge of what or why we are conducting this probe. Everyone, and I mean everyone, are on a need-to-know basis."

The section heads remain silent. It is custom in the ministry to listen to the assignment without comment.

Takeda scans the faces of the section heads for consent. When he feels comfortable that they understand the requirements of the mission, he proceeds.

Takeda "We will use our free-roving satellite, *Gengi*, to accomplish the mission. *Gengi*, right now, has acquired an orbit in close proximity to the target. Our geosynchronous communication satellite over the Malay Peninsula will coordinate with *Gengi* to narrow down the range of the probe. Hence, we will need constant communications capabilities between the operator assigned to *Gengi* and the operator assigned to the communications satellite. A third communications capability will be needed to monitor a distraction in Australia. Last, we will need an operator, preferably the section head, to maintain an open line with the Ministry for Information & Technology's Geophysics Laboratory. The Geophysics Laboratory will be the main recipient of the data collected by *Gengi*."

The section heads remain silent. Most of what Takeda has briefed is routine operation for such probes. Any use of *Gengi* is considered very sensitive and subject to heightened security requirements.

Takeda asks for questions from the section heads. The section heads respond that they understand the assignment.

Takeda "It is important that any unusual data received from the probe be identified. This anomaly may produce some bizarre data. We need to be vigilant in order to detect anything out of the ordinary."

The group understands. Takeda concludes the meeting by ordering the section heads to prepare to conduct the probe.

After the section heads have departed his office, Takeda has his secretary contact Mr. Kajioka at the Technology Division of the Ministry for Information & Technology.

Takeda "Hello, old friend. I just called to inform you that we are a go on the Doll House engagement."

Kajioka delighted, "That is good news, Takeda."

Takeda "Your pleasure women should be on their way."

Kajioka "Do you have an estimate as to how long they will be gone?"

Takeda "Two days, at most, that is all. They will be back for the weekend."

Kajioka "This is good news. I would hate for them to miss a beauty parlor engagement or a manicure."

Takeda "Speaking of manicures, I will have someone call to schedule an appointment. I hope you will have someone available to receive his call."

Kajioka "Oh yes, I have alerted everyone to expect your call."

Takeda "Very good! Shall we meet two days from now in the Doll House?"

Kajioka "That would be excellent. I will be waiting for your confirmation call."

The strange conversation ends. It is customary to discuss matters of elevated security in illusive language during phone conversations. Japanese are suspicious of possible penetrating technology that could eavesdrop on their telephone conversations. Other ministries, desirous of intelligence for political aspirations, often eavesdrop on their fellow ministries. Japanese ministries have been conditioned such since the days of the early shoguns. Since Japanese communication often relies on barely perceptible gestures, a desire for an awareness of the current dispositions of the ministries fosters an intense sensitivity to camouflage intentions.

Immediately after receiving the go-ahead from Takeda, Kajioka approves the allocated funds for the travel of the astrophysicists to Australia. The astrophysicists will leave on the evening flight to Sydney. Kajioka smiles at the thought that for a few days he will not need to be mindful of the presence of females. It will be wonderful to return, even for a few days, to how things were before Japan was shamed into allowing females to enter the bureaucracy in capacities above entry-level, administrative staff. The thought of having to refer to some educated housewife as a doctor has never set well with him. Women belong in the home with the children.

Later in the day, Kajioka receives a visit from the head of the Geophysics laboratory. He is carrying an overflowing valise, as he maneuvers his way into Kajioka's office.

Kajioka "I was not expecting you."

Geophysics Head "I should have called, but I felt that this was too urgent."

Kajioka admires how the Geophysics head manages to sit down and maintain all the contents of his valise.

Kajioka smiles, "Well, if it is that important, then please entertain me."

Geophysics Head rifling through his valise, "As you know, we are in contact with Dr. Yanagi in New Guinea. He managed to send us some bark samples from a tree of unknown origin. Accompanying the bark samples was a startling statement about the contents of the bark. Apparently, the botany laboratory at the University of Penang in Indonesia determined the bark to contain magma and seawater. Actually, they referred to it as a concentrated form of seawater. Well, our laboratory has confirmed their results. The bark contains excessive amounts of the compounds identified by the University of Penang."

Kajioka leans forward, "You have not reported this finding to anyone else, have you?"

Geophysics Head "No, of course not, Mr. Kajioka. Outside the laboratory, you are the only one to receive this information."

Kajioka "Go on."

Geophysics Head locating another data sheet, "According to our findings, the magma in the bark is composed of similar compounds and elements as would be expected deep in the earth's mantle."

Kajioka interjects, "Correct me if I am wrong, Doctor, the mantle is a few hundred kilometers below the earth's crust, is that not correct?"

Geophysics Head "That is correct, Mr. Kajioka."

Kajioka "Then, how is it possible that the laboratory acquired these results."

Geophysics Head "We double-checked our findings, Mr. Kajioka, the results are correct. How mantle material got into the bark of that tree, we have no idea."

Kajioka "Obviously, there must have been a volcanic eruption there some time ago."

Geophysics Head "No, Mr. Kajioka, there has been no eruption in that part of New Guinea for millennia. Actually, we have the results of a ground survey taken not six months ago in that very area…less than ten meters from the tree in question…that indicates no volcanic activity at all. None of the compounds and elements found in the bark sample matches any of those found in that survey."

Kajioka surprised, "What was the reason for this recent ground survey?"

Geophysics Head "The survey was performed in compliance for permission to invest in the natural gas project in New Guinea. It was a routine geophysics survey required for approval of any construction project. We sampled the entire area in which the tree in question is located. I have reviewed all the data taken for that survey. None of the survey sites reveal anything like what we have in this tree bark."

Kajioka puzzled, "Does not this tree bark require some input from the environment from an ecological perspective?"

Geophysics Head "That has been our understanding of ecology to this date. Now, Mr. Kajioka, I am not so sure. This tree seems to defy all our prior understanding of ecological balance."

Kajioka changes the subject: "Tell me about this seawater in the bark sample."

Geophysics Head "Actually, we do not have the seawater as of yet. The Penang laboratory reported that the tree bark decomposes into concentrated seawater. It takes a few days to do so. However, the compounds and elements contained in the concentrated seawater are present in the bark."

Kajioka "How does this seawater decomposition happen?"

Geophysics Head "That is our second mystery, Mr. Kajioka. Right now, we have no idea. From the data received from the Penang laboratory, the bark simply decomposes into concentrated seawater. Actually, from the constituents of the concentrated seawater, the mixture resembles those seawater concentrations observed whenever beach sand is kicked up along the shore from children playing. Of course, the silicate concentration is less represented because of the magma."

Kajioka leans back in his chair, "As I recall, the site in New Guinea is some kilometers from the ocean. Are the rivers in the area of the salt water variety?"

Geophysics Head "No, all the rivers in the area are fresh water types. The largest is the Sepik River; however, it is so far from the ocean in the vicinity of the site that only fresh water is detectable."

Kajioka "So what you are telling me is that there is no geophysical explanation for the seawater, is that right?"

Geophysics Head "That is right, Mr. Kajioka. We have no explanation for the seawater. As we see it, the bark or the tree in question is self-generating the seawater, and, for that matter, all the other compounds and elements."

Kajioka "Self-generation is a powerful expression. We will need to explain how this tree does that, before I can breathe a word of this."

Geophysics Head "I understand perfectly, Mr. Kajioka. There is one more item that I need to tell you. When a portion of the tree bark is removed, the tree regenerates the missing portion."

Kajioka resting his head against the palm of his hand, "The tree has regenerative capabilities…plants do regenerate to some extent. When the bark is carved, a tree will attempt to cover the area carved out."

Geophysics Head "According to Dr. Yanagi's report, this regeneration is quite extraordinary. The tree actually replaces the area removed in its entirety, and there are no signs that the bark had been disturbed at all."

Kajioka "Regeneration of that magnitude is unusual; however, some life forms display that ability…some reptiles."

Geophysics Head "Yes, I have heard of reptiles having regeneration capabilities. According to Dr. Yanagi, this tree reproduces an exact replicant."

Kajioka "Of course, Dr, Yanagi refers to a field observation. The exact replicant claim may not pass scrutiny in the laboratory."

Geophysics Head "Yes, we will need to verify that assertion under laboratory conditions. However, the claim itself warrants concern, given the other strange properties of the tree."

Kajioka in deep concentration, "It truly does warrant concern."

Geophysics Head "Given all that Dr. Yanagi has reported and the indestructibility claim, I would have to conclude that this is the strangest tree that has ever been brought to my attention."

Kajioka looks at the Geophysics Head a while before he responds, "It is the strangest tree for me, as well."

The men think on the matter a while. The Geophysics Head attempts to get up to leave, but Kajioka gestures for him to remain.

Kajioka "Entertain me. How could a tree of unknown origin become indestructible and create regenerative properties?"

Geophysics Head "I have no idea, Mr. Kajioka."

Kajioka "No, I mean how could something like this be explained?"

Geophysics Head "Are you asking me for a brainstorming explanation?"

Kajioka "Yes, I am. Free-think for a moment. How could indestructibility and regeneration be accomplished?"

Geophysics Head leaning back in his chair and gazing at the ceiling, "Well, the indestructibility part would require a realignment of the crystalline structure into a tightly-compacted configuration. The compactness would need to attain a density that I find incompatible with living organisms. Hence, the degree of compactness, required for indestructibility, would work in contradistinction to the ability to regenerate. In order for both processes to function, the crystalline structure would need to have an adjustable fluidity. By that, I mean, the crystalline structure employed for indestructibility would need to realign itself into another less compact configuration to permit regeneration. It would require a governing or controlling mechanism operating at the crystalline structure level. This is a capability that we have not even imagined in today's science."

Kajioka smiles, "That was a superb hypothesis. Please continue. How could this be accomplished?"

Geophysics Head shrugging his shoulders, "As you are aware, Mr. Kajioka, this is way over my head and expertise."

Kajioka smiles, "Of course, share your thoughts with me on this matter."

Geophysics Head "The key to this controlled, fluid crystalline structure would be the force field, enabling the process. There exist four, known force fields: gravity, electromagnetic energy, strong and weak forces. And, there is a hypothetical field referred to as the Higgs field that in the early days of the universe supposedly contained the electromagnetic, strong and weak fields. It has been postulated that all matter was created by an interaction between energy and the Higgs field. Matter, in this sense, defined as a manifestation of energy...from Einstein's energy equals mass times the speed of light squared ($E = MC2$). If the postulation proves meritorious, then crystalline structure could be reconfigured, instantaneously. In order for our theorized, controlled, fluid crystalline structure to exist, it would require some form of interaction with the Higgs field. It would also presuppose some form of intelligence guiding the reconfiguration."

Kajioka "Doctor, what you have just elaborated is amazing. Do you suppose this 'guiding intelligence' would be conscious?"

Geophysics Head "That question has many answers, Mr. Kajioka. First, if we believe Western thoughts, then the answer is yes. However, if we follow Eastern thoughts, the answer vacillates between yes and no. Recall the Indian philosophical belief that humans are composed of three minds: physical, emotional and intellectual. Recall how the physical mind is believed to operate 1800 times faster than the emotional mind. The emotional mind, in turn, is 1800 times faster than the intellectual mind. Consequently, if the energy interaction with the Higgs field occurs within the area of the physical mind, then consciousness, attributed to the area of the intellectual mind, would be unaware of its operation. A similar comparison exists when our bodies heal from cuts or bruises. Another example is that we are unaware of our digestive processes. There are many delicate processes going on in our bodies of which we are totally unaware."

Kajioka "I see your point, Doctor."

Kajioka requests a moment in order to contemplate what the doctor has just told him. The reality of the situation takes a while to settle in his mind. No such phenomena has been detected thus far any place in the world. Actually, no such phenomena has even been discussed anywhere in the world. Could what the doctor hypothesizes even be possible? If it were possible, to any extent, then it would be unique. Those in possession of such a capability would soon rise to the summit of civilization either through academic accreditation or military expansion. Japan must resolve this matter in New Guinea. As thoughts such as these bombard Kajioka's mind, one ominous thought emerges: could this tree be an alien presence? If it were alien to this earth, it would be formidable. How could Japan, or for that matter the entire world, deter this presence?

Kajioka breaks his contemplation to ask, "Doctor, how could we assess the capabilities of this tree in New Guinea?"

Geophysics Head "The energy to mass conversion that I described will not be ascertained until sometime after 2007 when the new European supercollider begins operation. The reason, given for constructing the supercollider, was to be able to detect the Higgs boson. The boson has been theorized to be the carrier of the Higgs field. Discovering the Higgs boson will confirm the existence of the Higgs field. To date, we have no capability of ascertaining what I have just hypothesized to you, Mr. Kajioka."

Kajioka "If I am understanding you correctly, Doctor, we could be dealing with a technology far in advance of anything we have ever experienced, is that correct?"

Geophysics Head "That is correct, Mr. Kajioka. The technology, being employed by this tree, if I am correct in my hypothesis, would be far in excess of anything known or even imagined by humankind."

Kajioka "What do you suppose this tree is doing here, Doctor?"

Geophysics Head "I have no idea, Mr. Kajioka. However, if the tree had evil intentions, it certainly has not displayed them to date. If it is alien in origin, then it may just be a probe."

Kajioka pleased with the assessment of benevolence, "Yes, you are correct, Doctor. The tree has not displayed any evil intentions at all. We have removed its bark, and it merely regenerates new material. There are no reports of anyone being harmed by the tree. I would have to conclude that the tree, whatever its possible intentions, will not be harmful to humans. Well, the intentions may not be harmful, at least not yet anyway."

Kajioka pauses a moment before he continues, "Let me see here, let us proceed with the idea that the tree is some form of technologically-advance entity. How do we deal with it?"

Geophysics Head realizing that he is being requested to propose a plan of action, "Communication has to be established with the tree. I realize how incredulous that sounds, but if it is an advance entity, we need to know its intentions. One way would be to ask it. We need to develop some form of communication with this tree."

Kajioka smiles, "It is good that this conversation is private and secure; otherwise, I fear we would both be on our way to a physical examination for suggesting communication with a tree."

The two men laugh at the comment. However, they both realize how embarrassing such an idea would be, if it ever got public attention. They also appreciate the specter of uncertainty emerging and enveloping their most cherished beliefs. To even suggest that the shamans of old were somehow in tune with some cosmic reality would devastate the notion of progress of civilization. Have we turned down a dark alley with allegiance to science?

Kajioka "When the probe results are available, we shall return to this matter. In the meantime, please brainstorm how we could communicate with this tree, if and when it may be become necessary."

Geophysics Head "I will do that, Mr. Kajioka. We should have the probe results in a few days."

Kajioka "Please keep our conversation within the circle of your most trusted scientists, Doctor. We need to submerge this idea in secrecy, until we have had time to prepare others for its promulgation. Something like this would be too shocking for even the most liberal and peripherally-oriented thinkers in our department."

Geophysics Head "I will, Mr. Kajioka."

Kajioka "Get back with me as soon as the probe results come in."

CHAPTER 8

▼

ENCAMPMENT, NEW GUINEA

Captain Djarmat wipes the dust, swirled up when the helicopters departed, from his face. Afternoons are the dry times in this part of the world. He has just received more dispatches. Lately, a postal delivery person seems to resemble his assignment more than the senior officer of advanced detachment. On his way to Dr. Leong's tent, he drops off his dispatches in his own tent and asks the second lieutenant to review them. After Dr. Leong's dispatches are delivered, he follows the pecking order to Dr. Yanagi and then on to Mr. Del Rosi. The walk to Mr. Del Rosi's tent often is not required, as he seldom receives any news. It is a good thing Connors spends time with Mr. Del Rosi; otherwise, he would go crazy in this isolation. How a Manila playboy got involved in all this mess, the captain cannot figure out? He must have been expendable.

Upon returning to his tent, following the dispatch deliveries, the second lieutenant appears eager to share something urgent with him.

Captain Djarmat gesturing to the Second Lieutenant to allow him time to settle into his chair, "I will just need a moment, Second Lieutenant."

The second lieutenant is grinning from ear to ear. Apparently, something in the dispatches aroused his spirit into a humorous frenzy.

After he takes a seat, the Captain exhales, "What is it, Second Lieutenant?"

Second Lieutenant "Captain, do recall how we asked for the size of a snake that could swallow a 163 cm (5'4") human?"

Captain Djarmat "Of course I do, Second Lieutenant. It was yesterday."

Second Lieutenant trying to keep from laughing, "They responded, Sir."

Circling his index finger, the captain gestures for the second lieutenant to continue.

Second Lieutenant reads from the dispatch, "The Military Command Jayapura acknowledges the inquiry of the Officer Commanding regarding the consumption by a snake of a human 163 cm (5'4") in height and requests additional information as to how many pieces of the human in question the Officer Commanding intends on feeding to the snake…respectfully."

The second lieutenant cannot hold his composure and bursts out in laughter.

The captain, stunned by the message, stares at the second lieutenant bent over gasping. For the life of a Muslim, what on this earth does the Military Command Jayapura think he is doing out here at this outpost? He thinks of asking the second lieutenant to re-read the message but realizes that the young man is over-entertained as it is.

The soldiers on post outside the captain's tent are laughing as well. Truly, it is no laughing matter. However, the sheer idiocy of the Military Command Jayapura is being confirmed. The captain wonders just what sort of macabre tales are being told about him in Jayapura concerning his past assignments. How bizarre others must think of him? He realizes that most of his career he has been assigned to the frontier posts at the farthest reaches of the republic, but he never dreamed that it would evoke such weird perceptions.

Finally, the Second Lieutenant regains his composure, "Captain, how shall we respond to the Military Command Jayapura?"

Captain Djarmat just stares at the second lieutenant without uttering a sound. It is an intense stare that communicates dissatisfaction. The second lieutenant realizes that the captain is lost in angry thoughts. Since the stare is peripheral, the second lieutenant understands that he is not the object of the captain's displeasure. The second lieutenant remains motionless and waits for the captain to speak.

After a pause that seemed to last all afternoon, the captain manages to look away and stand up.

Captain Djarmat pats the second lieutenant on the shoulder, "We will not respond, Second Lieutenant. I will seek the advice of Dr. Leong. She is probably the most knowledgeable person in New Guinea anyway."

The second lieutenant watches the captain walk slowly toward Dr. Leong's tent. The second lieutenant realizes that the Military Command Jayapura struck a very sensitive cord in the captain with this ridiculous message.

As Captain Djarmat approaches Dr. Leong's tent, he can overhear her discussing the tree with Dr. Yanagi. He ponders whether or not he should pose any questions to her regarding the snake while she is in Dr. Yanagi's company. With some residual furor still eating away at him over the message from Jayapura, he decides to chance it with Dr. Yanagi in attendance. At the entrance to Dr. Leong's tent, the captain has the sentry announce his wish to enter the tent. The sentry relays the captain's request to Dr. Leong. With good fortune, Dr. Yanagi upon hearing the request announces to Dr. Leong that he must be returning to his own tent.

Dr. Leong "Yes, by all means, Captain, enter. Dr. Yanagi was just leaving."

Dr. Yanagi exits the tent with the sentry.

Captain Djarmat allowing Dr. Yanagi time to make some distance from the tent, "Dr. Leong, I have a question for you. It concerns the consumption of a snake. Are you familiar with snakes?"

Dr. Leong thinks a moment about the nature of the question, "Yes, I am familiar with snakes. They are not my specialty, but I may be able to help. What is it you desire to know?"

Captain Djarmat "How large would a snake have to be in order to swallow a human?"

Dr. Leong responds quickly, "Large constrictors swallow children and small females. I have read reports on that matter from the Amazon in Brazil."

Captain Djarmat sensing that Dr. Leong has not made the connection with the disappearances in the area, "How large exactly, would you say, these constrictors would have to be?"

Dr. Leong "In the Amazon reports, six-to seven-meter constrictors have been known to swallow children. There are less frequent reports of constrictors swallowing small female adults. The last report that I read was dated some twenty years ago in which a nine-meter constrictor swallowed a small female. Since the size of snakes is diminishing, there are fewer reports of snakes swallowing humans."

Captain Djarmat "A nine-meter constrictor could swallow a small human, is that correct, Doctor?"

Dr. Leong "Yes, twenty years or so ago it actually happened. It was a small female. The people in the rainforest of South America are small people."

Captain Djarmat takes a deep breath and says, "How large would the snake have to be to swallow a human 163 cm (5'4") tall?"

Dr. Leong ponders the Captain's question a moment before she responds, "Captain, there are no snakes that large in the world."

Captain Djarmat "With respect, Doctor, how large would a snake have to be to swallow a human that size?"

Dr. Leong sensing the seriousness in the Captain's voice, "Well, let me see here, this would be hypothetical, of course. I would say a snake of some fifteen meters could do it."

Captain Djarmat eyes bulge open, "It would take a fifteen-meter snake, is that right?"

Dr. Leong exhales, "Captain Djarmat, I am guessing at the length. Recall the Amazon report that I quoted. It took a nine-meter snake to swallow a small rain-forest female. She could not have been more than a meter and half in height with a very small frame. To extrapolate her size into an adult human of Malay proportions would require a much larger snake. But yes, I believe a fifteen-meter snake could swallow an adult Malay."

Captain Djarmat "Do not these snakes adjust their jaw bones when they swallow?"

Dr. Leong "Yes, they do, and I took that into consideration when I quoted the fifteen meters."

Captain Djarmat "That is a huge snake."

Dr. Leong consoling the Captain, "There is no need to worry, Captain. Snakes of that size do not exist. Well, let me rephrase that. Snakes of that size no longer exist. They have been extinct since the last Ice Age."

Captain Djarmat startled by the Doctor's correction, "Are you saying that snakes of that size once existed?"

Dr. Leong "Yes, they were probably even larger in the eons before the last Ice Age. Those huge ones disappeared when the dinosaurs perished some one hundred and sixty million years ago."

The captain ponders the doctor's response. He recalls a whisper of information that he eavesdropped on once in Jayapura when two scientists from Jakarta mentioned a pre-historic bat being found thriving in a cave in New Guinea.

Captain Djarmat "Dr. Leong, was there not a discovery here in the not too distant past of a pre-historic bat living in New Guinea?"

Dr. Leong "Yes, there was. As a matter of fact, the Australians have discovered a number of creatures, long believed to have been extinct, in this very area of New Guinea. Are you thinking we have a pre-historic snake roaming about?"

Captain Djarmat cannot hold back his embarrassment, "Yes, I was thinking just that."

Dr. Leong thinks a moment, "Of course, all the missing persons. Yes, if there were such a creature, it would need to feed on large mammals to survive. It is hard to imagine though that one could have escaped notice for so long."

Captain Djarmat "It could be that the snake has not escaped detection."

Dr. Leong smiles, "Of course, this is an isolated area. No one understands the language of the natives in this area. The natives could be aware of its presence. No one else noticed the snake, because until this natural gas project, few non-native people ventured into this part of New Guinea. And, the vegetation has been removed that in turn removed the food supply of the snake. The snake is an opportunist. It would prey upon whatever was available. We are now what is available."

The doctor, realizing what she has just concluded, tightens her knees, sucks in a deep breath of air and frantically begins to look around her tent.

Captain Djarmat "Relax, Doctor, all reports of disappearances have occurred while the individuals were alone in the jungle. Soldiers surrounded the encampment. You are safe here."

Dr. Leong regains her composure, "You are right, Captain. I am sorry. I just frightened myself with the thought of a huge snake roaming about outside."

Captain Djarmat "Doctor, my men have been alerted already to shoot any huge snake on sight if it approaches the encampment."

Dr. Leong looks strangely at the Captain, "How long have you known about this snake?"

Captain Djarmat "Actually, Doctor, I do not know if the snake even exists. We have been theorizing that our disappearances could be the result of a snake. I came to seek your counsel, because Jayapura has not taken my queries seriously."

Dr. Leong breathing a sigh of relief, "For a moment there, Captain, I thought you knew the snake actually existed."

Captain Djarmat "I do not."

Dr. Leong nodding her head, "Will that be all, Captain?"

Captain Djarmat "Yes, I just needed some frame of reference for the disappearance cases."

As the Captain is about to take his leave, Dr. Leong says, "Captain, if it would not be too much trouble, could I have an extra guard around my tent?"

The captain smiles and assures the doctor that he will have an additional guard posted around her tent.

Taking his leave from Dr. Leong, the captain is approached by one of his senior enlisted soldiers.

Soldier "Captain, the American and the Australian have gone into the jungle."

Captain Djarmat "Do you know why they went into the jungle?"

Soldier "The sentry, following your orders, just allowed them to pass. He mentioned that they told him that they were scavenging. The Australian does not speak our language properly, so it is difficult to understand what it is he is saying. The American is even worse with our language, Captain."

Captain Djarmat "Scavenging, is that what they said?"

Soldier "Yes, that is what the sentry reported. They carried a huge sack with them. According to the sentry, the sack looked like a number of feed bags sewn together."

Captain Djarmat smiles, "That is fine. Just leave them alone. They should not get into too much trouble scavenging around out there."

The captain walks back to his tent, enjoying the thought that these two kooks are trying to catch the snake. The humor aspect of this assignment is beginning to make his time out here worthwhile.

Entering his tent, the second lieutenant presents him with a rundown on the content of the dispatches. The gist of the correspondence from the Military Command Jayapura concerns the status of the investigation on the tree. He understands the concern; however, his response is hampered by the speed with which the scientists acquire their data and are willing to share their findings.

In a passing comment, the captain mentions the two Caucasians wandering about in the jungle trying to catch the snake. The second lieutenant cannot control himself and regains the humor pitch he attained earlier. The captain begins to wonder whether or not the second lieutenant has matured enough to warrant a frontier post. As the young man is about to regain his composure, the captain relays that Dr. Leong estimated the snake would have to be some fifteen meters in length in order to swallow a Malay adult. This news overwhelms the second lieutenant. The captain is forced to wait until the young officer regains his composure, before he tells him to post an extra guard around Dr. Leong's tent. He explains that Dr. Leong is concerned that she might be correct about the size of the snake.

Second Lieutenant "Should not we be alerting the others about the possible danger of a snake this size?"

Captain Djarmat "No, let us not alert anyone until we have more concrete data on this snake. Besides, the Australian bush monkey and his Manila playboy associate are in the jungle right now trying to catch it."

Second Lieutenant bursts out laughing then says, "Do they know that the snake could be fifteen meters in length?"

Captain Djarmat "No, remember, we are not supposed to know about the snake. The snake is their soldier of fortune fantasy. Besides, from the data that I have extrapolated from the dispatches, the two kooks are too large for the snake to swallow. The snake will just pass them by."

Second Lieutenant "Are we to let them remain in the darkness on this matter?"

Captain Djarmat sitting down, "Yes, Second Lieutenant, we will let them enjoy their fantasy. Relax, Second Lieutenant, if a snake eats one of the kooks, I will take responsibility. Remember, we have no proof that there is such a creature out there. What those two Caucasians fantasize is out of my control. When we acquire definite proof of this creature, we will alert everyone. For time being, we will remain quiet. Right now, I am concerned for my troops. Many of them qualify as candidates for the snake's next meal. The troops have been ordered to shoot the snake on sight. Oh yes, please make the rounds and inform all the troops that the snake could be as large as fifteen meters in length."

Second Lieutenant realizes for the first time that his height qualifies him as a snake meal. Suddenly, it dawns on him that this is nothing to laugh about at all. While he was ridiculing the Caucasians, the snake could have been sizing him up for dinner. He doubts his sidearm would be of any value in deterring a hungry snake of that size. On that matter, he needs to check the weaponry at the encampment. Did the detachment bring along a rocket propelled grenade launcher? He does not recall one being listed on the manifest. For a fifteen-meter snake, maybe the detachment should request armor support. That is it! The encampment needs a tank. It is amazing how one's priorities shift so swiftly when one realizes how close and personal the danger lurks. A moment ago, a sidearm and a good laugh were sufficient. Now, a tank is needed. Truly, if a fifteen-foot snake is slithering about looking for a meal, maybe more tanks are warranted.

The second lieutenant's mind races from one extreme to the next. Like an animal recently incarcerated, his mind endlessly follows the periphery of the encasement. When it reaches one far boundary, it merely turns about and follows the periphery backwards. The thought on his mind, as he leaves the captain's tent to inform the sentries, is the need for a tank. He wants a tank.

Jungle setting

Connors and Joe have been walking along some two-wheel-wide, vehicular, beaten path in the middle of the Northern New Guinea jungle for quite some time. The path is the only viable means of travel, as the jungle area surrounding the path consists of tall grasses. The grass is taller than both Connors and Joe. Venturing out into that grass would be a disaster. Within minutes, the two men would part company as a result of the terrain and obstacles hidden in the grass. Constant communication would be the only means by which the two men could maintain some form of contact. In the distance some tropical trees mark the boundary into the denser vegetation areas that would provide for even more perilous adventures.

After what seems to be an eternity, Joe finally breaks the silence to ask where they are going. Actually, his query is more focused on whether or not Connors has any idea where they are headed. Connors informs Joe that there is a village just up ahead where they can get some information about a possible snake. Joe begrudgingly tags along. Comments about San Miguel beer spout from Joe's mouth with every other step. To Connors, Joe is a typical pampered American. Connors has second thoughts about bringing Joe along on this expedition.

Walking under the afternoon sun near the equator is a foolish venture to start; however, Joe's constant grumbling exacerbates the situation. The constant drone of mosquitoes and other member of the native New Guinea Air Force fuel the discontent. The equatorial environment provides no sanctuary from life's unpleasantries.

Finally, the two arrive at this open area of land, seemingly a fresh candidate of slash and burn agriculture. Joe scopes out the village. He counts about four huts and, in the distance, a lean tube type of arrangement. Pigs run about chasing each other. This is Connors' village! We walked all this way for this sorry excuse for a pigsty.

Connors wipes his brow, "There you go, Mate. I thought it would still be here."

Joe still looks around for some semblance of civilization. His facial expression communicates volumes about his disappointment. Connors does not need to query him.

Joe nodding, "This is it. Is there anyone living here besides the pigs?"

Connors chuckles, "Sure. They are just napping. It is naptime now. Come on let us wake them."

Connors walks up to one of the huts and slides under a matted cover that seems to serve as an entrance. Some strange sounds erupt from within the hut. Connors comes scurrying out.

Connors out of breath, "Sorry about that, Mate, it was the wrong hut. My old girlfriend lives there, and she was entertaining. Let me check the headman's hut."

Repeating a similar entrance strategy, Connors slides under another matted cover. This time the sounds are less perceptible. Meantime, a native emerges from Connors' girlfriend's hut with a spear. He is barely five feet tall but seems up to the task of tossing that spear. The native eyes Joe for some time, before he re-enters the hut. Without question, Joe is beginning to sense a sanity problem with Connors.

Connors slides out from under the cover of the headman's hut and motions for Joe to join him. As Joe enters the hut, Connors introduces him to the headman. The headman had been napping, as Connors had predicted. Now awake, he offers Connors some fluid. Connors graciously accepts. The smile on Connors' face gives Joe the impression that the real reason for this trek was to sample this fluid, whatever it is.

Connors smiling: "Try some of this, Mate."

The aroma of the fluid quickly energizes Joe's senses. It is an alcoholic beverage.

Joe "What is it?"

Connors "Why, it is jungle juice, Mate, the finest jungle juice in all of New Guinea."

Joe sniffs the fluid. If his nose is any true tester, this juice is made from near pure alcohol.

Joe "Brad, this is almost pure."

Connors "Well, of course it is. They make it pure...well, near pure for the jungle...then they add some local vegetation to make it tasty."

Joe sips some of the fluid. It reminds him of the rotgut tequila he drank in South America.

Joe exhales, "This stuff is rough."

Connors "There are no brand names in the jungle, Mate. Go ahead; take some more. The headman has plenty."

Joe sips once more then reminds Connors of why they came to the village.

Connors speaks to the headman in a strange language that includes all sort of gesturing. Joe suspects that neither man can speak the other's language.

Connors, after some deliberating says to Joe, "The headman has seen the snake. He said that it comes down from a rocky area not far from here. Now, I am not proficient in the headman's language, so he could mean the president of Indonesia lives up there."

Joe folds his arms across his chest, "What do you mean the president of Indonesia?"

Connors taking a generous sip of the jungle juice, "The word for danger is similar to the word for the president of Indonesia in the headman's language. In a sense, the words mean the same thing."

Joe "Well, Brad, I do not believe that the president of Indonesia lives in a rocky area. Are you sure he has seen this snake?"

Connors, after he has asked the headman again, "Yes, the headman confirms that he has seen the president of Indonesia in this rocky area not far from here. He says the best time to see the snake is in the early morning."

Joe "This is late afternoon."

Connors "I know, the headman has offered us the use of his home for the evening. We can wait until morning then go see if the snake comes out."

Joe "People will miss us at the encampment. What does the headman mean, if the snake comes out?"

Connors asks the headman for an explanation.

After the headman responds, Connors turns to Joe, "The headman says the president of Indonesia might not be hungry. The snake only comes out when it is hungry."

Joe "Are you sure of what the headman is saying?"

Connors generously sipping the jungle juice again, "No, I am not entirely certain. Like I say, I have a limited command of his language. But, I agree with you. The president of Indonesia does not live in a pile of rocks not far from here."

Joe "We could go up to see almost anything this guy feels is danger."

Connors exhaling, "Listen, Mate, why don't we just enjoy the headman's hospitality and check this out tomorrow morning?"

The way Connors is sipping the jungle juice Joe doubts he will leave this evening anyway. Walking the path back to the encampment at night would be too much trouble anyway, so Joe acquiesces to Connors' suggestion.

Whatever the cause for the celebration between Connors and the headman, the jungle juice never stops flowing. As soon as one bowl is empty, the headman's hostesses bring another. Within an hour, the alcohol has Joe sweating profusely. The high alcohol content causes the body to excrete in order to maintain system equilibrium. Joe has trouble keeping his eyelids open. Soon, his body just falls to one side. He barely perceives his shoulder hit the matted floor of the headman's hut.

Connors comes to his assistance and whispers in his ear, "Do not you worry, Mate, the headman will fix you up with a sheila for the night."

Joe mumbles, "Just let me sleep."

Connors and the headman continue their conversation and weird gesturing late into the night. By midnight, the three men are sleeping on the matted floor, overcome by the alcohol.

About an hour before dawn, hostesses enter the hut and awake the three men. It is time that they ready for the trip to the rocky area. Since the snake appears only in the early morning, they need to get to the site and find a suitable observation post.

As Joe is trying to regain his consciousness, one of the hostesses offers him what looks like a jerky strip. He declines and requests water. It takes some gesturing before the hostesses bring him some fresh water. Though thirst motivated the request, Joe realizes that this water is not purified. This is malaria country. He has not brought any quinine. Scooping up some of the water in the bowl, he douses his face with the water to wake up.

Within a few minutes, the three men are awake on their way to the rocky area. It is cooler before dawn, so the walk is pleasant. There is little conversation. The men allow their bodies to recover from the alcohol abuse in silence.

Joe eventually speaks up to Connors, "Brad, what were you and the headman celebrating last night?"

Connors "The headman's main squeeze was eaten by the snake. He was honoring her absence and misfortune."

Joe shakes his head from side to side: "He lost his wife to the snake!"

Connors "She was not exactly his wife. He sleeps with all the hostesses we met last night. She was one of his favorites. You should have stayed up. One of the sheilas would have made you forget Manila."

It is a bit of walk to the rocky area. Connors entertains Joe with tales of his sexual prowess the entire trip. Joe listens, because Connors is the only one he can speak to without gesturing like a monkey.

The moonlight is sufficient to illuminate the path that the men are following. Connors remarks that the moon being so bright might encourage the snake to come out earlier. Whenever the moon illuminates the terrain, the animals feed earlier. By dawn, most animals are resting after moonlit nights.

The headman stops the procession to point out the rocky area. At first glance, the site reminds Joe of how a doctor or dentist would inspect a person's mouth. The rock formation resembles a gravel tongue protruding from a cave, set back into the rocks. A depression in the tongue-shape appears to have been frozen in time like after a doctor just removed the popsicle stick he used to hold the tongue down to inspect the throat.

The headman locates an observation area and has Connors and Joe settle in. Since it is almost dawn, the malaria-carrying mosquitoes serenade them. Both Connors and Joe cover as much of their exposed skin as possible. Another thing the two men forgot to bring was mosquito repellant. Some of the salve that they applied yesterday still remains on their skin. Its effectiveness is questionable, since the two men wiped a lot of sweat of their bodies. The excessive perspiration from the alcohol removed a good portion of the salve as well.

The headman disturbs the two men, deep in thought over the effectiveness of their mosquito repellant. One of the headman's aids points toward the opening of the cave. At first, only the faint sense of movement attracts the two men. Joe makes out the movement to be the slurping motion of a snake's tongue. It is a long tongue. Soon, a head, four-fifths the size of Joe's head, protrudes from the cave opening. The camouflaged-green head stands out amongst the reddish-brown background of the rocky area.

Like lava or cold molasses, the snake begins to emerge from the cave. The movement of the snake is so slow that any other movement in the area distracts Joe's attention away from the snake. The creature eases his way down the depression in the gravel tongue. All the time, the tongue of the creature is flickering about.

By the time the creature fully emerges, Connors comments, "Mate, he looks about twelve meters in length."

Joe nervously concurs.

Though most of the body of the snake is larger than its head, Joe concludes that the expansive capacity of the snake body could hold a human. From the lax, deflated shape of its body, it is not hard to sense that the snake is hungry. This makes the men nervous.

When the snake reaches the base of the gravel tongue, it enters the tall grassy area. Unfortunately, that happens to be the area the men will traverse on their way back to the encampment. Some communication between the headman and Connors reveals that the snake is on its way to the river. Plenty of game comes to the river after dawn to drink. The snake will have easy pickings.

As Joe watches the tall grass give way to the snake's movement, Connors and the headman discuss something. After what appears to be an eternity of gesturing, Connors tells Joe that the snake that they just saw was not the president of Indonesia. It was one of his ministers.

Joe shocked, "Brad, is the headman saying that there are more snakes the size of the one we just saw out here?"

Connors "The best I can make out from his gesturing is that there are three snakes. There is another about the same size, as the one we just saw, and another larger one."

Joe "How much larger?"

Connors trying to get some estimate from the headman, "Mate, these people do not know the English or the metric system. He just keeps saying bigger."

As Connors is trying to explain the headman's comments to Joe, two of the aids burst out in laughter. They are pointing to Connors' bag that he brought with him.

Joe, identifying the humor, "Brad, I think we need a bigger bag for this snake."

Connors starring at the two aids making fun of him, "You are right, Mate. This was a pretty dumb idea, wasn't it?"

The headman gestures for the group to return to the village. The two men, now knowing of a larger snake, are in a hurry to return as well.

CHAPTER 9

▼

INTERNATIONAL AIRPORT, SYDNEY AUSTRALIA

Although Sydney is the largest city in Australia, it is not frequented as much as one would expect. Most flights into Sydney are their ultimate destination. People fly into Sydney to visit or do business in Australia. A more transient character describes most other cities around the world with international airports. The international airport in Paris, for example, acts as a hub for all of Europe and destinations in other continents.

Today, liaison personnel from the Australian Space Agency await the arrival of three astrophysicists from Tokyo. The itinerary for the astrophysicists includes a short get-acquainted stay in Sydney, transit to the observatory in the Northern Territories, and a two-day tour of the facilities at the Space Observatory.

The three astrophysicists arrive on Japanese Airlines. As expected, the three astrophysicists are females. Unlike the cordial greetings of the South Pacific, there are no leis or tropical dancers. Greetings in Australia are bland. Simple introductions and the transfer of itinerary material conclude the greeting. Liaison personnel escort the three women through customs and immigration. Within a half an hour, the astrophysicists board a military transport craft destined for the Space Observatory.

During the flight to the Space Observatory, the military personnel operating the airplane say little to the astrophysicists. Other than offers of refreshments, the astrophysicists make conversation in Japanese among themselves. Since the air route to the Northern Territories flies over some scenic areas, the astrophysicists take the opportunity to operate their cameras. The noise from the passenger cabin becomes a strange mix of Japanese, camera flicking and sounds of excitement.

In less than two hours, the military aircraft lands on a deserted runway in the middle of a sea of desert, speckled with a few islands of radiotelescopes. Everywhere the eye can see resides deserted landscape. The wind generated by the military aircraft's propellers creates mini-dust storms that seem to be absorbed by the endless desert.

After the plane's engines are cut, liaison personnel will escort the astrophysicists to their accommodations. As the passengers disembark the plane, the officer in charge (OIC) of the Space Observatory greets them and introduces their counterparts during their stay. The interchange mimics the greeting the astrophysicists received in Sydney.

The lead scientist at the Space Observatory is Dr. Greene, a very tall Caucasian with a distinct Australian accent. Compared to the Japanese gals, Dr. Greene seems twice their height. Fortunately, Dr. Unni, a person only a few centimeters taller than the Japanese gals, assists Dr. Greene. Dr. Unni, though an Australian citizen, has South Asian ancestry.

Following the introductions, the astrophysicists are shown their accommodations. They will be housed by themselves in modern barracks abutting the Space Observatory. The accommodations offer a single room for each of the astrophysicists. Each room contains ample living space, far in excess of what the astrophysicists are accustomed to in their own country. The living space includes individual showers and bath area, huge closets, a double bed, TV with international access, and a desk assembly. The entire barracks are air conditioned. The astrophysicists believe they have been accommodated in suites. The desk assembly is larger than the cubicles in their office areas back in Tokyo. To the astrophysicists, the large accommodations will take some acclimatization.

After the astrophysicists have been left alone to settle in, the officer in charge requests the presence of Dr, Greene. The officer in charge has a large office next to the Space Observatory. Although he oversees the Space Observatory, it is clear that his primary responsibilities are military. He intentionally refrains from entering the observatory, allowing the observatory staff to conduct themselves as they please. Military decorum ends at the entrance to the observatory.

Being a typical senior military officer, his office walls are draped with certificates and awards for past accomplishments. Entering his office is like any office of a senior military officer: a desk set back from the door to give the impression of space, desk items meticulously organized, a huge, ten-line, black telephone, and the flag of Australia in the corner. About the only non-military item in the office is the *espresso* coffee maker.

As Dr. Greene enters the Office in Charge's office, the OIC bellows out, "Come in, Doctor, have a seat."

Dr. Greene settles in a chair in front of the office in charge's desk.

OIC "What do you know of this tour of the Space Observatory?"

Dr. Greene "Only what I read in the correspondence. As I understand, the tour is a work-appreciation benefit for the astrophysicists and our staff."

OIC "Why did they just send females?"

Dr. Greene "I can only guess on that."

OIC "Give me your best guess."

Dr. Greene "Japan has a gender problem. They probably have nothing else to do with these women. Assignments overseas are given to males. I suspect that this tour is a way of balancing an inequity in their assignment protocol."

OIC "I am a bit more suspicious of the Japanese. They are sneaky characters. Somehow, I am getting the impression that the females are a diversion. Why send young females to a deserted outpost? Would not they be better served at some international conference, like say in Paris or New York?"

Dr. Greene "I seriously doubt that these women could be spies. They hardly seem to be the type."

OIC "I did not mean to suggest espionage, Doctor. I meant to suggest a diversion. Our mission here is satellite tracking in the Southern Hemisphere, is it not?"

Dr. Greene "Yes, primarily, we track satellites; however, we do not necessarily track any Japanese satellites. However, most of our time, currently, is devoted to listening for unusual noises emanating from space."

OIC "From the correspondence, these women work for the Technology sector of the Japanese Ministry for Information, is that right?"

Dr. Greene "I believe that is correct. I am not sure."

OIC "According to our Foreign Office, the Science & Technology sector serves as a black-bag agency for the Japanese Foreign Ministry. The inner workings of the Foreign and Information ministries of Japan are an intrigue to everyone in the intelligence field. Most visas issued to Japanese government personnel assigned to non-diplomatic posts in the Japanese High Commission are given to personnel from the Ministry for Information. Sometimes, it is called the Ministry for Information & Technology."

Dr. Greene "I have no knowledge of that."

OIC "I know you do not, Doctor. That is why I am telling you this. I have a hunch these woman are a diversion. What I am going to propose is that you have your staff, as best you can, be on alert for anything unusual while these women are here."

Dr. Greene "Most of the scientists will be entertaining the women."

OIC "Do you see what I mean? Most of your staff will be away from their posts."

Dr. Greene "I see your point. I can alternate having one scientist on watch at all times. The observatory operators will not participate in the tour, so I can post them around the clock. I can have one scientist and two operators on watch during the entire stay of the astrophysicists."

OIC "Good! Make sure the scientist reports any anomaly that his operators detect. We need to determine what the bloody Japs are up to, if anything."

Dr. Green "You really do not trust the Japanese at all, do you?"

OIC "No, I am afraid that I do not. Some of my relatives were killed during the battle for New Guinea. If there was one thing I learned from experience, it is that you cannot trust the Japanese. They are sneaky people that will stab you in the back in an instant when you are not looking. Whenever the bloody creatures are around, I look cautiously at every thing that they do. Trust me, Doctor, there is something going on here. We need to determine what it is."

Dr. Greene "I will post the watch."

OIC "One more thing before you go, make no mention of this to the females. Tell your scientists to keep their lips sealed about what we just discussed. We dare not alert the females that we distrust them. Show them a good time while they are here, but keep the observatory on alert."

There is not much to see when touring a space tracking facility. The main devices are the radiotelescopes. Those are huge saucer-shaped pieces of equipment that resemble the glove of a baseball player waiting to shag a fly ball. Once you have seen one of them, you have seen them all. For the most part, each disc is identical to every other disc. Generally, they are all aligned to focus on one spot in the sky, like soldiers in a firing squad formation.

Nonetheless, the itinerary has the Australian scientists escorting the astrophysicists to the site of each radiotelescope. Interestingly, the Australians try to say something different about each disc. Sometimes, it is an old story about some difficulty they had to resolve with the alignment of the disc. In other discs, the story concerns more the maintenance history of the item. Living around the year in the desert can make anyone appreciate the little nuances of life.

The astrophysicists spend the entire day inspecting the scopes. Although they convey expressions of interests, they are bored. Japanese culture trains one to control expression, a practice that dates back to the days of the *samurai* and the *bushido* code. Since these are female Japanese, they are much better trained than their male counterparts at hiding their true feelings.

The evening, following the day tour around the discs, features an attempt by the Australians to create a Japanese delicacy: shrimp tempura. The astrophysicists politely enjoy the company of their hosts. Regrettably, the batter for the tempura is missing a few ingredients, making the shrimp taste more like a corndog. Dipping the concoction in lots of soy sauce makes the treat palatable. The one welcomed feature of the evening is the Australian wine. The Australians are new at winemaking, but the quality of their efforts indicates that they researched the process well. Each of the astrophysicists pleads to be able to take a bottle of the wine back to Japan. The Australians agree to assist with the customs requirements to export the wine. As it turns out, the gals want a case of the wine each. They liked the wine.

While the astrophysicists are being entertained, the observatory watch monitors the satellites in the night sky. It had been determined that if there were something amiss, the Japanese would use their satellites. Accordingly, the interests of the observatory focus in on their satellites. Other than routine communication with their geosynchronous satellites, the watch uncovers no abnormal activity from the Japanese.

The second day commences with a tour of the space observatory and its associated electronics facilities. This tour is more interesting, as it traces the space observation process and how the observation data is interpreted and stored. The low hum of the massive computer banks evokes a sense that secrets of the universe are being collated within the huge steel frames of the consoles. During this tour, the astrophysicists constantly query the Australians about this and that operation. For certain, the astrophysicists are interested in the data collection arrangement. The familiarity of their questions implies that they operate similar equipment in Japan.

By mid-afternoon, the tour comes to an end. The astrophysicists have offered to prepare a meal for their hosts. Most of the items that they request are available in the facility's food storerooms. The physical location of Australia offers the cuisines of both the East and the West. The influx of immigrants to Australia likewise provides a diversity of cuisine. It is not uncommon to have a South Asian grilled cheese sandwich being served to a table next to a table offering cold noodle soup. Fried eggs and hash browns are as common as Japanese *miso* soup for breakfast.

Without reservation, the evening meal, prepared by the astrophysicists, proves tastier than the prior one. The Australians, maybe for the first time, enjoy Japanese cuisine. Naturally, more wine is served. Actually, the gals let their hair down a little and enjoy the company of their hosts. The evening produces some impromptu dancing. By the time the evening winds down, both parties desire a few more evenings like this one.

The unfortunate scientist assigned to the observatory keeps his crew alert. Though the early evening is as uneventful as any day in the desert, some unusual communication traffic begins to emerge as midnight approaches. A coded signal from the Japanese main island is being transmitted to their communication satellite over Singapore. The code consists of an elevated encryption like those used by the military. The facility's computers can identify only the bandwidth.

Quickly, the on-watch scientist calls Dr. Greene and informs him of the activity. Dr. Greene leaves the party area, as if he were just going to the restroom. No one notices his sudden absence.

Upon arriving at the main control station in the observatory, the on-watch scientist provides Dr. Greene with an overview of the activity with the communications satellite. The encrypted code startles the doctor.

Main Observatory Watch Stander "Doctor, they are repositioning their communications satellite."

Dr. Greene and the on-watch scientist observe the monitors and confirm that to be the case. Dr. Greene beeps the office in charge.

Main Observatory Watch Stander announces, "The communication satellite is transmitting an encrypted code to a location over New Guinea."

Dr. Greene "What is the destination of the signal?"

Main Observatory Watch Stander "It has no recognizable destination, Doctor. It is just aimed at a debris field. There are no known satellites in that mess of refuse."

The office in charge responds to Dr. Greene's pager beep.

Dr. Greene on the phone, "You were right. Something is happening. We will track it and get back to you."

Dr. Greene orders the watch to track and store all that transpires.

Dr. Greene confers with the on-watch scientist concerning such a strange event. The on-watch scientist proffers that the Japanese might just be conducting an operational test of their satellite. Why else would they transmit to a refuse field?

Just as Dr. Greene is about to concur with the on-watch scientist, the Main Observatory Watch Stander yells, "We have activity from the debris field. Something in the debris field is pulsing the northern tip of New Guinea."

On-watch Scientist "Can you determine the area being pulsed?"

Main Observatory Watch Stander "Yes, Doctor, I have recorded the coordinates."

The main observatory watch stander displays the coordinates pulsed over a background of a map of Northern New Guinea.

Dr. Greene looking over the New Guinea area, "There is nothing there but jungle and rainforests."

On-watch Scientist, "Operator, what kind of pulse was it?"

Main Observatory Watch Stander "It was an intense pulse, unlike a photo-pulse. They were not taking pictures. This was a probe."

On-watch Scientist to Dr. Greene, "What do you suppose the Japs are up to?"

Dr. Greene "I have no idea. We get an intensified probe pulse from a debris field, controlled from a communications satellite in receipt of an encrypted code. This is an event that needs to be brought to the attention of national security."

On-watch Scientist "I agree. If the Japs have some hidden military satellite that they can release this intense probe anytime they like, we need to put everyone on alert."

Dr. Green "Operator, did you record the strength of the pulse?"

Main Observatory Watch Stander "Yes, I did, as best as our equipment could measure it. From what I could read on the instruments, it was strong enough to penetrate this facility. We might have been harmed by the pulse."

Dr. Greene "Was it just one solid, short pulse?"

Main Observatory Watch Stander "No, Doctor, it was an intense varied pulse. The data that I recorded indicates that a number of frequencies were pulsed at these coordinates. The entire pulse lasted less than a minute. It was focused on these coordinates the entire time. Also, the data that we recorded indicates some form of feedback from the site coordinated."

Dr. Greene looks over the recoded data on a computer console, "The feedback was relayed from the debris field back to the communication satellite and then onto Japan."

Main Observatory Watch Stander "The communication satellite is repositioning to its original orientation, Doctor."

On-watch Scientist "The Japs must have completed whatever that they were doing."

Dr. Greene "Yes, they must have completed their operation. This is very strange."

Some discussion follows over what the men observed. The issue of national security is raised with all those present. Not a word on what was witnessed is to leave the room, until the national security people have has a chance to peruse the data.

With that being said, Dr. Greene leaves the observatory area and returns to the party.

Early the next morning, Dr. Greene enters the office of the OIC. The OIC is eager to hear the doctor's summation of the strange events of the prior evening. After a rendition of the events as they transpired, the OIC acknowledges his grasp of the matter.

Dr. Greene sheepishly, "How did you know the Japanese would do something like this?"

OIC "It comes from years of experience in dealing with these bloody characters. The Japs cannot be trusted. They never could be. Even far back in Chinese history, the Japs were a problem. During one dynasty, the Chinese overlords moved all the activity and settlements on the coast of China so many miles inland to protect them from sudden raids from Japanese seaman. They used to call them the Eastern Sea devils."

Dr. Greene "Are you not concerned about the astrophysicists?"

OIC "No, they were just a diversion. Those women have no idea that they were being used as decoys. I am going to let them go as if nothing happened. That is one thing about the Japs, if you do not raise a concern, they will believe that we are none the wiser. It is best we just allow the gals to return without incident. This way, the Japs will never know that we are on to them."

Dr. Greene "I understand."

OIC "Do you have any idea what the bloody Japs tried to accomplish?"

Dr. Greene "That is one thing we do not know. From what our data reveals, they somehow transmitted a multi-frequency, intense signal at a set of coordinates in northern New Guinea. Why the signal was multi-frequency remains a mystery?"

OIC "Could they have been testing a military weapon?"

Dr. Greene "No, for a military weapon, the efficiency would lie with a single-frequency, intense beam, like a laser. This was something else."

OIC "How about a simple reconnaissance photo?"

Dr. Greene "Then again, a single-frequency beam would suffice. No, the purpose of this pulse was something different. I suspect the Japanese have developed some new technology."

OIC "A new technology would explain why they went to so much trouble to hide it. Can you conjecture what this new technology could have been used for?"

Dr. Greene "I am clueless. Our data will need to be turned over to physicists with expertise in this area."

OIC "I will request some defense physicists accompany the plane coming to pick up the astrophysicists. You do agree that this event warrants the attention of national security, do you not?"

Dr. Greene "Yes, I concur that national security needs to be apprised of this event."

After breakfast, little gifts are exchanged between the astrophysicists and their hosts. The scheduled military aircraft arrives to transport the gals back to Sydney for further travel to Japan. By 10:00 AM, the Space Observatory routine has returned to normal.

As the plane carrying the astrophysicists takes off, Dr. Greene escorts the two physicists from the national security agency into the Space Observatory. Dr. Greene provides a rundown of the events; after which, the physicists interview each watch stander thoroughly. Once the interviews are completed, the physicists peruse the data collected during the event with Dr. Greene. Shockingly, the physicists are at a loss to explain the multi-frequency pulse.

Dr. Greene "It is an interesting event, is it not?"

Senior Physicist "Yes, it most certainly is. The only multi-frequency transmission that I can postulate is one associated with single- or multi-sideband transmission, similar to that used in radio and television transmission. But, according to this data, this multi-frequency transmission was not a sideband variety. These frequencies were of similar amplitude and magnitude. Where Radio/TV transmission consists of one main carrier frequency with little sidebands affixed to it, this multi-frequency pulse was all main carrier frequencies, each independent of the other. This is strange indeed. We have never encountered anything like this, aimed at a set of coordinates. This is without question some form of new technology."

Dr. Greene "Will you require copies of our data?"

Senior Physicist "We will be taking all your data with us. For the concerns of national security, all this data, as of this minute, has been impounded. When we return to Sydney, I will have military intelligence personnel fly back out here to debrief all of you that were involved. You will be required to sign non-disclosure agreements. I am sorry, but for something like this, national security dictates strict compliance with regulations."

Dr. Greene "I will need to brief the Officer in Charge."

Senior Physicist "I will accompany you to this brief to insure the Office in Charge understands the severity of this matter."

CHAPTER 10

▼

SCIENCE & TECHNOLOGY DIVISION, FOREIGN MINISTRY, JAPAN

The scientists bustle about checking and double-checking the computer consoles. Any computer card that indicates signs of substandard performance is replaced. The satellite control system for *Genji* has to be up to perfect performance standards.

By mid-afternoon, only designated control personnel and supervisors are permitted in the operational spaces. Once the control room attains the level of restriction dictated by procedure and regulations, Mr. Takeda commences the evolution.

Encrypted code is transmitted to the communications satellite over the Malay Peninsula. The code directs the communications satellite to activate its transmission center and orient its transmission device in the direction of the island of New Guinea. This process takes time for the satellite to decipher the code with its internal computers and conduct the change in orientation.

Time is of the essence as the recipient satellite, *Genji,* is not geosynchronous. *Genji* follows a more flowing, wave-like pattern between the Tropic of Cancer and the Tropic of Capricorn. Timing is of the essence in order for the communications satellite to activate *Genji,* as it passes over the intended target. If the opportunity is missed, the evolution will require a few days wait for the next chance. The island of New Guinea was never considered a point of interest when the *Genji* orbital program was created. Fortunately, the area of concern is located just a few degrees south of the equator. If it were farther away from the equator, the wait time between opportunities would be much longer, because of the wave-like pattern of *Genji*'s orbit. On one revolution of the earth, *Genji* might be on the crest of the wave, as it passed over the band containing the island of New Guinea area, making the satellite out of range for the intended coordinates to be probed. Yet on another revolution, *Genji* might find itself on the trough of the wave, creating a similar problem for probing a location in the top of the band. Since the target location of concern lies near the equator, every two days *Genji* presents an opportunity for probing.

The control center reports to Mr. Takeda that the communications satellite has activated its transmitting device. Mr. Takeda requests a scan of the satellite probing of the area. The report states that only routine monitoring of the area can be detected. The opinion in the control room is that the satellite monitors in Australia are distracted or asleep.

Mr. Takeda orders the transmission from the communications satellite to commence. An encrypted code is transmitted to *Genji,* as it approaches the island of New Guinea. It takes only a few moments for *Genji* to orient its transmitter to the desired coordinates and commence the pulse. The pulse lasts less than a minute. Though a minute would seem to be an eon for an intense pulse, *Genji* is transmitting a series of pre-selected frequencies. After the pulse is transmitted, *Genji* activates an array of tiny receptors, each one sensitized to a special frequency. *Genji* waits for a response from the coordinates. Once the responses are collected, *Genji* transmits the data to the communications satellite and shuts down. The communications satellite acts as a relay station to the main computers in Geophysics laboratory in the Technology Division of the Ministry for Information & Technology.

Shortly after Mr. Takeda is notified that the evolution has been completed, he receives word from the Geophysics laboratory that the data from the evolution has been collected, and the computers are analyzing the data. He understands that it may take some time to receive any results from the Geophysics people. They are painstaking prodders that function more in the mode of snails than scientists. They will double- and triple-check all their data, before they present it. After all, based upon their recommendations, Japan may choose to invest trillions of yen in exploration. They have to be certain.

Per prior direction, Mr. Takeda makes an appointment with Deputy Minister Kawamoto to report on the conduct of the evolution. Interestingly, the office of the deputy minister is readily available to him. Mr. Takeda is asked to appear before the deputy minister almost as soon as he set the receiver of his telephone back in its cradle. Upon arrival at the office of the deputy minister, the secretary informs Mr. Takeda that the deputy minister is waiting for him.

As Mr. Takeda enters the inner office, Deputy Minister Kawamoto greets him, "Takeda, I have been waiting to hear the results of the evolution. Please come in, and take a seat."

Takeda "Thank you, Deputy Minister. We completed the evolution early this morning. The computers in the Geophysics laboratory are analyzing the results, as we speak."

Deputy Minister Kawamoto "Tell me of the personnel that you sent down to Australia as a distraction."

Takeda "They have not returned yet, Deputy Minister. They should be en route to Tokyo right now. As I understand, they left Australia a few hours ago."

Deputy Minister Kawamoto "Have they communicated any concerns about their trip?"

Takeda "No, Deputy Minister, they have not. They were not briefed on the nature of their function. This trip to Australia, to them, was merely an inspection tour of the space tracking station."

Deputy Minister Kawamoto "Have you heard from them at all, since the evolution?"

Takeda "I have not heard from them personally, Deputy Minister. However, they did call from the airport prior to their departure for Tokyo to express thanks to their supervisor for allowing them to go on this tour. As I understand from the supervisor, the astrophysicists never mentioned anything disturbing concerning their trip. They seemed quite happy with the trip."

Deputy Minister Kawamoto "Be sure that Kajioka's personnel debrief the young ladies thoroughly when they return. We need to be certain the Australians were not eavesdropping on us during the evolution."

Takeda "One comment that Kajioka relayed to me was that, apparently, during the evolution, there was a party with dancing and wine that seemed to attract all personnel at the tracking station."

Deputy Minister Kawamoto smiles, "I can appreciate the timing. Our Australian friends were too busy inhaling perfume and fantasizing about our women. It was a good idea to send young women into an isolated area. I suspect those hairy, Caucasian beasts were distracted enough. I will need a brief nonetheless after the women return. The minister will demand assurances. You understand my position here, do you not?"

Takeda likewise smiles, "Yes, Deputy Minister, I understand. I will prepare something for you to report to the Minister."

Realizing how much of their time is wasted in these briefings causes the two men to chuckle. There are too many layers of responsibility in Japan.

Deputy Minister Kawamoto "On another issue, we gathered all the data that we set out to acquire, did we not?"

Takeda "I believe so, Deputy Minister. The actual results are being processed. There has been no report to the contrary. As far as I know, all the data we required has been acquired."

Deputy Minister Kawamoto "Is it not amazing how we have accomplished so much with this strange satellite?"

Takeda "It was a brilliant idea to launch a huge communications satellite then expose to the world that our engineers miscalculated some of the requirements for existence in earth's orbit in order to explain the communications satellite's unexpected decomposition."

Deputy Minister Kawamoto "It was truly brilliant. We have some very sharp minds in the Science & Technology Division."

Takeda "Just the other day, one of my section heads marveled at the value of the debris field surrounding *Genji* in deterring the approach of other satellites."

Deputy Minister Kawamoto "It is convenient to have a debris field act as boundary, camouflaging our satellite."

Takeda "Yes, we are most fortunate. Our success in resource exploration has gone on undetected for quite some time now."

Deputy Minister Kawamoto "With continued good fortune, we should be able to detect the exact location of most of the earth's resources within a few years. The discovery by *Genji* of the huge natural gas deposit in Iraq was precious to our future. Some 500 years worth of natural gas reserves was at our disposal. Continued successes like that will elevate Japan to world dominance within the next few generations. We must be cautious, however, so as not to alert the Americans. We know how greedy they are."

Takeda "Truly, Deputy Minister, we assure the continuity of our existence with these clandestine explorations."

Deputy Minister Kawamoto "Clandestine is only for the present, my dear Takeda. In the future, we will conduct our affairs openly and with the pride that accompanies dominance. We work for a better Japan."

Takeda "Yes, we work for a better Japan."

A pause in the conversation allows the two discussants to ponder the glory evolving each day, as Japan rises to a position of dominance.

Deputy Minister Kawamoto breaks the contemplative mood, "Be sure to brief me after the women return, and as soon as Kajioka has analyzed and compiled the results from the evolution."

Takeda senses his cue to leave the deputy minister to his affairs.

Takeda "I will, Deputy Minister."

Upon completion of the session with the deputy minister, Takeda is anxious to meet with his section heads in order to extend his gratitude for the success of the evolution. As soon as he arrives at his office, he has his secretary call the section heads. Within minutes of her calling, the section heads have all assembled in Takeda's office.

Takeda to section heads, "I just wanted to tell you how much the Deputy Minister appreciated our professionalism in conducting the operation of the deep-earth probe. He was truly impressed."

As expected, none of the section heads comment. They just smile and wait to be dismissed. A smile from the section heads translates into esteem for the acknowledgment of their performance.

Takeda dismisses the section heads, and they begin to file out of his office.

Soon after their departure, Takeda receives a call from Kajioka. Kajioka relays some anomalies that the Geophysics laboratory received from the probe. Takeda asks to meet with Kajioka and the Geophysics laboratory head, immediately.

Sensing urgency in Kajioka's voice, Takeda tells his secretary to let Information & Technology Ministry personnel into his office as soon as they arrive. Takeda orders tea from his secretary. Green tea will settle his stomach for any disturbing news Kajioka's group reveals to him.

Within thirty minutes, Kajioka and his Geophysics head settle into Takeda's office. Takeda has the secretary close the door.

Takeda "Alright, what disturbs you, Kajioka?"

Kajioka "The Geophysics laboratory has uncovered some strange results from the data received from the deep-earth probe."

Takeda "Do you have some strange results to tell me?"

Cued by Kajioka, the Geophysics Head interjects, "Yes, Mr. Takeda, there is something we need to tell you. We have some strange anomalies emerging from the data. Although we do not have all the data processed yet, we do have some results that we are having difficulty deciphering."

Takeda "Are you saying that the data received is giving our computers difficulty processing?"

Geophysics Head "I believe I would rephrase the question, Mr. Takeda, our computers are working fine. The data being processed by our computers is alarming."

Takeda looks over at Kajioka. With facial gestures, Kajioka relays to Takeda that the opinion of the Geophysics head is to be trusted.

Takeda to Geophysics Head, "Go on, Doctor."

Geophysics Head "Mr. Kajioka informs me that you are familiar with deep-earth probes, so I will not elaborate on the procedure."

Takeda nods in acknowledgment.

Geophysics Head "As you are aware, when we conduct the deep-earth probe we direct intense multi-frequencies at the intended coordinates in order to measure their reflection. What the data we are receiving indicates is that some frequencies in the select multi-frequency band were not reflected. Other frequencies returned with much lower amplitudes than we had expected…and they were distributed in the harmonic ranges. Mr. Takeda, we have never received results like this in all of our deep-earth probes."

Takeda confused "What does this all mean?"

Kajioka gestures to the Geophysics head that it is safe to continue.

Geophysics Head nervously continues, "Mr. Takeda, the deep-earth probe works similar to radar and sonar in a sense. You send a radar or sonar frequency wave out, and when it interacts with something, it bounces back, so to speak."

Takeda nods that he understands the phenomena.

Geophysics Head "We sent out selected frequencies that would resonant with certain elements, compounds, geophysical layers, etc. At least one of those selected frequencies never returned. Other selected frequencies retuned at much lower energy than expected and had expanded into their harmonics."

Takeda "How is it possible that a selected frequency did not return?"

Geophysics Head "There are two possibilities that come to mind, Mr. Takeda. One is that the selected frequency resonated with the intended target and continued penetrating the target longer than our satellite remained in the receptor-orbit area. In a sense, it took so long for the selected frequency to strike a non-resonating surface below the target that our satellite passed out of range before the bounce back could return and be acknowledged by the receptor circuitry. Second, we uncovered some form of natural stealth structure to this selected frequency."

Takeda "How far would the selected frequency have to penetrate the target for our satellite to miss the bounce back?"

Geophysics head looks over at Kajioka for permission to respond. Kajioka gestures with a nod to respond.

Geophysics Head "Given the selected frequency in question and the speed with which it would propagate through the intended target, it would had to have traveled over one hundred kilometers. The exact distance, I would need a computer to calculate."

Takeda exhales, as he leans forward, "Over one hundred kilometers!"

Geophysics Head "It would be at least that distance, Mr. Takeda."

Takeda "What was the intended target?"

Once again the Geophysics head waits for permission from Kajioka to respond. Kajioka pauses moment.

Kajioka "Mr. Takeda, you do understand that this discussion is still premature, as we have not analyzed all the data, do you not?"

Takeda anxious for a response, "Of course, Kajioka, what was the target?"

Kajioka motions for the Geophysics head to respond.

Geophysics Head "For this selected frequency, it was heavily-concentrated iron-based materials."

Takeda "You are saying that iron was the target, is that right?"

Geophysics Head "That is correct, Mr. Takeda. We targeted iron with this selected frequency. We are concerned about iron resources for our steel industry."

Takeda laughs, "Doctor, if your data is correct, you have uncovered a mother lode of iron ore for Japan."

Kajioka "We thought you should be the first to know of this discovery. If it is, in fact, iron, then we will need to commence acquiring mining privileges in northern New Guinea."

Takeda is taken by the revelation that Japan's need for iron could be satisfied forever. He remembers his discussion with the deputy minister about the survival and dominance of Japan. If these results are true, dominance it shall be.

Kajioka, sensing Takeda elation, conveys to him that as soon as all the results are deciphered and analyzed that he will return for a formal brief.

Takeda just nods.

Kajioka and Geophysics head exit Takeda office. As they leave, Kajioka pats the Geophysics head on the shoulder.

Later that evening, the Astrophysics section head reports to Kajioka that the astrophysicists returned safely and were briefed thoroughly. Kajioka queries the section head on the brief. The query uncovers no unusual occurrences during the entire stay of the astrophysicists in Australia. Their departure went as smoothly as their arrival. The two-day tour at the Space Observatory was uneventful. The section head even mentions that the astrophysicists were allowed to return with a case of Australian wine each.

Kajioka focuses in on the comments during the time of the probe, "Did the astrophysicists mention any change in the Australians during the festivities of the second evening?"

Astrophysics Section Head "They only recall the Space Observatory leading scientist being paged. To them, it seemed like a routine matter."

Kajioka leans forward, "This is very important to our national security. Was there any noticeable difference in the lead scientist's behavior when he returned after attending to the page?"

Astrophysics Section Head "According to the astrophysicists, the lead scientist was away for some time. They were not sure how long. He returned while they were dancing. However, he seemed normal in every respect. The astrophysicists assured me that nothing out of the ordinary was detected during their entire stay in Australia."

Kajioka "Was the lead scientist the liaison for the astrophysicists?"

Astrophysics Section Head "No, the liaison was a Dr. Unni. I believe the astrophysicists identified him as the second in command in the Space Observatory. Dr. Unni remained with the astrophysicists all the second evening."

Kajioka "The morning of their departure, did the astrophysicists meet with the military officer in charge?"

Astrophysics Section head looks over his notes a moment, "Gifts were exchanged prior to their departure. The officer in charge presented the astrophysicists with a plaque, commemorating their tour of the outpost. It was a semi-formal affair."

Kajioka "Did the astrophysicists mention anything unusual in his demeanor?"

Astrophysics Section Head "No, he was just military, as they put it."

Kajioka concludes the report on the brief. After the Astrophysics section head departs his office, Kajioka reviews his report. Certainly, if the Australians suspected something, there would have been some indication of change in their disposition. Australians have difficulty hiding their emotions. Our females would have sensed it. Kajioka concludes that the Australians have not detected the intention behind the touring of the space tracking station.

Kajioka relays his summation of the brief of the astrophysicists to Takeda. Takeda expresses his thanks for choosing females to distract the Australians. The two men commend the intermeshing arrangement of the Foreign Ministry and the Information Ministry in creating the opportunity for such ventures in furthering national interests. Takeda remarks how the intrigue between the ministries resembles that of the court of the ancient emperors of Japan. Kajioka responds that they still drink the same fine *sake* and frequent the same *geisha* establishments. The two men agree to visit the Doll House, once the evolution has concluded.

By the end of the next day, Kajioka informs Takeda that the Geophysics laboratory has compiled and deciphered the data and requests an audience. Takeda graciously agrees and asks them to come to his office after hours. He will hear the brief, immediately.

Although it is normal time for the close of the office on this day, Takeda requests that the secretary and staff remain until after the brief. It is understandable and routine in the ministry to make such a request and expect compliance. After all, the first duty in a Japanese work environment is to your co-workers for the benefit of the enterprise.

Kajioka arrives with the Geophysics section head. Their arms cradle rolls of computer data. Takeda makes room on his sketch table for their printouts. When all is assembled in Takeda's office, the Kajioka tells the Geophysics section head to commence the brief.

The Geophysics section head overviews the background of the data collection processes. Percentages of assurance are highlighted. A list of targets of geological interest is provided. He then focuses on the target list for this evolution. Indications of natural gas deposits are abundant.

With good reason, the area in question has been singled out previously as a huge natural gas resource being development by a Japanese multi-national enterprise (MNE) in cooperation with a multi-national effort.

Next, he discusses the presence of an unusual amount of magma material, suggesting recent volcanic activity in the area. This data stuns Takeda. Kajioka who has been silent on this issue remains so during this brief. Takeda queries the Geophysics section head on the magma. The questions are basic, and the response satisfies his interest. The mention of volcanic activity nearby in Papua New Guinea, and the plate shift along the coast, not far from the site, comforts Takeda's concerns.

Water becomes the next topic. The data reveals a series of underground tunnels feeding the Sepik River along the border of the province containing the site. This is a routine revelation for locations on islands close to the ocean. For the most part, the underground tunnels are remnants of old lava tubes. The Geophysics section head points to the abundance of fresh water that could be exploited to support the general development of the area, including the huge natural gas facility soon to be constructed.

Before he settles into the conversation of the iron discovery, the Geophysics section head runs through the list of other elements of interests; such as, gold, copper, silver, zinc, and others found in quantities in excess of minimum extraction capacities. Truly, this probe highlighted the need to negotiate a variety of exploration licenses for the area with the Indonesian government.

Lastly, the Geophysics section head brings up the topic of a huge iron deposit. According to the data, a mother lode of rich iron ore exists directly below the coordinates probed. To determine the exact extent of the mother lode, an on-site test would need to be performed. The Geophysics section head describes the test as a sounding exercise in which the upper surface of the mother lode is sounded with a technical apparatus. Allowing the sound to propagate through the mother load from different surface points will enable the Geophysics laboratory to estimate, with some degree of accuracy, the capacity of the resource.

Takeda asks how this could be accomplished without alerting the site personnel. Kajioka interjects that the on-site expert, Dr. Yanagi, is qualified to perform the test. The apparatus used in the test is portable and could be flown to the site with instructions for Dr. Yanagi to follow. A cover story for the test could be almost anything. As Kajioka understands from Dr. Yanagi's communications, the site personnel are busy trying to determine what the tree is anyway. Any assistance provided by our government would be seen as aid to that effort. Sounding the tree and its environs would seem natural in order to determine the extent of the roots.

Takeda questions Kajioka's reasoning about a sounding test done on a tree. Takeda feels that the test and the tree are not complementary. Kajioka disagrees in that the concern on-site is to determine the consistency and nature of the tree. Since the Indonesian scientist has reported the presence of magma in the tree bark, it would follow to reason that the tree contains some metallic material. The sounding test would consist of an effort to determine the extent of the metallic presence in the tree.

Takeda still expresses doubts about the idea but acquiesces to Kajioka's retort. Takeda further questions whether or not Dr. Yanagi can perform the test without having to divulge its true nature. This concerns Kajioka, as well. Dr. Yanagi would need to mask the results.

The Geophysics section head suggests altering the meter readout gage. It is a simple procedure to overlay a fake readout on top of the actual meter readout. Since the meter readout is encased in glass, observers will be unable to determine the actual data being collected by the test apparatus. With each sounding, Dr. Yanagi will record the reading as visible on the fake meter readout. Later, when he is alone, he can dismantle the test apparatus meter face, remove the fake meter readout and determine the correct readings by comparing the two meter readout faces with his recorded data.

Kajioka smiles at Takeda and nods approvingly. Takeda agrees that the idea has merit. After some further discussion, Takeda tells Kajioka to create a fake meter face and get the device to Dr. Yanagi as soon as possible. Takeda insists that an encrypted dispatch be sent to Dr. Yanagi ahead of the sounding apparatus in order to allow him time to prepare a cover story for its use.

Before the session concludes, Takeda asks for an estimation of the size of the iron deposit. The Geophysics head reports that from the data collected, thus far, the estimate would be some 160 kilometers below the earth's surface. This estimate startles Takeda. He asks for percentage accuracy for the estimation. Kajioka responds that the sounding test will make the accuracy of the estimation over ninety percent. Right now, Kajioka explains that all we have is a mound of bizarre data that needs some form of on-site grasp for authentication.

Takeda realizes for the first time that 160 kilometers is a long way below the earth's surface. He questions the magnitude of the thickness of the earth's crust. The Geophysics section head responds with a series of references designed to couch his estimate. When the list of references, and some caveats, has been explained, the Geophysics section head states that the deep-earth probe data remains well within the depth of the earth's outer crust. Takeda seems relieved. Why, he does not know. Takeda supposes if the depth of the iron deposit exceeded the thickness of the earth's crust, he would suspect the readings to be too bizarre to take seriously.

The session winds down with the direction to the Geophysics laboratory to prepare the test apparatus for transport to New Guinea. A recommendation follows to include a technician to operate the sounding apparatus for Dr. Yanagi. The technician idea has merit. This way, there will be someone accompanying the sounding apparatus to New Guinea, ensuring the device is not tampered with in any manner. Also, there would be no chance or error in the instructions to Dr. Yanagi. Takeda approves the idea and reminds Kajioka of the confidential nature of their association in this matter.

The session ends with Takeda promising to brief the upper echelon on the findings and the intended course of action.

Takeda needs to brief Deputy Minister Kawamoto quickly for two reasons. One, he requires permission to authorize the transfer of a sounding apparatus to New Guinea, accompanied by a skilled technician. Second, the deputy minister will have to brief the foreign minister on the urgency to commence negotiations with the Republic of Indonesia for mining rights in the area encompassing the coordinates probed by the satellite *Genji*.

The deputy minister is eager to receive Takeda. As expected, the deputy minister desired Takeda presence, as soon as he rested the telephone handset in its cradle. Takeda gathers his thoughts and hurries to the deputy minister's office.

Deputy Minister Kawamoto, on seeing Takeda walk up to his secretary's desk, motions for him to enter his office post haste.

Deputy Minister Kawamoto "Takeda, I have been quivering with anticipation to meet with you. How did things go?"

Takeda smiling, "I believe that they went as expected, Deputy Minister."

Deputy Minister Kawamoto smiles, "You believe that they went well, is that it? Why do you only believe that things went well?"

Takeda "We have the data results deciphered, Deputy Minister; however, there are some grossly-unusual findings."

Deputy Minister Kawamoto "Now, there is a phrase that I am not used to hearing: 'grossly-unusual.'"

Takeda "Deputy Minister, our findings seem to indicate an iron deposit extending some one hundred kilometers into the earth's crust."

Deputy Minister Kawamoto frowns, "One hundred meters?"

Takeda "No, Deputy Minister, what I said was one hundred kilometers."

Deputy Minister Kawamoto pauses a moment, "Takeda, one hundred kilometers is a long distance. Have these results been verified?"

Takeda "At least one hundred kilometers has been verified by the Geophysics laboratory, Deputy Minister. We desire to perform a more accurate, on-site verification in order to ascertain the exact depth of the iron ore deposit."

Deputy Minister Kawamoto "Are you certain of this, Takeda?"

Takeda "Yes, I am fairly certain, Deputy Minister. The Geophysics laboratory head is certain."

Deputy Minister Kawamoto pauses a moment to reflect on the significance of the report, "Does anyone else know of this?"

Takeda "No, Deputy Minister, the report and this entire evolution have been kept in strict compliance with the dictates of national security."

Deputy Minister Kawamoto nods approvingly, "Well done, Takeda. Do what is necessary to conduct this on-site verification."

Takeda expresses his thanks for the permission to proceed.

Deputy Minister Kawamoto rethinking the report, "One hundred kilometers, if my recollection of geology from my university days is correct, falls below the estimated boundary of the earth's outer crust."

Takeda "We have not established that to be the case, Deputy Minister, which is why we need to conduct this additional on-site test."

Deputy Minister Kawamoto "Takeda, I believe this to be the case indeed. One hundred kilometers exceeds the known boundary depth of the earth's outer crust. I admit that in some areas of the world the outer crust could be thicker, but, as best as I can recall, your one hundred kilometers approaches that boundary."

Takeda remains silent, as he awaits the deputy minister's summation.

Deputy Minister Kawamoto "Takeda, this could be the greatest iron ore deposit discovery in history. Do you realize that? One hundred kilometers represents an unlimited supply of iron ore."

Takeda "I concur, Deputy Minister."

Deputy Minister Kawamoto smiling, "We need to acquire mining rights, do we not?"

Takeda smiles, "Yes, Deputy Minister, mining rights was my second request of Your Excellency."

Deputy Minister Kawamoto "I understand. I will brief the minister, personally. Our embassy in Djakarta will make the request so as not to alert anyone."

Takeda "Thank you, Deputy Minister."

Deputy Minister Kawamoto "Tell me the results of the brief of the astrophysicists."

Takeda "The brief revealed no unusual concerns expressed by the Australians, Deputy Minister."

Deputy Minister Kawamoto nods his head up and down, "Good, Takeda. I will take this matter through the proper channels. Report back to me when the results of the on-site verification have been completed."

Takeda takes his leave of the deputy minister. The brief was short, indicating the deputy minister's excitement with the results.

Everyone involved seems excited over the results of the deep-earth probe.

CHAPTER 11

▼

GEOPHYSICS LABORATORY, MINISTRY OF INFORMATION & TECHNOLOGY

Walking into a typical Geophysics laboratory is akin to wandering around the underground space of a medieval castle. Strange contraptions of every which type adorn the cement walls. To the unknowing eye, the purpose of such apparati bewilders the imagination. There are huge gages larger than cattle weight scales, piston assemblies that resemble the pipes of a church organ, huge sledge hammers and anvils, large gearing assemblies designed for digging, and dirt. Loose dirt, in the form closely resembling dust from cement work, blankets every surface of the stowage rooms. One desperately desires a surgical facemask in order to roam the spaces.

Kajioka has just arrived to meet with the selected technician designated to accompany the sounding apparatus to New Guinea.

Geophysics Head makes the introductions, "Mr. Kajioka, this is Sugai. He has been assigned to operate the sounding apparatus."

Sugai is an average Japanese, slender built, some 165 cm (5'5") in height with noticeable front teeth that seem to pop out of his mouth when he smiles.

Kajioka looks him over and concludes, with a nod, that he will do. The Geophysics Head dismisses Sugai.

After Sugai has entered one of the storage spaces, the Geophysics Head reminds Kajioka, "Mr. Kajioka, we have not overlooked Dr. Yanagi's reports from on-site, have we?"

Kajioka startled by the inquiry, "What do you mean?"

Geophysics Head "Dr. Yanagi reported a phenomenon of regeneration associated with the tree's bark."

Kajioka "I fail to see the relevance. We have a huge iron deposit to assess."

Geophysics Head realizing that he has spoken prematurely, "I understand, Mr. Kajioka. We need to focus on the task before us."

Kajioka "Whatever those Indonesian scientists and Yanagi are imagining should not distract us. Given this new discovery, we need to position ourselves quickly in order to reap whatever benefits we can. We must keep in mind that our division receives its allowances from the government. Should we let such an opportunity slip by us, I fear we would be rationed severely. We need to move quickly."

Geophysics Head sheepishly responds, "I understand, Mr. Kajioka."

Kajioka impatiently, "Get this fellow, Sugai, and the apparatus on the next plane to New Guinea."

As Kajioka is about to leave the Geophysics laboratory, he turns and asks, "By the way, have we heard anything else from Dr. Yanagi?"

Geophysics Head "He has communicated, but there is nothing new in his correspondences. The content of the messages amounts to just updates, Mr. Kajioka. Dr. Yanagi has acknowledged that we are sending a sounding device and a technician."

Kajioka, feeling the cement dust on the side wall near the exit door, "This is a dusty business, isn't it?"

Geophysics Head "The dust comes with the job, Mr. Kajioka. Now and then, I have the workers wash down all the surfaces to minimize the build up."

Kajioka shakes his head, "It appears you are close to another wipe down."

Geophysics Head "I will have it done today, Mr. Kajioka."

Kajioka likes to hear that his opinion is taken seriously. It is one of the things he likes most about his job. If the capacity of this iron ore deposit proves to be correct, he can expect a promotion. A promotion would mean that more people would take him seriously.

After Kajioka has departed the laboratory, the Geophysics Head excuses all workers from their assignments, except Sugai and those assisting him to prepare the apparatus for shipment, and orders the workers to wipe down the space.

After some thought, the Geophysics Head decides to confide in Sugai concerning some of the happenings that have been reported in New Guinea, so he will be prepared to confront a bizarre environment.

Geophysics Head, after looking around the spaces for Sugai, "Here you are, Sugai. I have been looking everywhere for you."

Sugai "I am sorry, boss. I was preparing a shipping label for Indonesian customs."

Geophysics Head gestures for Sugai to accompany him, as they return to the secure space where the sounding apparatus is being altered.

Geophysics Head upon entering the secure space, "Sugai, as you may be aware, you have been assigned to a sensitive mission. Secrecy will be the prime issue, once you depart this secure space. You are not to divulge anything to which you have been a witness. Is that clearly understood?"

Sugai "Yes, I understand, boss. I have been on similar assignments in the past."

Geophysics Head "Show me how you have altered the meter readout."

Sugai goes through the procedure he used, step by step, describing the altering of the meter face.

Geophysics Head looking over the overlaid meter face, "I see that the new readout is labeled in increments of meters. That is an excellent innovation."

Sugai "I thought having the increments in meters would not alert anyone, regardless of what the final readout turned out to be."

Geophysics Head exhales, "Yes, even if the reading is off-scale, no one should take alarm."

Sugai laughs, "I believe so, as well."

Geophysics Head "Now, Sugai, there are some anomalies associated with this assignment that I need to share with you. Listen very carefully to me. You will be sound testing what appears to be a tree in the middle of a jungle area in northern New Guinea."

Sugai interjects, "A tree!? The sounding apparatus will be of no use on a tree. The device's intended use is on metal."

Geophysics Head "I understand the intended use of the sounding apparatus; however, it is believed that this tree is made of some form of metal."

Sugai chuckles, "How can that be?"

Geophysics Head "I wish I knew that answer, Sugai. The reports coming in from Dr. Yanagi indicate that this tree is made of an extremely strong material. Some tests have likewise supported that contention."

Sugai "What tests are these, boss?"

Geophysics Head begins to respond to Sugai but stops, "Sugai, I cannot share the content of those tests with you. You will have to trust me. We believe this tree to be made of some metallic form."

Sugai "I trust you, boss."

Geophysics Head "Good, let us move on to another issue. This tree appears to be indestructible. A few attempts to cut down the tree have resulted in broken tree-cutting equipment. The tree appears to have no indication of visible damage, after the attempts to cut into it failed."

Sugai "Are you serious, boss?"

Geophysics Head "I am afraid that I am, Sugai. Anyway, those are the reports that we are receiving. There is another issue of which you need to be aware. This tree has regenerative properties."

Sugai "Most trees have the ability for some form of regeneration."

Geophysics Head rubs his chin, "This tree seems to have regeneration perfected. Do not be alarmed, if one day you cut off a piece of bark to do your sound test, and the same piece that you cut off reappears a few days later."

Sugai smiles, "This tree is amazing, isn't it?"

Geophysics Head "Sugai, you are going down to New Guinea to sound the roots of the tree."

Sugai is taken by surprise, "I was told I was going to sound a huge iron ore deposit."

Geophysics Head "It is the same assignment, Sugai. It appears that the tree's roots are the huge iron ore deposit."

Sugai stunned, "I understand the secrecy now, boss."

Geophysics Head "Good, remember, you represent all of us down there. Stay close to Dr. Yanagi. Follow his directions to the letter. He has been there for some time now. He will advise you on how to proceed. Remember, the on-site area is under the control of the Indonesian Army. In that part of the world, those soldiers are on the fringes of the fanatical. Most of those soldiers have participated in wholesale massacres. They will not hesitate to discharge their weapons. You may witness summary executions of the natives. If you do witness such an event, control yourself and remain calm. Most of all, try to forget what you witnessed, and never bring it up in conversation while you are on-site."

Sugai sheepishly asks, "Does the Indonesia Army still harbor resentment over Japan's occupation of the area during the last big war?"

Geophysics Head "Everyone in South East Asia resents us, Sugai. They remember our forced-labor camps. Try not to upset anyone down there. Just do your job and remain close to Dr. Yanagi. Dr. Yanagi is accepted by the international community and respected by the Indonesian government."

Sugai "I will remain close to Dr. Yanagi, boss."

Geophysics Head "There is one other caution. Since we are dealing with an unknown here, try to make note of anything unusual that you witness while you are sound testing. Make note of the little things that seem odd. The little anomalies may become important, as we attempt to make sense of what we have discovered."

Sugai "I will surely do that, boss."

Geophysics Head mulls over whether or not he should share with Sugai that people are disappearing down there. He decides against it. Sugai has enough on his mind already. The thought that this trip might be his ultimate destination would be too much for him. It is best Sugai just concentrate on his assignment. Besides, once he joins up with Dr. Yanagi, he will be considered expendable.

Geophysics Head "Have you packed all the equipment that you believe that you will need?"

Sugai points to huge duffle bag leaning against one of the walls, "Yes, I have my electronic supplies, equipment and tools in that bag. I think I have enough of everything that I can imagine. I should be able to rewire the sounding apparatus, if necessary."

Geophysics Head "Have you itemized everything for Indonesian customs? The Muslims can be sticklers."

Sugai "I was filling out the Indonesian customs forms when you asked to speak to me, boss. I am almost done. I have everything listed. They will be able to tell that I am a working technician."

Geophysics Head chuckles, "Maybe you can improve Dr. Yanagi's communication ability while you are down there?"

Sugai smiles, "Well, boss, I will be bringing enough extra wire to build a transmitter."

Geophysics Head "I was joking, Sugai. All looks well here. Good luck, Sugai."

Sugai smiles, "Thank you, boss."

The Geophysics Head departs the working spaces and makes his way toward Mr. Kajioka's office. Fortunately, he sees Mr. Kajioka in the hallway and catches up to him. The greeting is informal, and they decide on refreshments. The Geophysics area contains a mini-cafeteria where short-order meals can be purchased through vending machines. A favorite drink dispensed from these machines is ice-cold, sweetened milk coffee.

Kajioka "I am glad to see you. The last time we talked I sensed that you had something important to tell me."

Geophysics Head "Actually, Mr. Kajioka, my reason to see you has more to do with the status of the delivery of the sounding apparatus to New Guinea."

Kajioka "How is that going?"

Geophysics Head "The sounding apparatus will be on the next flight to Singapore. The technician is packed and ready to accompany it. I just finished briefing him."

Kajioka "Did the brief go as expected?"

Geophysics Head "Yes, the brief went as expected. There was no hesitation on the part of the technician."

Kajioka nodding, "How did the technician handle the missing people phenomenon we are experiencing in New Guinea?"

Geophysics Head "Actually, I chose not to discuss that issue with the technician. He has many things on his mind right now, and I felt that knowledge of those disappearances would distract him."

Kajioka surprised by the response, "He does not know then, is that it?"

Geophysics Head sensing disapproval, "No, Mr. Kajioka, the technician does not know anything about the disappearances. Besides, there have been no reports of disappearances in Dr. Yanagi's transmissions."

Kajioka looks at the Geophysics Head a moment, "You might lose the man's trust by not telling him. Are you aware of that?"

Geophysics Head "Yes, I considered that possibility, but I feel confident that the technician will not see my decision in that manner."

Kajioka "You know this man, Sugai, well, do you?"

Geophysics Head "I know him well enough to spare him this distraction, Mr. Kajioka."

Kajioka nods, "I see. Let us hope things turn out well down there. We are gambling our future on Dr. Yanagi and this technician. We have to be right."

Geophysics Head "I am confident in Sugai's ability, Mr. Kajioka."

Kajioka "Tell me now, was there anything else you wished to discuss with me?"

Geophysics Head "There is, Mr. Kajioka, but it can wait until more data has been received."

Kajioka finishes his iced coffee drink, "I see you are becoming a man of caution. That is good to see. I can appreciate someone with caution. In these trying times of global enterprise, caution is needed."

Geophysics Head sensing approval, "Thank you, Mr. Kajioka, for the kind words."

Kajioka "The regeneration issue concerns you, does it not?"

Geophysics Head looking around for eavesdroppers, "Yes, it does, Mr. Kajioka."

Kajioka smiles: "Do not be so worried, there are few people here who understand what we are talking about. But, you are right such a discussion warrants the confines of my office."

Geophysics Head "I feel such a discussion would be premature. We should await the results from the sounding test."

Kajioka nods, "You are right. We should await the results of the sounding test. However, once the results have been analyzed, I want to hear your concerns. Do you understand?"

Geophysics Head smiles, "I understand completely, Mr. Kajioka."

The Geophysics Head realizes that the regeneration capabilities have not escaped Mr. Kajioka's evaluation of the situation. Truly, Mr. Kajioka is braving uncertainty.

Kajioka extends his departing greeting, as he tosses his empty coffee can into a trash bin and exits the cafeteria area. The Geophysics Head has made his point and believes that it has been well taken. Some anxiety will build as the Geophysics Head awaits the test results of the sounding. Given the bizarre reports that have been received thus far, almost anything could materialize from this sounding test. The bizarre appears to have become the norm in the Geophysics laboratory.

Looking around the row of vending machines, the Geophysics Head remembers that he has not eaten yet, today. He selects a broth vender and deposits the right amount of yen. Unfortunately, the paper cup drops down upside down, and the broth pours over it into the drain below. The Geophysics Head prays his luck does not imitate that of the broth cup.

CHAPTER 12

▼

VILLAGE, NEW GUINEA

Connors and Joe commence their walk back to the encampment. It is early morning, so the path is fresh with dew. A strange coolness that often accompanies early mornings near the equator refreshes the air. For whatever reason, the mosquitoes have decided to take a rest.

Connors still feeling the effects of the jungle juice from the night before, "Mate, I tell you, you should have partaken in one of them little brown sheilas. Keeps the plumbing primed, you know."

Joe somewhat disgusted with Connors' comments, "I just did not feel up to it, Brad."

Connors chides Joe, "Mate, do you have a special sheila back in Manila?"

Joe looking for an escape from this conversation, "Yes, Brad, as a matter of fact I do have someone back there."

Connors "I knew it. I knew there was a reason you passed up some relief."

Joe is now thoroughly disgusted with Connors animalistic habits. During the evening, Joe could not help awaking to the sounds emanating from Connors' extravagances. The girl looked too young to be engaging in carnal knowledge. As a matter of fact, the way Connors handled her Joe got the impression that Connors had experience with sheep. All Joe needed to hear was a "bah" sound from the little girl to authenticate his suspicions about Connors.

Walking the path a ways from the village, a bird of paradise takes flight and startles Connors and Joe. Joe smiles at the thought that the bird took flight so as

not to be sexually abused by Connors. Whatever the reason for the sudden departure of the bird, something scared it. Those birds seldom move in the presence of
humans. It is as if they have a sixth sense that humans do not prey upon them.

Joe enjoys the silence during the walk, as Connors wipes the sweat off his neck
constantly. The jungle juice is oozing out of Connors. He did consume much
more than he should have. Had Joe consumed that much, he would still be sleeping it off in the village hut.

Finally, Joe breaks the silence, "Brad, do you think that they missed us in the
encampment?"

Connors chuckles, "Of course they did, Mate. Question is: how much did
they miss us? It could not have been too much, because I saw no searchlights
scanning the tall grass for us last night or this morning."

Joe "Do you think we have some explaining to do when we return?"

Connors "We should tell them a little to pacify their anxiety. The Captain will
be furious. He is responsible for you. You will need to appease the Captain, if you
expect to be allowed outside the encampment ever again."

Joe exhales deeply, "I was afraid of that."

Connors "I would not let it worry you too much, Mate. The captain understands you needed some relief. He knows you left with me, and he is a smart
man. He probably knows we went into the village to improve foreign relations."

Joe chuckles, "Brad, do you ever worry about anything at all?"

Connors "Of course I do, Mate. I worry about how we are going to catch one
of those bloody snakes. I cannot pass up a chance for a million dollars US."

Joe "Brad, did you see the size of that snake this morning?"

Connors "That I did, Mate. I plan on catching that one. To hell with the
larger one is what I say."

Joe smiles, "Well, I am sure am glad your senses returned, Brad. Do you not
think the snake we saw might be too much for you as well?"

Connors "Mate, I tell you. It is just a matter of mind over matter. Let me
think a while on this, and I will come up with a sure fire way to capture that
beast. One million dollars US creates a lot of determination."

Joe "Are you sure it is not the jungle juice?"

Connors smiles, "I am sure, Mate. I only had a few sips of the jungle juice
anyway."

Joe realizes that Connors must have drunk the headman out of all his liquor.
Connors must be a habitual drunk. That is probably the reason that he prefers
these isolated assignments. He probably cannot cope with the rigors and sobriety
of civilization.

After a few kilometers of walking and evading the tall grass encroaching into their paths, Joe notices a tree lying across the road. It seems strange, because Joe does not recall encountering such an obstacle during the trek to the village. No matter how hard he tries to remember, a tree hindering traffic seems out of place. If the tree were there on the way to the village, Connors and he would have had to walk over it. Could they have been so lost in conversation and just stepped over it? It is possible. The tree is not that large.

Joe to Connors, "Brad, do you recall stepping over a tree on the way out here?"

Connors looks down the path ahead and notices the tree, "No, Mate, I do not recall a tree in the road on the way out here."

Joe pointing up ahead, "Well, there is a tree there now."

Connors rubs the back of his hand against his chin, "It is not that big of a tree. I would not worry about it."

Joe "Do you see any trees around this road that could have fallen?"

Connors looks around the road and over the tall grass, as best he can, "Mate, I do not see any trees around here at all. It is just tall grass everywhere."

Joe "Where did this tree come from? I do not recall seeing any trees in the vicinity of this road."

Connors takes a second look around, "You are right, Mate. There are no trees around here. Do you suppose the natives are blockading the road? They do that, you know, to extract toll fees. Maybe they intend to ambush us and demand money or cigarettes."

Joe "You cannot be serious. There is nothing out here."

Connors "The rebels run through this area en route to other destinations. Maybe the rebels need some money."

Joe "That is all we need to be held up in the jungle of New Guinea."

Connors "Do not worry, Mate. If you give them something, they will leave you alone. The rebels are not so bad. Besides, we are white. The rebels only hate the Indonesians."

Joe "Are you sure Brad? I would hate to ruin such a beautiful morning by getting a spear in my guts."

Connors chuckles, "Relax, Joe, these rebels have automatic weapons. If you get something sharp in your gut, it would be a bayonet or a survival knife. These rebels are sophisticated."

Joe, as they get a little closer to the tree, "Thanks for the comforting words, Brad."

As the two men approach the area of the roadway where the tree lies, they notice the tree move. It appears that someone is pulling the tree into the tall grass to one side of the roadway.

Connors "See, Mate, the natives are moving the tree out of the way for us. We should be fine. They must have set the roadblock for some anticipated motor vehicle. Mate, they are probably the headman's people."

Joe notices after a while that the tree is tampering as it is being pulled into the tall grass. He senses that the root end must be the one the natives are pulling on. Although from his experiences with lumberjacking, the tapered end of the tree is the end pulled. Everything else is backward in this part of the world, why not tree pulling?

Joe "Where did they get the tree in the first place?"

Connors "The river bank is not more than a kilometer from here. They might have cut the tree down there. There are lots of trees that size along the river bank."

Joe "Brad, the river bank is on the same side of the roadway that the natives are pulling the tree into the tall grass. Besides, the roadway up ahead is over ten meters wide. Why would they cut down a ten-meter-plus tree and lug it a kilometer in order to block a road?"

They are some twenty meters from the tree when they notice the tapered end of the tree drag cross the road slowly.

Connors alarmed, "Mate, the end of that tree looks more like a tail than a tree top."

Joe inhales deeply. He can feel his heart slamming against his chest. All he can say to himself is: "My God, that thing is alive. It is a snake!"

Connors speaks first, "It is a snake! Holy Mother of God, it is a snake."

Seeing the roadway clear ahead, both men begin running down the road toward the encampment. They have a few kilometers to traverse, but their bodies are energized. They have never felt so willing to run in their lives. Despite their ages and poor physical conditioning, they run like Olympic dashers. Both men cover the distance to the encampment without slowing down. Covered in sweat and out of breath, they race past the guards into the encampment. Connors, upon reaching the inner confines of the encampment, falls to his knees and commences expectorating. He throws up at least a week's worth of tuna and vile fluids.

The encampment personnel soon gather around the two men. Neither man can speak for loss of breath or expectorating. The guards attempt to query Connors, but he continues to heave. Connors' disposition causes laughter amongst the guards. Some descriptive phrase in Indonesian that roughly translates into white monkey spits off their lips, like old chewing tobacco.

One of the guards leaves the scene of the two exhausted men to fetch Captain Djarmat. The other guards continue to admire the two white monkeys. It is clear from the position of the guards that the two men are being detained. Their abrupt breach of the outer perimeter is a violation of the rules of the encampment. If the outer sentries had not recognized them, they might have been summarily executed, as they approached the encampment. Connors is aware of this and realizes his report with the soldiers probably saved his life and the life of Del Rosi.

Connors soon regains his composure and leans backward to the point of falling over backward on the ground. Joe attempts to help Connors up, but Connors is too exhausted to rise. Connors closes his eyes and seems to pass into sleep or some deep state of contemplation.

Joe leans over to whisper to Connors, "Brad, I think we have to tell the Captain what we just saw out there."

Connors swats Joe away, "Leave me be, Mate. I think I am going to have a heart attack."

Joe "Brad, I cannot keep quiet about something like this."

Connors "Bloody hell, just let me rest a while, Mate."

After a few attempts to revive Connors, Joe just takes a seat on the ground next to him. The run has caused him to sweat profusely. His shirt is drenched. As the morning sun warms his clothing, Joe watches the sweat evaporate. The evaporation resembles an aura permeating out of his body. Even the mosquitoes keep their distance from the aura of transforming sweat. Joe admits that he enjoys the sanctuary from the New Guinea air force.

Captain Djarmat arrives on the scene, accompanied by a few of soldiers. The soldiers are smiling. Something humorous must have been exchanged to make them so joyous. From the avoidance of eye contact with Joe, he suspects whatever the content of the joke that Connors and he were the topic.

Captain Djarmat speaks up, as he approaches the two men, "I am sorry for the delay. I was in the middle of my morning prayers."

The captain is a devout Muslim and makes every attempt to perform his five prayers a day.

Joe "We needed a few moments to catch our breath, Captain."

Captain Djarmat smiles, as he looks at Connors asleep, "Looks like this fellow is in need of a few nights rest. I could have waited until tomorrow to visit with him."

Connors does not even stir during the captain's speech. Apparently, the mixture of sudden exercise and an overdose of jungle juice have placed him into a coma.

Joe looking over Connors' lifeless body, "We had a rough time of it out there, Captain. Bradley should be fine."

Captain Djarmat "I am sure that he will be. You are aware that you violated my security checkpoint, are you not?"

Joe "Yes, Captain, we were disrespectful to your guards and for that I apologize."

Captain Djarmat "You know that I have issued orders to shoot anyone trying to breach our containment, are you not?"

Joe "Yes, Captain, I am aware of your orders. I do not know what got into us. We were racing each other and just forgot."

Captain Djarmat knows Joe is lying, "It is a good thing my soldiers recognized you. It is an even better thing that they like you, Mr. Del Rosi. Were you and your comatose associate here not a matter of humor for my soldiers they would have shot you. You can count your blessings, Mr. Del Rosi. My soldiers have difficulty finding humor in this forsaken jungle environment."

Joe remains silent. The captain's admonishment should be the extent of their punishment for breaking containment. Connors begins to snore. Laughter breaks out amongst the soldiers. The white monkey phrase erupts whenever the soldiers can catch their breath from laughing. Joe realizes that the soldiers enjoy Connors' company for his humor value.

The captain looks around the encampment. All of his soldiers are smiling or laughing. It is good to laugh once in a while in such an assignment. Laughter brings back a sense of camaraderie that the soldiers have missed for some time now.

Captain Djarmat "Alright, Mr. Del Rosi, you can drag your associate into your tent. Get some rest and freshen up. I have some dispatches that came in while you and your associate were roaming about in the jungle. You should find them on the table in your tent. If you feel the need to talk with me later on just have one of the sentries outside your tent pass the word to me."

Joe senses a form of tent detention being imposed upon Connors and him in the captain's comment. It is in Joe's best interest not to try this Indonesian officer. He will do as the captain implies and remain in his tent until told otherwise.

Captain Djarmat, as he is about to walk away, "If you need some help dragging your associate into your tent, my men will assist you. Although, I must warn you, Mr. Del Rosi, my men are not too keen on the scent of alcohol. They are good followers of Islam."

Joe understands the gist of the captain's comment: drag the white monkey's carcass in your tent and be quick about it. Joe gets up and grabs Connors under the armpits and commences dragging his lifeless body into the tent. The sight of Connors' mouth open with his tongue peeking out one corner drives the soldiers into another frenzy of laughter. Truly, dragging Connors into the tent is a humiliating experience for Joe. From now on, he will be associated with white monkey jokes in the presence of the men.

Joe tugs the best he can to get Connors inside the tent. Once Connors' body crosses the threshold of the tent, Joe immediately releases the knot holding the tent flap open. Like a curtain coming down at the end of a play, the white monkey show ends. Joe struggles to get Connors onto his field bed, a camouflage-colored, Indonesian army variety. By the time Joe has Connors prone on the bed the laughter from outside the tent subsides. Joe crumbles into his director's chair and rests, as he watches Connors peacefully breathe. The run into the encampment really overtaxed Connors' bio-system. Connors is in deep sleep. He may not recover for days. The bathtub of jungle juice Connors consumed did not help either. How can people destroy themselves so? Joe is amazed at the way Connors exists. Even in this desolate environment, Connors seems to suck the marrow out of life. What strange people these Australians are. Maybe, being surrounded by kangaroos, koala bears and all the other strange creatures produces this strange behavior in Australians. Let us not forget the Tasmanian devils and the dingoes in this formula for over-indulgence.

Joe is alarmed when the tent flap suddenly flies open. Dr. Leong enters the tent without an introduction from the sentry.

Dr. Leong, out of breath, "I just heard you were back. Thank God, you are safe."

Joe is taken back by the doctor's show of emotion. He had not realized that his romp in the jungle with Connors would worry her.

Joe stands to greet the doctor, "I am fine, Doctor."

Dr. Leong smiles, "It is Rachael, remember."

Joe sensing her comfort, "Yes, of course I remember, Rachel."

Joe opens his arms to gesture an invitation to embrace. Dr. Leong enthusiastically accepts to Joe's even greater surprise. Dr. Leong embraces Joe firmly. He takes a while to respond, more from uncertainty than appreciation. Once Dr. Leong senses Joe's response, she releases her embrace and tends to Connors. Joe just observes her examine Connors for life signs.

Dr. Leong after a few life checks on Connors, "He has had quite a bit to drink, hasn't he?"

Joe smiles, "Yes, some headman from a village not far from here encouraged him to celebrate. You could say they over-indulged a bit."

Dr. Leong "Yes, I could say that he consumed way too much. His liver is recuperating. I have some vitamin C that I can bring him. See that he gets plenty of water. He is dehydrating from all the alcohol."

Once her preliminary diagnosis is complete, she hugs Joe again and says, "I was worried about you. Do not wander off like that again. It is dangerous out here. You could have been killed."

Joe promises her that he will remain within the confines of the encampment. His assurances comfort the doctor. Joe senses that his response pleases Rachael. She excuses herself from Joe's tent, and says she will return, immediately, with some vitamin C for Connors.

The distinct sound of helicopter blades whipping serenades Dr. Leong's departure from Joe's tent. A new set of dispatches from Jayapura will be delivered soon. Although for Joe, the dispatches are few and far between. He wonders if the ADB has forgotten him. Long periods in isolation evoke such thoughts.

Connors turns over on his side. It is a first sign of life. Joe breathes a sigh of relief. For a while, he felt Connors had deserted him. Joe adjusts the blanket covering Connors. Connors is perspiring a lot, as his body attempts to excrete the foul jungle juice from its blood system.

Joe resettles into his folding chair and allows his mind to reminisce the wonderful times that he experienced in Manila. He wishes he had a radio to let the romantic sounds of the Philippines comfort his soul. In desperation, he attempts to replay those sounds that he cherished most in his mind. As for women, there are always women who haunt men's minds in isolation. At first, he recounts favorites from Manila. Next, he moves backward to his collegiate experiences. After that, he enjoys the backseat romances of his high school days. It is only after all those favorites have played out that he thinks of Rachael. She is soft and desirable. He recalls with advantages how she felt in his arms just a few moments ago. How, for just a moment, he felt himself come alive. Envisioning an evening with Rachael in this god-forsaken place pleases Joe. He realizes that he desires her company. Even though he knows that any future with this woman would be impossible, he longs for the comfort of her loins.

Joe's daydreaming is interrupted with a sudden opening of the tent flap. The object of his daydreams enters the tent and quickly attends to Connors. Rachael force feeds Connors some vitamins and bottled water. Connors' grimace conveys that he preferred whatever she gave him to have been chased with jungle juice. Connors is a diehard alcoholic.

Offering a forward advance, Joe comments that he was just thinking of Rachael. Rachael returns one of those smiles sweeter than the morning after, and tells Joe that she thought of him a lot while he was away.

Joe "You know this is impossible for us, don't you?"

Dr. Leong "Yes, I do know. I even know that whatever happens, Captain Djarmat will report it."

Joe "You would be ruined in a Muslim culture. We cannot allow this to proceed any further."

Dr. Leong smiles, "You know, I never figured you for a gentleman, Mr. Del Rosi."

Joe Chuckles, "I am not a gentleman, but I cannot hurt you this way."

Dr. Leong sighs approvingly, "You are a gentleman, Mr. Del Rosi. I appreciate your concern for my reputation. It is nice to feel appreciated and respected by a true gentleman."

Joe somewhat embarrassed, "Rachael, I do desire you."

Dr. Leong "I know. I see it in your eyes, and I feel it in your touch."

Joe is suddenly lost for words. He remains silent to allow his mind to subdue his emotions that are boiling over with raw desire.

Dr. Leong turns toward Connors and takes a deep breath, "He will be fine. Just keep him warm and give him lots of water."

Joe understands, in his act to be proper, he let a wonderful moment pass. He also understands that this opportunity will never appear again. How strange it is that we allow some of life's greatest pleasure to pass us by, because we assume, through habit, some role in culture that is quite alien to us. Why cannot Joe be like Connors and just experience life for what it offers?

After a few moments of silence, Dr. Leong turns to face Joe and says, "The reason I was so worried about you was that Captain Djarmat has this theory that a huge snake is the cause of the disappearances."

Joe finds himself in a dilemma. If he says nothing to Rachel, she will distrust him forever.

Joe offers an evasive response, "How big did the Captain think this snake was?"

Dr. Leong "Well, once he shared his idea with me, I did some extrapolations on the size of known snakes and estimated the snake would need to be some fifteen meters or more in length."

Joe decides he has to come clean with Rachael, "Rachael, Brad and I saw a snake some twelve meters in length. On the way back to the encampment, we came across a portion of a snake crossing the roadway ahead of us that could easily be the snake that you extrapolated."

Dr. Leong "Are you saying that you have seen this snake?"

Joe "I am saying that I have seen two huge snakes, Rachael."

Dr. Leong obviously petrified, "Did Connors see the two snakes too?"

Joe looks at the ground in the tent, "Yes, Rachael, Brad saw the snakes too. That is why we were so exhausted from running. We were running to escape the bigger snake."

Dr. Leong in disbelief, "Tell me truthfully, Mr. Del Rosi. Are there actually two huge snakes out there in the tall grass?"

Joe thinks a moment before he responds, "Actually, Rachael, I believe that there are three huge snakes out there. One is the size that you extrapolated, and two smaller ones of about twelve meters or so in length."

Dr. Leong "Does the Captain know this?"

Joe, once again, finds himself gazing at the ground, "No, Rachael, the Captain does not know."

Dr. Leong forcefully slaps her hands on her hips, "And why does he not know of these snakes, Mr. Del Rosi. I saw him talk to you when you returned. You had ample time to tell him."

Joe says nothing.

Dr. Leong forcefully exhales as she turns away from Joe, "It was the million dollar US prize, wasn't it?"

Joe still says nothing. He just stands there like a defendant that has just pleaded "no contest" to the charge brought against him.

Dr. Leong storms out of the tent mumbling, "I knew it. Soldiers of fortune never let you down, even the stupid ones."

The sentry, seeing Dr. Leong's disturbed demeanor, enters the tent and asks what happened.

Joe just responds, "Women, you know how they get."

The soldier expresses displeasure with Joe's appraisal of Dr. Leong. The soldier reminds Joe that Dr. Leong is an esteemed citizen of the Republic of Indonesia. The sentry admonishes Joe to treat the doctor in such a manner that she does not get angry.

Meanwhile, Dr. Leong heavy-foots it to Captain Djarmat's tent. The sentry, seeing her mood, halts her and asks her business with the captain. She explains as best she can without being rude. The soldier, satisfied that her disturbed composure will not offend the captain, announces her and allows her to enter the captain's tent.

Captain Djarmat reading over recent dispatches, "What gives me the honor this morning, Dr. Leong?"

Dr. Leong "May I speak freely, Captain?"

Captain Djarmat looks over at the second lieutenant and asks him to leave the tent.

After the second lieutenant exits the tent, Captain Djarmat says, "Yes you may speak freely, Doctor. We are alone now."

Dr. Leong exhales, "Captain, Connors and Del Rosi have seen the snake you asked me about. Actually, they have seen two snakes, and they believe that there is a third out there in the tall grass."

Captain Djarmat drops the dispatch folder onto the table, "Are you sure?"

Dr. Leong "Mr. Del Rosi just informed me that the huge snake was the reason they were running back to the encampment. They saw a portion of it cross the road."

Captain Djarmat "They saw a portion of the snake and not the whole snake, is that it? How do they know the snake was the snake we discussed, if they only saw a portion?"

Dr. Leong "Mr. Del Rosi informed me that he has seen a twelve-meter snake earlier, and the snake that crossed the road was larger. The size of the snake that crossed the roadway scared Connors and him in flight. That is why they were so exhausted this morning from running."

Captain Djarmat "I understand, Doctor. I will have a talk with Mr. Connors and Mr. Del Rosi. Thank you for informing me of this."

Dr. Leong realizing the Captain's displeasure over the news, "I will take my leave now, Captain."

Captain Djarmat "Thank you, Doctor."

After Dr. Leong leaves the captain's tent, the captain summons the second lieutenant. As he waits for the return of the second lieutenant, he finishes reading over the dispatches. One dispatch is of interest: the Indonesian government has approved a visa for a Japanese technician with a device designed to measure the root depth of the tree. Since he is copied on the main document, Dr. Yanagi should have received the same memorandum. According to the dispatch, the technician should arrive tomorrow from Jayapura.

The second lieutenant enters the captain's tent.

Second Lieutenant "Did you ask to see me, sir?"

Captain Djarmat "Yes, Second Lieutenant, please take a seat. There are two things that I need to discuss with you. First, our theories about a snake, apparently, have materialized. Dr. Leong just informed me that the bush monkeys saw two huge snakes of the size we discussed."

Second Lieutenant gasping for air, "Where did they see them?"

Captain Djarmat "One of the snakes was just a few kilometers from this encampment, squirming about in the tall grass."

Second Lieutenant "Is that why the white monkeys were running into the encampment?"

Captain Djarmat nodding, "I am afraid so. The size of this snake scared them. Given their recent bout with the jungle distiller, the snake must be as large as Dr. Leong predicted for those two creatures to be frightened."

Second Lieutenant "Captain, may I speak freely?"

Captain Djarmat amused by the Second Lieutenant's request, "Speaking freely seems to be all you do, Second Lieutenant, even to the point of insubordination. Of course, please tell me what is on your mind."

Second Lieutenant "Now, that a huge snake has been sighted, could we request an armored vehicle to combat it?"

Captain Djarmat smiles, "Second Lieutenant, it is only a snake. Surely, we can handle any intrusion by this creature with our small arms."

Second Lieutenant "Begging the Captain's pardon, but I do not believe we can combat a creature this size with out current weapons. Captain, we have no rocket propelled grenade launchers."

Captain Djarmat thinks over the Second Lieutenant's point, "You might be right, Second Lieutenant. Small arms fire might not deter a creature that size. Do you have a tank in mind?"

Second Lieutenant pauses, "Actually, Captain, I had two tanks in mind."

Captain Djarmat "Two tanks, is it? Well, I could not request two tanks, Second Lieutenant."

The second lieutenant realizes that a request for two tanks would be tantamount to asking for the captain to be relieved of command. A senior captain or a major would accompany two tanks; whereas, a first lieutenant would command one tank.

Second Lieutenant "I will settle for one tank."

Captain Djarmat thinks over the situation, "Yes, I agree. Request the support of one tank from the Military Command Jayapura. If they question our requisition, tell them the tank is backup support in the event this project proves provocative. They will understand our concern. Do not mention a huge snake just yet."

Second Lieutenant breathing a sigh of relief, "Thank you, Captain."

Captain Djarmat "There is one more thing. Dr. Leong mentioned that there could be three snakes out there in the tall grass."

Second Lieutenant "A tank should be able to deter three huge snakes."

Captain Djarmat chooses to initiate the second topic rather than continue with the snake discussion.

Captain Djarmat "The second item I wished to discuss with you, Second Lieutenant, was this latest dispatch informing us that a Japanese technician will arrive tomorrow morning on the airlift. He will be bringing some sophisticated equipment to test the tree. When he arrives, billet him with Dr. Yanagi."

Second Lieutenant writes the captain's orders into his notepad.

Captain Djarmat "That was all I had for you, Second Lieutenant."

Second Lieutenant "Captain, some of our soldiers have come down with a form of sunburn. Only a few of the soldiers are affected. I did some checking as to why only a few have sunburns. I found out that the only time those soldiers were together were on a night watch around the tree a few days ago."

Captain Djarmat "It is hard to be burned by the sun at night, Second Lieutenant."

Second Lieutenant "I understand that; however, when I spoke with Dr. Yanagi, he mentioned something about a solar flare."

Captain Djarmat nods, "Yes, I suppose, a sundog could cause a pulse of ionizing radiation to pass though our atmosphere. Did any of the soldiers witness strange lights in the sky?"

Second Lieutenant "I do not follow you, Captain."

Captain Djarmat "When sundogs affect our atmosphere, the ionization effect produces strange light formations in the sky. They are generally green, red and yellow in color."

Second Lieutenant "None of our soldiers mentioned anything strange that night."

Captain Djarmat "Let us see here. If the hole in the ozone layer passed over this area, then the radiation from the sundog would pass right down to us without attenuation by any ionizing shield. If that happened, our soldiers could have been sunburnt. But, I still think that it has to be daytime for such a phenomenon to affect us. Do some more research into this sunburning and get back to me. I find this very interesting."

Second Lieutenant "I will, Captain. Meantime, I will request the support of one tank and prepare for the arrival of the Japanese technician."

Captain Djarmat "You might want to have a few soldiers standing by to assist the technician with this device. I have no idea how big it is. The technician might need some help unloading it from the helicopter."

Second Lieutenant "Will that be all, Captain?"

Captain Djarmat "Yes, you are dismissed, Second Lieutenant."

CHAPTER 13

▼

ENCAMPMENT, NEW GUINEA

The sound of flapping helicopter blades accompanies sunrise. The airlift is early today. Soldiers scurry, here and there, readying the landing site. The encampment did not expect the helicopters for another few hours. Some prayer sessions had to cease abruptly.

Seeing the confusion on the ground, the helicopter pilots commence circling the encampment, allowing time for the ground crews to stage the area. With the landing site clear and receiving the signal from the grounds crew chief, the helicopters descend, one by one, in order to offload their cargo and personnel.

The second lieutenant hurries to gather and collate all the outgoing correspondences from the tents of Dr. Leong, Dr. Yanagi, and Mr. Del Rosi. Waking the tent occupants takes up most of his time. By the time the last helicopter has offloaded its cargo, the second lieutenant delivers a satchel of dispatches to the pilot. The handover of the satchel is routine. The pilot knows the recipients.

Waiting to be greeted, after the last helicopter lifts off, is Sugai and his equipment. The second lieutenant makes introductions, has soldiers assist with the gear and escorts Sugai to Dr. Yanagi's tent. Once the apparatus and Sugai's belongings are stowed in Dr. Yanagi's tent, the second lieutenant leaves Sugai in the hands of Dr. Yanagi and returns to his routine morning assignments in the encampment.

Dr. Yanagi having finished freshening up, after his sudden awakening by the second lieutenant, queries Sugai on the intricacies of the sounding equipment. He finds Sugai quite knowledgeable and experienced. Sugai unpacks the sounding apparatus and provides Dr. Yanagi a simulated run through of the equipment's operation. Dr. Yanagi is impressed. He is even more impressed when he learns from Sugai that the true meter readout has been masked by a fake readout in order to deceive any unauthorized observers.

After some discussion, Dr. Yanagi schedules a sounding test of the tree through Captain Djarmat. The captain will coordinate to have sufficient tree bark removed, in advance, in order to accommodate the test. The group agrees that early afternoon, today, will be the first opportunity to conduct the test.

Dr. Yanagi informs the captain that the sounding test will estimate the root depth of the tree. The captain is left with the impression that the expected root depth is a matter of a few meters below the surface. The test duration will take a matter of minutes and should not interfere with the activities in the encampment. Since the encampment should not be disturbed, the captain considers the sounding test a routine scientific measurement and may not be necessary for him to be present in observance. This conclusion by the captain pleases Dr. Yanagi and Sugai who were concerned with the secrecy of the evolution.

After the meeting with Captain Djarmat, Dr. Yanagi and Sugai, accompanied by a few soldiers, carry the sounding apparatus to a site near the tree. The soldiers erect a shade covering over the sounding apparatus in order to protect the operators and the equipment from the equatorial sun's rays. Dr. Yanagi and Sugai, upon staging the sounding equipment for the test, return to their tent to await the word that the tree bark has been removed. Captain Djarmat orders a few of his men to remove two meters of the bark all around the tree. Sugai has concurred that a two-meter exposed area around the tree should be sufficient for the conduct of the test.

By noontime, Captain Djarmat reports to Dr. Yanagi that the tree is prepared for the test. Dr. Yanagi and Sugai accompany the captain to the tree in order to inspect the tree preparations. Sugai climbs into the hole dug around the tree from prior attempts to determine the root depth and inspects the exposed area. After a few minutes of inspection, he notifies Dr. Yanagi that the tree is ready for the test.

Dr. Yanagi and Sugai commence installing the three detector-transmitters around the tree. The detector-transmitters are aligned 120 degrees from one another in order to establish a triangular pattern. The triangular pattern enables maximum ping effectiveness into the interior of the tree and maximum reception flexibility. Both Dr. Yanagi and Sugai take turns checking and double-checking the alignment of the detector-transmitters. Once they are satisfied with the alignment, they inform Captain Djarmat that they are ready to sound test the tree. The informing of the captain is more of a polite gesture than procedural. Dr. Yanagi does not require the captain's permission to conduct the test. The captain just nods his acknowledgment to proceed.

Sensing the conclusion of his responsibilities with the sounding test, Captain Djarmat returns to his tent to read over the latest dispatches from Jayapura, leaving the two Japanese scientists to attend to the test. In departing, the captain reminds, in Bahasa Indonesian, the three soldiers guarding the periphery of the inner boundary to the tree to be alert and notify him, immediately, if they suspect anything unusual occurring during the sound test.

Dr. Yanagi directs Sugai to energize the sounding apparatus and establish a threshold level in order to account for stray and background noise levels. Sugai turns on the machine and performs the basic operational checks. The machine checks out satisfactorily. Sugai next energizes the sound detector-transmitters in order to establish background levels for the ensuing sound test. Strangely, the meter readout fluctuates as it moves up scale. Sugai repeats the procedure by first de-energizing the detector-transmitters and then re-energizing them. He observes the same erratic up scale movement. Stunned by the readout from the detector-transmitters, he just stands there a moment observing the continual climb of the meter needle until it wiggles erratically near the top of the first scale. Sugai realizes that this initial readout is too high to be accepted as the background noise threshold. Something is terribly wrong.

Sugai requests the assistance of Dr. Yanagi.

Dr. Yanagi "What do you mean you are having difficulty with the machine? Are you not qualified to operate this piece of equipment?"

Sugai nervously responds, "Yes, Dr. Yanagi, I am qualified to operate the test device. However, I have never witnessed anything like this background reading."

Dr. Yanagi looks over the readout. The needle is hovering at the top end of the scale.

Dr. Yanagi "This cannot be right, Sugai. Turn the machine off and start over. This time make sure you double-check each step in the startup procedure. With readouts like this, obviously you have erred on one of the start up steps."

Sugai looks over the machine. He is certain that he followed the start up sequence in verbatim compliance with the procedure. Nevertheless, he repeats the start up procedure, as Dr. Yanagi has directed.

Certain of his accuracy in the start up procedure Sugai, once again, attempts to set background noise levels. Once again, the needle moves erratically up the meter readout. He reports the same results to Dr. Yanagi.

Dr. Yanagi is now furious. He takes the procedure from Sugai and reads it over, now and then quizzing Sugai on its contents. Satisfied with Sugai's competence, Dr. Yanagi decides to redo the start up procedure with him reading out each step and Sugai performing the step in the doctor's presence.

Dr. Yanagi and Sugai complete the start up procedure with the order and repeat back mode. Satisfied that each step was performed properly, Dr. Yanagi orders the detector-transmitters energized. In shock, Dr. Yanagi witnesses the needle move up the meter readout in the same manner observed with Sugai.

Dr. Yanagi pauses a moment to gather his thoughts. Without question, the machine is operating properly. The start up procedural steps authenticated proper operation. Since there is no appreciable noise being generated in the encampment, the background level noises, being detected by the sounding apparatus, must be coming from inside the tree. He confides his theory to Sugai. Sugai concurs with the doctor's assessment. The tree is generating noises.

Sugai "Doctor, what do you make of the erratic movement of the needle?"

Dr. Yanagi "That kind of needle movement generally implies multiple, frequencies amplitudes being pick up by the detectors."

Sugai "Are you saying that the tree is generating many sounds of different loudness levels?"

Dr. Yanagi "Yes, I am. Apparently, no singal noise level dominates the others. From the erratic movement of the needle, many noises are in competition. It would be like the cacophony of competing noises generated from foundry machinery."

Sugai "The sounding apparatus is not designed for this type of situation."

Dr. Yanagi exhales, "I am afraid that I must agree with you, Sugai. Looks like you took a long trip for nothing. We need to input these noises into a filtered sound system."

Sugai "We have such a system in the electronics technology laboratory in Tokyo."

Dr. Yanagi chuckles, "That we do, but such a system does not do us any good here."

Sugai "I understand you have transmission capability, Doctor."

Dr. Yanagi "Yes, I can transmit to Tokyo when the conditions permit."

Sugai smiles, "Doctor, I could patch the output of these detectors through to your transmitter. Our people in the electronics technology lab could patch the signal that they receive from your transmitter into the filtered sound system."

Dr. Yanagi "Can you do that, really?"

Sugai smiles, "Yes, Doctor, I can. I brought an ample supply of wire in order to do something similar."

Dr. Yanagi thinks over Sugai's idea. The sounding apparatus is useless with such a high background level. Why not try it? It would save having someone else having to take a long trip to New Guinea.

Dr. Yanagi "I am in agreement with you, Sugai. Wire your idea up, and we will see if it works. While you are wiring, I will transmit to Tokyo to inform them of our intensions."

Sugai goes back into Dr. Yanagi's tent to collect all the tools and wire that he will need to do the job.

Dr. Yanagi enters the tent as Sugai is assembling his tools. They exchange nods and go about their business. Sugai leaves the tent with his equipment and proceeds to the tree site to alter the wiring of the detector-transmitters. Meanwhile, Dr. Yanagi transmits his intentions to the Ministry of Information & Technology in Tokyo. The transmission is short and to the point: a signal will be coming from New Guinea within the hour that needs to be fed into their filtered sound system. The sounds are those emanating from the strange tree. The doctor requests that they tape the transmission for future reference.

Dr. Yanagi feels that by the time Sugai alters the wiring the electronics technology laboratory will be set up to receive the signal. His only concern is if his recipient-associate is away at a meeting somewhere. Nevertheless, he intends to transmit when Sugai is done.

Before Dr. Yanagi can leave his tent, he receives a confirmation green light from Tokyo that his transmission has been received. Smiling, he wanders down to the tree site to see how Sugai is coming along with the wiring.

At the tree site, Sugai opens the main terminal section of the sounding apparatus and disconnects the detector-transmitter leads (wire ends). The leads are the commonly used plug-in type in the Japanese electronics industry. He has brought an ample supply of female connectors to match the male connector leads from the sounding apparatus' terminal board. Some quick crimping of the female connectors to some of the wire that he has brought enables him to bypasses the sounding apparatus.

Dr. Yanagi arrives on scene and asks how things are coming along.

Sugai smiles, "I am waiting for you, Doctor. This end is wired up."

Dr. Yanagi hands Sugai his transmitter. Sugai is impressed by its miniature size. Delicately, Sugai, using a tiny jeweler's screwdriver, opens the transmitter's encasement. Immediately, Sugai notices the tiny wiring contained in the transmitter. He does not have wire that small. Improvising is what will be needed. There is scant room within the transmitter terminal section to disconnect and re-wire. He has some small alligator clamps that he can use to attach to the terminal lugs where the transmitter's input signal is attached. As long as the transmitter is only receiving inputs from the detector-transmitters, the signal should be unadulterated.

Sugai discusses the change in plans with Dr. Yanagi.

Dr. Yanagi "The way the transmitter operates is that once I press the transmission key the transmitter is active. The transmitter would be sensitive to the noises from the encampment."

Sugai recommends disconnecting the transmitter's transmission section. Dr. Yanagi looks at him strangely, until Sugai explains that he would be merely removing the transmission's audio input device. Sugai explains that it is a screw out type of device. Actual transmission would not be effected.

Dr. Yanagi reluctantly agrees to allow Sugai to proceed. He watches attentively, as Sugai dismantles the transmitter's audio input section and screws out the audio input device. Sugai shows the transmission' audio input device to Dr. Yanagi.

Sugai "With your permission, Doctor, all I need to do now is to remove these two leads in order to disconnect the transmission's audio input device."

Dr. Yanagi looks over the two leads and notices that they are screw in types. He tells Sugai to remove the leads. Sugai unscrews the leads and places the audio input device into his spare parts' pouch.

With the audio input device removed, stray noises from the encampment will not interfere with the intended transmission of the tree sounds. Sugai hurries to solder up the small alligator camps to the leads from the sounding apparatus bypass. Covering the fresh soldered connection with shrink tubing to seal the connection, he reports the bypass is complete. Dr. Yanagi has Sugai perform an additional continuity check to insure the circuitry is complete. Once done, Dr. Yanagi orders Sugai to complete the transmission circuitry. Sugai attaches the alligator clamps to the hand-held transmitter's terminal board input section. With one press of the transmission key by Dr. Yanagi, the sounds being generated from the tree are on their way to Tokyo.

Electronics Laboratory, Ministry of Information & Technology, Tokyo, Japan

The crew chief of the Electronics Laboratory announces the reception of the incoming signal from New Guinea. The initial stage of the recipient electronic system demodulates, filters and amplifies the incoming signal. Demodulation removes the carrier frequency portion from the incoming signal, leaving only the information portion: the sounds transmitted from the tree. Filtration removes previously selected frequencies, often referred to as common background noises. Amplification raises the level of the incoming, informational signal to the audible range.

Without question, the noises emanating from the speakers in the sound system are eerie. These sounds are not recognizable. They do not even resemble weird street noises. To the electronic technicians operating the sound filtration system, the noises seem to have been subjected to an intense muffling. The muffling effect is more pronounced than anyone in the laboratory has ever sensed. Truly, everything about the incoming signal is unrecognizable.

The crew chief orders the sounds taped and data identified. When asked by a member of his administrative team for a labeling suggestion, the crew chief responds: "Tree from New Guinea." Recording commences by another bank of electronic devices.

When the incoming signal is viewed on an advanced, oscilloscope readout, many sine waves appear. Interestingly, other strange, unexplained shapes appear on the readout as well. The readout baffles the electronic operators. Once again, nothing like this has been received or processed through this equipment.

One of the operators suggests to the crew chief that the incoming signal should be processed through their new three-dimensional, sound analysis apparatus. The crew chief, overcome with awe, acquiesces to the suggestion. Another of the operators, witnessing the weird readouts, reminds the crew chief that some phases of the new sound analysis system are down for maintenance. The readout would be partial under the current system status. The crew chief, in an attempt to understand what he is witnessing, permits the hook up to the three-dimensional apparatus.

With the hook up to the three-dimensional, sound analysis apparatus complete, the crew chief and his team witness, yet another, even more eerie display, as it appears on the TV-like monitors. The sine waves on the oscilloscope readout have transformed into strange, irregular shapes that appear to pulse irregularly. Whereas, the three-dimensional, sound analysis apparatus' readout has been programmed to provide a standard, three-dimensional display for ease of identifying incoming frequencies, this readout even defies the programming.

The sound analysis team realizes that their mental capacities for the interpretation of sound have just bottomed out. What displays before their eyes challenges the furthest reaches of their imagination. Truly, again, in three-dimensions, the readout baffles even more attempts at interpretation.

As the crew chief slowly walks around the different monitors, trying to make some sense of the displays, he realizes that all the sound analysis equipment is functional. He recalls the caution from one of the operators, concerning some of the equipment being down for maintenance.

Crew Chief "I thought one of you said some of this equipment was down for maintenance."

One of the Operators "It was down this morning when I checked on the status of the maintenance, Chief."

Crew Chief "Would not someone from the maintenance crew have informed you of any change in status?"

The same Operator "They sure would have, Chief."

Crew Chief puzzled, "Check the maintenance log to see when they brought the system back up."

The same Operator checks the maintenance log and says, "Chief, according to the maintenance log, the equipment is still down for maintenance."

Crew Chief looks over at the operator then back at the obvious, visible display, "How can that be? Clearly, it is operating."

The same Operator "The maintenance group must have cleared the isolations and prepared the system for some operational test. We must have energized the entire system."

Crew Chief to his team, "Was there anything else unusual that any of you observed during the system start up?"

Another Operator "Chief, this may not mean much, but I noticed that the entire system responded to the incoming system without the usual warm up pause."

Crew Chief "What do you mean?"

Same Operator "Well, usually when we receive a signal, the system takes a little time adjusting to it before we actually receive any readout. In fact, we can hear the system warm up in order to produce the readout. In the case of this signal, there was no observable warm up time and no sound indicating the system needed to increase power to deliver this three-dimensional display. It was like it just happened, instantaneously."

Crew Chief pauses a moment to think this over, then says, "Check the isolations on the portion of the equipment reported to be under maintenance."

A few moments pass while the operators check the isolations. Meanwhile, the crew chief realizes that what he is witnessing is way beyond his comprehension.

One of the Operators reports, "Chief, the isolations are tagged open."

Crew Chief "What did you say?"

Same Operator "I said the isolations are open, and they are tagged open."

Crew Chief's face turns red, "That's impossible!"

All the operators turn toward the display on the monitors. Awe does not come close to describing their expressions.

Crew Chief commands "Shut it down, now!"

One of the operators opens the main isolation breaker to the entire three-dimensional, sound analysis system. Another operator removes the patch-in lead from the filtered sound system to the three-dimensional portion. The system shuts down. The displays go blank.

The Crew Chief assembles all his team and informs them that the dictates of national security are in effect. No one is to mention anything about what they witnessed, until after they have been debriefed.

The crew chief orders the incoming sound taped and data recorded separately from all other files. The electronics laboratory continues to receive the transmission from New Guinea. Meanwhile, the crew chief requests an immediate audience with the deputy minister for information.

In the interim of between the audience request and the granting, the crew chief assembles his team to brainstorm reasons for what they just observed on the displays of the sound analysis equipment. The team members are at a loss for explanations.

One member of the team volunteers that the display consoles in the sound analysis system are interconnected in order to assure synchronization. Few members of the team knew that. This information partially explains why the displays operated even though the isolation breakers to them were open. Although this is the first time the phenomenon has been witnessed, the crew chief buys into the explanation. Power from one display console simply powered the others interconnected with it. A check of the maintenance procedure currently underway on that portion of the sound analysis system revealed that only the amplification circuitry was under test. The connections to the display consoles were not disturbed.

When the subject of the strange, irregular shapes, observed on the oscilloscope readout and the display monitors, comes up, the team has no explanations. Those shapes have never been seen before by any of the team members. The oscilloscope operator swears that he has never read or heard of any such anomaly in all his years of training and experience. The shapes remain a mystery.

The multiple sine waves on the oscilloscope are explained simply as a result of multiple input frequencies. Different frequencies would produce different sine waves. The erratic behavior of some of the sine waves was more difficult to explain away. One team member offered the notion that different sounds were in competition with one another at similar frequencies. The oscilloscope is not designed to differentiate amongst a multitude of similar frequencies; hence, the resultant sine wave displayed on the readout was a composite or alternating-dominant sine wave. This explanation seemed to satisfy most of the team members, including the crew chief.

The pulsing of the irregular shapes on the sound analysis system displays was another troubling issue to bring up. Somehow, the sine waves from the oscilloscope transformed into irregular shapes that pulsed. One team member hypothesized that the pulsing of the irregular shapes seemed to mimic the variations in amplitude of the sine wave displayed on the oscilloscope. In further support, the team member stated that, in reality, a sine wave is merely a circle viewed over time. In that respect, he felt the irregular shapes could be seen as a multi-dimensional representation of the oscilloscope readout. The team deliberated a bit over whether the representation was two- or three-dimensional.

The strange dots that littered the background of the readout and displays were yet another issue. They could not be flaws in the readout or displays. And, they too seemed to become brighter and dimmer in a sort of irregular, pulsing cadence. For those dots, the team had no explanation.

The crew chief took elaborate notes during the brainstorming session. After he dismissed the team and repeated the national security caution, he commenced organizing his notes for presentation to the deputy minister. He allowed the taping of the incoming signal to continue until the signal ceased. In all, the New Guinea signal lasted about an hour. The data banks of the electronics laboratory contained the full measure of the signal's content.

While the crew chief organizes his presentation, one of the administrative personnel informs him that the deputy minister will see him. Also, he is informed that Mr. Kajioka from the technology division section will be in attendance.

The deputy minister receives the electronics laboratory crew chief in his office. Mr. Kajioka is already seated when the crew chief arrives. The deputy minister makes the formal introductions. Although Mr. Kajioka and the crew chief work in the information ministry, they have not worked together. Other than attending some of the same functions, the two men are strangers. For whatever reason, they have never been seated together at social functions, sponsored by the ministry.

Deputy Minister Kawamoto "Crew Chief, Mr. Kajioka was the person who requested a sounding test in New Guinea. However, the on-site person, Dr. Yanagi, is the one who transmitted the sound signal to your laboratory. I have asked Mr. Kajioka to attend this meeting, because of his familiarity with the project in New Guinea. Mr. Kajioka is not a sound engineer, so you may be asked to explain, in secular terms, some of the things that you are about to tell me."

The crew chief and Mr. Kajioka nod acknowledgments.

With a gesture from the deputy minister, the crew chief begins a run through of the events, as they transpired in the electronics laboratory. Mr. Kajioka listens attentively. Clearly, it is not the intention of the deputy minister or Mr. Kajioka to divulge anything beyond a "need to know" to the crew chief about the anomaly in New Guinea.

After the crew chief's run down of the events, he provides some of the brainstorming ideas that he and his team proposed as explanations for the strange occurrences. Mr. Kajioka remarks on the sharp imaginations of the electronics laboratory.

Kajioka poses a question to the Crew Chief, "Would you say that the sounds that you witnessed on the readout and display monitors represented an intentional organization of some kind?"

The crew chief seems puzzled by the question.

Kajioka rephrases, "Do you think the sounds came from machinery of some kind?"

Crew Chief ponders the question, "It is hard to tell. It certainly would not be any machinery of which I am aware."

Kajioka smiles, "I understand, but what I am looking for here is if the sounds imitated in any way some form of machinery."

Crew Chief "I would have to say 'no.' The sounds were too irregular."

Kajioka "What about those irregular shapes that you mentioned did any of those appear to represent something mechanical?"

Crew Chief "I would have to say 'no' again. They were just too irregular, and the pulsing was irregular."

Kajioka "Tell me about the sounds again. What did they most resemble?"

Crew Chief "Like I said in my brief, we had never heard these sounds before. They resembled nothing like we had ever heard."

Kajioka "Are you saying that these sounds were so strange that they defied all comparison?"

Crew Chief becoming a little nervous, "Yes, Mr. Kajioka, that is what I am saying."

Mr. Kajioka looks over at the deputy minister. The deputy minister shrugs his shoulders in disbelief.

Deputy Minister Kawamoto nods his head, "Fine, thank you, Crew Chief, for the brief. I will discuss a few things with Mr. Kajioka and get back to you on this matter. Well done."

After the crew chief has left the deputy minister's office, the deputy minister raises his concerns to Mr. Kajioka.

Deputy Minister Kawamoto "Mr. Kajioka, we need to find out, in a hurry, what we are dealing with here."

Kajioka "First, I will direct Dr. Yanagi to sound the tree, even if the background noises are indicating at the upper end of the lower scale. We can extrapolate the results from the second scale, as best we can. We need to ascertain the depth of the iron ore deposit in order to estimate its resource capacity. Second, I recommend we continue to analyze these sound signal frequencies in order to determine their potential origin."

Deputy Minister Kawamoto "Mr. Kajioka, we cannot waste time here. This tree in New Guinea is becoming more bizarre each time I receive a brief. I hate to say this, but it is sounding more and more like this thing came from another world. We need to get a handle on this thing, quickly. I hope you can appreciate the stir something like this would make in parliament. Currently, we have geophysics lab and electronics lab personnel who have experienced this thing. Our list of 'need to know' personnel is growing exponentially. We will achieve critical leak mass, if any other laboratory gets involved with this. Kajioka, put this mess to rest."

Kajioka does not need to wait around for the deputy minister's last statement to be clarified. He has his cue to get busy resolving this anomaly, before the entire world gets alerted. Kajioka just nods and exits the room, hastily.

Upon returning to the electronics laboratory, the crew chief is swamped with inquiries concerning the meeting. About all the crew chief can do is calm his team and tell them that all is well.

One of the team members informs the crew chief that he has something to show him on the oscilloscope readout. The crew chief makes his way through the team encircling him to the main oscilloscope. Once at the main oscilloscope, the team member points out the fine definition of the sine waves. The crew chief is unimpressed, until the team member tells him to watch the sine wave change after a little blip appears on the readout.

Crew Chief astonished, "The wave is becoming more defined."

The crew chief looks at each sine wave on the readout and notices their definition improve with each blip, as well.

Crew Chief in awe, "This is amazing!"

Team Member "The readout is self-correcting, Crew Chief."

Crew Chief "I can see that."

Team Member "That's not all it is doing, Crew Chief. Watch this!"

The team member purposely off-focuses the readout so that the sine wave is blurry. Right before their eyes, the readout refocuses to the same definition previously observed. Then, the team member readjusts the focus back to where it was originally. Miraculously, nothing changes on the readout. The readout somehow remembered the original setting of the focus.

The crew chief just stares at the team member. The team member is smiling while the crew chief has his mouth open. To both, this is too bizarre for even a brainstorming session.

CHAPTER 14

▼

SPACE OBSERVATORY, NORTHERN AUSTRALIA

Continuously monitoring the southern hemisphere for unusual occurrences, the space observatory staff maintains round the clock surveillance watches. Due to funding restrictions, most watches are twelve hours in duration. There are no days off *per se*. While a watch stander is away from his or her post, doubling up on watch assignments creastes periods for time off. Consequently, the staff turn over rate exceeds other scientific assignments within the Australian government.

Dr. Unni is standing in for the usual scientist assigned to this watch section. It is early afternoon in Northern Australia when one of the watch standers reports an unusual signal being transmitted from Northern New Guinea. Dr. Unni recalls the coordinates of the strange transmission, as those belonging to the intense pulse that caused so much concern during the astrophysicists' visit.

Dr. Unni to the discovering watch stander, "Can you identify the transmission frequency?"

Watch Stander "Yes, Doctor, I have it locked in."

Dr. Unni "Can you determine if there are any sideband frequencies?"

Watch Stander "Let me plug the signal into our frequency identification circuitry. This should provide us readout of all the frequencies, if any, in any sideband."

The watch stander connects the locked-in frequency to the identification circuitry console. Soon, a display appears on a monitor, visualizing a multitude of frequencies. As the watch stander and Dr. Unni observe the frequencies on the monitor, strange shapes begin to form.

Dr. Unni to Watch Stander, "What do you make of these strange shapes?"

Watch Stander rubbing his chin, "I have never seen anything like those shapes before. I had not realized that the identification circuitry could display such shapes."

Dr. Unni "Why are they changing size?"

Watch Stander "The shapes must represent some form of new frequency that the Japanese have developed."

Dr. Unni puzzled, "Why do you say the shapes are frequencies?"

Watch Stander "They are behaving like a frequency, Doctor. Notice how the shapes increase and decrease in size, as if responding to a change in amplitude that is characteristic of a frequency."

Dr. Unni "Do you mean that these shapes could represent some form of multi-dimensional frequency?"

Watch Stander "That is my best guess, Doctor. I suspect the Japanese have pushed the envelope of communication technology one step further."

Dr. Unni ponders the watch stander's comments a while, as he observes the strange shapes alter their size. Could the Japanese have created an advanced frequency system? It would appear to be the case with this visual evidence.

Dr. Unni "Are we taping this?"

Watch Stander "Yes, Doctor, we are. It is loading into our data banks, as we speak."

Dr. Unni to the Watch Stander, "Can we redirect some of this signal to our more sophisticated detection equipment for analysis?"

Watch Stander "Yes, Doctor, we just have to patch in the output from the identification circuitry into the other analysis equipment. Shall I have that done, Doctor?"

Dr. Unni "Yes, let us checkout this dimensional theory of yours."

The watch stander orders his assistant to leave his observation post and make the necessary patch in. The assistant leaves the observatory surveillance area and enters the computer room. In the computer room, he patches the signal from New Guinea into the high-tech analysis console and activates its readout.

While his on-watch section prepares to analyze the Japanese transmission, Dr. Unni requests the presence of Dr. Greene.

Watch Stander's Assistant to Watch Stander "I patched in the signal to the high-tech console."

Watch Stander "Doctor, we are patched in. We can observe the signal on the monitor to your right. Just select 'Analysis' on the mode selector switch."

Dr. Unni moves the mode selector switch to "Analysis." The display screen immediately produces some 1960s, pulsating, lava-lamp-type shapes.

Dr. Unni "These shapes are stranger than the ones depicted on the standard monitor."

Watch Stander straining his neck to see the "Analysis" display, "You are right, Doctor. I have never seen anything like those shapes."

Dr. Greene enters the observation area of the space observatory. He greets Dr. Unni at the "Analysis" console. Dr. Unni provides Dr. Greene a synopsis of their actions concerning the Japanese transmission from Northern New Guinea.

Dr. Greene, admiring the contrast on the "Analysis" monitor, mentions, "This imaginary on this display is remarkable. Is this new equipment?"

Before Dr. Unni can respond, the Watch Stander interjects, "Bloody hell no, Doctor. That monitor is an antique. Remember, it was removed from a university laboratory during a technology upgrading. It was a hand-me-down, Doctor."

Dr. Greene looking over, again, at the quality of the display, "We sure made good monitors in the old days, didn't we?"

Watch Stander, amazed at the quality of the display, stutters, "Yes, we must have, Doctor."

After the initial shock from the display quality subsides, Dr. Greene discusses the shapes on the screen with the watch section. Dr. Greene is suspicious of the hypothesis that the Japanese have created a new frequency-transmission package for communication. However, he acquiesces to what he observes on the "Analysis" monitor. This has to be a new innovation of some kind.

Suddenly, the transmission from Northern New Guinea ceases.

Watch Stander checking his frequency ranges, "Doctor, they have stopped transmitting."

Dr. Unni "Can you decipher where the signal was transmitted?"

Watch Stander "Yes, Doctor, the signal came from Northern New Guinea at the precise location of the intense pulse that we tracked. It was bounced off the Japanese communications satellite over Singapore and redirected to Tokyo, Japan."

Dr. Greene requests, "Can you determine the type of transmitter of origin?"

Watch Stander "At this carrier frequency, I would say that the signal of origin came from a portable transmitter or even a hand-held variety."

Dr. Greene surprised, "To think the Japanese have developed an advanced hand-held transmitter is astonishing. This transmission must be some new form of encryption."

Watch Stander "The prior transmissions in and out of these coordinates in Northern New Guinea were encrypted, Doctor."

Dr. Unni puzzled, "If the other transmissions were encrypted, then why not encrypt this one? Or, if you possess this type of technology, why bother with encryption at all?"

Dr. Greene "You have an excellent point, Dr. Unni. Why would the Japanese change their mode of transmission so abruptly? This new signal, carrying these strange shapes on our display monitor, might be something else."

Dr. Unni "I realize that I have raised the possibility of optional explanations; however, we must keep in mind that the signal did originate from the same coordinates as the other strange activities. I believe that what we are observing is an advanced form of communication. Perhaps, the data being transmitted is more voluminous than the standard encryption mode can process."

Dr. Greene "Whatever this is, we need to inform the authorities. I will brief the Officer in Charge. We have copied this transmission, have we not?"

Watch Stander "Yes, Dr. Greene, we have copied this transmission. We have some forty or so minutes in our data banks."

Dr. Greene "Copy the data from the signal to a disc while I brief the Officer in Charge."

Dr. Greene leaves the observatory area and proceeds out of the space observatory to officer in charge's operational area.

After Dr. Greene leaves the observatory area, Dr. Unni comments on the quality of the displays on the "Analysis" monitor, "These displays are incredible. Frankly, I have not seen displays of this quality in the top-end electronics stores in Sydney. How old did you say these monitors were?"

Watch Stander somewhat in agreement with Dr. Unni's appraisal, "I believe the monitor that you are looking at, Doctor, is over a decade old. It might be as much as fifteen years old. There should be a date on the manufacturer's label plate, located somewhere on the rear of the equipment."

The watch stander has his assistant go around behind the monitor and look for the manufacturer's label plate.

Watch Stander's Assistant "1986!"

Dr. Unni "Bloody hell, the monitor is almost twenty years old! How can this display be so perfect?"

Watch Stander "Maybe, congratulations are in order for the upkeep crew that maintains our equipment."

Dr. Unni smiles, "Bloody good job those maintenance lads have done, indeed."

Watch Stander "The wiring might be old, but the replacement circuit boards the maintenance crew put in are state of the art. That might account for the increased quality of the display."

Dr. Unni smiling, "I am still amazed at the incredible picture quality. They must use similar circuit boards in the civilian electronics industry, yet these pictures are far superior to any I have seen in the electronic stores."

Watch Stander "Maybe, the civilian industry skimps on the wiring and uses substandard transmission materials to reduce the costs."

Dr. Unni "Certainly, the civilians are doing something wrong. These pictures present a superb quality. The peripheral demarcations of the shapes are incredibly distinct. The boundaries are so sharp that they appear to have been cut by a sharp razor. This is absolutely incredible."

The watch stander and his assistant sense the doctor's mind has wandered off into a far realm of aesthetics. Truly, to them, the doctor is expending too much time admiring the quality of the displays.

Within fifteen minutes or so after his leaving the observatory, Dr. Greene returns with a directive from the officer in charge to transmit the signal received from New Guinea to the Advanced Technology Laboratory at the University of Australia in Canberra. Upon receipt of the directive, Dr. Unni summons the microwave communications support team to the observatory. Microwave communication provides the main means of communicating sensitive information to other parts of Australia.

Dr. Greene reports that the officer in charge has made the necessary arrangements for the Canberra team to receive the transmission. As Dr. Greene explains the directive and the requirements of national security, the Canberra team is preparing to receive the signal from the space observatory and store it in a secure, electronic file in their data banks.

Dr. Unni oversees the microwave transmission. In a matter of minutes, the signal is away. Canberra will analyze the New Guinea signal. Other than the awe effect that the observatory watch section experienced, their responsibilities, other than the security of national interests, ceases with the transmission to Canberra.

Advanced Technology Laboratory, Canberra, Australia

Dr. Goodwin leads the electronic research division in the Advanced Technology Laboratory (ATL). Having performed his doctoral work at the prestigious Massachusetts Institute of Technology (MIT) in the United States, he reigns supreme as the *avant guarde* mentality in technology in Australia. The Canberra repository of innovation overflows with his designs and patents.

The officer in charge of the space observatory insisted that Dr. Goodwin, personally, analyze the signal received from New Guinea. Since Dr. Goodwin is cleared for the highest security disclosure in Australia, his opinion on the nature of this strange signal will be invaluable to national interests. Dr. Goodwin is standing by in the communications analysis room of the ATL when the signal is received and demodulated.

Dr. Goodwin directs the demodulated portion of the signal fed into a filtered sound assembly, equipped with two- and three-dimensional display readouts. He and his staff listen and observe the signal evolve through the stages of the sound analysis assembly. Akin to their counterparts in the space observatory, Dr. Goodwin and his staff are overcome with awe over what they observe. Truly, current electronic technology is inadequate in describing what appears on the display monitors. Dr. Goodwin is quick to notice the continuous improvement in contrast and definition of the images on the display.

Like an aesthetician admiring a painting, Dr. Goodwin takes a seat and contemplates the anomalies and nuances of the imagery on the displays. His imagination works overtime to make sense of the strange shapes and their odd and subtle movements. Likewise, his staff joins him in a period of contemplation. The entire advanced electronics area becomes as silent as a Buddhist monastery.

Finally, Dr. Goodwin offers, "Our reference, built into our electronic analysis equipment, is inadequate. That is why these strange features present themselves before us."

Staff Member "I was thinking the same thing, Dr. Goodwin. This appears to be a case of mismatching dimensions."

Another Staff Member "Could the Japanese have developed such a leap in communications technology?"

Dr. Goodwin "If the Japanese did develop this technology, what would they use it for? Our current communication technology provides sufficient adequacy for all our transmission needs. What would be the purpose of this new technology?"

Original Staff Member "If they have developed this technology, they must have developed the new reference, as well."

Dr. Goodwin "Those are my thoughts exactly. The beauty inherent in this advancement lies not in these bizarre displays but in the creation of the reference."

Original Staff Member "I think this possible reference is dangerous to national security, if it, in fact, exists."

Dr. Goodwin "Yes, the Japanese are operating on an advanced dimension. There is no telling what they could do with something like this. Think of the advanced encryption opportunities available. We could never decipher their codes, if they were hidden in another dimension."

Original Staff Member "Should we share this with the Americans?"

Dr. Goodwin "We have to share this with the Americans. Something like this comes under the jurisdiction of our international defense agreement with the United States and New Zealand. Contact the Defense Ministry and inform them of our discovery. The Defense Ministry will coordinate with the Foreign Ministry to enable us to transmit this data to the Americans for their analysis. Meanwhile, let us analyze these shapes more."

The original staff member leaves the ATL to contact the Defense Ministry. All the secure telephones are located in the main administrative office area.

Dr. Goodwin pays particular attention to the strange assortment of black dots in the background of the display. To him, these black dots represent something very odd. His does not discount how the black dots seem to enlarge from time to time.

Dr. Goodwin to the remaining staff, "Do any of you suppose the black dots in the background could represent vertices?"

The room falls silent as the scientists ponder the idea proposed by Dr. Goodwin. Buddhist temples do not achieve the quiet permeating this room in the ATL.

After some fifteen minutes of pure silence, One Staff Member says, "Are you suggesting, Dr. Goodwin, that those are vertices of figures existing in advanced dimensions?"

Dr. Goodwin "Yes, I am thinking along those lines. The reason we can only discern the vertices is because the actual dimension is not available to our senses."

Another Staff Member "Dr. Goodwin, I doubt the Japanese could have leaped their technology this far without anyone having been alerted to their progress. The Japanese are quite good at sharing their developments…at least in the original stages of development. Nothing of what we are considering has ever graced the pages of the scientific journals."

Dr. Goodwin "I understand your skepticism, Doctor; however before our eyes lies proof positive that someone has developed a multi-dimensional communications technology. And, this signal did originate from a Japanese transmitter, tracked by our space observatory in Northern Australia. Somehow, we have to assume that the Japanese have this technology. Gentlemen, it would appear that we have some fast catching up to do in electronics."

The original staff member returns from the administrative offices and informs Dr. Goodwin that the Defense Ministry will make the necessary arrangements to transmit the signal data to the Americans.

One of the Staff "Dr. Goodwin, have you noticed how the display continuously improves in definition?"

Dr. Goodwin "Yes, I have observed that phenomenon. I believe the improvement in definition is related to the multi-dimensional character of the signal interacting with our limited-dimensional, inherent, electronic reference. Succinctly, as the different dimensions interact, our reference adjusts in an attempt to accommodate the multi-dimensions. That is why, I believe, our contrast and definition on our displays are improving."

Same Staff Member "Self-correcting displays would monopolize the television market."

The entire group chuckles at the notion of a sales bonanza for the television market in Australia. Surely, they have a feature on their displays that would antiquate the current top of the line television systems.

Another Staff Member "I never realized that advanced dimensions were even possible."

Dr. Goodwin "I have to concur with your original notion of impossibility, Doctor. Nevertheless, what lies before our eyes is an array of advanced dimensions. From what I can imagine, those shapes represent the fourth dimension and the vertices represent dimensions above the fourth. Certainly, the fifth dimension is present before us. Since the vertices offer only a tiny glimpse of a dimension, the exact advanced degree of the dimension is unknown."

Same Staff Member "We could have six or seven dimensions here, is that what you are saying, Dr. Goodman?"

Dr. Goodman "Doctors, I believe, we have many more than six or seven dimensions here. Whatever this is it presents us with a possibility of unlocking an access to the advanced dimensions. This is an amazing feat, if the Japanese have done this. Actually, it could represent the greatest feat in the history of scientific innovation. If the Japanese have accomplished this feat, they would reign supreme in the world of science for decades to come. Their technological advancement in the fields of electronics would leave our industries in the Stone Age. National security, gentlemen, was never so threatened, as it is today. The technology we see before us would devastate the world market place. Stock markets would crumble, driving the world into the most severe depression in history."

Another Staff Member "Dr. Goodman, do you suppose the strange sounds we heard from the signal were advanced dimensional sounds?"

Dr. Goodwin "No, I believe the sounds originate from events taking place in the advanced dimensions that are perceived in our dimension. The strange sounds are somehow being muffled, like they were underwater or propagating through some dense medium. Remember, our ears have our dimension as a reference. It is my belief that our ears would be incapable of hearing sounds from another dimension. Just as we can only see the vertices of advanced dimensions on the displays, our ears would have a similar difficulty perceiving the sound emanating from advanced dimensions."

An administrative aide brings a message to Dr. Goodwin that the Foreign Ministry has authorized the transmission of the New Guinea signal to the United States and New Zealand.

Defense Laboratory, Massachusetts Institute of Technology, Cambridge, MA, USA

The Advanced Intelligence Section of the Defense Laboratory received a message from the Pentagon that the space observatory in Northern Australia intercepted a strange, unidentified signal. The Australian Advanced Technology Laboratory in Canberra has been unable to decipher the contents of the signal. Assistance has been requested from the Defense Laboratory at the Massachusetts Institute of Technology (MIT) in interpreting the content of this signal.

In compliance with the Pentagon's message, an ensemble of scientists has gathered in the Defense Laboratory to commence analyzing the signal from Canberra. Dr. Lars Hansen, Head of the Defense Laboratory, will facilitate the analysis effort.

After receipt, a group of graduate students, directed by Dr. Hansen, commence a thorough evaluation of the signal's content. A content identification map is produced, categorizing different characteristics of the signal, and distributed to the attendees of the analysis symposium.

Dr. Lars Hansen, a tall, slender, Nordic fellow, opens the discussion with a rendition of the events, leading up to this symposium. Some prior postulations, obtained from Canberra, are presented in an attempt to orient the discussion. The prior postulations fail to convince the attendees.

First, few of the attendees subscribe to the notion that this signal is some form of advance communications technology developed by the Japanese. This is not a racial put down but a matter of scientific reality. Such an advanced signal, with multi-dimensional characteristics, would require elaborate advancements in supporting technologies. To the attendees, this would require an improbably degree of stealth in order to conceal such progress from the rest of the scientific community.

Second, the identification of the medium within which the sound would have had to propagate as iron-based evokes a cornucopia of imaginative scenarios. Ideas, ranging from alien spacecrafts to high-strength, steel foundries, abound in the discussion. Clearly, Dr. Hansen must employ a delicate touch in restricting the imaginative extravagances of the attendees.

Third, the self-correcting effect of the signal on the electronics catches the attentions of all the attendees. Watching the displays improve the definition and contrast of their imagery is nothing short of astounding.

Dr. Hansen concurs with much of the input provided by the attendees. Surely, the sound originated from within some dense, iron-based material. Most of the attendees agree that the sound originated from within an iron-based material rather than merely propagate through the material. This concurrence eliminates any notion of a spacecraft, alien or otherwise. Data received from the analysis of the signal's content supports this agreement.

Most of the attendees consider that the signal contains multi-dimensional characteristics. Yet, only a few of the attendees are willing to support as many as twelve dimensions. Most of the attendees accept the presence of at least six dimensions. A few tests, run on the signal with a simulation of the resultant imagery exposed on a display, reveal inter-dimensional activity ongoing within the signal. For some attendees, it was the first time that they had ever been exposed to a discussion of dimensions beyond the fourth.

With the displays clearly visible to attendees within the confines of the symposium, Dr. Hansen proposes that not only the electronics supporting the imagery on the monitors self-corrects, but somehow our own physiology undergoes a form of self-correction. Dr. Hansen proffers that our optical senses are likewise improving. Specifically, Dr. Hansen transforms the notion of our senses improving to one of reactivating. Naturally, this idea evokes an intense debate. The connotations of the idea erupt in controversy.

To even consider the notion of our senses reactivating implies that we humans have experienced a multi-dimensional world in the distant past. That world remains locked within our genes, awaiting the correct signals for its reactivations. Dr. Hansen continues his elaboration on the idea of reactivation with an expose on the amount of inactive spaces contained in our brains and other critical organs. To the doctor, that idle space within us was once active and not some excess designed into our bodies for some intended future use. One has to admire the persuasive reasoning of the doctor's position. Everywhere we look in the biosphere, we see the remnants of past environmental exposures. From our spleen to our tailbone, examples abound.

As the debate on Dr. Hansen's proposal evolves, more and more of the attendees begin to accept the idea of reactivation. Not only are the pixels on the display's imagery realigning to provide a clearer and more distinct definition, our optical capabilities are honing, as well, as idle portions of our brain and nervous system activate.

By the culmination of the symposium, most attendees are astounded by the realization that an ancient experience is reactivating within them. Genes of no prior particular function are activating. Parts of our nervous system regarded as relics from pre-human evolution, reactivating to ancient environmental stimuli. Question is: what is this stimulus?

To a person, the attendees concur that whatever this signal contains needs to be quarantined, until it can be further analyzed in order to insure the safety of the human species. Regrettably, the spirit of cooperation that brought this signal to the Defense Laboratory will not be permitted to return. The Pentagon has determined that national security dictates that this new information remains within the confines of the Defense Laboratory until such time that it is deemed appropriate for unrestricted release. The Pentagon has directed the Defense Laboratory to stall the Advanced Technology Laboratory in Canberra on the results of their analyses. Likewise, the Pentagon will smoke and mirror the Australian Foreign Ministry.

In the interim, the Pentagon has directed that the origin of this signal be identified and subsequently contained. A defense priority just short of that authorizing hostile action is assigned to the project.

Within a few hours of the Pentagon's quarantine, the names Watson and Del Rosi are on the whispering lips of every American foreign service officer in East Asia. The dossiers of Watson and Del Rosi kiss the scanning surface of every

Xerox machine in the foreign service sector of the State Department. Smiles abound on the faces of the foreign service officers perusing Del Rosi's dossier. How could a character like Del Rosi maneuvering himself center stage into this arena of intrigue?

CHAPTER 15

▼

ENCAMPMENT, NEW GUINEA

Following the morning airlift, Captain Djarmat makes his rounds, delivering dispatches. Interestingly, there is a rather heavy dispatch for Mr. Del Rosi. Apparently, the Asian Development Bank has not forgotten about him. The sheer size of the contents of the dispatch alerts the captain that something is amiss. Why, suddenly, would the ADB become concerned about this project and this white monkey Del Rosi?

The captain drops off dispatches to Dr. Leong and Dr. Yanagi on his way to Mr. Del Rosi's tent. He notices with interest how Dr. Yanagi waits for him to depart his tent prior to opening his dispatch bag. Dr. Yanagi is a strange and secretive fellow. The captain has noticed Dr. Yanagi's secretive manner increase, since the technician, Sugai, arrived. There is no doubt in the captain's mind that Dr. Yanagi has not been forthcoming with respect to his findings. Also, given the paucity of reports from the Japanese-speaking sentry assigned to the doctor's tent, it is too clear that the doctor and his technician are hiding something.

Entering Mr. Del Rosi's tent, the captain finds him, once again, dining on tuna from the can with Connors.

Captain Djarmat smiling, "I see you are enjoying the epicurean delights of the area. Tell me, Mr. Del Rosi, what is it exactly that you find distasteful with our Indonesian cuisine?"

Joe, a little lost for words, wipes some tuna off his lips, "It is just that I prefer foods with which I am familiar. I mean no disrespect to your cuisine, Captain."

Captain Djarmat just nods. He realizes that Connors' propaganda about the illicit bush meat trade has been effective on Mr. Del Rosi.

Captain Djarmat handing Mr. Del Rosi his dispatch, "You have a heavy one today, Mr. Del Rosi."

Joe, feeling the weight of the dispatch, is surprised and responds, "Wow, this is heavy. I wonder what Watson is sending me."

The captain makes note of the fact Mr. Del Rosi truly was not expecting the heavy dispatch. To the captain, Mr. Del Rosi is a babe in the woods in this environment. How he ever got sent down here to New Guinea is a mystery. But, the captain senses a kind of honesty within Mr. Del Rosi that he admires. It is the kind of honesty not shared by Dr. Yanagi or the bush monkey Connors. The captain feels at ease in Mr. Del Rosi's presence.

Captain Djarmat "Watson is your contact in Manila, is that it?"

Joe "Yes, Watson is the one who sent me down here. We were chums in our university days."

Joe removes the contents of the dispatch in front of the captain. He offers the captain a seat, and Connors begins to prepare some tuna fish for the captain. The captain declines the tuna fish, before Connors can fill a tin for him. The captain does accept Connors' tea, however, and takes a seat near Mr. Del Rosi.

Joe skims through the correspondences, mostly copiers of funding authorizations. While Connors entertains the captain, Joe discovers an interesting letter from Watson indicating international interest in the encampment. Watson cites a recently-received State Department memorandum directing Watson to make reports to the US Embassy in Manila under the cognizance of national security. This directive alarms Joe. There is more going on here than the investigation into a seemingly indestructible tree. Interestingly, Watson does not even mention the tree in his letter. This too is strange for Joe. Why did Watson avoid mentioning the tree? The danger of the huge snakes seeps into the background, as Joe realizes the intensity and intrigue of the assignment increase.

Captain Djarmat, sensing that something has disturbed Mr. Del Rosi, says, "Is everything alright, Mr. Del Rosi?"

Joe, slow to respond, "Yes, Captain, Watson has just conveyed that I might be here much longer than I had anticipated from his prior correspondences."

Captain Djarmat chuckles, "Maybe you can finally get the opportunity to sample our cuisine."

Joe, still recovering from the letter, mumbles, "That I might, Captain. I just might be able to do that."

Connors interrupts the moment between the Captain and Joe, "Looks like we are out of water for tea. I will be right back. I am going to get some more water."

Captain Djarmat to Connors, "Check the trucks that came in yesterday. They are parked about thirty meters from my tent near the roadway into the encampment. Those trucks contain the freshest water."

Connors, as he exits the tent, "I will do that, Captain, thanks."

After Connors has left the tent, Joe decides on sharing Watson's letter with the captain.

Joe, handing Captain Djarmat Watson's letter, "You might like to read this."

The captain takes his time reading the letter. He pauses a while, as he reads over the section concerning the interest of the US State Department.

Captain Djarmat handing the letter back to Joe, "It would appear that there is more going here than we have been informed to believe."

Joe nodding, "Those are my thoughts exactly, Captain. However, there is little else that I can tell you, simply because I do not know anything else. This tree seems to be in the hands of Dr. Leong and Dr. Yanagi. They have shared precious little with me on their findings."

Captain Djarmat "Why would the American State Department develop a concern over this matter?"

Joe "Captain, I have no idea. They must have some other source of information unbeknownst to me. To the best of my knowledge, Watson gets all his information from me, so he does not know anymore than I do. Dr. Yanagi, however, is the ADB's scientific representative. He would be a likely suspect as a source of scientific information."

Captain Djarmat just nods and proceeds to leave the tent when suddenly he turns around and says, "The snakes that you are looking for feed, about once a week, near the river bank a few kilometers from here. If you like, I can have a cadre of my men assist you and Connors in capturing one of the smaller ones. Either of the smaller ones will meet the requirements that have empowered you."

Joe is speechless. The captain knows about the snakes. He knows what Connors and he have been doing in the tall grass.

Joe manages to respond in a low voice, "Thank you, Captain."

Captain Djarmat just smiles as he departs Joe's tent. As the captain makes his way to his tent, Connors, carrying two huge water containers, greets him with a nod and a smile.

Dr. Yanagi emerges from his tent, as the captain walks past it. Dr. Yanagi requests permission to sound test the tree again. He explains to the captain that his laboratory in Tokyo has developed a new testing technique that Dr. Yanagi would like Sugai to attempt. The captain agrees without any request for amplification. Dr. Yanagi states that Sugai can remove whatever bark may have regenerated over the original sound test area of the tree.

With the captain's consent granted, Dr. Yanagi hurries down to the tree with Sugai and the sounding apparatus. Some bark has regenerated, but Sugai removes it quickly and prepares the tree for the detector-transmitters of the sounding apparatus. Within fifteen minutes, Dr. Yanagi and Sugai are ready to sound test the tree.

Dr. Yanagi reminds Sugai, "Try to get the background level as low as possible on the second scale. We will run the test on the second scale for better accuracy."

Sugai adjusts the calibration and waits until the meter readout stabilizes low on the second scale. He informs Dr. Yanagi when stabilization has been achieved.

Dr. Yanagi "Stand clear of the tree and the detector-transmitters, Sugai."

When Sugai climbs out of the mini-trench dug around the base of the tree, Dr. Yanagi powers the detector-transmitters and releases a ping sound into the tree. Sugai watches the meter readout for any change in the meter reading. Minutes go by without any response on the meter readout. Dr. Yanagi and Sugai begin to get nervous over the overdue results. Truly, it is taking too long for the meter readout to respond.

Just as Dr. Yanagi is about to redo the sounding, Sugai announces the meter readout rising. The meter readout climbs to a little above mid-scale on the second scale. Although the fake readout on the second scale is measured in tens of meters, the actual readout indicates in tens of kilometers.

Sugai waits for the meter readout to level out and reports to Dr. Yanagi, "I have thirty-one meters, Doctor."

Dr. Yanagi looks strangely at Sugai, "Did you say thirty-one meters?"

Sugai looks back at Dr. Yanagi, "Yes, Doctor, the meter has leveled out at thirty-one meters."

Dr. Yanagi decides on performing another sounding test to compare the readouts. He reminds Sugai to remain clear of the tree and the detector-transmitters and pings into the tree again.

While Dr. Yanagi and Sugai await the response to the second ping, Dr. Yanagi queries Sugai, "What is the accuracy range for the second scale on the sounding apparatus?"

Sugai thinks a moment and responds, "Doctor, the second scale's accuracy ranges are plus 20% and minus 50%."

Dr. Yanagi applies the accuracy ranges to the meter readout, "The first meter readout would fall within the range of sixteen meters to about thirty-eight meters."

Sugai "Yes, Doctor, the true distance into the earth would fall somewhere between sixteen meters and thirty-eight meters."

Both men realize that they are talking about a range between one hundred and sixty kilometers to three hundred and eighty kilometers. The depth to which the roots of this tree descend into the earth defies the imagination.

Sugai announces the next readout as thirty-two meters. Dr. Yanagi is satisfied that the original calculated range of depth is sufficiently accurate. Sugai and he de-energize and disassemble the sounding apparatus and then proceed to Dr. Yanagi's tent.

Captain Djarmat greets them, as they pass his tent. The captain asks if they achieved any results. Dr. Yanagi reports that they have some preliminary results that need to be confirmed. The doctor informs the captain that he will apprise him of the result as soon as they are available.

Once inside Dr. Yanagi's tent, the two quietly begin to discuss the results.

Sugai "Doctor, don't our readings exceed the depth of the earth's upper crust?"

Dr. Yanagi "Yes, Sugai, even if we use the lower end of the accuracy range, we are below the earth's upper crust. Without question, the roots of this tree extend into spaces below the surface of the earth's crust that contain, at least, partially molten material."

Sugai "Lava?"

Dr. Yanagi "I admit it is just a matter of terminology, but yes, lava, in a sense. Lava is the term applied to molten material when it breaches the earth's surface. While underground, it is called molten material."

Sugai "I did not know that, Doctor."

Dr. Yanagi "The disparaging news is that if we use the high end of the accuracy range, then we find the roots of the tree in the mantle. The mantle is composed of fluid, molten material."

Sugai stunned, "How far down is the mantle?"

Dr. Yanagi "The experts have the mantle at about two hundred kilometers below the earth's surface. As you can visualize, Sugai, there is a good chance that we are close, if not inside, the mantle."

Sugai "The roots of the tree could not extend inside the mantle, if the mantle is fluid. Our sound test would have detected the change in density."

Dr. Yanagi "Theoretically, you maybe correct, Sugai, but we must remember that glass is a fluid that retains most all of the characteristics of a solid. The mantle may presumably function in a similar manner as glass. Certainly, the material filling the space between the mantle and the earth's crust…some one hundred kilometers or so thick…would resemble the characteristics of glass. Furthermore, we have never ventured into the mantle in order to determine its exact characteristics. All we have are theories about the mantle. Our sound test might shed some light on the attributes of the mantle and the space between the mantle and the earth's upper crust."

Sugai continues his probe of Dr. Yanagi's assumption: "If what you are concluding is correct, Doctor, how could this tree exist? Would it not have to be flowing lava and not some solid structure?"

Dr. Yanagi "I have to admit, Sugai, that there are far more questions than answers, right now. However, the tree's appearance can be explained by a process known as subduction. In subduction, the upper flow of lava from the space between the upper earth's crust and the mantle (*asethenosphere*) causes the ocean floor to spread out and force other parts of the ocean floor, abutting the continental crust, to be pulled under the continental crust and back into the mantle. Most of the time, the process of subduction merely draws upper earth's crust material into the upper mantle area and re-circulates it back to the earth's surface in the form of slow flowing lava from the ocean ridges. However, under certain conditions, the earth's crust material is drawn all the way down into the bottom of the lower mantle area where it is jettisoned back up to the earth's crust in the form of spouting volcanoes. We have experienced such activity in this area lately. I bring your attention to the recent Aitape disaster in which the geological plates shifted and caused a tidal wave. Aitape is not that many kilometers from here. And, volcanic activity abounds just across the border in Papua New Guinea."

Sugai "Either way or despite the recent geological activity in this area, Doctor, we should be seeing lava and not a solid structure."

Dr. Yanagi "True, Sugai, we should see flowing lava, if, in fact, only the laws of geology were at work here. However, this solid structure exhibits some rather strange characteristics that defy our understanding of solid structures, would you not agree?"

Sugai chuckles, "I would have to agree that this tree has the longest roots in the world."

Dr. Yanagi "Sugai, how many trees do you know of that are made of iron-based materials?"

Sugai "None, I am certain of that, Doctor."

Dr. Yanagi "This tree is made of iron-based materials, and it regenerates its bark. How many iron structures regenerate anything, but rust?"

Sugai "Regeneration is restricted to biology."

Dr. Yanagi "Precisely, Sugai, regeneration is a property associated with living organisms. Right here before our eyes lies a structure that defies the boundaries between the animate and the inanimate. And today, we discovered that this structure could reach all the way down to the mantle. Think for a moment of the implications here."

Sugai "Doctor, my assignment was to take soundings in order for you to be able to determine the capacity of a huge iron ore deposit. I am unsure if I want to contemplate anything beyond that."

Dr. Yanagi smiles, "You have chosen wisely, Sugai! Unfortunately, I do not share your luxury. I have to make sense of all this."

Before Dr. Yanagi can continue his discussion with Sugai, a strange clunking and roaring sound trembles the tent. The two men exit the tent to see what could be making such a terrible racket. Coming down the dirt road leading into the encampment, puffing smoke and tearing up dirt, is a tank with its turret aimed directly at Dr. Yanagi.

Sugai in awe: "What do you suppose that this is all about, Doctor?"

Dr. Yanagi sighs, "The Indonesian military moves in mysterious ways, Sugai."

Sugai "But, why do we need a tank?"

Before Dr. Yanagi can respond, the Second Lieutenant rushes past him screaming in Bahasa, "Praise be to Allah, we are saved!"

Soon the captain and the second lieutenant are greeting the tank commander and directing him where to park the awesome contraption. After a few more grunts from the metallic beast, the encampment quiets with the flick of an ignition key to the "off" position.

Dr. Yanagi shakes his head and motions for Sugai to rejoin him in the tent.

Meanwhile Captain Djarmat and the second lieutenant escort the tank commander, a first lieutenant, to his new accommodations in the encampment. A special tent has been arranged for the first lieutenant and his tank crew. After a brief inspection of the tent, the first lieutenant indicates his acceptance of the living space. Since one of his crew will be on watch inside the tank at all times, the tent provides adequate spaciousness.

With the accommodations in order, the captain commences a discussion about the assignment of the tank crew. The captain makes it clear that the tank is to be used in a defensive posture only. The first lieutenant concurs that his understanding of the assignment is defensive.

The second lieutenant provides the first lieutenant with a cup of tea.

Captain Djarmat states, "Under no circumstances will we be entering the tall grass to engage these snakes."

First Lieutenant "I concur, Captain. Colonel Ulang was quite specific. Territorial conditioning remains our highest priority. Since these snakes assist us, in a manner of speaking, in that effort, we are to leave them alone."

Captain Djarmat "It has been my experience with large snakes that they do not exhibit aggression toward humans. Naturally, I have never encountered creatures of this magnitude. Most snakes are docile creatures that are easily handled. Large snakes are meals in this part of the country. I am not expecting any assault on the encampment by one of these creatures. My scouts inform me that the snakes currently restrict their feeding habits around the river bank not far from here."

First Lieutenant "You do have soldiers missing though, do you not?"

Captain Djarmat "Yes, one of my long time soldiers went missing one morning. Apparently, he must have strayed into the tall grass at an inappropriate moment. Since I have forbidden entering the tall grass during the early hours of the morning, we have not had any more disappearances."

First Lieutenant "Why did you request a tank, if you felt you had the situation under control?"

Captain Djarmat "The sheer size of these creatures made me realize that our small arms would be useless against one, if one decided to enter the encampment. I could not take the chance, given the nature of what we are doing here."

First Lieutenant "I understand, Captain. If one should enter the encampment, what I recommend is to have your men force the snake to coil up. Any aggressive action on their part would cause the snake to react reflectively and coil. In a coiled position, the tank could easily inflict lethal damage to the snake. The shrapnel from one projectile would tear the snake to pieces."

Captain Djarmat "I will insure my men force the snake to coil."

Turning to the Second Lieutenant, the Captain says, "Have the word passed to all the men that if one of the huge snakes enters the encampment, we are to maneuver in such a manner as to have the snake coil up."

Second Lieutenant "It will done, Captain."

Seeing the first lieutenant finishing his cup of tea, the captain offers to show the tank commander around the encampment. The second lieutenant is dispatched to alert the troops of the new orders. Captain Djarmat decides on introducing the first lieutenant to the distinguished encampment guests.

Meanwhile, Connors and Joe, rousted by the unusual sounds emitted by the tank, are pondering why such drastic military action would be required. It is not like anyone is expecting an invasion from Papua New Guinea. The small arms, carried by the army, are sufficient to deter any rebel activity. Connors suspects the strange tree has something to do with the sudden appearance of a tank in the encampment. Whatever the reason, a tank is here.

On another note, Joe informs Connors, "Brad, the Captain knows about the snakes."

Connors surprised, "Does he now? What did he say about the snakes?"

Joe "He said if we needed some assistance, he would provide some of his men to help us."

Connors smiles, "And, just how much did he want for his help?"

Joe "He asked for nothing, Brad. I believe that he genuinely wanted to help us. He even mentioned that any of the snakes would meet our requirements. So, he knew about the million dollar US bounty."

Connors sips some tea, "Well, Mate, we still have to get the critter out of the country. I bet the Captain has something in store for us at that point."

Joe "I do not think so, Brad. I suspect the Captain wants something from us, but whatever it is it has nothing to do with the snake or the bounty on the snake."

Connors "Bloody hell, Mate, the Captain is no dummy. You bet your life he wants something."

Joe "Brad, once we have the snake, all we need do is to contact the press. The bounty people will come out here to see the snake."

Connors smiles, "You are right, Mate. We actually do not have to remove the snake from this hellish place. We just have to capture one of them."

Joe "Oh yes! The Captain said we could take either of the smaller snakes. For some reason, he does not want the larger snake disturbed."

Connors chuckled, "The larger snake probably ate his man. I suspect the Captain has something special in store for that one."

Just as Joe is about to pour himself a cup of tea, the captain enters his tent and introduces the first lieutenant. Joe offers them both a cup of tea, but they decline. They are just making the introductory tour. The offer of tea can be saved for another occasion. After the usual nods of acknowledgment, the captain and the first lieutenant give their adieus and exit.

Connors "What do you make of this new fellow, Mate?"

Joe "Indonesian military officer…he resembles the Captain…looks like he has been in New Guinea a while."

Connors "Yes, the new fellow is very much like the Captain. I would guess that both those men have spent a lot of time in forward deployed positions. Those are the kind of men the Indonesian Army just leaves out in the periphery and forgets to promote. The military is a sad life without any political connections."

Joe "Maybe they just like being soldiers."

Connors "Trust me, Mate, no one likes being a soldier on the periphery of civilization, surrounded by hostiles. They do it, because it is all that they can do and feel respectable."

Joe "I never looked at it that way."

Connors "We come from more advanced countries with ample opportunities. In Indonesia, the opportunities are few, and those few are reserved for the politically connected. It is a crying shame, too. The Captain is a good man. If he were politically connected, he would be a colonel or brigadier general in Djakarta. Instead, he endures the jungle environment of New Guinea, taking orders from men with half his experience and a quarter of his dedication."

By now, Dr. Leong has taken an interest in the tank. She is waiting outside her tent when the captain and the first lieutenant stop in on her.

After the formal introductions, Dr. Leong is quick to query the Captain, "I was under the understanding that this encampment was for scientific research, Captain. Why do we need a tank?"

Captain Djarmat smiles, "I thought it would be best to have a tank in the encampment in order to soothe your concerns over the huge snakes."

Dr. Leong places her hand over her mouth to hide her embarrassment, "Really, Captain! I believe I am more concerned about this tank than any snake, regardless of how large it might be."

The First Lieutenant breaks in, "Doctor, you can be certain of one thing. This tank will not eat anyone. I promise."

Captain Djarmat tries to restrain his chuckling.

Dr. Leong just stares at the tank commander a moment then retreats into her tent. Captain Djarmat motions to the first lieutenant to join him, as he follows the doctor into her tent.

Once inside the doctor's tent, Captain Djarmat says, "I apologize for imposing upon you, Doctor, but I need to know if you have any more information on the bark samples that you sent to your laboratory."

Dr. Leong, obviously upset from the First Lieutenant's ill humor, "Yes, from what my lab has reported, the tree bark poses no threat whatsoever to life. The bark is completely safe, whether as bark or in its liquid form."

Captain Djarmat "Once again, I apologize if anything the First Lieutenant and I said upset you, Doctor. Thank you for the information."

With that having been said, the captain and the first lieutenant leave the doctor's tent and proceed to meet with Dr. Yanagi.

The sentry outside Dr. Yanagi's tent comes to attention when the captain and the first lieutenant approach. The military courtesy acts as a signal to the captain that Dr. Yanagi is discussing sensitive information within his tent. The captain motions to the sentry to announce his presence to Dr. Yanagi.

Sentry "Dr. Yanagi, Captain Djarmat is here to see you."

Dr. Yanagi immediately ceases his conversation with Sugai: "Thank you. Please have the Captain come in."

Captain Djarmat and the first lieutenant enter Dr. Yanagi's tent and exchange formal introductions. Dr. Yanagi introduces Sugai to the first lieutenant.

Captain Djarmat "Have you achieved any results from the sound test, Doctor?"

Dr. Yanagi "We were just discussing the test when you entered, Captain. I will need some more time to compare the sound test readings with my charts and tables, before I can release any information. Rest assured, Captain, that I will inform you as soon as I have some results."

Even the first lieutenant knows the doctor is lying. Graciously, the captain and the first lieutenant thank the doctor for his time and leave his tent.

On the walk to the first lieutenant's accommodations, Captain Djarmat says, "I never trusted that guy, Yanagi. Since his sidekick has showed up, I trust him even less. They are up to no good. Something serious is under that tree, and Yanagi is hiding it from us. I know it."

First Lieutenant "Well, you have a tank here now, Captain. Believe it or not, a tank is a mighty persuasive weapon."

Captain Djarmat stops in front of the tank commander's tent, "Unfortunately, Yanagi and his sidekick are our guests. If you can believe this, the Asian Development Bank appointed Yanagi as their scientific liaison in the encampment."

First Lieutenant "I can believe it. Japan is the major donor to the Asian Development Bank. But I agree with you, Captain, there is more going on here than that Japanese scientist is letting on. Did you know that Jayapura has been inundated with copies of memos from the Japanese Embassy in Djakarta to our government?"

Captain Djarmat tilts his head toward the First Lieutenant, "What kind of memos?"

First Lieutenant invites the captain inside his tent.

With the Captain inside his tent, the First Lieutenant whispers, "The Japanese Embassy in Djakarta is negotiating for mining rights under this encampment."

Captain Djarmat brings both his hands to his chin, "Are they mentioning any particular kind of mining?"

First Lieutenant "Well, I have not read any of the memos, but the word around headquarters is iron ore. The Japanese want to mine iron ore here. And, according to the staff at headquarters, some big money is being stuffed into pockets all around in Djakarta."

Captain Djarmat "Are you sure of this, First Lieutenant?"

First Lieutenant "Captain, I have swallowed some of the same dirt that you have out in the provinces and so have the people who shared this information with me. I trust the information that I just told you. Iron ore is what the Japanese are after. Since I am a civil engineer by formal training, I suspect what your Japanese scientist is doing here is determining the capacity of the iron deposit under this encampment."

Captain Djarmat "Dr. Yanagi is performing sound tests on the tree to determine the depth to which its roots reach into the ground."

First Lieutenant "Captain, trees do not need to get sound tested. Sound testing is reserved for metallic or liquid entities. The sound test the doctor is performing is for iron. The Japanese want to know how far the iron ore reaches into the ground."

Captain Djarmat "That may be true. The tree has been determined to be composed of mostly iron-based materials."

First Lieutenant "Captain, the tree is not a tree at all. Whatever it is; it is made of iron-based materials…just like my tank."

Captain Djarmat thinks a moment, before he tells the first lieutenant anything else. He decides to leave the conversation where it is and say nothing of the other anomalies.

Captain Djarmat just nods and says, "Iron ore, I got it."

First Lieutenant "Iron ore is what the Japanese want."

With the captain and the first lieutenant a safe distance from his tent, Dr. Yanagi has Sugai guard the entrance while he transmits their sounding results to Tokyo.

CHAPTER 16

▼

KAJIOKA'S OFFICE, MINISTRY OF INFORMATION & TECHNOLOGY, TOKYO

The secretary informs Mr. Kajioka that the Geophysics Head is waiting to see him. Kajioka, overwhelmed with response demands from the Foreign Ministry, attempts to avoid any new meetings or interviews. He needs the time to draft responses.

Kajioka responds, "I was not aware that a meeting had been scheduled with the Geophysics Laboratory."

Secretary "The Geophysics Head says that it is urgent that he speak with you."

Kajioka "Very well, postpone my next meeting, if necessary. Send the man in."

The Geophysics Head enters Mr. Kajioka's office and notices the stacks of papers and file folders on his desk. Mr. Kajioka resembles a machine gunner entrenched behind a barricade.

Geophysics Head "Sorry to interrupt you, Mr. Kajioka. I know you are busy."

Kajioka "Get on with it. Can you not see that I am swamped with paperwork? What is it?"

Geophysics Head "We received a transmission from Dr. Yanagi in New Guinea, Mr. Kajioka. I felt that you should be the first to read his message."

Kajioka pops up from behind the barricade of papers and file folders, "You felt right. Let me see it."

The demands of the correspondences suddenly dissipate. Kajioka realizes what this message contains. His priorities just shifted.

The Geophysics Head hands the message to Mr. Kajioka, as Mr. Kajioka walks to the front of his desk and takes a seat next to the Geophysics Head. With keen interest, Mr. Kajioka reads over Dr. Yanagi's message.

Kajioka "According to Dr. Yanagi, the iron ore deposit reaches a depth of at least one hundred and sixty kilometers. This is incredible news."

Geophysics Head "I thought you would appreciate the results of the sound test, Mr. Kajioka."

Kajioka ponders the content of the message a while and asks, "Why does Dr. Yanagi quote such a wide variation on the possible depth of the deposit?"

Geophysics Head "The second scale of the sounding apparatus contains those parameters of accuracy. If you recall, Mr. Kajioka, we had to conduct the test on the second scale because of the high background level noises."

Kajioka "In actuality, we should be quoting the precise reading of some three hundred kilometers and append the caveat of the accuracy range, wouldn't you say?"

Geophysics Head "I suppose it would depend on the geological background of the audience, Mr. Kajioka. Certainly, the members of parliament would prefer the one reading at three hundred kilometers."

Kajioka "Your man, Sugai, verified these readings, did he not?"

Geophysics Head "I am sure that he did, Mr. Kajioka. He operated the sounding apparatus. Dr. Yanagi would have conferred with Sugai, before he allowed anything to be transmitted outside New Guinea."

Kajioka "Fine! I will brief the Deputy Minister. Thank you for bringing this to my immediate attention."

After the Geophysics Head has left his office, Kajioka contemplates the implications of an iron ore deposit some three hundred kilometers into the earth. It dawns on him that three hundred kilometers is well into the theorized region of the upper mantle. This realization forces Kajioka to question the accuracy of the readings.

After some thought, Kajioka decides on reporting the lower end of the accuracy range, only. At some two hundred kilometers below the earth's crust, Kajioka can avoid the embarrassing question of explaining how the molten material of the mantle could be considered extractable by our current mining technology. On that thought, Kajioka realizes that anything over ten kilometers into the earth's crust will pose a substantial technological problem. Kajioka refuses to consider explaining how a metallic tree is connected with this discovery. That topic is just too bizarre and defies explanation.

In no time, Kajioka's secretary informs him that the deputy minister is expecting him. Once again, as he approaches the deputy minister's secretary's desk, she is quick to usher him within the office and close the door.

Deputy Minister Kawamoto "I was hoping to hear from you sooner, Kajioka. What do you have for me? Good news, I hope."

Kajioka "Perhaps, the news is much better than either of us could have ever imagined, Deputy Minister."

Deputy Minister Kawamoto "Believe it or not, Kajioka, I would not be surprised at anything you brought to me after our last few meetings. You have a flare for the bizarre, Kajioka. As I recall, no other officer in our ministry has ever displayed your talents. Well, at least, they have not exhibited them openly."

Kajioka suddenly feels uncomfortable with the deputy minister's jocular demeanor. For a moment, he realizes that the deputy minister could dismiss him for being a lunatic. Caution envelops Kajioka and settles tightly around him.

Kajioka, experiencing difficulty to speak, mutters, "We have the sound test results from New Guinea, Deputy Minister."

Deputy Minister Kawamoto, sensing Kajioka sudden withdrawal, gestures with his hand to proceed.

Kajioka "Dr. Yanagi reports that the iron ore deposit reaches a depth of some two hundred or so kilometers."

Deputy Minister Kawamoto stops what he is doing in order to fathom the information that Kajioka just spoke. The deputy minister seems to stop breathing for a moment. It is as if his heart just stopped pumping.

Deputy Minister Kawamoto "Did you just say: 'two hundred kilometers?'"

Kajioka looking down at his shoes, "Yes, Deputy Minister, Dr. Yanagi reports two hundred kilometers."

Deputy Minister Kawamoto "How can that be possible?"

Kajioka now realizes how fortunate it was for him to mention only a number from the low end of the accuracy range.

Kajioka shakes his head from side-to-side, "I do not know, Deputy Minister."

Deputy Minister Kawamoto speaking firmly, as he leans toward Kajioka, "You have to know, Kajioka. I cannot possibly relay some ridiculous number like this to the Minister. His Excellency will have me committed to a loony bin."

Kajioka, sensing intense displeasure emanating from the Deputy Minister's facial expressions, simply states, "Those are the numbers reported by Dr. Yanagi, Deputy Minister. I am not in a position to discuss the plausibility of those numbers with the good Doctor."

Deputy Minister Kawamoto "You just mentioned 'numbers.' Are there other numbers? Perhaps, those numbers are more convincing."

Kajioka, realizing his slip of the tongue, says, "I fear not, Deputy Minister. I just reported to you one of the most conservative numbers. All the other numbers reach further into the realm of absurdity, Deputy Minister."

Deputy Minister Kawamoto leans back in his chair, "Really? Tell me what they are, Kajioka."

Kajioka clears his throat, "Two hundred kilometers represents the lower end of the accuracy band, Deputy Minister. The actual reading reported was three hundred and ten kilometers with an upper accuracy range of three hundred and eighty kilometers."

Deputy Minister Kawamoto takes a moment to respond, then says, "I spoke prematurely earlier, Kajioka. Your reports continue to outdo one another. You truly are the champion of champions of the bizarre. What I admire most about you Kajioka is that you say these things, as if you believed them. Are you in need of some time off, Kajioka? I can arrange for you to have a much needed vacation. I can arrange for the time off not to be counted against you. Would you like that?"

Kajioka is convinced the deputy minister views him as a misfit, driven into lunacy by the demanding workload.

Kajioka taking on a positive stance, "Deputy Minister, I am reporting what Dr. Yanagi has transmitted. My Geophysics Head has confirmed the accuracy of the data. There has been no error in transmission. These incredible numbers are what they are, subject to the accuracy and sensitivity of our test instrumentation."

Deputy Minister Kawamoto pauses to reflect on the report and his comments toward Kajioka.

Deputy Minister Kawamoto breaks the silence with, "You do realize, Kajioka, that these numbers are too incredible to go beyond this room, do you not?"

Kajioka "With respect, Deputy Minister, I believe that these numbers are too incredible not to go beyond this room. We have been rejoicing in the belief that we had discovered a huge iron deposit. I believe now that we may have discovered something far more serious to our national interest. Yes, the numbers are incredible beyond belief, but if they are accurate, then we need to determine, immediately, what we have discovered."

Deputy Minister Kawamoto "Kajioka, these numbers could take us into the earth's core. I find that too difficult to comprehend."

Kajioka "You have stated my concern, as well, Deputy Minister. Let me remind the Deputy Minister that this tree, that we now have data connecting it to molten material in the mantle, has regenerative properties and has exhibited indestructibility. To me, that is a very serious concern that far exceeds that of any huge iron ore deposit."

Kajioka pauses his oration to stand and pound on the Deputy Minister's desk, "Deputy Minister, this three-hundred-kilometer, iron tree could be alive!"

Deputy Minister Kawamoto, in awe over Kajioka's sudden outburst, retreats into silence in order to give him time to respond appropriately.

Both men stare at the deputy minister's desk while they await one or the other to speak. Silence permeates the room. Kajioka can hear the deputy minister breathing.

Finally, the Deputy Minister speaks, "Kajioka, this tree cannot be alive."

Kajioka "With respect, Deputy Minister, what are you basing that statement on? The tree regenerates bark material designed for camouflage, Deputy Minister. Furthermore, it defies all our attempts to penetrate it. Deputy Minister, this tree exhibits some strange, if not alien, form of intelligence."

Deputy Minister Kawamoto "You must excuse me, Kajioka, I am not prepared or qualified to respond to this line of discussion. I plead my ignorance to you, Kajioka. I just do not believe that we even are discussing something like this."

Kajioka, "Deputy Minister, I believe the data that we have collected on this tree propelled us into the sanctuary of the unthinkable. We should not shy away from the challenge. We should embrace it with full vigor. As incredible as the numbers appear, the greater incredibility is what they conceal."

The secretary distracts Deputy Minster Kawamoto. She informs him that his scheduled appointment is waiting.

Deputy Minister Kawamoto "I have to break this conversation, Kajioka. Give me time to think all this over. Try to understand that my expertise is not science, Kajioka. We both have our entire careers on the line here, if we go through and publicize these numbers. Let us meet again tomorrow afternoon. I will have my secretary vacate the entire afternoon for us. Bring your most trusted staff members with you. We need to hash this out thoroughly. Now, I must adjourn this meeting. Duty calls me to another matter."

The next afternoon, Kajioka has assembled with the Geophysics Head outside the deputy minister's office. As he waits for the deputy minister to finish with an appointment, the Electronics Laboratory Crew Chief and two sound analysis personnel take seats in the waiting room next to the Geophysics Head. Kajioka recognizes the Electronics Laboratory Crew Chief.

Kajioka to the Electronics Crew Chief, "Did the Deputy Minister request your presence for this meeting?"

Electronics Crew Chief "He sure did. I brought along my two experts."

The Electronics Crew Chief introduces his two sound analysis experts (SAE1 & SAE2) to Mr. Kajioka and the Geophysics Head. Before any further communication can proceed, the deputy minister orders the group into his office and has his secretary close the door. Kajioka immediately notices the extra chairs and realizes that the deputy minister means business.

After all are seated, the deputy minister introduces everyone and the purpose of the meeting. Clearly, everyone in attendance understands that the topic is not so much the tree in New Guinea, as it is the precise identification of the tree. After the intent of the meeting is declared, the deputy minister offers the floor to Kajioka.

Kajioka does his best to promote the idea of intelligence at work within the tree and its accompanying iron ore deposit. The Geophysics Head supports the idea and provides the information on the regenerative properties of the tree. The notion of regeneration shocks the Electronics Crew Chief and his two experts. This is the first time such information has been introduced to them. Their shock increases when Geophysics Head reveals the indestructible nature of the tree.

Clearly, the two anomalies are difficult for anyone in the room to complement. Regeneration establishes connotations of living organisms: whereas, indestructibility evokes notions of strong and tough metallic substances. The characteristic of indestructibility can be rationalized through an advanced mechanism of crystalline structure rearrangement. Although, this mechanism currently is far beyond our capabilities, it can be theorized as a plausible explanation. The Geophysics Head covers the theory in a palatable detail.

Kajioka tackles the regeneration issue with a weak connection to the same mechanism described by the Geophysics Head. In essence, Kajioka hypothesizes that if the tree has the ability to alter, at will, its crystalline structure to suit the situation, it would have a similar ability to regenerate itself and other similar materials.

Interestingly, after Kajioka and the Geophysics Head have had their turn of explaining this anomaly in New Guinea, the Electronics Crew Chiefs turns the discussion over to his senior sound analysis expert (SAE1). SAE1 describes the interesting features that he and SAE2 have been analyzing from the sound transmission. According to SAE1, the visual display of the sounds indicates interplay of dimensions at work. SAE1 is convinced that at least some six dimensions are involved in the creation of the sound.

For the benefit of the deputy minister, SAE1 offers one of Zeno's examples of dimensions: The zero dimension could be represented as a single dot. For example sake, the dot is considered to have no length, width or depth. The first dimension, in Zeno's example, would be a single line. Once again, the line is considered to have length but no width or depth. Hence, the one dimension line could be viewed as a series of dots. A dot moving along the line would not recognize the line but merely the motion of moving along the line. The second dimension could be seen as a plane or a two-dimensional figure with length and height but no width. Likewise, a line embedded in the plane would not see the plane but only the motion of moving through the plane. A dot in the plane would be two dimensions removed from the plane and be oblivious to the existence of a plane. The third dimension would be represented by a cube with length, width and height. Similarly, a plane embedded in the cube would not see the cube but only sense the motion of moving through the cube. The dot and the line both would be oblivious to the existence of the cube. The fourth dimension could be thought of as a dimension in which a three-dimensional cube moves through without realizing its existence.

At this point, SAE1 translates our idea of time as our three-dimensional explanation for motion through the fourth dimension. Time is used to explain the phenomenon of motion. Likewise, analogies are made to the first and second dimensions from the examples. Zeno's ideas of ancient time prove successful in explaining current phenomena. As for the higher dimensions: five and six, the examples are provided via extrapolations of the lower dimensions. Specifically, the sixth dimension would have a fifth dimensional entity moving through it. The sixth dimension would be oblivious to anything in the fourth dimension.

From this launching position, SAE1 proposes that an entity operating in an advanced dimension would be able to create the anomalies witnessed in New Guinea. With some assistance from SAE2, SAE1 connects the strange sounds emitted from the tree as inter-dimensional activity capable of realigning crystalline structure. SAE1's expose is persuasive to say the least. The group confers their appreciation for his rendition.

After some reflection time, the Geophysics Head states that the ease and speed with which the crystalline structure realigns might require activity in the twelfth dimension, as theorized as interaction between an energy field with the Higgs field. Activity in the sixth dimension was difficult to accept. However, once the group granted the possibility, theorizing activity in the twelfth dimension followed easily.

The meeting took most of the early afternoon set aside by the deputy minister. Prior to closing the meeting, one strange question emerged: if this tree has acquired these multi-dimensional capabilities, how did it do it? The deputy minister reserves time on the following afternoon to discuss that issue.

On closing the meeting, the deputy minister mentions that he has a conference with his daughter's teacher in Narita.

Before the Deputy Minister can collate his notes on the meeting, SAE2 states, "Deputy Minister, you will have extreme difficulty getting to Narita. There was an accident on the main artery to Narita from here. Cars will be tied up until after 5:00 PM."

Deputy Minister Kawamoto to his secretary, "Check the radio for the status of the accident and traffic to Narita."

The rest of the group is surprised that SAE2 would make such a comment.

After a few moments, the Secretary reports, "Deputy Minister, there is no traffic problem on the road to Narita. No accident has been reported."

Deputy Minister Kawamoto stares at SAE2 and says, "What gave you the idea that there was an accident?"

SAE2 "Deputy Minister, there was a three-car accident at approximately 3:30 PM on the road to Narita, do you not remember?"

The deputy minister looks at his watch, as does the rest of the group. His watch reads 3:10 PM.

Deputy Minister Kawamoto "Kajioka, what time do you have?"

Kajioka looks at the Deputy Minister and at SAE2, "I have 3:10 PM, Deputy Minister."

Deputy Minister Kawamoto "I have 3:10 PM, too."

Everyone stares at SAE2.

SAE2 looks at everyone staring at him and says, "Don't you remember, two of the drivers were killed, and a little girl was rushed to the hospital. What is wrong with you people? You are looking at me like I am crazy."

SAE1 says to SAE2, "It is not 3:30 PM yet. Are you sure you are not referring to some other accident?"

SAE2 "No, the accident occurs today at about 3:30 PM and ties up all the traffic to Narita from this part of Tokyo. Don't you remember?"

Kajioka is in total disbelief. He stares with his mouth open at the Electronics Crew Chief intently. The Electronics Crew Chief just shrugs his shoulders.

Deputy Minister Kawamoto, inundated with the bizarre, actually decides to remain in his office until after 3:30 PM. He requests the other members of the meeting to remain as well. While they wait, the deputy minister asks what assignments SAE2 has been involved in recently. The Electronics Crew Chief explains that SAE2 did the majority of the hands-on work in deciphering the multi-dimensional characteristics of the sounds from New Guinea. According to SAE1, SAE2 spent nearly twelve hours a day analyzing the sounds and their visual displays. The deputy minister realizes that SAE2 has been overworked and recommends some time off for him.

At about 3:35 PM, the secretary informs the deputy minister that the radio has reported an accident on the Narita artery. It is a three-car accident. By 3:45 PM, two people have been reported killed in the accident, and a third has been rushed to a hospital. By 4:00 PM, the two people killed have been identified as the drivers of two of the cars, and a child, a young girl, was taken to the local hospital in critical condition.

Deputy Minister Kawamoto collapses at his desk. Kajioka and the Electronics Crew Chief rush to perform CPR and revive the deputy minister.

By 5:00 PM, everything SAE2 had foretold concerning the accident had come to pass. SAE1 had known SAE2 since their university days. Never had SAE1 ever witnessed SAE2 make any kind of prediction. SAE2 was someone dedicated to reason and firmly rooted in facts. Yet, here he was accounting the future with precision.

Though nothing was said in the deputy minister's office, clearly every mind, but SAE2's, was racing to find an explanation. SAE2, on the other hand, acted as if nothing unusual had happened. SAE2's demeanor was another concern for the group. Kajioka asked that the Geophysics and the Electronics Crew Chiefs join him in his office while SAE1 and SAE2 returned to the Electronics Laboratory.

In his office with the door closed, Kajioka queries the Electronics Crew Chief, "I will not ask you what kind of person SAE2 is. I think what we just observed was nothing short of remarkable. Do you believe the sounds from New Guinea could have anything to do with his sudden ability to predict the future?"

Electronics Crew Chief "Mr. Kajioka, I can think of no other explanation."

Geophysics Head "If what SAE1 outlined, concerning the dimensions, could be taken as a starting point for an explanation, then SAE2's exposure to the sounds and the visuals of the signal from New Guinea could have affected his mind sufficiently as to create some form of disturbance, allowing him to see the future."

Kajioka to the Electronics Crew Chief, "What do you think of that idea?"

Electronics Crew Chief "We have to take the idea seriously, Mr. Kajioka. Fortunately, I restricted access to the signal from New Guinea. Only SAE1 and SAE2 have had access to that signal."

Kajioka "We have to add Dr. Yanagi and your sound technician to that list."

Electronics Crew Chief "Yes, we do, but SAE1 and SAE2 had much more exposure to that signal than anyone else. SAE2 was exposed far more than SAE1. SAE1 did not exhibit any signs or willingness to predict the future."

Kajioka "So, you are thinking that a period of exposure to this signal produces an ability to predict the future, is that it?"

Electronics Crew Chief "Yes, I am inclined to support such a theory. Long periods of exposure could have caused SAE2's ability to predict the future."

Kajioka to the Geophysics Head, "Do you concur?"

Geophysics Head "I would have to concur, Mr. Kajioka. Some time ago, you and I discussed the anomalies of this tree. This notion of inter-dimensional interaction presents a new frontier. We have no idea what to expect. However, allow me to reiterate one idea. If we exist within a fourth dimensional experience and we are three-dimensional entities, then we would only experience motion, as we passed through the fourth dimension. Suppose SAE2's exposure to the proposed higher dimensions: fifth and sixth, provided him with a mountain top consciousness, so to speak, and enable him to experience the fourth dimension, as it truly exists. If that were the case, then SAE2 would have been relieved of the experience of motion and been able to experience the entire fourth dimension, as it exists. Since time has been proposed as a tool employed to explain motion, without the experience of motion, time becomes meaningless. Experiencing the fourth dimension would have meant experiencing all of it at once, without the aid of time. That would explain, SAE2's repeated statements to us: 'Don't you remember?'"

Electronics Crew Chief "My compliments! Yes, SAE2's mind must have undergone something similar."

Kajioka likewise impressed, "Are you saying SAE2 experienced the fourth dimension?"

Geophysics Head "Yes, I am. Actually, I am proposing that SAE2 might have experienced the higher dimensions, as well."

Kajioka "Let me grant a leave of absence for SAE2. Meanwhile, have him debriefed. For that matter, debrief SAE1, as well. And, do not allow anyone to go near those New Guinea sounds until further notice."

The meeting adjourns with the sense of restriction on the entire meeting with the deputy minister.

Entering the electronics laboratory, the Electronics Crew Chief greets SAE1 and SAE2: "Mr. Kajioka is going to ask the Deputy Minister to grant you both leave without penalty."

SAE2 chuckles, "Could you have Mr. Kajioka countersign the leave slips?"

Electronics Crew Chief "Why on earth would he do that?"

SAE2 calmly, "Don't you remember, the Deputy Minister suffered a stroke on Thursday. Mr. Kajioka was appointed as the interim deputy minister."

The Electronics Crew Chief realizes that today is only Tuesday.

CHAPTER 17

▼

ENCAMPMENT, NEW GUINEA

.

Joe awakes to a commotion outside his tent. He fumbles around trying to find his watch. In the darkness of the tent, its florescent dial and moving arms indicate 4:30 AM. It is way too early for anything. The commotion continues. Excited soldiers ramble on in Bahasa. Joe can distinguish Captain Djarmat's voice amongst the cacophony of other noises. Realizing that the captain seldom awakes this early, Joe decides to check out what is happening.

Opening the tent flap, Joe notices that the area around the tank is teeming with soldiers. Also, it is not as dark, as he had anticipated for 4:30 AM. Although there are extra lights alit around the encampment, particularly in the vicinity of the tank, Joe notices that the heavens are brighter than normal. There is a full moon, resembling a harvest moon. The encampment could extinguish many of its lights. The harvest-like moon provides ample illumination.

Joe follows two soldiers, who were awaken, as well, by the commotion, to the tank. Once in the immediate vicinity of the tank, a sentry prevents Joe from approaching any closer. An English-speaking soldier informs Joe that one member of the tank crew is missing. Little else on the missing crewman is released; other than he was working inside the tank and suddenly came out of the tank and ran into the tall grass.

Satisfied with sentry's information, Joe makes his way back to his tent. Upon entering the tent, Joe finds Connors awake, preparing a pot of tea.

Connors wiping sleep from his eyes, "What is going on out there? Doesn't the army know how to sleep?"

Joe "One of the tank crewmen ran into the tall grass."

Connors chuckles, "Now there is a dumb thing to do at night. Poor soul is probably lost, wandering about out there."

Joe "Those are my sentiments exactly, but the soldiers are too worked up for the tank crewman to have just gone crazy. I think something terrible happened to the crewman."

Connors "He should have slept in the tank."

Joe "Brad, as I understood from the sentry around the tank, the crewman was inside the tank. He, apparently, got out of the tank and ran into the tall grass."

Connors "Do you think he was sampling some of the local marijuana inside the tank and went crazy?"

Joe "No, I don't, Brad. The entire tank crew looked like professional soldiers. Something terrible happened."

Connors testing the teapot for warmth, "How terrible could it have been, he was inside a tank. There is no better place for protection in this encampment."

Joe "Brad, I tell you the soldiers are concerned. I have never seen them this worried."

Connors notices the tea boiling, "The tea is ready. Care for a cup, Mate?"

Joe finds his teacup and hands it to Connors.

As Connors fills Joe's teacup, he says, "Tell you what, I will speak to our sentry."

Sipping his tea, Connors calls the sentry and asks him in Bahasa what happened. The sentry responds similar to what Joe had just told Connors.

Connors to Joe, "He tells the same story, Mate. The guy just went nuts."

Joe "These soldiers just do not go nuts, Brad. You know that."

Connors joins the sentry back outside the tent and notices the moonlit night. It is an unusually bright moonlit night. Connors recalls that during full moons, such as this one, animals feed earlier. The bright moonlight illuminates their feeding habitat. This way, they can avoid the daylight predators.

Connors reentering the tent says to Joe, "Did you notice the full moon?"

Joe "Yes, it was exceptionally bright for 4:30 AM when I awoke to the commotion."

Connors "Do you suppose our snakes were up early, causing some mischief?"

Joe stunned by the comment, "I do not know much about snake feeding habits."

Connors "Our snakes feed at dawn, Mate. They wait for the first light. Tonight, it is bright enough to equate to first light. Experience would have taught them that their prey fed in the pre-dawn hours on a night such as this."

Joe "No one mentioned a snake was involved in the crewman's disappearance, Brad."

Connors sipping some more tea, "The soldiers are probably right. The guy just went crazy."

Meanwhile Captain Djarmat and the first lieutenant are interviewing witnesses to the disappearance of the tank crewman. Two sentries observed the crewman disembark the tank and run into the tall grass.

First Lieutenant to First Sentry, "What exactly did you observe?"

First Sentry "I heard an unusual noise coming from inside the tank. As I approached the tank, the noise decreased. Then, I noticed the tank's access cover open and the crewman crawl out and slide down the side of the tank. Once he touched the ground, the crewman ran into the tall grass. I called out to him to halt, but he ignored me. All I saw was the tall grass part, as he ran further into it."

First Lieutenant "Could you identify the noise coming from inside the tank?"

First Sentry "It sounded like someone grunting from lifting something heavy. It must have been heavy, because a loud noise followed like something heavy was set down. It sounded like someone slapping or punching the inside wall of the tank."

First Lieutenant "Are you sure the tank access cover was shut when you heard the initial noises?"

First Sentry "I am not entirely certain, but the access cover was shut before the crewman exited the tank. I saw him slide out from under the cover."

Captain Djarmat interjects, "Are you sure the crewman slid out from under the cover?"

First Sentry "Yes, he did not open and latch the access cover, as the tank crewmen usually do. He just slid out from under the cover. I remember, because the cover slammed shut, after he slid out."

First Lieutenant continues the probing, "Are you sure he slid down the side of the tank rather than climb down?"

First Sentry thinks a moment before he responds, "Yes, he slid down the side of the tank. It was difficult to see him, as he wore his camouflage clothing rather than his usual tank attire."

First Lieutenant stunned by the mention of camouflage clothing, "Are you certain of the camouflage clothing, Sentry?"

First Sentry "I am positive, First Lieutenant. The camouflage clothing was distinctly the bright-and-dark, green-patch variety."

First Lieutenant to Captain Djarmat, "Captain, my crewman have no such camouflage clothing. Actually, when I interviewed the other crewmen, they reported that the missing crewman wore only an undershirt and regulation trousers when he entered the tank to perform some maintenance."

Captain Djarmat "Are you saying that your tank crew has not been issued camouflage clothing?"

First Lieutenant "We have never been issued camouflage clothing, Captain. Why would we need camouflage clothing inside a tank? Even if we had camouflage clothing, it certainly would not be any green variety. We are inside a tank. We do not need camouflage."

Captain Djarmat to the Second Sentry, "What can you tell us about the events that you witnessed?"

Second Sentry "I saw similar things. I was on the other side of the tank, so I did not see the crewman slide down the side of the tank. However, I did notice that he seemed to be dragging something behind him, after he came out from behind the tank and entered the tall grass."

First Lieutenant "Are you certain that he was dragging something?"

Second Sentry "Yes, First Lieutenant, he was dragging something that appeared to have on the same camouflage clothing as the First Sentry described. It was hard for me to tell what it was, but it looked like a person that the crewman was pulling head first into the tall grass."

First Lieutenant "Why do think he was pulling a person head first?"

Second Sentry "The person he was pulling tapered off. He was wider at the front than the rear."

First Lieutenant "Are you certain that the person being pulled was wearing camouflage clothing?"

Second Sentry "Yes, I am positive, First Lieutenant. It was definitely bright-and-dark, green, camouflage clothing."

First Lieutenant to Captain Djarmat, "Do you suppose the local rebels killed my crewman, dressed him up in camouflage clothing then drug his body into the tall grass?"

Captain Djarmat laughs, "Absolutely not, First Lieutenant! The local rebels hardly have any clothing to wear at all. Their best attire is hand-me-down clothing from Papua New Guinea or donated clothing from the religious missions.

Contemplating the local rebels with camouflage clothing is like imagining them with artillery or a tank."

First Lieutenant asks both sentries if they saw anyone enter the encampment from the tall grass. Both sentries deny any sighting. A survey of all sentries on watch that night likewise revealed no unusual sightings. All sentries confirmed that the full moon allowed them to see everything in the encampment. Visibility was exceptionally good.

Captain Djarmat and the first lieutenant dismiss the sentries and retreat into captain's tent in order to discuss the disappearance. Joined by the second lieutenant, the captain and the first lieutenant bring up the idea that one of the huge snakes could have eaten the tank crewman. From the first lieutenant's description of the crewman, he fits the profile of the other missing persons. The question for the three officers now is: how did the snake get inside the tank?

First Lieutenant "Both sentries affirmed that the access hatch was shut. It would have been impossible for a huge snake to wedge open a spring-shut, access hatch from the outside. The sentries would have heard the sound of the hatch closing. Chances are the noise from the trials and errors of the snake attempting the entry would have alerted the sentries. The snake could not have come inside the tank through a closed access hatch."

Second Lieutenant "Are there any other accesses into the interior of the tank?"

First Lieutenant smiles, "There are no portals in the tank that a person could get through. The access hatch is it."

Captain Djarmat "Yes, I can understand a tank's construction, but we are not talking about a human here. We are talking about a snake. Although these snakes exceed ten meters in length, they are not very tall or wide. What about the viewing portal for the tank driver? How large is that?"

First Lieutenant "It is certainly large enough for a person's head to pass through. Actually, the driver's window opening allows for a good degree of peripheral vision. I believe the view-scope is designed for something like one hundred and twenty degrees. There is no way a person could crawl through such an opening without cutting off his shoulders."

Captain Djarmat "Would you say it is large enough for a huge snake to pass through?"

First Lieutenant "I do not think so. The large constrictors that I have seen get quite bulky in the space between the head and the center of the snake."

Captain Djarmat to the Second Lieutenant: "Second Lieutenant, would you ask Dr. Leong to join us?"

The second lieutenant acknowledges the captain's request and exits the tent promptly.

Captain Djarmat to the First Lieutenant, "Dr. Leong is our resident expert on the biological sciences. She can provide us with a scientific opinion as to whether or not one of these huge snakes could enter the tank through the driver's window."

Sooner than expected, the second lieutenant returns with Dr. Leong. The captain offers the doctor a seat.

Captain Djarmat to the Doctor, "We were just discussing whether or not a huge snake, like the one you and I discussed during an earlier conversation, could enter a tank through the driver's window. We were wondering if you could provide us with an expert opinion."

Dr. Leong "Well, I would need to examine the window."

Captain Djarmat to the Second Lieutenant, "Take the Doctor to see the window."

Captain Djarmat to the Doctor, "Please follow the Second Lieutenant, he will show you the window in question."

Second Lieutenant taking the Doctor's hand to assist her rising from her chair, "Come follow me, Doctor."

After the second lieutenant and the doctor exit the tent, they walk briskly to the tank. The second lieutenant points out the driver's window.

Dr. Leong merely has to sight the window, "It is large enough for one of those huge snakes to enter."

Second Lieutenant in shock, "Are you sure Doctor?"

Dr. Leong "Yes, I am quite sure."

The two return to the captain's tent.

As they enter the tent, the Second Lieutenant says, "She says it is large enough for a snake to enter."

First Lieutenant looks at the Captain, "May I ask a few questions of the Doctor?"

Captain Djarmat nods in acknowledgment.

First Lieutenant, after the Doctor has re-seated, "Have you considered the larger portion of the snake between the head and the mid-section?"

Dr. Leong "Yes, I have. Although that section of a snake appears large at rest, it can be made thinner, just as we can suck in our bellies. It is one of the advantages of snakes to be able to adjust their body sizes to fit the situation."

First Lieutenant "So, what you are saying is that the snake underwent some form of contortion in order to get inside the tank through the driver's window, is that it?"

Dr. Leong "Yes, I am stating that, if, in fact, the snake did enter through the driver's window."

Captain Djarmat steps into the conversation, "Do you have another theory as to how the snake got inside the tank, Doctor?"

Dr. Leong "Captain, the snake could have entered the tank via the access hatch. It is much larger, and snakes like holes."

Captain Djarmat "Two sentries and the missing crewman's partner averred that the access hatch was closed."

Dr. Leong "Was the access hatch closed all the time? The snake could have entered while the hatch was open, before the crewman even entered the tank. The tank had been running earlier, the snake could have been attracted by the warmth."

First Lieutenant asks, "Why would not the crewman have spotted such a huge snake inside the tank when he first entered?"

Dr. Leong "Snakes of any size are experts at concealment. One of their greatest forms of concealment is to lay motionless. If the crewman had maintenance on his mind, he might not have noticed anything unusual, unless it was right out in the open, blocking his path or in motion. Without moving, a snake is difficult to see. Our eyes interpret it as something else."

First Lieutenant nodding in agreement, "It is possible. I suppose that the snake could have entered before the crewman. It explains the shut hatch."

Captain Djarmat "Even if we grant that the snake could have entered before the crewman, Doctor, we cannot explain the crewman's disappearance."

Dr. Leong adds affirmatively, "Captain, the snake suffocated your crewman; then, it devoured him inside the tank."

First Lieutenant "How did the snake get out of the tank with the crewman inside it?"

Dr. Leong "If the snake used the access hatch to enter, then it exited via the same route. Snakes remember their tracks. The bulk of the crewman would be contained within the snake's belly. The snake would have appeared to have a huge, pronounced lump in its belly."

Captain Djarmat "Second Lieutenant, sorry to have to bother you again, but would you go and get Mr. Connors."

Once again, the second lieutenant hurries out to comply with the captain's orders. The first lieutenant comments to the captain, after the second lieutenant has departed, that the captain has the young man well trained. Both officers laugh. Eventually, even Dr. Leong laughs at the second lieutenant's naivety.

With the personnel in the captain's tent still smiling from the first lieutenant's comment, the second lieutenant returns with Mr. Connors. The captain offers Mr. Connors the second lieutenant's chair.

Captain Djarmat "Mr. Connors, I understand that you got a good look at one of the huge snakes, is that correct?"

Connors embarrassed, "Well, Captain, I saw two of them pretty well, why do you ask?"

Captain Djarmat "What did they look like?"

Connors smiles, "They looked like bloody snakes, only larger."

Captain Djarmat smiles to convey his displeasure with Connors' humor, "I meant what color were they?"

Connors, with a more serious air in his response, "Both snakes were camouflage green, Captain. It was not the dark green of usual military camouflage. It was brighter, like the color of freshly-moistened, jungle vegetation."

First Lieutenant utters a sound, "Gulp!"

Connors, distracted by the First Lieutenant's noise, "Did I say something wrong, Captain?"

Captain Djarmat "No, Mr. Connors, that will be all. Thank you for your assistance."

After Connors departs the tent, Dr. Leong tends to the first lieutenant. He is in shock. The thought of a snake devouring his trusted friend inside the tank overcame him with fear. At that moment, Captain Djarmat realizes that the first lieutenant may not be able to re-enter the tank without having a relapse.

In reflection, the tank crew considers the interior of the tank their sanctuary from harm. To have that sanctuary violated destroys all the comfort they achieved. The inside of the tank now becomes a horror chamber…a death trap…where one of their friends was violated, unspeakably.

Dr. Leong "Captain, the First Lieutenant will need some rest. He may require a few days to hash out this tragedy. And, if I may speak frankly, Captain, you need to improve the safety of this encampment from these snakes. Personally, I suggest you seek out these creatures and destroy them with the tank, before any more of us get eaten."

Speaking out of turn and disrespectfully, the Second Lieutenant demands, "We have to kill these things, Captain."

The Captain looks at the Second Lieutenant disapprovingly, "Control yourself, Second Lieutenant."

Captain Djarmat to the Doctor, "I will take that under advisement, Dr. Leong."

Dr. Leong more insistent in her retort, "There is no advisement needed, Captain. One of those creatures sneaked past your guards, entered a tank and had one your men for breakfast. What damned advisement do you need in order to act? Kill the damned things, before they devour us all."

Captain Djarmat to the Second Lieutenant, "Escort Dr. Leong back to her tent, Second Lieutenant. See to it that she remains inside her tent. Post extra guards around her tent. And, for the love of Allah, order your sentries to be alert for snakes. Double the sentries, if you think it is required."

As the Second Lieutenant is about to leave with Dr. Leong, the Captain says to him, "Have the remaining tank crewmen assemble in my tent."

Before the Second Lieutenant can take two steps, the Captain says, "Get the two bush monkeys in my tent, as well."

As the Second Lieutenant is escorting Dr. Leong to her tent, she asks, "Where are these bush monkeys?"

The second lieutenant just ignores the doctor's query and delivers her to her tent.

Connors and Joe enter the captain's tent and ask why they were summoned. The captain explains to them that the snakes have devoured another victim, one of the tank crewmen. The captain makes it clear to them that the snakes will need to be destroyed. He orders Connors to accompany the tank crew when the first lieutenant has recuperated to the site where he saw one of the snakes emerge from the rocky cliffs.

Connors pleads with the captain to be able to capture one of the beasts in pristine condition. The captain informs Connors that they will make every effort to preserve one of the snakes for him. Right now, the captain has made the decision to seal off the tunnel entrance of the snake hole in the rocky cliffs. The captain encourages Connors to create any form of trapping device that he feels will contain one or more of the snakes, before the tank makes its way to the rocky cliffs.

Connors exclaims that the tank will make hamburger out of the snakes' bodies, if they are subjected to the tank's projectiles. The captain understands; however, he reiterates that he must protect his men and the encampment inhabitants. He reminds Connors that his primary duty is to preserve the research effort ongoing in the encampment. Unfortunately, the snakes are threatening that safety in a most macabre of manners.

Joe pleads with the captain, as well, to be more realistic about the snakes. He states that the snakes truly are harmless, as long as the encampment institutes the proper procedures to safeguard against them. The captain is hearing none of that nonsense. According to the captain, the snakes are too cunning for their own survival. Devouring local wildlife and natives is one thing, but when the snakes devour members of the Indonesian army, they exterminate themselves. The captain reminds Connors and Joe that he has exercised considerable restraint already with these beasts. Their feeding habits need to be addressed with extreme prejudice. No, it is the captain's intent to destroy them, if Connors has not captured one of them by the time the first lieutenant has recovered from the shock of his crewman's death.

Reluctantly, Connors tells the captain that he understands the situation. Connors and Joe exit the captain's tent and begin plotting how they can capture one of the beasts. Joe discounts any large canvas bag idea as lunacy. They need some form of huge cargo net with a small mesh in order to contain one of the snakes. Connors agrees and says he will enlist the help of the second lieutenant in order to acquire the net. Connors believes that he can get the headman to have his villagers set the trap to ensnare a snake.

In their tent, Connors and Joe share some tea and curse the misfortune of the snakes' eating habits. Connors asks Joe if he wants to return to the headman's village for some more jungle juice. Joe emphatically declines. Before Connors can offer, Joe declines a bout with a little brown sheila, as well. Joe is quite satisfied with his tea, surrounded by armed members of the Indonesian army.

CHAPTER 18

▼

KAJIOKA'S OFFICE, MINISTRY OF INFORMATION & TECHNOLOGY, TOKYO

Kajioka's secretary informs him that he has a call from the Foreign Ministry, a Mr. Takeda. Kajioka recognizes the name immediately but not the title. He is somewhat at a loss, as to whether or not he should answer the phone. The last time they spoke Takeda insisted that their arrangement be kept confidential.

Kajioka "Yes, Mr. Takeda, I was not expecting a call from you."

Takeda in a serious tone, "I assure you, Mr. Kajioka, it was never my intention either ever to call you. However, circumstances dictate that our arrangement needs to be compromised."

Kajioka, suspecting the worst, "It is terrible for me to hear those words, Mr. Takeda."

Takeda "Let me get right to the reason for this intrusion. Do you know a Lars Hansen?"

Kajioka "I cannot say that I do. Why do you ask?"

Takeda "Let me refresh your memory, Mr. Kajioka. Do you know a Dr. Lars Hansen from MIT in the United States?"

Kajioka, shaking his head, "I am sorry, Mr. Takeda, the name Lars Hansen does not ring a bell with me. I tell you that I know him not."

Takeda "Well, apparently, he knows you, and he has some knowledge about our anomaly in Northern New Guinea."

Kajioka shocked, "I swear to you, Mr. Takeda. I do not know this man. Actually, I have never knowingly made the acquaintance of anyone from MIT."

Takeda "He is quite adamant that he knows you, Mr. Kajioka. Furthermore, he is quite knowledgeable of your anomaly in New Guinea."

Kajioka, speaking affirmatively, "Takeda, stop playing with me. I tell you I do not know this person."

Takeda "Can you explain how he acquired a copy of your sound recordings from New Guinea?"

Kajioka stunned, "No, I have no idea how he may have acquired them."

Kajioka gets his secretary's attention and motions for her to come to his desk. As she approaches, he scribbles something onto a memo pad and gives it to her. The memo reads: Get the Electronics Crew Chief in here right now!

Takeda "Let me fill you in on Dr. Hansen's call to the Science & Technology Section of the Foreign Ministry. This Dr. Lars Hansen called to confirm his availability for the teleconference call that you scheduled for tomorrow."

Kajioka puzzled, "I have not scheduled any teleconference call at all. I swear to you, Mr. Takeda. My office does not even have teleconferencing equipment."

Takeda "I understand your lack of teleconferencing equipment. That is why the venue for the teleconferencing call is listed as the offices of Science & Technology."

Kajioka "Mr. Takeda, I swear to you. I have no knowledge of any teleconferencing call."

Takeda "What struck me as most odd when I took the call from Dr. Hansen was that he said you informed him of the teleconferencing call on Friday."

Kajioka "Mr. Takeda, the Electronics Laboratory had not even finished analyzing the sound recordings from New Guinea last Friday."

Takeda "Ah Kajioka, here comes the best part. Dr. Hansen said that you informed him of the teleconferencing call this Friday."

Kajioka "Mr. Takeda, it is only Thursday. Are you sure he said this Friday?"

Takeda "I am positive, Mr. Kajioka. I even had him check his calendar. He read out this Friday coming's date. And, he confirmed that you scheduled the actual teleconference on Thursday, the day before."

Kajioka "I am afraid that I do not follow what you are trying to tell me, Mr. Takeda."

Takeda "Trust me, Mr. Kajioka; I have no idea what to make of my entire conversation with Dr. Hansen. However, he said that you could straighten this all out for me."

Kajioka "Did he actually say that?"

Takeda "Yes, he did, and he was quite serious about it."

Kajioka, stunned beyond belief, "I am speechless, Mr. Takeda."

Takeda "I pray you will not be so inclined when you brief me on this matter this afternoon. Shall we say 2:00 PM?"

The secretary informs Kajioka that the Electronics Crew Chief is waiting to see him. He asks for a minute, before she lets him into the office.

Kajioka "Certainly, I will report to your office promptly. Would you mind if I brought one of my section supervisors?"

Takeda "For this matter, Mr. Kajioka, you can bring the Lord Buddha Himself."

After getting off the phone with Takeda, Kajioka remembers that the Electronics Crew Chief is waiting outside his office. He tells his secretary to let the Electronics Crew Chief into his office.

As the Electronics Crew Chief enters, Kajioka says, "I just received a most disturbing call from the Foreign Ministry. Perhaps, you can shed some light onto the subject for me."

Electronics Crew Chief somewhat hesitant to respond, "I will do all I can, Mr. Kajioka."

Kajioka gesturing toward one of the chairs, "Please, take a seat. The Foreign Ministry received a call from an American scientist who claims to have a copy of our sound recordings from New Guinea. What do you now of this?"

Electronics Crew Chief stunned, "I know nothing of this, Mr. Kajioka. I assure you that no one in the electronics laboratory has mentioned anything of our work outside our section."

Kajioka "You are certain of this, is that correct?"

Electronics Crew Chief feeling the pressure of an investigation coming, "Yes, Mr. Kajioka, I am certain. All our people in the section can be trusted unconditionally."

Kajioka suspected that the security was tight within his ministry. The question now is: how did the American find out?

Kajioka "The American somehow knows about our sound recordings. How could he have found out?"

Electronics Crew Chief "Perhaps our security in New Guinea has been penetrated."

Kajioka "Dr. Yanagi is a careful and experienced fellow. I cannot imagine him letting anything slip. People might suspect him of something, but suspicion would be as far as they get. His technician, Sugai, is another experienced person. I doubt either of them breathed a word of any of this to anyone. Do you have any other ideas?"

Electronics Crew Chief "The only vulnerability we have is our transmission frequency from New Guinea. If someone was eavesdropping, they could have intercepted our frequency, demodulated it and copied it."

Kajioka pauses a moment, "Are not those frequencies encrypted?"

Electronics Crew Chief "The carrier frequency is not encrypted. It is the sideband information that is encrypted, Mr. Kajioka. However, in the case of pure sounds, like those transmitted from New Guinea, there would have been no encryption necessary. The information, or text, contained in the sideband is what we encrypt."

Kajioka "Are you saying that the sounds recorded in New Guinea were available to anyone listening to our transmission frequency?"

Electronics Crew Chief "Yes, Mr. Kajioka, anyone tuned into our frequency could have recorded the sounds. It works similar to a radio receiver. Question is: why would anyone have been tuned into our frequency. Our frequency resides way above the normal radio bands? If they were tuned in, then they were doing so intentionally. Our listeners were probably foreign military."

Kajioka "Where is the closest American listening post?"

Electronics Crew Chief smiles, "In Yokosuka, Mr. Kajioka, at the American 7th Fleet Liaison Office. They are military and employ encryption in all their transmissions."

Kajioka "Could they have been the ones who might have intercepted our transmission?"

Electronics Crew Chief "I would not think so, Mr. Kajioka. The American Liaison Office is just that. They merely liaise. They are not equipped, to the best of my knowledge, to eavesdrop on our encrypted transmissions. Besides, they are under some form of bi-lateral agreement not to do so as an understanding for their right to operate in Japan. If I were to guess a location, I would have to say the American installations on Okinawa. They do a considerable degree of eavesdropping."

Kajioka "I had not thought of Okinawa."

A few moments of silence pass as Kajioka ponders the implications and connections.

Kajioka "Let me share this with you. The Foreign Ministry informed me that the American was a scientist from MIT in the United States."

Electronics Crew Chief smiles, "Really, I did my graduate work at MIT. Perhaps I know this scientist. What was his name?"

Kajioka "I believe the Foreign Ministry said 'Hansen.'"

Electronics Crew Chief really smiles, "Lars Hansen!"

Kajioka surprised at the sudden enthusiasm from his guest, "Yes, I believe the Foreign Ministry said 'Lars Hansen.' Do you know this man?"

Electronics Crew Chief "Mr. Kajioka, Lars Hansen is the head of the Defense Laboratory at MIT. He is the most respected scientist in the United States. Are you certain it was him who called?"

Kajioka "The Foreign Ministry mentioned him by name."

Electronics Crew Chief "My congratulations, Mr. Kajioka, you must be an important man to receive Dr. Hansen's attention."

Kajioka attempts to lower the enthusiasm bubbling over from his guest, "I believe Dr. Hansen was interested in our sound recordings and not me. The Foreign Ministry mentioned that Dr. Hansen had a copy of our recordings. And, from the conversation Dr. Hansen had with the Foreign Ministry, I suspect that he has been listening to them."

Electronics Crew Chief "Did the Foreign Ministry mention if he approved of the recordings?"

Kajioka looks up at the ceiling in order to prepare his retort, "Actually, according to the Foreign Ministry, Dr. Hansen's conversation resembled more that of SAE2's."

Electronics Crew Chief "That reminds me, SAE2 predicted that Deputy Minister Kawamoto would have a stroke, and you would be appointed the interim deputy minister."

Kajioka nods at the absurdity emerging the past few days, "Thank you for telling me. When did SAE2 say the Deputy Minister would suffer this stroke?"

Electronics Crew Chief "Today!"

Kajioka suddenly feels his stomach welling up with butterflies, "SAE2 said it would happen today, is that right?"

Electronics Crew Chief "Yes, Mr. Kajioka, he said 'Thursday'…'today.'"

Kajioka breaks the conversation and asks his secretary to call the deputy minister, immediately. A few moments pass before the secretary informs Mr. Kajioka that the deputy minister is ill and had to be rushed to the hospital. Kajioka's secretary says that the deputy minister's secretary asked if he would care to leave a message. Kajioka declines and thanks his secretary.

Retuning to the conversation, Kajioka says, "It was precisely that prediction capability of SAE2 that the Foreign Ministry wanted me to explain about Dr. Hansen. The Foreign Ministry has summoned me to their offices this afternoon. I have received clearance to bring you along with me. Please put together a brief on SAE2's observed capabilities and a plausible explanation for them. It appears this prediction capability is becoming contagious. Anyone who spends time with our sound recordings seems to become infected to some degree."

At 2:00 PM sharp, Kajioka and the Electronics Crew Chief check in with the secretary at Mr. Takeda's new office in the Foreign Ministry. She checks their clearances and has them take a seat in the waiting room.

The waiting room contains comfortable, leather upholstery, glass coffee tables, the latest news magazines from around the world and excellent temperature control. Soothing, semi-classical music serenades the guests. Kajioka cannot wait to achieve a comparable status in order to enjoy these comforts. Although, he expects he has a good many years of dedication yet to endure, before something this prestigious comes his way.

Both men sit in silence, as they await their meeting. Kajioka realizes that something this important could ruin his ambitions if handled improperly. He enters sacred space, today. In sacred space, one must act as if the Lord Buddha Himself were in attendance, judging one's conduct. Just thinking of the matter makes Kajioka fidgety and restless.

The Electronics Crew Chief is not as concerned. To him, this is a routine brief in which he gets to expound somewhat on the work done by his laboratory. He has been a lead sectional supervisor for years, and he does not expect to be advanced any further for the remainder of his career. A position such as Mr. Kajioka's is beyond his reach, regardless of how many years of dedication he might serve.

The secretary informs Kajioka that Mr. Takeda will see him now. Kajioka, followed closely by the Electronics Crew Chief, enters Takeda office.

Upon entry into Takeda's new office, Kajioka realizes how much he over-valued the waiting room. Takeda resides in a showcase. All the amenities of the waiting room are here with the added benefit of expensive Japanese prints adorning all the walls. The window section on the far wall provides a spectacular view of the Tokyo Tower area. Promotion in the Foreign Ministry is worthwhile.

Takeda smiling, "Please, make yourselves comfortable. I will have the secretary bring us some Japanese green tea and some tasty rice cakes."

Kajioka, obviously impressed with Takeda's new office, takes a seat. The Electronics Crew Chief settles into a cushioned seat to the left of Kajioka. The allocation of amenities, provided to the upper echelons of the Foreign Ministry, far outweigh those of the Information Ministry.

Takeda, adjusting his chair in order to lean back comfortably, "I need you to explain to me about Hansen, Kajioka."

Kajioka "I brought my Electronics Crew Chief with me to assist with that explanation, Mr. Takeda."

Takeda "That is fine. First, why did Hansen mention a call from you took place tomorrow for a teleconference set up for later today?"

Kajioka "Mr. Takeda, we have been experiencing some strange happenings that we believe are somehow connected with the sound recordings that we received from New Guinea."

Takeda "Does this have anything to do with the surveillance that you requested?"

Kajioka "Yes, Mr. Takeda, it does. The sound recordings were created as a result of an on-site sound test performed to confirm the surveillance results."

Takeda "I see. Go on Kajioka."

Kajioka "It appears that anyone who spends a good deal of time listening and viewing the graphic displays of these sound recordings develops an ability to predict the future."

Takeda "How does that happen?"

Kajioka "We are not certain of why, just yet. All we know, right now, is that the phenomenon evolves somehow. Can I have my assistant provide a theory that we have been entertaining on this matter?"

Takeda "Yes, please do."

Kajioka introduces the Electronics Crew Chief and asks him to proceed with an explanation.

Electronics Crew Chief "Mr. Takeda, we have theorized that the sound recordings emanated from an entity possessing multi-dimensional processing capability. By that, I mean that the sound recordings represent the noises created in dimensions above the fourth dimension."

Takeda interrupts, "Kajioka, do you subscribe to this theory?"

Kajioka "Yes I do, Mr. Takeda. Can we have my assistant proceed with the explanation?"

Takeda "That will not be necessary. I believe I comprehend the theory, already. Let me explain: If the sound recordings represent dimensions above the fourth dimension and our scientists are being affected by them, then Hansen was existing in the fourth dimension...or higher...when he called me and spoke of future events."

Electronics Crew Chief "Precisely, Mr. Takeda."

Takeda to Kajioka, "We need to restrict access to those sound recordings, immediately. You and your assistant will teleconference, at the appointed time, with Dr. Hansen and explain to him what is happening. He must be alerted to restrict access to those sound recordings."

Takeda pauses a moment before he continues, "Can someone really predict the future after being exposed to these recordings?"

Kajioka "It seems to be the case, Mr. Takeda."

Takeda "How far into the future?"

Kajioka smiles, "From what we know so far, a few days seem to be the norm."

Takeda "Do you have examples?"

Kajioka "One of our sound technicians predicted the three-car accident...the one that happened a few days ago...a few minutes earlier than the accident occurred. And, the same technician predicted that Deputy Minister Kawamoto would have a stroke two days in advance."

Takeda "Has the Deputy Minister suffered a stroke?"

Kajioka "We are not sure if it was a stroke, but he was rushed to the hospital this morning."

Takeda "This is very interesting, indeed. Where is this technician now?"

Kajioka looks over at the Electronics Crew Chief.

Electronics Crew Chief responds to the question, "He is on leave of absence, Mr. Takeda. We felt he needed some time off to clear his mind."

Takeda "We need to put this technician under close observation. Bring him back in and check him into the Foreign Ministry's medical facilities. There is no telling what he might expose, if he wanders out and about in Tokyo, babbling about future events."

Kajioka to the Electronics Crew Chief, "Call him back in as soon as we finish here."

Takeda "Let us not wait that long, Kajioka. Have your assistant see my secretary and get it done right now."

The Electronics Crew Chief leaves the room to attend to the matter with the aid of Takeda's secretary.

Takeda "If Deputy Minister Kawamoto is incapacitated, we cannot allow this matter to be without a responsible manager. You will act as interim Deputy Minister. I will process the appointment, immediately."

Kajioka shocked at the sudden turn of events, "Thank you, Mr. Takeda."

Takeda laughs, "Do not thank me yet, Kajioka. You still have a teleconference in which to persuade the Americans to restrict access to those sound recordings. You could say that teleconference will make or break you for upward mobility."

Kajioka "I understand, completely, Mr. Takeda."

Takeda "Additionally, I want your Electronics Crew Chief to confer with the Foreign Ministry's medical personnel in order to apprise them of what they are dealing with here. Have him do that as soon as he orders the technician back."

Kajioka "I will make it happen, Mr. Takeda."

Takeda "Good! I will see you then for the teleconference."

At 10 PM, Tokyo time, Kajioka, the Electronics Crew Chief and Takeda are standing by to receive the teleconference from the United States. A few minutes after 10 PM, an American appears on the teleconference screen. The Electronics Crew Chief identifies the American as Dr. Lars Hansen.

Short introductions are exchanged in Japanese. Dr. Hansen has arranged for a Japanese interpreter to conduct the exchange of ideas. The Electronics Crew Chief remembers the interpreter as someone who applied for a position with his laboratory. He is Japanese, and his family resides in Yokahama.

Dr. Hansen commences the meeting, "Thank you for inviting us to this meeting, Mr. Kajioka."

Dr. Hansen has three other scientists seated beside him.

Kajioka somewhat at lost for words, "Yes, Dr. Hansen, I felt we could meet in this manner in order to exchange ideas about the control of access to these sound recordings."

Dr. Hansen responds, "I appreciate your concerns, Mr. Kajioka; however we believe that these sound recordings are useful in expanding our consciousnesses. We feel that their availability should be expanded."

Kajioka "Please understand, Dr. Hansen, these sound recordings are something new, and as such, would need to be controlled until we understand their impact on our civilization."

Dr. Hansen "We believe that our preliminary tests on subjects have shown these sound recordings to be harmless. With the exception of being able to predict short term future events and corresponding diminishing memory of past events, they do not seem to have any adverse side effects."

Kajioka surprised at the advancement the Americans have made with the sound recordings, "Are you saying that you have undergone tests with sound recordings?"

Dr. Hansen "Yes, we have. We organized and compared a volunteer test group with a control group. Our results indicate as I have spoken."

Kajioka "Are you saying that you have documented a loss in memory?"

Dr. Hansen "Let me re-state what I said earlier. We have documented a diminishing memory. It is not the case that memory is lost. What we have observed is that the immediate past has been shown to be less certain in the test group than the control group. Subjecting both groups to the same experiences has proven that the test group is not as certain in recalling events of the immediate past. For example, both groups order morning coffee at a local establishment. During their end of day interview, the control group recalls with certainty how they ordered their gourmet coffee: Cappuccino, Latte, etc.… The test group has difficulty remembering what they ordered. They recall ordering coffee and drinking it, but the specific selection that they chose, for the most part, remains blurry."

Kajioka with interest, "The test group exhibited predictive tendencies, did they not?"

Dr. Hansen "Immersion in the sounds and the visual displays of the sound recordings produced predictive tendencies in every member of the test group. We took precautions to insure that the test group was debriefed thoroughly following each experimental session. We believe we have the effects of the sound recordings under control with no danger to the general population."

Kajioka looks over at Takeda. Takeda nods to proceed.

Kajioka "This is such good news to hear, Dr. Hansen. We were quite concerned when we first witnessed the accuracy of the predictive powers. We also expressed concerns about the future itself."

Dr. Hansen "We investigated future concerns, as well. Our findings indicate that our comprehension of the future changes it somewhat. The future, in our belief, is merely at set of alternatives. We do not consider the future deterministic in any way; other than, sometimes our own actions produce what appears to be a deterministic outcome. This was an interesting insight for us. After a good deal of discussion, we determined that our beliefs about the past were what we reflected into our beliefs about the future. Our development of history, and writing in general, allowed us to codify a version of the past that brought meaning into our existence in the form of a narrative. We now conclude that has never been the case. The past is as alternative-ridden as the future. Succinctly, although events did occur in the past in which we may have participated, their happening was as subjective as their interpretation and codification."

Kajioka astounded by the observation, "Correct me, if I am wrong, what you are stating is that our ability to write history masked our former understanding of the past. Is that your position, Dr. Hansen?"

Dr. Hansen "It is close enough, Mr. Kajioka. Through the exposure to these sound recordings we have been able to better understand ourselves and our intentional construction of the past as a meaning-laden narrative."

Kajioka "From your report, Dr. Hansen, it appears that you are further along investigating these sound recordings than we are."

Dr. Hansen "Thank you for the compliment, Mr. Kajioka. What I would like to propose is that we work in unison in exploring the source of these sound recordings."

Kajioka looks over at Takeda for permission to respond. Takeda's facial expression is one of awe over the frankness of the conversation and information being conveyed by the Americans. Takeda nods his approval.

Kajioka "Dr. Hansen, we would relish such an arrangement."

Dr. Hansen "One of the things we would like to entertain is an attempt at a communication with the source of these sound recordings. Do you believe that would be something your government would condone?"

Kajioka stunned, "We have never considered such an action."

Kajioka has to take a moment to comprehend the implication of Dr. Hansen's proposal.

Kajioka "Are you suggesting that these sound recordings emanate from a conscious source, Dr. Hansen?"

Dr. Hansen smiling, "Mr. Kajioka, where else would such sounds emanate? These are sounds from multi-dimensional activities. Their precision suggests that they are being controlled consciously and with intent."

Kajioka "We are not so certain of their conscious control, Dr. Hansen."

Dr. Hansen "Our research into their origin unearthed a reported anomaly in New Guinea. It is our understanding that they came from a tropical tree."

Kajioka hesitates to say anything.

Takeda "Dr. Hansen, I am Mr. Takeda, and I am representing the Foreign Ministry in this teleconference. Mr. Kajioka is restricted in saying anything about an anomaly in New Guinea. We would need a higher clearance from our Foreign Ministry in order to continue this discussion with you."

Dr. Hansen "I understand your secrecy concerns, Mr. Takeda. If you could acquire those higher clearances, I would be willing to bring a scientific delegation over to Tokyo in order to discuss a plan of action in order to further understand this phenomenon for the benefit of both our countries."

Mr. Takeda "I will take your request to my higher authority. If and when we get approval for this joint investigation, I will have Mr. Kajioka contact you in order to facilitate the arrangements for a meeting in Tokyo."

The teleconference attendees sign off. The screen goes blank.

Electronics Crew Chief "Did you hear what Dr. Hansen said? We could be dealing with a new life form!"

Kajioka to Takeda, "I entertained such a possibility. The facts were right in front of my eyes, and I must have chosen to ignore them."

Takeda "Kajioka, I am sure that the Foreign Ministry will approve of this joint effort, given the suggestion of the eminent Dr. Hansen. Do not be too hard on yourself, Kajioka; I was praying the Americans would not mention something like this. We cannot oppose them now. The Americans know too much, and we all know how aggressive they can get. Kajioka, I will have the approval by tomorrow. You should prepare to receive the American delegation."

CHAPTER 19

▼

ENCAMPMENT, NEW GUINEA

Captain Djarmat has just informed Connors and Joe that he will lead an armored column into the area near where the snakes are said to be nesting. Connors realizes that their time is up. From the captain's conversation, he is aware of the rocky cliff where the snakes rest. Connors and Joe decide to take up the captain's offer to accompany him on the mission.

The low pitch growls waking Connors and Joe remind them that the tank is being warmed up for the mission. Connors and Joe scramble about getting whatever they decide to bring along with them. This time, they both remember to bring water. They each take two quart size bottles of pure water. The thirst that they endured lingers on in their memory from their last misadventure into the tall grass.

Exiting their tent to the request of the sentry, they notice that the column is ready to get underway. Captain Djarmat and two soldiers occupy the jeep that will lead the procession. The tank will follow closely behind the jeep. Last in the procession will be a military truck carrying about ten soldiers. The canopy has been removed from the truck to provide natural air conditioning for the passengers.

Captain Djarmat "Climb aboard the tank. We are ready to go."

The first lieutenant, half visible in the turret access hole, tells Connors and Joe to relax on the inclined portion of the rear of the tank. Connors and Joe manage to climb onto the rear of the tank. They find the accommodations quite pleasant. Despite the cacophony of sounds emanating from the crude combustion engine and the warmth permeating the metal below their bodies, the accommodation is surprisingly comfortable. The two men are able to lounge and sun themselves.

Captain Djarmat gestures for the column to get underway and orders the jeep driver to accelerate. As the column passes Dr. Leong's tent, she waves to the captain. She then waves to the first lieutenant in the turret. Seeing Connors and Joe lounged out on the rear of the tank makes her smile, at first. Then, she just bursts out in laughter. These two characters are so out of place in this military environment. The captain must be bringing them along to humor the men. With smiles on their faces, the men in the rear of the military truck wave back to Dr. Leong. Dr. Leong wonders if the troops are smiling because they are glad to see that she greeted their departure, or if they are overcome with the sight of Connors and Joe on the rear of the tank. White monkeys, like Connors and Joe, provide a constant source of humor to the young Indonesian soldiers. Dr. Leong sometimes wonders how the young soldiers view her.

The road to the village retains the dampness from the morning moisture, making the travel pleasant. The usual afternoon dust clouds that often hamper travel do not test the drivers. Visibility is clear. The captain was correct to travel early.

The usual vegetation that encroaches into the roadway does not pester the troops in the canopy-less truck. The tank doubles as a road plow that crushes and discards anything in its path. Even the order of the column's vehicles proves effective. It is good to have an experienced soldier lead a column.

Entering the village, the captain notices that it appears to be deserted. The racket from the tank must have scared the natives into the jungle. The captain halts the procession when all vehicles have entered the clearing around the village. He orders the engines of the tank and the other vehicles turned off. The silence encourages one native to emerge from the jungle and enter the village. Connors identifies the native as the headman of the village and informs the captain of such.

Speaking through an interpreter, the captain explains to the headman his purpose in his village. The headman acknowledges and agrees to assist the soldiers. Once the headman spots Connors, he yells to him to confirm the soldiers' good intentions. Connors gestures and persuades the headman that the villagers have nothing to fear from the soldiers. Connors prays that he is right. The Indonesian soldiers have a nasty reputation for abusing the natives.

After some strange sounds from the headman, a few younger natives emerge from the jungle. One native, interestingly, brings Connors a bowl of jungle juice. The interchange between Connors and native over the jungle juice brings the troops in the truck to laughter. The captain has to remind them to be respectful of the monkeys. As difficult as it may be for the troops, they are the guests of the monkeys while they are in this village.

With the help of an interpreter, the headman informs the captain that two of the young natives will escort his column to the site where the snakes rest. The headman tells the captain that Connors and Joe have seen the site, so they will be able to confirm it when his village people point it out to his soldiers. The captain looks over at Connors for assurance. Connors, as his sips from the jungle juice bowl, raises his index finger as a gesture of confidence to the captain.

With escorts leading the way, the captain and one of his men mount the front of the tank and take seats on either side of the turret cannon. The tank proceeds to the rocky cliff area, mowing down whatever vegetation and other obstacles in its path. The captain has the troops disembark the truck and follow behind the tank. Connors and Joe are permitted to remain on the rear incline of the tank. The smiles of the troops, marching behind the tank, irritate Connors who understands that they are laughing at Joe and him.

The jeep driver and another soldier stand guard on the remaining vehicles. The headman attends to their every need. Although as Muslims they decline the jungle juice, the soldiers graciously accept the offer of wild berries and jungle fruits. It has been a while, since they tasted fresh fruits.

As the tank approaches the rocky cliff area, the captain has the troops fan out to form an arc around the front of the cliffs. The sound of M-16 rifles being prepared for automatic mode of operating serenade Connors and Joe. It is hard to forget the eerie ratcheting sound made when an M-16 is readied. Connors realizes that it would only take a second for the soldiers to turn those weapons on Joe and him. At this moment, he wonders why they would not do so. The snake trophies could make them all rich, if they were to dispense with Joe, the escorts and him. Connors breathes easier when he sees the soldiers begin to fan out as directed by the captain. Connors thanks his good fortune that these Indonesian soldiers are professional. Too many times, he has witnessed similar soldiers execute natives just for the fun of it.

Connors overhears one of the escorts point out one of the snakes emerging from the huge hole in the rocky cliffs. The captain orders the tank commander to take aim on the beast. The captain and the soldier sitting in the front of the tank disembark quickly in order to avoid being struck by the moving turret cannon. Before the snake has completely emerged from the hole in the cliffs, the first lieutenant reports that the tank has aim on the snake. The captain looks at Connors and Joe for a moment then orders the first lieutenant to fire upon the snake.

A loud noise erupts from the cannon that trembles the tank. Connors has to grab onto a railing welded onto the rear of the tank to prevent from falling off. Joe braced himself as soon as he heard the order to fire upon the snake. The projectile from the tank strikes the snake in the enlarged portion of his midsection just behind its head. Connors and Joe watch the flesh of the beast burst into the air. The head of the snake is tossed some five meters forward. The snakes tongue continues to sample the air a few moments after being severed from its body. The remaining rear portion of the snake attempts to coil near the entrance to the hole in the cliffs. The coiling is unsuccessful as the portion loses direction and just trembles. Where the midsection of the snake resided, just before the impact from the projectile, now exists a sizeable crater. Snake flesh and blood drips from the leaves of the surrounding vegetation.

Connors utters, "Poor bastard!"

Soon, the area around the snake's body parts settles into the calm that existed prior to the impact from the projectile. It is as if nothing happened at all. It is often that way in the jungle. One creature's misfortune only lasts for a few moments and then like the ocean swallowing up its victims, an eerie calm returns. Death is that way. Although, we seem important while living, our demise happens as quickly as it is passes into the past.

The captain orders the first lieutenant to fire a round into the overhead of the hole in the rocky cliffs in order to seal the hole and trap the remaining snakes inside. Another loud noise jerks the tank. Those present watch a portion of the overhead collapse. A small exit hole still remains. The captain orders a second round into the hole. Once again, the tank jerks. This time, the projectile collapses the entire overhead, sealing the hole.

The captain orders a cadre of his troops to inspect the hole and the surrounding area for any visible signs of the snakes or other possible accesses into the rocky cliffs. Some of the soldiers rush up to the rocky cliffs and commence inspecting the area. Others wander around the rear of the cliffs in order to detect any other entrances.

The two natives depart the group and wander a ways down the far end of the rocky cliffs where they observe two of the snakes squirming into the tall grass, making distance from the tank and the soldiers. The natives just smile and say nothing about the fleeing snakes. Once satisfied that the snakes have escaped, the two natives return to where the soldiers are assembled.

One of the soldiers has identified a possible entrance into the rocky cliffs. The captain orders the soldiers to grenade the small opening. A few moments pass before a moderately large explosion tosses dirt into the air from the side of the rocky cliffs. A report is heard that the opening has been sealed.

The captain offers Connors a canvas bag in which to carry back the snake's head as a trophy. Connors thanks the captain for his generosity and climbs down from the rear of the tank to fetch the head. According to the captain, the whole body might not be present, but at least he has the huge head that might be used to extrapolate the size of the beast. Joe accompanies Connors to retrieve the snake's head.

Upon reaching the site, Joe notices how much of the snake's head was preserved from the blast.

Joe to Connors, "Brad, you might be able to estimate the length of the snake from its head size. Captain Djarmat just might be right."

Connors "Mate, when it comes to a million dollars US, even the Americans want positive proof. I have been down this road before, you know. It all seems easy when you talk about it. But when it comes time to receive your rewards…well…things seems to get complicated. The person with the authority to make the award never seems to be available. And, when you finally meet that person, he refers to some committee approval as a requirement. Mate, you face an uphill battle all the way. However, if you are entitled to a reward and you can endure the gauntlet of letdowns, it eventually will come to you. My problem always has been enduring the letdowns. See, the letdowns take up time that could better be used doing other things that are more enjoyable. The key, I believe, is to make your claim for the reward and then just go about your life."

Joe nods approvingly, "I can go along with that, Brad."

Connors smiles, "I was hoping you would see it my way, Mate. I will submit the head via the Australian Biological Society in both our names. When the prize money comes through, I will contact you in Manila. Like I say, there is no need hanging around waiting for these blokes to make up their mind on the matter."

Joe smiles, "I surely do not want to spend any more time away from Manila…and civilization, then I have to. You got a deal, Brad."

As the two men are discussing the head size, the captain joins them.

Captain Djarmat "It sure is a good size head, isn't it?"

Connors smiles, "You bet it is, Captain. By the way, can we count on your assistance in exporting this head?"

Captain Djarmat "Yes, Mr. Connors, you can count on my assistance. I can have this snake's head airlifted to Jayapura tomorrow morning. Just provide me the instruction and the destination. I will do my best to see to it that your prize gets to where it needs to go."

Connors "Why are you being so accommodating, Captain?"

Captain Djarmat "We are not out of this encampment yet, Mr. Connors. Quite frankly, I suspect it will be a long haul for all of us. Anything, within reason, I can do to make your stay here comfortable, I will do for you. You have my word on that. In return, I only ask your cooperation and support."

Connors "I could offer you some of the prize money."

Captain Djarmat "I know you could, Mr. Connors, but I am a frontier soldier. I have been one all my career. Only Allah knows how I would fare, if I suddenly became wealthy. I believe wealth would detract from my ability to command in the field. Thank you just the same, Mr. Connors, but I enjoy the clarity of my life too much to muddy it."

Having said that, the captain returns to the tank where the soldiers are amassing. Connors and Joe remain silent and contemplate the captain's words. The words were powerful and made them examine their own lives.

Connors eventually speaks, "Well, Mate, we better be getting along, if we intend to return to the encampment with the column."

Joe nods in acknowledgment and walks behind Connors back to the tank. Both men walk back slowly. It is as if the captain's words were tugging on their legs, beckoning them to leave the snake's head where the found it. Connors' eagerness for sudden wealth prevails, and he snuggles the canvas bag containing the snake's head closer to his body. For Connors, the snake's head is an opportunity to leave this jungle environment forever.

Joe, on the other hand, is affected by the captain's words. Whether or not Connors lives up to his promise is no longer important to him. What would he do differently with a large amount of money? He would still remain in Manila, drinking and whoring his life away. Right now, the lack of a large sum of money enables him to recuperate between nights out on the town. He chuckles at the thought that more money might actually lead to a quicker death. His body demands the recuperation time.

Once assembled at the tank, the captain, through an interpreter, thanks the headman and then orders the troops into the vehicles. Surprisingly, the natives are all smiles when the column departs the village. The headman presents Connors another bowl of jungle juice to comfort him during the trip back. Connors suspects that the natives pulled something over on the soldiers.

The trip back is somewhat more uncomfortable than the morning travel. The equatorial sun has evaporated the moisture in the roadway. Dust clouds rise up as the vehicles press the earth under their wheels and tracks. The driver of the military truck has to slow down in order to allow the dust cloud to clear and enable him to see the road ahead. Although the vision of the tank driver is little affected, the dust cloud created by the lead vehicle seems to settle down upon the after portion of the tank's turret...where Connors and Joe are resting. There is little protection for the two men, as the dust piles up on their bodies and the area behind the turret. Within the first few kilometers of travel, Connors and Joe are covered with dirt. They decide to endure the misfortune rather than disembark the tank and walk back to the encampment.

Upon entering the encampment, Dr. Leong is shocked to see Connors and Joe adorned in a blanket of road soot. They look like they have survived an artillery barrage. She hurries to their aid, as the tank comes to a halt. Both men spend a few minutes trying to brush and shake the road debris from their clothing and person. For the most part, they are unsuccessful. Hurrying into their tent, they quickly disrobe and apply generous amounts of water to their hair and bodies. There are no showers, so bird bathing with bottled water has to suffice.

While Connors and Joe attend to their persons, Dr. Leong inquires of the captain how the mission went. The captain informs her that the snakes have been neutralized. One has been confirmed dead while the other two are presumed trapped inside an underground grave. The captain directs Dr. Leong to assist Connors with the trophy head. He asks if she could provide whatever scientific assessment on the snake's head that she could in order to help expedite Connors' aspirations.

After Dr. Leong departs to assist Connors, the second lieutenant informs the captain that dispatches arrived during his absence. One of the correspondences from Djakarta alerts the encampment that a scientific team will arrive any day to conduct additional testing on the tree. Though there is no mention of the size of the incoming party, Captain Djarmat orders two more tents erected to house the newcomers. Interestingly, in another dispatch from Djakarta, the Mining Ministry commends the encampment military staff for assisting the ongoing scientific research that has produced a large mining contract with the Japanese government. Captain Djarmat can sense his promised promotion being awarded soon. For the first time, he can feel his long years in the frontier paying dividends to his career.

Lastly, the Military Command Jayapura has recommended to the officer commanding that the alert status be reduced at the encampment. According to their memo, joint international research has concluded that the potential for danger from the tree anomaly is considered to be insignificant. This news startles the captain, but he welcomes it. With the snakes neutralized, he orders the second lieutenant to reduce the number of perimeter sentries. Naturally, this action will enable the troops to have more leisure time. According to the captain, this may not be a blessing. He needs to be innovative and keep his troops busy with other assignments. Too much free time eventually leads to breaches in discipline.

After Joe finishes bird bathing and changing his attire, he notices a new dispatch on the table. He settles into a chair and opens the envelope. It contains a letter from Watson at the ADB informing him to expect a joint American and Japanese scientific delegation. He has been directed to provide whatever assistance desired. Nothing specific is requested in the memo, and the reason for their coming is left unannounced. Joe believes that the memo is too vague. There is something terribly wrong, but he has no idea what to do about it. For whatever reason, his buddy Watson is keeping him in the dark. Watson does not even place cues in the memo to alert Joe, but the very nature of the letter alerts Joe that something is amiss.

Joe shares his concerns with Connors who just laughs them off. Connors is satisfied with his snake's head. Other concerns take a backseat to the million-dollar bounty occupying center stage in his mind.

Dr. Leong enters the tent and asks to see the snake's head, commenting on Captain Djarmat's request. Connors opens the canvas bag and shows the doctor the head. After careful examination, the doctor concludes that Connors should have no trouble convincing the Australia Biological Society that this head belonged to a creature in excess of ten meters in length. Connors produces an ear-to-ear smile and exclaims: "Bloody hell, I am rich!" Dr. Leong and Joe are taken by surprise over Connors' sudden burst of enthusiasm. Both realize that many miles and pitfalls exist between where the snake's head sits currently in the tent and its eventual appearance before an Australian committee.

In Dr. Yanagi's tent, the news of the demise of the huge snakes does not produce any excitement whatsoever. To the Japanese, the snake adventure was merely a distraction. Apparently, to Dr. Yanagi and Sugai, the encampment personnel just embarked on a big game hunt to kill some time and liven up the assignment. News from Japan that does alert them, however, is the announcement of an additional scientific team. Although the purpose of the visit from the new team remains unspoken, Dr. Yanagi can feel the sensitivity of the investigation increasing. These new scientists are not coming to the encampment to assist him. They are coming for an entirely different purpose.

In a related correspondence from Tokyo, Dr. Yanagi takes pride in learning that the Japanese government has concluded successfully the rights to mine the area around the encampment for iron ore. He envisions tremendous potential for Japan in this acquisition.

This evening the encampment personnel are more upbeat than any previous time. The news in general is good and promising. All this time wasted in the jungle is paying off for everyone involved. The general opinion is that it will not be long before this assignment is over, and the encampment personnel are released from quarantine.

CHAPTER 20

▼

NARITA INTERNATIONAL AIRPORT, TOKYO

The first thing that strikes someone as odd upon entering Japan is the vision of their security forces. Their entire uniform, including the helmet, is jet black in color. Unlike the uniforms of security personnel in other parts of the world, these uniforms are designed to fit snuggly. Pant cuffs are neatly stowed, in the military fashion of the First Great War, into calf-high, laced, black boots. The helmet is fastened securely in a manner reminiscent of an American football player's headgear. The shoulder-strapped weapon, also black, is the latest model, German-made, machine pistol. This security force evokes the sense of readiness, so much so, that one gets the impression that they are robots.

The second striking feature is the orderliness with which the passengers go about their business within the terminal. People take their proper seats in waiting lounges. People stand in long lines for refreshments and exhibit no signs of annoyance. Silence, despite the roar of the airplane engines and the intermittent announcements over the loudspeaker, permeates every corridor of the airport.

In Tokyo to the residents, Narita is not known foremost for its airport. The large Buddhist Temple is the magnet that attracts visitors and residents alike. Even if one's religious preference is not Buddhism, Narita houses a number of fine cultural exchange establishments. One in particular is a bookstore that features titles, in both English and Japanese, written by the nation's most prominent writers. The certainty of obtaining any copy of one of Yukio Mishima's or Yasunuri Kawabata's works, in English or Japanese, is guaranteed. Narita is a haven for Westerners attempting to appreciate Japanese culture.

Mr. Takeda and other members of the Japanese Foreign Ministry meet the MIT delagations, as they disembark their plane. Since Foreign Ministry personnel are escorting the delegation, passage through customs and immigration goes unhindered. The delegation is awed by the efficiency with which the Japanese maneuver their way through the airport bureaucracy and the streets of Tokyo to the Foreign Ministry buildings. Similar, robot-like, security personnel mark the entrance to the Foreign Ministry. The delegation feels like they have entered a military regime.

Once inside the office spaces of the Foreign Ministry, past the entry checkpoint personnel, the attitude becomes more relaxed and ameliorating. Seated in a plush reception area, the delegates are indulged with gourmet teas and French-style pastries. Waiters attend to their every epicurean desire. Bus boys from the hotel, assigned to their accommodations, gather their travel bags and provide the delegates their room keys. Without exception, the delegates conclude that this trip will be enjoyable.

Having won the admiration of the American delegation, Mr. Takeda outlines their itinerary. Following a short familiarization tour of the areas within the Foreign Ministry where they will be working, the delegation is ushered to their five-star accommodations for a few hours of refreshing and relaxing. It has been a very long flight from Boston to Tokyo. The delegates require time to adjust to the time zone change and refresh themselves in a hot shower. Regrettably, the Foreign Ministry felt it was too sudden to indulge their guests in a Japanese-style hot bath. That pleasure to the skin will have to wait another time.

By early afternoon, the delegates have been assembled in a conference room to meet with their counterparts from the Japanese Ministry of Information & Technology. Mr. Takeda will moderate the meeting with Mr. Kajoka chairing for the Information Ministry.

This conference room is smaller than the usual meeting rooms for dignitaries. However, it is large enough to accommodate the participants, and it has the benefit of being far enough away from the routine traffic of the Foreign Ministry. There are no windows in order to prevent surveillance from the outside areas. In a sense, it is an ideal location for the topic under discussion.

Adhering to the usual protocol, the Americans are seated to one side of the oval-shaped, conference table while the Japanese occupy the other side. The entrances to the room are located to the back of the Japanese participants in order to facilitate to and from administrative traffic. The staff provides hot tea and an assortment of tasty rice cakes to the participants.

After a short greeting, Kajioka introduces the members of the Japanese team. Dr. Hansen reciprocates with an introduction of the American team. All team members from both countries have either worked with the sound recordings, or they possess expertise in the issues to be discussed. Some of the Americans represent the *avant guarde* class of their scientific discipline.

Interestingly, after the introductions, it is Dr. Hansen that commences the discussion.

Dr. Hansen "Mr. Kajioka, it is our understanding that your government has conducted a series of tests in New Guinea on the source of these sound recordings, is that correct?"

Kajioka, hesitant to responds, "Yes, we have, Dr. Hansen, but, for the most part, those tests were just preliminary. They were more in line with acclimatizing ourselves with the anomaly."

Dr. Hansen, in a bold move, "Mr. Kajioka, is that why your government utilized a secret satellite in conjunction with your communications satellite over Singapore?"

The pleasant atmosphere of cooperation, established since the Americans arrived, just dissipated. The Japanese are embarrassed. How did the Americans find out? No one on the Japanese side of the table wants to respond to Dr. Hansen's question.

Moments pass, as Kajioka and the rest of the delegation just stare into the eyes of Dr. Hansen. Silence flows over the table like an incoming wave gushing inland from the shoreline.

Finally, Dr. Hansen says, "I am sorry. Did I speak out of turn?"

Kajioka "No, Dr. Hansen, you did not. We were hoping we could discuss that issue a little later in the conversation."

Dr. Hansen "There is a time and a place for everything, is that it?"

Kajioka "It is something like that, yes."

Dr. Hansen "Alright, are you prepared to discuss any of the preliminary tests that you conducted on this anomaly in New Guinea at this time?"

Kajioka "Dr. Hansen, you have to understand we did not know what we were dealing with here when the anomaly was first reported. Actually, the initial request for us to investigate came from the Asian Development Bank in Manila. Initially, our position was that we were trying to resolve a hold up in a development project. Some very strange reports were emanating from a little known part of the world, and we were requested to check them out. The initial reports were of such a bizarre nature that we just discounted them as nonsense. However, since our country was a major donor to the Asian Development Bank, and we invested heavily into this particular project in New Guinea, we felt obligated to go through the motions of an investigation."

Dr. Hansen "So, you could say that this anomaly took you by surprise, is that it?"

Kajioka "Without question, this anomaly appeared without warning and, quite frankly, defied our wildest imaginations. We had no idea what to do, so we resorted to our investigative procedures employed in other recent, exploration projects. We went into default mode, so to speak."

Dr. Hansen "Are you willing to share what you have discovered thus far?"

Kajioka looks over at Takeda for approval to continue. Takeda nods to proceed.

Kajioka stutters a bit, "Dr. Hansen, please understand that what we have to share with you is difficult for us to reveal. We consider ourselves rational individuals and dedicated to the scientific method. However, our discoveries appear to cling to the periphery of our beliefs, and I am being polite by stating such."

Dr. Hansen chuckles, "My, my, what have you discovered, if I may ask?"

Dr. Hansen looks over at the faces of the three scientists in the American delegation, as if to say, "Brace yourselves, fellows!"

Kajioka "If you will permit me, Dr. Hansen, allow me to reveal our findings one at a time."

Dr. Hansen, now expressing a serious concern, "Of course, by all means, proceed as slowly as you feel necessary, Mr. Kajioka."

Kajioka "First, the anomaly, a tree, is composed of iron-based compounds."

Dr. Hansen looks intently at Mr. Kajioka. His lips roll up together, as his head bows down, as if to say: "What are you talking about?"

Kajioka "We have double- and tripled-checked these results. A biological laboratory in Indonesian has confirmed our results."

Dr. Hansen "You have discovered a metal tree, is that what you are saying, Mr. Kajioka?"

Kajioka, being careful in his choice of words, "To be accurate, Dr. Hansen, we have discovered a metal structure that, for some reason, is masquerading as a tree."

Dr. Hansen gapes, "Did you say 'masquerade?'"

Kajioka "Yes, I did. The word 'masquerade' brings us to our second discovery: the metal tree creates a bark-like covering that resembles that of similar trees in the jungle area."

Dr. Hansen still gaping, "There is bark, too!"

Kajioka "Yes, the bark of this metal tree is composed of a mixture of iron-based compounds, some hydrocarbons, magma and silicates. The bark acts as an epidermis for the metal tree."

Dr. Hansen "Do you have samples of this bark?"

Kajioka "We had samples. That brings us to our third discovery. The bark, after being removed from the metal tree for about three days, decomposes into a concentrated seawater solution. Both our laboratory and the laboratory in Indonesian have confirmed that the resultant seawater solution is harmless."

Dr. Hansen "This is very interesting, Mr. Kajioka. Does the metal tree resemble the other trees in the jungle?"

Kajioka "According to our expert in New Guinea, the metal tree resembles similar trees in the immediate area of the jungle. However, its leaves are not sensitive to the changing position of the sun. The metal tree does not exhibit any signs of photosynthesis."

Dr. Hansen "If what you are telling us is correct, this metal tree is camouflaging itself."

Kajioka "Camouflage was our determination, as well."

Dr. Hansen "It must have been difficult to identify this tree."

Kajioka "Actually, we were called in to research this tree for another reason. Our first introduction to this metal tree was the inability of the on-site forestry crew to cut down the tree. This brings us to the fourth discovery: the tree is indestructible."

Dr. Hansen "How can that possibly be the case?"

Kajioka "After a series of top-of-the-line chainsaws were destroyed, and dynamite failed to tarnish the inner tree's surface, we came to that conclusion."

Dr. Hansen "I take it you can remove the bark."

Kajioka "Yes, the bark is removed with ease. That brings us to our fifth discovery: the bark regenerates in a few days. By regeneration, I mean that the entire bark area removed regenerates, as if it had never been disturbed."

Dr. Hansen glancing over intently at his colleagues, "Are you saying that this metal tree has regenerative capabilities?"

Kajioka "Yes, I am, Dr. Hansen. However, the regeneration resembles more that of reptiles than that of ordinary trees. The regeneration is not a healing process, observed in regular tree bark. It is, in fact, a complete regeneration."

Dr. Hansen "This is unbelievable!"

Kajioka "I hope you can begin to appreciate the state of our minds, as we began to accumulate these discoveries. Quite frankly, we felt that we had stepped out of our world into another one in which we roamed about in awe and without any sense of direction."

Dr. Hansen "It must have been a wonderful world to be in, even for just a moment, was it not?"

Kajioka smiles, "Yes, as a matter of fact, it was wonderful. For once in our lives, we felt alive and overflowing with excitement at the possibilities."

Dr. Hansen thinks a moment over what Kajioka has just said: "Our research has unearthed some startling discoveries, as well. Shall I go on, Mr. Kajioka?"

Kajioka, feeling relieved, just gestures affirmatively, "Yes, Doctor, please go on."

Dr. Hansen "Our research has indicated that unusual abilities seem to evolve within us as a result of our exposure to the sound recordings, and they are not novel."

Kajioka interrupts, "What do you mean?"

Dr. Hansen "These unusual abilities adapt to us too easily, Mr. Kajioka. Our research has concluded that we have experienced these unusual abilities and the other effects from the sound recordings at some earlier period."

The facial expressions of the entire Japanese delegation transforms into one of confusion.

Dr. Hansen, sensing the bewilderment of his Japanese counterparts, explains, "What I mean by 'an earlier period' is an earlier time in the history of our species."

From the sustained, confused expression on the faces of the Japanese delegation, their comprehension of Dr. Hansen's explanation has not improved.

Dr. Hansen embarks on another tack, "In the last half of the century, much data concerning our brain power has indicated that there are large portions of the organ that remain idle. The general response has been orchestrated to provide hope for the future evolution of our species. Interestingly, our other observations of natural development within our species, and other species, provide a response quite the contrary. Without exception, additional organs...idle in recent generations...have been explained as refuse from our progressive evolution. Our exposure to these sound recordings 're-awakened' some of those 'idle portions' of our brain. To us, the implication that at some earlier period we employed those idle portions of our brain haunts our perception of reality."

Kajioka leans back in his chair, "You are saying that we have experienced the multi-dimensional world contained within these sound recordings. Is that your conclusion, Dr. Hansen?"

Dr. Hansen "Yes, Mr. Kajioka, our species has adapted, through evolution, to this multi-dimensional world. We once lived in such a world. We once communicated in the language of such a world."

Kajioka looks around at the other members of the Japanese delegation. Disbelief would be an understatement of the interpretation from their facial expressions.

Kajioka "How could this be, Doctor?"

Dr. Hansen "Over the millennia, we have taken great strikes in codifying our experience of the world. Much of that codification has come from a preference of reason over the other modes of interpreting reality. Taking a notion from Eastern philosophy, our Western ideas have evolved from an intentional discarding of the emotional and physical senses in difference to our intellectual abilities. Recent research in brain response to stimuli has proven what Eastern philosophy has known for millennia: the emotional sense, or mind, responds faster than the intellectual power of choice. Succinctly, our bodies do, in fact, select choices before we can reason the existence of those choices. We in the West have walked down the wrong path into the darkness. It is our own mental constructs that have blinded us from reality."

Kajioka "I am not sure that I am following you, Dr. Hansen."

Dr. Hansen provides another example: "What I am trying to say is that Quantum Mechanics better ascribes reality than our Newtonian constructs."

Kajioka "I believe that science has accepted that reality of Quantum Mechanics."

Dr. Hansen "Yes, it has but not in the manner presented by these sound recordings: a multi-dimensional reality."

Kajioka "Quantum Mechanics does not suggest a multi-dimensional reality, Dr. Hansen. Quantum Mechanics is a probability laden enterprise."

Dr. Hansen "Mr. Kajioka, the probability of Quantum Mechanics is our means of explaining the phenomenon of interacting with a multi-dimensional reality that we have yet to comprehend. In a sense, the probability of Quantum Mechanics is an extension of our limited scientific vocabulary. Clearly, when we observe the visual displays of the sound recordings, we can identify how some things suddenly appear then disappear as a result of passing through various dimensions. Recall the standard example of an encased treasure chest existing in the second dimension that can be easily entered via the third dimension, as if magic had been spelled, and the contents of the treasure chest made to disappear."

Kajioka smiles, "Correct me if I am mistaken, Dr. Hansen. What you are proposing is that multi-dimensionality is reality. Is that correct?"

Dr. Hansen "Yes, Mr. Kajioka, the multi-dimensionality contained within the sound recordings represents our true reality."

Kajioka has to take a short pause in order to internalize the implications. He discusses in Japanese with Mr. Takeda. Mr. Takeda encourages him to continue the meeting.

Kajioka shares some doubts, "How could we have overlooked these capabilities for so long?"

Dr. Hansen "As I spoke earlier, we in the West have given dominion to reason over the other senses. We have discarded the inputs from the other senses as nonsense. We even discarded some of our intellectual inputs, as well, like myths. The last two millennia underwent great efforts to subdue all myths that conflicted with reason. Reason is a construct of our experience in the third dimension and our struggles to understand the fourth dimension. It is our creation of reason with its confines within the third and fourth dimensions that has blinded us from reality."

Kajioka chuckles, "You cannot be saying that our myths were once real, can you?"

Dr. Hansen smiles, "Our myths originated from another dimension above the fourth. They only seemed difficult to comprehend within the confines of the third and fourth dimensions. If you find our myths of old incomprehensible, I urge you to revisit our latest constructs of reality with string theories. Just because we label something as scientific does not make it any more correct than the ramblings of a shaman. As I observed the visual displays of the sound recordings, more and more, I began to realize how closer to reality those ancient shamans were. What seems ridiculous to us today about the activities of the shamans of old, now, turns the tables upon our own activities and reflects our own ridiculousness back to the shamans."

Kajioka "Dr. Hansen, the shaman talked to rocks and trees for guidance."

Dr. Hansen smiles, "Interesting that you should mention that, Mr. Kajioka. One of our goals in this meeting is to arrange for a joint effort between our governments in order to 'talk' to your tree in New Guinea."

Kajioka politely explains to Takeda what the Americans have just proposed. Takeda speaks perfect English and does not require translation. However, Takeda does need the time to refocus his sense of reality. In disbelief, the Japanese delegation agrees to the joint effort proposed by the Americans.

Kajioka after some deliberation with Takeda, "How do you plan to 'talk' to the tree, Dr. Hansen?"

Takeda realizes that it was a wise choice to use an out of the way meeting room for this discussion. If anyone overheard this conversation, the Tokyo press would feast on the absurdity.

Dr. Hansen "We have developed a crude multi-dimensional language that we can feed into the tree. We just need your support to hook up the electronics for the transmission."

Kajioka "Have you brought this language with you?"

Dr. Hansen "Yes, we have. It is contained in a software package and able to be generated with our latest electronic constructions."

Kajioka "What are the transmission requirements?"

Dr. Hansen "We can transmit the language on a carrier frequency in resonance with the tree, or we can input directly with physical contact."

Kajioka gets a suggestion from the Electronics Crew Chief, "What are the power requirements?"

Dr. Hansen "Our electronics have been designed to operate with your power characteristics."

Kajioka gestures to the Electronics Crew Chief to speak directly to Dr. Hansen.

Electronics Crew Chief "Dr. Hansen, we have a sounding apparatus on-site with which we can attach transmitters directly to the tree. In addition, we have a similar apparatus here for your team to inspect and evaluate for compatibility with your equipment."

Dr. Hansen thanks the Electronics Crew Chief for the offer and information. Members of the American delegation are assigned to check out the sound apparatus.

Dr. Hansen to Kajioka, "You said that you have a sound apparatus on-site in New Guinea. What were you sounding?"

Kajioka looks over at Takeda for permission to responds. Takeda nods to go ahead.

Kajioka "We were sounding the depth of the roots of the tree."

Dr. Hansen with a strange look on his face, "What did you find out from the soundings?"

Kajioka "Our sounding estimate the depth to be some two hundred or so kilometers into the earth."

Dr. Hansen places both hands on the meeting table firmly, "My God, two hundred meters! This tree is a monster!"

Kajioka "Let me restate that figure, Dr. Hansen. I said two hundred KILO-meters not two hundred meters."

The eyes of the American delegation seem to be readying to launch out of their heads.

After a long period of silence, Dr. Hansen says, "Two hundred kilometers would place the roots in the mantle."

Kajioka nods his head up and down, "Yes, Dr. Hansen, we came to that realization, as well. Whatever we are dealing with extends into the mantle of the earth. Whatever we are dealing with possesses regenerative powers, is indestructible, operates in dimensions above the sixth and is at least two hundred kilometers long."

Dr. Hansen in disbelief, "Are you certain of your soundings?"

Kajioka "We are as certain as the accuracy of our instruments. As for certainty in general, I believe our discussion today calls for a re-definition of certainty."

Now, the American delegation, once confident, exhibits signs of exhaustion and bewilderment. Although no words are spoken, it is clear that on the minds of each member of the American delegation is the same question: Are we sure that we want to communicate with something this large and powerful? Size has a strange way of differentiating what matters!

CHAPTER 21

▼

ENCAMPMENT, NEW GUINEA

After having tested the language hardware assembly for proper operation with the on-site sounding apparatus, the Americans inform Dr. Yanagi that they are ready to attempt to communicate with the tree. Dr. Yanagi perplexed by the entire proposal requests a brief on the process. Since communication with his superiors in Japan has been limited, he has to be certain of the intentions of what is being proposed here.

Only a few Japanese technicians accompanied the American delagation, headed by Dr. Hansen. Since they just arrived earlier this morning, Dr. Yanagi was caught unprepared. Other than a note on their coming, Dr. Yanagi has no idea what was expected.

Dr. Hansen, with some support from his scientific colleagues, outlines the communication effort to Dr. Yanagi. As a backup, the Americans' rendition is translated into Japanese by one of the accompanying Japanese technicians in order to insure Dr. Yanagi's comprehension. Essentially, the software program is generated in the Americans' electronic assembly and patched into the sounding apparatus for transmission into the tree. Rather than pinging into the tree, the sound apparatus' detector-transmitters will be inputting information.

Additionally, a modified, visual display of the sounds emanating from within the tree during the communication effort will be available. During the interim between a pulsed communications into the tree, the visual display will enable the technicians to monitor the changes in the sound patterns, as the tree responds to the input signals from the sound apparatus.

After listening to the proposal, Dr. Yanagi asks, "From your brief, Dr. Hansen, I am getting the impression that you believe that this tree possesses intelligence. Is that correct?"

Dr. Hansen "Yes, Dr. Yanagi, we hold the belief that whatever this tree is that it possesses intelligence. When I refer to intelligence, I am restricting the definition to the 'emergence' phenomenon."

Dr. Yanagi "I see. As you are aware, Dr. Hansen, 'emergence' is not a widely accepted concept. There exists strong opposition to any such a notion."

Dr. Hansen, looking around the tent a moment to assess the audience, responds, "Most of that opposition originates from religious based organizations that have not had enough time to internalize the implications of the concept. And, I admit, Dr. Yanagi, it is a troublesome concept for them to accept. However, I believe the Eastern philosophies are more adaptable to the notion of 'emergence' than their Western counterparts."

Dr. Yanagi "Correct me, Dr. Hansen, if I am wrong. Does not the idea of 'emergence' propose that our intellectual capacity 'emerges' out of the inter-functioning of our other bodily processes?"

Dr. Hansen "Yes, you could explain it simply in that manner. I prefer to use an Eastern philosophical example in which 'emergence' is equated to our intellectual mind. With that equation established the intellectual mind evolves out of the emotional mind, as the emotional mind evolves out of the physical mind. Interestingly, recent research in the United States has confirmed that the emotional portions of our brain respond before our intellectual capacities recognize the stimulus. Supporting data for 'emergence' is mounting."

Dr. Yanagi "I see your position, Dr. Hansen. I take it that you consider this tree to have attained some form of intellectual capacity through some form of 'emergence.'"

Dr. Hansen "Yes, we do, Dr. Yanagi. We also contend that the tree has attained an 'emergence' level somewhere between the sixth and the twelfth dimensions."

Dr. Yanagi "Why do you propose such a high level of dimensional capability?"

Dr. Hansen "In order for this tree to exhibit the strange phenomena that you have reported it would require an ability to re-align itself at the crystalline structural level. We have theorized that a feature like that could only materialize as a result of an interaction within the Higgs field that currently warrants activity in the twelfth dimension."

Dr. Yanagi "I see. I see. You have contemplated mass to energy conversion."

Dr. Hansen "We have considered much more than mere conversion, Dr. Yanagi. We have stipulated an intentional mass to energy conversion."

Dr. Yanagi smiles, "An intellectually guided crystalline structure re-configuration would account for the phenomena that I have been reporting to Tokyo."

Dr. Hansen "Yes, we read those reports thoroughly, Dr. Yanagi."

Dr. Yanagi "Does it not bother you when you consider how deep this tree's substructure extends?"

Dr. Hansen "Yes, we are awed by the size. However, the sooner we communicate with this entity, the better our understanding of its existence will become. We need to know why it is suddenly here."

Dr. Yanagi "It is so true. Anything, erecting a column of magma over five meters into the air and maintaining it that way, deserves our undivided attention. Theoretically, this entity could be spouting lava, emanating from the mantle, anywhere on the globe. When you consider its origin as the mantle, it could easily cover the earth with lava and extinguish all life."

Dr. Hansen "I must admit, Dr. Yanagi, when you highlight our situation in that manner, it is a scary thought. This tree could be the harbinger of doomsday…Armageddon, even!"

Dr. Yanagi shrugs off the comment, "Armageddon! The Christians do have colorful, yet macabre, endings to their creation stories, don't they?"

The Americans, realizing the Japanese are mostly Buddhists, a religion containing no such doomsday calamities, chuckle at their own subscriptions.

Dr. Yanagi, sensing the disturbance from his comment, continues, "When do we start this communication effort?"

With Captain Djarmat's permission, the American and Japanese scientists assemble their electronic apparati around the tree while Sugai clears the bark away from the area of the tree to be used as a connection for the detector-transmitters. Some of the Indonesian soldiers provide shade devices. Dr. Yanagi invites Dr. Leong to observe the communication effort. Connors and Del Rosi are left to their snake's head.

In an effort to reduce the amount of airborne dust, Captain Djarmat has some of his soldiers sprinkle water on the dry ground in the area surrounding the scientists' devices. This time of day is prone to mini-dust storms, as the breeze from the ocean massages the encampment.

Dr. Yanagi checks for proper connection of the detector-transmitters to the tree while Dr. Hansen monitors the proper operation of his electronic equipment. When both men are satisfied that the equipment is functioning properly, they agree to commence the test.

Dr. Yanagi orders Sugai to energize the detector-transmitters. Dr. Hansen watches the visual displays develop on his monitors. It is the first time that Dr. Yanagi and Sugai have seen the visual displays. Dr. Hansen provides them with an overview of what they are witnessing on the monitor. The key to the communication effort is to identify any change in the visual displays once an information signal has been transmitted into the tree.

With proper operation and a clear visual display established, Dr. Hansen transmits the first message into the tree. The Americans have devised five messages, ranging from geometry to strange, multi-dimensional abstractions. The first message is geometric in design.

After a few moments of observation, the monitors indicate no change whatsoever from the first message. Some of the scientists hypothesize that the geometric message must be too low in dimension to have been perceived. It is an appealing interpretation. After all, how often does one notice a perturbation from the first dimension? A one-dimensional entity could be screaming as loud as it could but would remain as simply static to a three-dimensional entity. This brings up another question for the scientists: Is sound dimensional? It must be able to transcend dimensions. After all, the visual displays from the tree's sounds seem to indicate various dimensional qualities. The next question poses a more serious concern: When does sound communicate intent? Static seems to have no intent. Are there dimensional thresholds to overcome in order to communicate intent?

The second message contains another, but more complicated, geometric component. Likewise, the monitors indicate no change or response. Dr. Hansen concludes that three-dimensional geometry, regardless of complexity, does not affect the tree.

The third message begins to introduce elementary abstractions. This time, the monitors indicate changes in a number of the visuals on the screen. The change is rapid, so Dr. Hansen has the message repeated a few times in order to decipher a pattern in the changes. Interestingly, after three messages, the tree stops responding to the messages. In subsequent trials, Dr. Hansen attempts to change amplitude and frequency to no avail. For some reason, the tree absorbs the message within three repetitions and then becomes immune to it, so to speak.

Dr. Hansen decides to send the fourth message containing more complicated abstractions. Once again, the visual displays change. With the input of these abstractions, Dr. Hansen observes a distinct pattern in the changes on the visual displays. In conference with the other American scientists, they theorize what is happening is that the tree is somehow categorizing the input signal in repositories of data of various dimensions. The threshold concept begins to emerge as a dominant force in communication with the tree. Specifically, in order to be sensed by the tree, the signal must overcome some dimensional threshold.

One of the American scientists proffers that what could be being witnessed on the displays is some form of multi-dimensional, antibiotic-like, defense mechanism: Strange signals enter the tree, and in turn, the tree's sensory systems classify the signal. If the classification is meaningless to the tree, like beneath a threshold requirement, then the intellectual component of the tree is not bothered by the input signal. The input signal, being of no interest to the intellectual portion, gets stored in a repository for future comparison and response.

Despite the weird nature of the idea, the analogy with biological systems succeeds in winning over supporters from the American scientists. Interestingly, biological systems agitate the discussion with respect to their origin. If, in fact, the tree does possess some sort of internal defense mechanism, as described, then it follows that it is quite possible that the tree's defense mechanism could be a primer for our biological systems. All of a sudden, the idea surfaces like a submarine broaching a calm sea: the tree might have come first. Biological creatures, as we know them, might have evolved from this entity or something similar.

Dr. Hansen proceeds with the last signal, a concoction of perceived multi-dimensional abstractions. The visual displays vibrate and elongate in response. Whatever the Americans created in the fifth signal got the tree's attention. Some of the similar changes observed in signals three and four are observed. Yet, the changes are now more distinct and vibrant. The displays continue to adjust. Dr. Hansen does not have to repeat the signal. The displays seem to be trying to unravel the signal. One scientist suggests that the tree is acting similar to a powerful computer that has been given a complex, mathematical problem to solve. Dr. Hansen agrees. Whatever they inputted might have overwhelmed the tree's defense mechanisms.

After moments of watching changes take place on the monitor, the scientists notice a small black dot appear to enlarge in the lower corner. As the dot enlarges, the changes on the display attenuate, until they cease. The screen becomes motionless. Nothing is moving. Another black dot enlarges in the upper corner of the monitor, as the black dot in the lower corner contracts. Soon the upper black dot contracts without any change noticeable anywhere on the monitor. It is over!

Repeated inputs of the fifth signal fail to produce any changes. Apparently, the fifth signal has been absorbed into the tree's repository like a vaccine. Although some success seemed imminent from the fifth signal, it would appear that the signal was insufficient to overcome the tree's threshold for communication.

Dr. Yanagi "The tree must know that we are here, Dr. Hansen."

Dr. Hansen "I believe the question now for us all is who are 'we' to this tree."

Dr. Yanagi "You would think an entity encountering another entity, for the first time, would want to communicate: if for anything at all, to express its defense mechanisms and scare us off."

Dr. Hansen smiles, "I do not believe this is the tree's first encounter with us, Dr. Yanagi. No, I do not believe that at all. I think it knows of us. The question is: what does it know of us?"

Dr. Yanagi affirmatively responds, "We are the human race. We have dominion over this world. That tree needs to communicate to us its intentions. If it knows us, then it must know we will destroy it."

Dr. Hansen "It would be difficult to destroy the mantle, Dr. Yanagi. Besides, if the tree wanted to harm us, it would have done so already. No, there is something else here."

Dr. Yanagi "I see this thing as dangerous."

Dr. Hansen "I do, too, but I think our sense of danger is misplaced."

Dr. Yanagi "We cannot allow something this humongous to exist. Its very size is threatening."

Dr. Hansen looking around the encampment, "Gentlemen, what do you see here?"

What to look at puzzles the other scientists.

Dr. Hansen "We see life all around us. We give preference to that which moves. Yet, that which moves dies. And, new life sprouts up everywhere to replace it. We notice this, because it happens within the time of our life. What if we were to suppose a time beyond that of our lives? What if we were to suppose a time beyond all our lives?"

The scientists remain quite and contemplate the possibility.

Dr. Hansen "Look at the heavens. There are times out there that certainly will exceed our existence as a species. There are entities out there, as well, that die and other entities that are born. I believe that we have encountered one such entity, today."

One of the American scientists, "I am not ready to conclude, Dr. Hansen, that our species is meaningless."

Other scientists express their opinions. The consensus is that humans are important and not some lost and meaningless by-product.

Dr. Hansen furthers the discussion, "How does a star suddenly appear?"

The group provides a number of explanations. Nonetheless, the issue of suddenness or epiphany puzzles everyone: How does that epiphany occur?

Dr. Hansen after a few moments of silence, "We cause the epiphany. We, we humans, make it happen, like sperm in an ovary."

One scientist "Are you comparing us as cosmic sperm, Dr. Hansen?"

Dr. Hansen "When was the last time, you received a message from your sperm?"

The biological analogy seems to take root in everyone. Each sperm is an individual entity, many times smaller than its human host. The similarity to what has been witnessed is astounding. The notion of humans as equivalent to individual cells in the body with respect to their possible composite within a larger, unmovable entity; such as a city, state or the planet, entertains the scientists.

Dr. Hansen "Why cannot we communicate with our sperm in order to insure the right one does the job? Why cannot our sperm communicate with us? Think of the lifetime of a sperm. What can a sperm possibly learn about the host he lives in or the one he will be deposited in? How does he learn? For that matter, how would we learn of a larger entity comprised of humans?"

Dr. Yanagi "I can appreciate your dimensional analogy, Dr. Hansen. But, how could this tree have acquired so much ability?"

Dr. Hansen "Your question is well put, Dr. Yanagi. I believe the difference lies with our separateness and biology. Our separateness has allowed us to venture into many side alleys. We have strayed afar from our origin. This entity has maintained the course because of its singularity. Alchemy versus chemistry is our dilemma. In alchemy, we look back to an origin for the source of knowledge. In chemistry, we follow science into the future to acquire knowledge. Both directions are circuitous and eventually lead us to where we desire to go. The entity remained at the origin. We, we humans, discarded our origin and embarked on relearning it via science."

Dr. Yanagi "You are referring to the ability of the entity to utilize the Higgs field to restructure itself as the origin, is that correct?"

Dr. Hansen "Yes, the Higgs field existed at the origin. As we moved away from our origins…or as time marched onward, it disassociated into other basic forces. Likewise, the perceptible multi-dimensions reduced with the advent of the other basic forces."

Dr. Yanagi "By side alleys, you are referring to our misconceptions throughout the ages, are you not?"

Dr. Hansen "Yes, our religious beliefs have done us a disfavor and blinded us from our true nature. Our entire education system has likewise removed us from our perception of reality. The Russian, Vygotsky, enlightened us so in his experiments with Uzbeks in the 1930s. Academia, chasing its tail for four centuries over a self-created dichotomy between mind and matter, has not even progressed to the point of reconnection. Academia is adrift in an expanding ocean of vocabulary. We seek sanctuary within vocabulary. The destruction of myths, again, masked our ability to witness the miraculous and sense the multi-dimensions."

Dr. Yanagi "Do you believe the shamans of old sensed something in nature that we today are unable to sense, Dr. Hansen?"

Dr. Hansen "Yes, I am beginning to think in that manner. What we have learned about this tree defies all our prior preferences...well, scientific knowledge, to be polite. Prior to encountering this tree, communication with inanimate objects had been rejected by the West. We have been satisfied to observe and categorize the inanimate. Now, we must embark on a reconstruction of our world. It will be difficult, because we have traveled so far down a wrong alley. The very idea that we cherish about life needs rethinking."

Dr. Yanagi "I doubt the world is prepared to embrace any Rousseau-an notion of a Noble Savage much less a Noble Tree or Noble Rock."

Dr. Hansen "I doubt they are ready either, but right here before us lies one."

Dr. Yanagi "I am not sure that I can conclude in my report that we have discovered a Noble Tree."

Dr. Hansen "We will need to couch our reports in scientific language; otherwise, we will come across as deranged shamans."

Dr. Yanagi "My challenge is not as severe as yours, Dr. Hansen. The Japanese are first *Shinto*, before they are a Buddhists. *Shinto* beliefs dovetail similar notions that we have wrestled with here."

Dr. Hansen "The peripheral Indonesian islanders with their animistic beliefs seem right at home with this tree and its implications. Have you ever noticed how they look at us scientists? I have often interpreted their facial expressions as awe over our advanced nature. Now, I believe their faces express awe over our obliviousness."

In silence, one by one the group of scientist begins to scan the encampment. Though there are no natives in the immediate viewing area, the group realizes that it has been them whom have been under observation. The eyes that once were thought to have communicated bewilderment were, in fact, eyes expressing bewilderment of another order. Then, the scientists had to take into account all the other eyes in the jungle about them. How aware of reality were they?

Dr. Yanagi "Dr. Hansen, even if you are correct, what could be our reason, as humans, for existence?"

Dr. Hansen exhales, as he looks up into the sky, "We are star-makers, Dr. Yanagi. We, we humans, cause the 'emergence' into a star."

Dr. Yanagi "As you know, Dr. Hansen, not all heavenly bodies evolve into stars. Just look at our solar system, we have, at least, nine examples. Other than our planet, I seriously doubt that any of the other planets will ever evolve into a star. Even our planet does not seem to exhibit any inclination to do so."

Dr. Hansen "I believe we have a window of opportunity in which to 'emerge'. If we miss that window, we join the ranks of the other inert heavenly bodies."

Dr. Yanagi "How would we determine whether or not we are in this window, as you put it?"

Dr. Hansen "Our window is now. Our window transpires as the sands of an hourglass. We, we humans, are the window, Dr. Yanagi."

Dr. Yanagi "I suspect the sands in our hourglass are many. We humans will be around for a long time, unless we destroy ourselves. We are our own worst enemy."

Dr. Hansen "I will differ with you here, Dr. Yanagi. The length of our window has been estimated as probably another 10,000 years or so."

Dr. Yanagi surprised, "How do you know this?"

Dr. Hansen "Our ecological balance is made possible by the orientation and movement of our planet. When that balance is interrupted, we perish."

Dr. Yanagi "I see. When the moon escapes the gravitational attraction of the earth, the moon will spin out of orbit. The earth will right itself, stop spinning or spin erratically in every which orientation for a period of time. Life, as we know it, will not be able to adjust."

Dr. Hansen interjects, "Precisely, Dr. Yanagi, we humans have until that time to determine whether we continue our evolution as a star or a lifeless planet...well, a biologically lifeless planet in the universe."

Dr. Yanagi "Speaking of lifetimes, the unexplained, sudden climatic changes that occurred some 800,000 years ago that enable our kind to propagate about the surface of the planet could have represented this phenomenal commencement: the standing of the hour glass, so to speak."

Dr. Hansen "I concur, Dr. Yanagi. Our ancestors marked time by the moon. How right they were! Time commenced for us humans when the moon succumbed to our planet's attraction. Our ancestors bequeathed to us the creation analogies. We just misinterpreted them. How arrogant and misguided we have been."

Suddenly, the notion of Armageddon 'emerges' into a new meaning: Armageddon is a universal phenomenon in which we humans participate. Dr. Yanagi's statement "...unless we destroy ourselves..." echoes in a reversal of intention into one of aspiration. The haze...shrouding all the incredible stories from every which affiliation that mesmerized generations for millennia...begins to clear. Truth permeates down through the multitude of dimensions: we humans understand our purpose. Truly, we are part of the miraculous in the universe. Like a mother with open arms, She welcomes us back into Her embrace.

CHAPTER 22

▼

ENCAMPMENT, NEW GUINEA

It is early morning in New Guinea. The helicopters are airlifting the last of the scientists out today. Farewells are often the hardest social courtesies to perform. Many of the group in the encampment had been there since the beginning. When all is said and done, no one will be left, except a few soldiers.

The Americans left on the first wave of helicopters. The Japanese occupied all the space on the second wave. Captain Djarmat and Joe are making their adieus to Dr. Leong, as the troops load her belongings and equipment onto the copters.

Dr. Leong invites the two men to visit her at the University of Pelang. Captain Djarmat realizes that he might have the chance to do so, now that he will be selected for rapid promotion to lieutenant colonel. The Military Command Jayapura has seen fit to have him spend six months in the rank of major, before officially advancing him to the rank of lieutenant colonel. As lieutenant colonel, he will be assigned to regional headquarters in Sulawesi. As chance would favor, Dr. Leong's laboratory is located on Sulawesi not far from the regional headquarters.

Joe, on the other hand, will return to Manila and the monotony of his previous status. Connors and he have made arrangements for the disbursements of any awards forthcoming from the snake's head. Accompanied with a letter from Dr. Leong, the snake's head cleared Indonesian customs and was sent, express delivery, to the Australian National University for evaluation. Bradley Connors and Joseph Del Rosi were named as the discoverers in Dr. Leong's letter for the purposes of accreditation. As for the imminent riches, the two men will have to await the decision and speed with which the awarding bureaucracy operates. Since that bureaucracy may have been idle since the early part of the 20th Century, it might take some greasing and tender loving care to reactivate. Nonetheless, both Connors and Joe intend to persevere and wait it out.

The helicopter pilot signals that it is time to lift off. Dr. Leong climbs aboard the copter, straps herself in securely and waves farewell, as the copter whirls upward. The scientists are now gone. All the excitement that they created has extinguished. Like water poured onto a dying campfire, the last fizzes of the fire die away with the diminishing sound from the departing helicopter blades.

Captain Djarmat, Connors and Joe watch the helicopters disappear over the horizon. There will be no more helicopters. Captain Djarmat will return with Connors and Joe via military convoy to Jayapura. Once in Jayapura, Joe will be taken to Sentani Airport for transport to Manila. Connors will be reunited with his forestry company and assigned to a new project somewhere in the central highlands areas of New Guinea. Truly, it will be the last time the three men see one another. Although invites are mutually exchanged, the men understand that this is it. Once in Jayapura, they will part company, perhaps for many years…perhaps forever.

The captain orders the second lieutenant to break camp and finish loading the transport vehicles. He expects to be on the way back to Jayapura by noontime. The captain would prefer to wait until the following morning, but there is little here to do now that the tree has disappeared into the ground. In a sense, the captain does not desire to camp here overnight in order to wake up to a new tree sprouting up somewhere.

Connors and Joe take one last stroll to the area where the tree once stood. Now, there is just a pile of bark, covering the void made by the tree when it slipped back into the earth. In a few days, Dr. Leong told them, the bark would turn into a form of harmless seawater.

Connors kicking some of the bark, "What do you make of this, Mate?"

Joe "I have no idea, Brad. Maybe the scientists found a way to cut the tree down. They did seem to get out of here in a hurry, once the tree was gone."

Connors wipes his chin, "That's what I think, too, Mate. Once they had it cut down, their job in this God forsaken place was over."

Joe "It sure attracted a lot of attention, didn't it?"

Connors, looking around the encampment: "It sure did, Mate."

Connors and Joe notice the soldiers working at their normal pace, as if nothing had happened here. To the soldiers, the time spent here represented just days in their military obligation. Connors and Joe convince each other that the American scientists cut down the tree with some new device that they brought with them. The tree, due to its oddity, was cut up into smaller sections and taken with the Americans.

With their tent disassembled by the soldiers, Connors and Joe check their carry-on belongings and board one of the trucks with the second lieutenant. Since the second lieutenant does not speak English well, the trip to Jayapura is quiet. Joe savors his last views of the jungle. He may never see this place again.

Within an hour of travel from the encampment, the convoy comes upon a stretch of dry road surface. The weight and traction of the vehicles causes a dust cloud to form. Joe resents how the dust cloud restricts his vision. He realizes that his memory of his experiences in the encampment will soon cloud, as well, once he returns to Jayapura. In Manila, they may well be forgotten altogether.

It is late afternoon when the convoy reaches Jayapura. At the entrance to the Military Command Jayapura, a sentry requests that Mr. Del Rosi disembark the truck. A jeep is waiting to take him to Sentani Airport. Joe extends his last farewells and boards the jeep. Within a few minutes, he finds himself rushing to the airport. The jeep driver is experienced in the streets of Jayapura. His ability to weave in and out of traffic reminds Joe of some Hollywood chase scenes. Joe is convinced that this guy has a future in stunt driving. The gate guards at the airport merely wave the jeep through without any ID check. Obviously, they were expecting the jeep and know the driver. The driver skids up onto the tarmac and helps Joe with his belongings. The driver encourages Joe to hustle to an old transport plane on the runway. As they approach the plane, a side door opens and someone lowers a ladder. Joe's belongings are loaded quickly, and the driver helps him to climb aboard. Before Joe can take a seat in a parachute stall, the door closes. One of the flight crew hands him a white, cardboard lunch box. Joe peeks inside: a bologna sandwich, a peanut butter and jelly sandwich, a carton of milk and an orange. Welcome back to the United States of America!

Manila

It is always a long flight in a military transport plane. The humidity of the equatorial regions does not improve the accommodations in a parachute stall. The noise from the drone of the engines makes speech difficult. Being alone in the cargo bay allows Joe to reminisce the time he spent in New Guinea and the life that awaits him back in Manila.

Upon arrival in Manila, the Asian Development Bank provided a car on the tarmac to take Joe directly to their main offices in Metro Manila. The car was not a limousine, but in Manila, any larger vehicle expresses the intent. Once inside the car, Joe's body is greeted with air conditioning. It has been some time, since he experienced such refreshment. A familiar melody soothes the entire interior of the vehicle, as the driver navigates through the crowded streets of the metro area. The melody is his favorite song: "*Maganda Oumaga.*"

Thoughts of Angelina pour into his mind. He imagines being attended to by this beautiful creature in a hot bath. Her hands, soft and gentle, ease over his shoulders like warm water. He can feel her breasts press against the naked flesh of his back. It is good to be back in Manila. Even the scent of the city arouses him. Senses, dulled in New Guinea, revive, as acquaintances begin to mount. Joe can feel his body come alive. His body recognizes this place and remembers, with advantages, the pleasures. Chemistry, once idle, works its magic anew in every capillary of his body.

Joe's pleasantries are interrupted as the vehicle stops in front of the entrance to the ADB. The driver hurries out of the vehicle to open the door for Joe. It is the first time in Manila that a driver extended to him such courtesies. Joe disembarks and makes his way to Bob Watson's office. Watson's secretary greets him and tells him to go right into Mr. Watson's office.

Upon entering Watson's office, Watson exclaims, "Thank God, you made it, Joe."

Joe just laughs.

Watson, emerging quickly from his seat to go around his desk to shake hands with Joe, "I was beginning to think we would abandon you in New Guinea."

Joe shaking hands, "It is good to be back."

Watson, gesturing for Joe to make himself comfortable, "Tell me, how did it go? Did they finally get that tree problem resolved?"

Joe nods affirmatively, "It took a while, but yes, they did manage to resolve the tree problem. There was no tree there when I left."

Watson smiles, "Thank God! You cannot imagine the amounts of extra financing that the bank processed for this fiasco."

Joe "I believe I can. There were many specialists down there from all over the world."

Watson is all ears. He had heard very little of what took place down there, other than processing paperwork for additional financing. Joe relates the overall problem with the tree's indestructibility. The tank issue evokes some laughter from Watson. The snakes were of interest to Watson even more. In summation, according to Joe, there was a tree problem, and it has been resolved. The forestry project is back on track.

Watson credits Joe with a job well done and awards him a well-deserved increase in salary and allowances. There is even a huge bonus in cash handed to him in an envelope. Watson knew that Joe needed some walking around money. Watson assures Joe that his position with the bank will be secure for many more years, and he promises Joe that he will not receive an assignment of this arduous nature in the future. Watson cannot apologize enough for sending Joe down there. Joe senses a real concern from Watson and is appreciative. The meeting ends with the usual words to standby for another assignment. Joe anticipates the standby time to be at least a year.

Joe leaves Watson's office and hires a jeepny to take him back to his apartment. He will shower and prepare for an evening with Angelina. This time, he will arrange for Angelina to stay a few days...maybe forever. Joe missed her.

EPILOGUE

▼

Although the tree in New Guinea did not exist, the question emerging from the novel does exist. Every narrative concerning this question has commenced with a hypothetical scenario. Rather than giving life to the original scenario, this novel abandons its origins and leaves the reader with the response. This novel does not require aspirants. There are no conversions, rituals or secret societies to endure. Advanced degrees are not required to become an esteemed believer. The question of the ages has been posed anew, and a response has been provided. The author believes the clarity of the response speaks for itself. One just needs the courage to accept our place in the miraculous, and one can dispense with millennia of narratives to the contrary.

ABBREVIATIONS/
DEFINITIONS

Abu Sayyad	Al Queda terrorist group active in the Philippine Islands
ADB	Asian Development Bank (Manila, Philippine Islands)
Aitape	Area on the north coast of Papua New Guinea near the Sepik River
AK-47	Russian made assault rifle
Animism	South East Asia spirit world belief religions
Asethenosphere	space of some 120 kilometers (75 miles) between the mantle and the earth's upper crust. Estimated at some 240 kilometers (150 miles) below the earth's crust
ATL	Advanced Technology Laboratory (Canberra, Australia)
Bahasa	Most popular Indonesian language
BSc	Bachelor of Science degree in the British Commonwealth
Bush meat	Jungle animal trade for consumption by isolated, overseas workers
Bush monkey	Caucasian soldier of fortune in South East Asia
Bushido Code	Warrior code of the 12th Century Miniamoto Clan in Japan
CLEO	Client Liaison Entertainment Officer
Containment	Military enforced quarantine of various classes of severity levels

Cm	centimeter
Crimping	squashing together electronic connections with special pliers
Dimension	in three-dimensional terminology: length, width and height
Demodulate	removal of the carrier frequency from an incoming signal
Emergence	Theory that intelligence "emerges" from the interaction of the other bodily functions with the nervous system: Whole being greater than the sum of the parts
Geisha	Skilled and refined entertainment woman in Japan
Genji	Secret sub-earth probing satellite
Geophysics	Geological and material testing
Geosynchronous	In synchronization with the earth's rotation
Harmonics	Exact multiples of the original frequency
Higgs Boson	Carrier of the Higgs Field: intermediate vector boson (IVB)
Higgs Field	hypothesized energy field existing just after the Big Bang that became the progenitor of the electromagnetic and nuclear (strong and weak) fields
IBRD	International Bank for Reconstruction & Development
IFC	International Finance Corporation
IMF	International Monetary Fund
Jeepny	Converted American Jeep into a passenger vehicle
Kanji	modern Japanese writing script
Karaoki	Signing style self-entertainment in Japan
Kilometer	$5/8^{th}$ of a mile
Kiwi	Slang for New Zealander
Lava lamp	popular lamp containing cohesive, slow-moving fluid in 1960s
LDC	Less Developed Countries

M-16	American made assault rifle
Magma	sub-earth lava: molten materials
Mantle	sub-earth layer composed of active magma surrounding the core Estimated at 2800 kilometers (1800 miles) thick
Meter	a few inches more than one yard: 39.37 inches
Miso	Japanese word for water…commonly refers to morning soup
MIT	Massachusetts Institute of Technology (Boston, MA, USA)
MNE	Multinational Enterprise
OIC	Officer in Charge
Oscilloscope	frequency measuring device with visual readout
Peso	Unit of currency in the Philippine Islands
Photosynthesis	process by which some plants produce carbohydrates from sunlight
Quantum Mechanics	Current scientific theory that matter and energy are quantized and behave like a particle and a wave: quantum electrodynamics (QED) and quantum chromodynamics (QCD)
Regeneration	process of growing back lost body parts
Ring of Fire	Active volcanic band running in an arc in the South Pacific near the equator
SAE	Sound Analysis Expert
Sake	Japanese rice wine
Samurai	Ancient Japanese warrior adhering to the Bushido Code
Sashimi	raw tuna
Sentani	Main airport for Jayapura, Papua, Republic of Indonesia Former headquarters for General MacArthur in New Guinea
SETI	Search for Extra-Terrestrial Intelligence
Shaman	Ancient seer and medicine man From the Siberian word *saman*

Sheila	slang for woman in Australia
Shinto	Japanese spirit world belief religion
Sideband	Information carrying frequency riding on either side of the carrier frequency
Silicate	silicon-based compounds
Sine wave	a circle or ellipse graphed in time
String theory	Theory that ultimate physical reality consists of a structure of multi-dimensional stings (like musical chords). As many as ten dimensions are theorized. Also: Loop theory and Super-symmetry theory.
Subduction	process of circulating the earth's crust into the mantle and back
Sumo	popular wrestling style in Japan
Sundog	eruption of fire from the sun's surface
US $	United States currency symbol
Vygotsky	Lev S. Vygotsky (1896-1934) Russian philosopher who proved that exposure to the education system alters our perception of reality. We become more geometric thinkers.
WB	World Bank
White Monkey	Slang for Caucasian in South East and South Asia
Zeno	Ancient philosopher who first tried to explain time via dimensions

0-595-34441-0

Printed in the United States
25982LVS00004B/224

9 780595 344413